CUSTODY

By the same author

DIFFICULT DAUGHTERS
A MARRIED WOMAN
HOME
THE IMMIGRANT

CUSTODY

MANJU KAPUR

PENGUIN BOOKS
An imprint of Penguin Random House

PENGUIN BOOKS

USA | Canada | UK | Ireland | Australia
New Zealand | India | South Africa | China | Singapore

Penguin Books is part of the Penguin Random House group of companies whose addresses can be found at global.penguinrandomhouse.com

Published by Penguin Random House India Pvt. Ltd
4th Floor, Capital Tower 1, MG Road,
Gurugram 122 002, Haryana, India

Penguin Random House India

First Published in Vintage by Random House India 2011
This edition published in Penguin Books by Penguin Random House India 2020

12 11 10 9 8 7 6 5

ISBN 9788184000283

For sale in India only

Typeset in Sabon by InoSoft Systems, Noida
Printed at Manipal Technologies Limited, India

www.penguin.co.in

FSC www.fsc.org MIX Paper | Supporting responsible forestry FSC® C043100

This is a legitimate digitally printed version of the book and therefore might not have certain extra finishing on the cover.

For

Amba Dalmia

&

Vimla Kapur

I

January 1st, 1998.

The couple lay among stained sheets and rumpled quilts, eyes closed, legs twisted together like the knotted branches of a low growing tree.

Slowly their breathing became less noisy. Her head grew heavier on his shoulder, his hand across her stomach became limp.

They dozed, perhaps for fifteen minutes, but behind their heaving eyelids lay uneasy thoughts. They had things to do, places to go, lies to tell, the woman particularly.

Eventually they dragged each other off the bed and into the bathroom.

They hated this, they said as they washed and dressed, simply hated it.

But they had kept their promise, they had heralded the new year by making love.

One final kiss and it was time to part. The woman left first; she believed that the spirits of the universe at the service of betrayed partners were tracking her movements, keeping note of incriminating times and places. Never mind that this was a relatively quiet street in one of the inner lanes of an elite colony in South Delhi. Guilt sees accusation everywhere, in the glance of a servant, the fretful cry of a child, the stranger staring on the street, a driver's insolent tones.

As she made her way towards the main road, she kept looking around but recognized no one, and decided it was her conscience that made her so uneasy.

She dragged her mind from love, as she readied herself to meet her two children, a toddler daughter, and a boy eight years older. She had a husband too, but of late the husband had been seen in altered hues, his irritating aspects rushing to the fore, his sterling qualities and all the years she had thought them sterling hurtling towards oblivion.

Every day she practised thinking badly of her spouse. Her lover encouraged this by providing a basis for comparison. The dissatisfaction that accrues in most marriages was not allowed dissipation; instead, she clung to reasons to justify her unfaithfulness.

The man set out on his evening round of social engagements in a chauffeur-driven car, untroubled by considerations of being spied upon. Initially he had wasted a few thoughts on the irony of falling in love with a married woman, chased as he had been through the years by so many single ones. He thrived on challenges but in this case had proceeded cautiously to make sure it wasn't the frisson of the forbidden that had sparked his interest.

Now he felt that so long as she agreed to remain in his life he would accept any condition she laid down. Whenever she worried about her children he assured her of his constancy. Once she was truly his, he vowed, no further sorrow would ever distress her.

He was a corporate man with a strong belief in hard work. As the days went by and his love grew, the effort he put into it became more vigorous. A trace of superstition lurked beneath his rational assumptions, and he liked to imagine their encounter to be the hidden purpose behind the two-year assignment that had returned him to his home country.

Except for this new interest, The Brand absorbed him completely. With a billion potential customers, sales in

India could touch the sky, and he wanted to reach those heights before he was transferred. It would be a spectacular achievement, both in personal and professional terms.

It was The Brand's second venture into India. In 1977, the giant company had been ejected due to changed political realities. The Janata Party, having won a surprise victory against the Congress, wanted to be seen as protector of both national capital and Indian manufacturers. If The Brand did not reveal its secret formula it would have to leave, which it did, and Indian integrity was preserved along with its diminutive bottled-drink industry.

Now all that Leftist euphoria was gone. It was the nineties and economic liberalization meant that rules regarding foreign direct investment were relaxed. The Brand was invited back. Some politicians objected: of what practical use were fizzy beverages? Resources should be spent on high-end technology. Such a view was outdated. The utility of The Brand lay in its image, its presence suggested a financially favourable market.

After five years and millions of dollars, Indian operations had yet to generate a rupee in profits. Ashok Khanna was summoned. Indian in origin, it was believed his insights would be helpful in tackling the vagaries of an indigenous market.

The man came with a formidable reputation for troubleshooting. In Brussels, he had moved swiftly after a connection between some sick children and The Brand had been established. TV cameras filmed the destruction of thousands of their bottled drinks, then filmed him saying that the health of their customers was more important than profit. After the scare, he had come up with the slogan 'Today more than ever we thank you for your loyalty', with its subliminal link between continuing purchase and moral probity.

Within a few months of arriving in India he saw the woman he knew he had been destined for. In her colouring, her greenish eyes and her demeanour, she was a perfect blend of East and West. A woman so pretty had to be married; besides, she had the look of someone who never had to compete for male attention. To woo her would thus be that much more difficult: he must first create a need before he could fulfil it. But he was used to creating needs, it was what he did for a living.

II

May 1997.

The building had a frontage of natural white marble, its rough expanses interspersed with polished stone. A yellow and blue geometrical frieze started from the top, meandered across the middle to disappear down one side. The architect said this was meant to give the impression of running water on a white sandy beach. In the centre of fume-choked Delhi, it was a nice conceit, but no one in the myriad office rooms had time to consider the poetry behind such an image. Time meant money, and multinationals were too devoted to its pursuit to waste even a minute.

The Brand's Delhi headquarters took up the whole second floor, divided, then subdivided into sections dealing with different products and different regions. At the end of a corridor of one such division was a large office, its status emphasized by the smaller rooms in that row. Here Ashok Khanna sat in the soft gold ambience created by tussore silk sofas and patterned bamboo blinds across the windows. Floor-to-ceiling shelves were packed with files along with company products in all their packaged avatars. Behind the big desk hung posters from the latest ad campaign enjoining all Indians from the peasant to the urbanite to savour the drink which would transfix their taste buds and allow them to relish every moment of the day.

The man behind the desk swivelled in his black high-backed chair, alternating his gaze between the window and Raman Kaushik, the Mang-oh! sales manager in front of him. From time to time he leaned forward, circling figures, underlining dates. Noise from the street below could be heard over the air conditioning; the wall clock ticked loudly and irritatingly.

This grated so on the nerves of the Mang-oh! manager that he couldn't help an annoyed glance up.

'Time does go on,' remarked the one behind the desk. 'It is good to keep that in mind.'

A reprimand. Targets were not being met, and that was the reason why he was sitting here, staring at his boss, feeling as wretched as a successful organization would wish him to feel.

He thought of the hours on the road, the miserable B and C towns where he had passed many lonely nights, sacrificing family life for the sake of his job. Now he wondered whether he was capable of more. Ever since he had joined The Brand, he had felt the sharp edge of competition nudging into every idea he had, sometimes to the point of paralysis.

As the one responsible for the India Mang-oh! account, his merit was continuously under surveillance. It was not as though other departments were not posting losses, but unreasonably it was felt that in India, mangoes sold themselves, and so he found himself fighting hard for every advertising rupee in the juice segment. In meetings he was told his projections had to be more ambitious—an opinion he shared—his sales pitch more aggressive, his ideas more dynamic.

He looked at the Mang-oh! Tetra Pak on the table with loathing. That little carton swam insouciantly about in the pool of anxiety that lay at the heart of his working life.

Ashok was thinking. Everything Raman had not been able to tell him revealed what he needed to know about the state of Mang-oh!. A man who was not obsessed by his marketing figures, eating, sleeping, dreaming to their rhythm, such a man rarely produced outstanding results. With only local products to compete against, making profits should have been fairly straightforward.

In a country as hot and populated as India, no hand should be without a beverage manufactured by The Brand. His job was to grind this belief into every employee of the company.

He could see from the hangdog look that Raman was anticipating blame. But Ashok Khanna did not do things that way. On his arrival, he had spent time getting to know everyone in the office before embarking on a three-week all-India tour, acquainting himself with the foot soldiers, he said, and incidentally letting every foot soldier know that he had his eye on them. Mang-oh! must be a success story: even the relative non-performance of a small fruit juice was demoralizing in a company as target driven as theirs. He gave Raman a few minutes to maunder on about how challenging the task was.

If despite its international image The Brand's signature cola was not doing well, what did they expect of a home-grown item? Right now he was counting on the inclusion of Alphonso, the king of mangoes, to add to its appeal. King Mang-oh!, how did that sound?

'Not bad.'

Raman looked alert, and decided to air some more difficulties.

'When it comes to buying drinks, people prefer lassi or orange juice made before their eyes. Fresh, tasty, with as much ice and spice as they want.'

Ashok felt fresh irritation. Never criticize your product: breathe it, believe in it, make it your religion.

'Have you considered other factors? Expense? Time? Cleanliness?' Here he shuddered, remembering the ubiquitous juice wallah, with his peeled, limp oranges displayed in glass jars, the dirty hands that reached to put them into heavy machines cranked manually, the pulp falling into an overflowing bucket on the pavement and flies buzzing everywhere. It was a civic duty to get people to drink Mang-oh!.

'Arre, in these mofussil towns people have a lot of time. What does it take to stand around and wait for juice to be pressed out of a few oranges? As for cleanliness, they think that just because they can see what is happening, it is all right. How can one change that?'

'What are oranges compared to mangoes? Mangoes are part of the Indian psyche, but they are available only in summer. Now—in this pack—' he tapped the Mang-oh! on his desk, while doodling on his pad, 'for the first time you can have mango all year round. *All year round.* How significant is that?'

'It does have possibilities,' conceded Raman.

'Listen:

In the country all around,
Mangoes can be found
In the North and in the South,
Cool and wholesome,

Natural, healthy, yum-yum,
In the East and in the West,
Mang-oh! is best, best, best.'

The Mang-oh! manager, a former ad man, blanched slightly as he asked, 'Did you make that up?'

Ashok looked modest. 'After college I thought of becoming a poet.'

'Really? What happened?'

'Oh, one has to earn a living. I was accepted in business school, then I had to pay off my loan. And I had much rather this, than starve in a garret.'

Raman did not know how to respond. Ashok's success was so well known that it was impossible to imagine his talents to lie in any other direction. Into his silence Ashok spoke, outlining a more focused sales pitch. Target three states in north India, sponsor local events in schools and colleges, build up loyalty, extend the awareness of The Brand to Mang-oh!. Tell the dealers to set up various schemes before you visit.

That he had to travel more and work longer hours Raman accepted as his due, but as he got up he couldn't help confiding, 'My wife complains she hardly sees me any more. We have got a small baby, it's hard on her.'

'Home life does suffer.'

'They say you never married, because of your commitment to The Brand?'

Ashok merely laughed. 'I'm sure inside here,' he said, tapping Raman on the shoulder, 'there is a marketing genius. We just need the right circumstances for it to emerge.'

Raman blushed at this image of himself. Ashok's reputation was based on his ability to get the best out of people, even the most dispirited campaign appeared more lively when he blessed it with his attention. That was why his salary was in the astronomical region of 50 lakhs a year, why his house was in West End and his car a chauffeured BMW. He had been in India only six months and already there was more confidence that the steady losses of the last five years could after all be stemmed.

*

Driving home, Raman thought of his wife and the distance he had begun to feel between them. Maybe it was the baby she hadn't really wanted, maybe it was all the travelling he had to do, had always had to do.

As he expected, she did say she was sick and tired of being alone. Immediately he felt anxious—her bad moods were like claws that clutched his heart. It was only later, when they were out with friends, drinking and dining as guests at the golf club, that her spirits lightened. The conversation had turned to the Cricket World Cup in England, still two years away. Somebody said let's go, and the others said yes, let's, and someone said it was during the children's holidays, it would suit everybody, and Raman said, by then Mango-oh! sales should earn him a good bonus, and Rohan said he was so good at marketing, his bonus could pay for all their tickets, and Shagun felt calmer about the travelling that was so essential to her husband. She looked about her; there was not one wife seated around the low table who didn't have to be alone most of the week, but the success of their husbands' jobs added to the things they could buy and the places they could visit. Even six or seven years ago, would it have been possible for people like them to consider going abroad to watch the Indian cricket team?

Raman's friend from the ad agency then asked whether he would be at the Hrithik Roshan do at the Oberoi Hotel. Yes, Raman would. Mang-oh! wouldn't collapse if he postponed his trip by a few days. Besides, with temperatures in the forties, it was good to remind himself that his job had perks, which was easy to forget when he was on the road in the middle of a heatwave.

Shagun quickly said she would love to meet Hrithik Roshan, but she also wanted to meet the new boss Raman talked so much of. She believed he was from Harvard Business School?

Arre, said another, what did Harvard Business School matter? The man was Indian, that was his saving grace, otherwise foreigners came here, didn't understand the Indian mentality and expected westernized marketing techniques to work. Well, they didn't. Look at that chicken fiasco that The Rival had spent so much money on. It took immense strategy to make Indians eat such stuff when they had their own delicious tandooris, tikkas and murgh masalas.

The crush at the Oberoi was stupendous. The Kaushiks were introduced to the movie star, then Shagun was introduced to Ashok Khanna, the company wonder man. Even though the crowd was glamorous, Raman found the evening long. The only aspect that pleased him was the delight Shagun took in the compliments her appearance elicited. Later on in the car she asked many questions about the boss, was it true he was a marketing genius? Had he managed to produce results so far? Where was his wife? How come he wasn't married? Raman was pleasantly surprised, her interest in company matters was usually limited.

That night Shagun was very tender to her husband, her body apologizing for the sullenness of the day before. In a happier frame of mind Raman left the next morning to enthuse regional marketing managers, to do unto others what had been done unto him.

A week later he was accosted by Ashok in the office. Would his wife be interested in acting in an ad? They needed a housewife to put a Mang-oh! Tetra Pak in a child's tiffin, he had thought she would be suitable, but there was no compulsion, the agency could always provide some model.

Raman hadn't realized such a project was in the offing, but he was sure it would gratify his wife to act.

He thought of this opportunity as a gift, knowing the excitement it would provide. When he first knew Shagun she had wanted to be a model, but her mother was strongly opposed to a career that would allow all kinds of lechery near her lovely daughter. 'Do what you like after you marry,' she had said, but after marriage there had been a child. Then the claims of husband, family and friends made a career hard to justify, especially since money was not an issue.

*

The screen test was promising and Shagun was chosen to appear as a mother in a thirty-second film. When they wanted a child, she suggested her son, and he too was taken. In one week, the exhilaration was over, but not over was the intensity of Ashok's gaze as he dropped in on the studio to see how it was going.

She put the visit down to the perfectionism she had heard so much about, but when he asked her to coffee, her pleasure was mixed with fear.

Had he been a home-grown Indian and not the boss, she would have found a way to refuse, but this man had been imported from abroad and she did not want to seem unsophisticated. So she went for coffee, and in the spirit of sophistication, dispassionately revelled in the admiration emanating from him, knowing she was still in a role, and it was nice to play away from home.

He encouraged her to talk. Once, she said, she had got modelling offers that might have led to screen tests, but then she had married very young and there had been the inevitable children. Now she was too old to start in films, but with so many new TV channels, and with countless soaps on offer she might have a chance once this ad was released?

Yes, an ad might open up opportunities. He was acquainted with someone who worked with Asha Kakkar, queen producer of practically every sob-inducing serial; would she like him to make a few enquiries? If she gave him her phone number he could get in touch with her directly should something materialize. Nervously she wrote her number down, then watched him insert the chit carefully into his wallet. He would do his best, but she was not to be disappointed if nothing came up.

Of course not, that was understood, she murmured.

He grinned dazzlingly at her. If anyone deserved to be in films it was the woman sitting before him, he said.

A week later found her in his house, after he had phoned about needing advice on furnishings.

Did you manage to get any information about the TV series? she asked as he opened the door, visions of the casting couch flooding her mind. Ashok Khanna didn't seem that type of man, but you never knew.

I have asked my friends, they will get back to me. But I must tell you, it will be necessary to relocate to Bombay if you are serious. It's unfeasible to think of an acting career from Delhi.

In that case, asked Shagun, was it not possible for Raman to be posted there?

He did not answer, and she wondered whether her question was too unprofessional to merit attention. She looked at him anxiously, he looked back unsmiling, she lowered her eyes and asked about the furnishings.

He showed her some nondescript beige drapes, did she think he should change the fabric?

Silk would look much better, she replied; these were a polyester mix, that's why they seemed on the shiny cheap side. There was a shop in Khan Market that sold excellent stuff, expensive but with tailoring thrown in. Who had done his decorating, by the way?

Obviously someone who didn't know very much. Now would she like some coffee, he wanted to get to know her, did she think that was permissible?

A giggle that sounded idiotic even to her ears. Of course it was permissible, she said. He made the coffee himself—there was not a single servant about, which seemed strange to her.

Not yet used to having them underfoot all the time, he explained. Though he'd grown up in India, he'd lived abroad for the past twenty-five years. But he wanted to hear more about her: what did she do with herself, how did she spend her day?

She was an ordinary woman, why did he want to know? He asked her to guess and as she blushed self-consciously he proceeded with his own history that had led him to this place, this sofa, talking to her.

Later she was to discover he had a strong sense of the significance of his own presence. But was it any wonder? Apparently he had been successful since the day he was born. And ever since he had joined The Brand, fresh out of Harvard Business School, the company had responded to his devotion with equal commitment.

Anecdotally he mentioned his recent trip to Africa. People thought capitalism was heartless, they never considered the great good achieved by multinationals. When the folk he met knew he represented The Brand, they practically fell down and kissed his feet, their community work—such as the fight against AIDS—was so well known. He wanted that impact in India as well.

III

Raman and Shagun's marriage had been arranged along standard lines, she the beauty, he the one with the brilliant prospects.

Their first child had been born within a year. On learning of his young wife's pregnancy, Raman had blamed himself. He should have been more careful, he wasn't sure he was ready to be a father. He made the mistake of divulging his doubts to his mother—he hadn't been married long enough to be wary of such confidences.

'I really wish this hadn't happened so soon. We need more time together,' he started.

His mother bridled. 'What will she do when you are in office? It is not as though you can be together night and day, particularly when you are in a travelling job.'

'She is only twenty-two.'

'It may interest you to know I myself was only nineteen when I had you.'

'There was less awareness then. And if you had me at nineteen, surely that was not good for you, Mummy. You don't want your daughter-in-law to go through the same thing.'

'Beta, it is good to have children early. By the time they settle down you are still young and free enough to enjoy.'

What she didn't mention was that as a grandmother she imagined she would have more of a role in her son's life. As it was she only saw him on Sundays, which just about broke her heart.

Shagun herself had no doubts. Everything was a glorious adventure, and being pregnant plunged her into the centre of all attention. She didn't throw up once, her skin glowed, her hair shone, her husband called her a Madonna, her mother said she was fruitful like the earth, her in-laws looked proud and fed her almonds and ghee whenever they could get near her.

The birth of a boy added to her glory. She had gotten over the duties of heir-producing smoothly, there would be no need to have another child. Her son had inherited her looks and colour, a further source of gratification.

To Raman's amazement her figure resumed its girlish curves, leaving only breasts that were more abundant. She now looked like those ideal women described in the Kama Sutra, their hair like a cloud of bees, their breasts like mountains of honey, their eyes like those of a deer, a waist that could be spanned by his two hands (well almost), a belly that folded over in three flat folds, and a walk that was like an elephant's. When he told her this she laughed and said you now have a private zoo.

These were the good years. Raman was doing well at work, his creativity at IndiaThinkTank was recognized by bonuses and awards. A happy moment with a Foot Fetish shoe ad had made his name. All that lies between you and the . . . various imaginative scenarios followed. He had taken special care with the visuals. Small feet, beautifully shod, stepping daintily across desert sands, rainwater puddles, muddy river banks, even the Arctic tundra. Who cared about logic in an ad? It was all about evoking desire.

When The Brand re-entered India, Raman was ready for a change. He wanted more challenge, more prestige, more salary.

No one was surprised when they hired him in the marketing department at 10 lakhs a year. Shagun and Raman celebrated by going to Europe for their summer holidays. Had his parents not refused, Raman would have taken them along, but later, beta, first you establish yourself, his father had said, not wanting that money should be spent on them, especially when the exchange rate was so high. They were used to guarding family resources.

In his new job Raman was in charge of Mang-oh!, a duty that took him up and down the country. It was a huge leap in status and responsibility, but as his time away from home increased, Shagun began to protest. 'But what to do, darling? We have to create brand awareness in every corner of the country. People will drink anything. The Rival is paying crores to film stars to endorse their products. Our sales figures have to outstrip theirs.'

So, money-swollen film stars were getting even more swollen, while her poor hard-working husband had to be content with 10 lakhs a year. Since Raman had moved to The Brand, Shagun had heard of salaries that at one time seemed unimaginable—40—50—60 lakhs a year, plus bonuses. Anything seemed possible if you worked hard enough. India was becoming a meritocracy, connections were no longer necessary for success.

Their lives assumed the pattern of so many in their set. Weekends with family, friends, clubs and parties. Weekdays shopping, restaurants, children afternoon and evening, nights drinks and parties. From time to time a book was read and knowledge of it displayed.

When Arjun was almost eight, Shagun found she was pregnant again. On a dearly paid holiday cruise around the islands of Hawaii, accompanied by parents (the treat of a lifetime), they fought and made up with hurried sex while Arjun was playing in the bathtub. Thus the conception.

Shagun was distraught. There might have been empty spaces in her life, but this was not how she chose to fill them.

'Why weren't you more careful?'

'Is this my fault?'

'You were supposed to get a vasectomy, but of course you did nothing. Too busy all the time.'

'A lot of people have two children. What's the big deal? We have the money, you can have all the help you want.'

'It's not that. I'll be thirty, Arjun is just becoming independent, I don't want to start all over again. Always tied to a child, is that what you want?'

He stared at her, deeply offended. He was the most committed father he knew, on holidays and weekends devoting himself to his son, giving his wife the break she needed. Another child could only be a blessing, and maybe he would get the daughter he longed for.

He was leaving the next evening for Bareilly, by the time he came back things would have settled down. One precaution he did take, though. Before he left he phoned his mother-in-law: please look after her, she is in a delicate condition, still somewhat upset, and I am worried.

Whatever the stratagems, whether Shagun's mother's delight, whether Arjun's steady demand for a brother, whether the life within made its own claims, Shagun did carry the baby to term, and gave birth to a daughter in June 1996.

Right from the beginning it was clear that Baby Roohi was a carbon copy of her father.

All mine, Raman joked, can't mistake her for anybody else's.

At least don't draw attention to her looks, snapped Shagun, when she had heard him once too often.

Raman looked at his wife in surprise. This is not how you talk of your child, no matter who she takes after. 'You'll see, she will blossom into a beauty—not like you, but a beauty all the same.'

'And how can you tell that?'

The father picked up the baby, now seven months old, and held her in his arms. He looked at the tiny features that held every promise of plainness. Like his own. But he was a man, this little thing would have more need of a pretty face, or life might treat her unkindly.

'If we treat her as beautiful she will think she is beautiful, and people will judge her by the way she judges herself. So I don't want to ever hear her called plain again.'

In Shagun's experience beauty did not work like that, but the little child was her daughter and Raman took her silence for assent.

IV

Indraprastha Extension, located in East Delhi across the river Jamuna, was an area furrowed with housing societies, and the poorer colonies devoted to servicing them. Tiny shops and roadside vendors intruded slyly into the chaotic traffic as rickshaws, cyclists, cars, scooters, pushcarts, buses and pedestrians jostled for space on the crowded roads.

Also known as Patparganj, here lay the hope of many of the salaried middle classes to own a home of their own.

Swarg Nivas was one of the largest housing societies in the area. Planned in blocks of six, the three A blocks in front had the larger flats, while the B blocks behind were smaller and cheaper. Three fenced-in gardens, lined with benches, divided the two sections. At the corner in the front was a small grocery store, the society offices and a little temple.

Here lived the brothers Kaushik, Raman's father and uncle, in flats that attested to the uncle's business acumen. He was a lawyer, and it was through one of his clients in the eighties that he had heard about the Swarg Nivas Co-operative Housing Society while still a dream on paper.

Knowing that you can't go wrong with real estate, Som Nath Kaushik made down payments on two flats. One in A block for himself, one in B block for his younger brother, Shiv Nath, who as an engineer in the PWD had to operate under the constraints of a government salary and honesty.

Each of the brothers had one son, with seven years between them. In Nandan's time things were not quite so competitive; with a minimum of study, he managed to qualify for law college. Once he got his LLB, he started sharing his father's office in the evenings, while working from slightly larger premises in the Tees Hazari grounds during the day.

He agreed to marry the first girl his parents showed him. Rohini was a niece of his mother's sister's husband, home-loving, pleasant features, medium height, nice smile. When she produced twins, Aditya and Abhilasha, the family was joyfully complete, and her charms further enhanced.

Raman meanwhile excelled in studies from an early age. His mother grew ambitious for him, as without any coaxing, he stood first year after year. He will be an engineer, she decided, only in a better position than his father, who all his life has had his talents wasted. In class XI she put him into a local coaching group, and for the next two years Raman attended school in the morning, coaching in the afternoon, then did the homework of both. When he cleared the entrance exam for IIT, his father insisted that it was all due to his elder brother's blessings, making an imaginative leap his wife didn't even begin to understand.

She didn't think there was any need to be quite so grateful, even though she was privy to the sums the older brother lent the younger. But she hated feeling this obliged.

When you are older, she told her son, you will earn more than all of them put together. They think because they have helped us with this flat we have yet to see, they have done something great.

Raman heard her without attention. He was still a student and for him the future was limited to the next exam.

Raman spent the next five years in IIT swotting. Then another two years of even greater toil in IIM, Ahmedabad, to finally land a job at IndiaThinkTank with a six-figure annual salary. His long hours, and the distances he had to travel, made it convenient for him to live with other corporate trainees in a flat near his office.

When he celebrated his twenty-seventh birthday, his parents decided it was time he marry.

I will ask Bhabhi to look for a bride, said Mr Kaushik, she has done such a good job with Rohini. Fits in perfectly. Such lovely children too.

But the mother wanted somebody with a little more class. Raman had a corporate job, the wife would need to look after his interests socially. While not disagreeing with her husband she quickly spread the word far and wide. Among its recipients was a cousin twice removed, living in Alaknanda.

Ami knew a neighbour's daughter, third-year college. The mother, a widow, vetted Raman's credentials, scrutinized his photograph and then allowed the young people to meet.

It took exactly a minute for Raman to fall in love. Two months of courtship followed before Shagun consented to marry him. His parents were then formally introduced to the girl.

How stunningly beautiful she is, realized a frightened Mrs Kaushik, can such a woman really be a homemaker?

She voiced her apprehensions to her son, knowing it was too late, cursing the modern need to love before marriage.

'Uff Ma, she is still in college—what do you want? That she spend all her time in the kitchen?'

'Even after you marry, I do not see this woman in the kitchen.'

Neither did Raman, but he did not care. If he could have her in his bed, what did the kitchen matter?

Mrs Kaushik could see there was no point saying anything to her son—he had a slack-jawed moronic look when it came to any discussion of his future after marriage.

Shagun herself had romantic visions of the two of them running their house on their own. Raman hadn't lived with his parents since he started work, it was too far, too inconvenient. Why should those reasons still not apply?

Whereas Mrs Kaushik had always considered her son's living arrangements temporary. As an only child she expected that his marriage would at last augment their tiny family. Knowing this, Mr Kaushik made an attempt to bring the boy closer.

'Nandan has put down a deposit for a flat in the building, he and his parents will be across the hall from each other once the apartments are finished,' he told Raman. 'You can do the same.'

'How many years ago were you promised this thing?'

'Such a big project—delays will take place. Now they are saying 1990. Latest.'

'That's three years away—ridiculous. If the corporate sector did things like this, nobody would get anywhere.'

'That's not the point. If nothing else it is a sound investment. People are already selling the 3-lakh flats for 6, but still you can afford it. You will be eligible for a good loan. When the new bridge is built it won't even take long to reach work.'

'I am not sure I see us in Swarg Nivas, Papa,' said Raman slowly. 'It is very far from Shagun's mother, and you know she is all alone.'

'Arre, she can always come to visit. Then she will be close to all of us. Once you have your flat there, you will be both independent and nearby.'

'If I rent a bigger house, we can stay together in South Delhi,' said Raman, valiantly trying to do his duty.

This possibility seduced his father for a moment, but only a moment. A pretty daughter-in-law, the son dancing attendance on her, an angry disappointed mother, such a situation would lead to daily tension. Perhaps it was better to change his expectations of their joint family life right now. Not every couple were Rohini and Nandan, so willing to adjust.

'Beta, your uncle has helped me so much with this flat, thinking we will all be together. How much we have planned and dreamt. Once Swarg Nivas is ready we should live there,' he said slowly. 'But perhaps you are right. It is not good to start your marriage caught between wife and mother. All we want is your happiness.'

Raman looked at the slight man before him, his heavy glasses, his thin grey hair. It was quite apparent he had altered his own ideas to accommodate the conflicting interests of those he loved. He bent to touch his father's feet. 'May we always have your blessings, Papa, that is all we want.'

Mrs Kaushik was devastated when it became clear that her separation from her son was to be permanent.

'Why won't they come to Swarg Nivas? What about my grandchildren?' she wailed.

'When they come, we will see,' said her husband sternly. 'In the meantime you will have plenty to occupy you with Rohini's children.'

A niece-in-law's children could never be like her own, though she was not allowed to think so, her husband expecting a saintliness of which she was not capable. To her grief after all these years he always seemed to be engaging with some quite other person.

Forced into being a spectator of her son's life, Mrs Kaushik had to make a virtue of necessity. Soon everybody knew how they did not believe in hanging around their child's neck, though actually that was all she had ever wanted to do.

Raman insisted on a weekly visit to his parents. Shagun was always careful to demonstrate daughter-in-law devotion. From time to time she complained to her husband, 'Your mother hates me,' but this was only because she wanted him to see how magnanimous she was. Raman did not respond to her comments. He knew his mother expected respect, deference and love from her daughter-in-law plus an undisputed supremacy in her little grandson's heart, all of which she was never going to get.

In 1991, the Swarg Nivas Co-operative Housing Society complex was finally ready. Nandan had a flat of his own across from his parents. The elder Kaushiks put a grille across the passage, black granite tiles on the walls and floor of their section of the corridor and hung a small chandelier with dangling crystal pendants in the middle. The door between their two flats was kept open all day long. The children dashed from room to room; Rohini declared she thought she was living in a palace, her new home was so grand, leading her mother-in-law to quickly circle her head with a green chilli and put it in the fire to counter the effect of the evil eye.

The happy togetherness in her brother-in-law's family showed Raman's mother how much she was missing and she took this knowledge badly, blaming her daughter-in-law for the loneliness she felt.

V

Mrs Sabharwal, Shagun's mother, got along excellently with Raman. For twelve years he had been more son than son-in-law. Shagun sometimes said you two are like lovebirds, making the mother uncomfortable at her daughter's understanding of the tenderness between them.

After all these years she still remembered the instinctive sense of relief that came upon her when she first saw him. Ami had already declared Raman steady, sober, an excellent wage earner, Punjabi and twenty-seven. In appearance he was good-looking, complexion wheatish, a lovely open smile, handsome white teeth, medium height with just the tiniest paunch and a head of thinning hair. She hoped Shagun was not going to fuss about that. Sensitive from the start, he had put her at ease, voluntarily supplying all the information a mother might need, carrying out his own interview as it were.

IIT—Delhi, IIM—Ahmedabad, graduated in '84, been recruited on campus for this job with IndiaThinkTank, India's number-one advertising agency, 5 lakhs had been the starting salary, the annual bonus handsome. He was responsible for ensuring customers remained satisfied, converting even the uncertain into the firm's loyal clients. As Raman talked, Mrs Sabharwal's understanding skipped away from his words and made straight for his heart. Clearly he was a sincere company worker, hard-working, ambitious, obviously talented. The man radiated dependability.

The more she got to know Raman, the more secure she felt. He was punctual to the minute, coming over with fruit, chocolate, biscuits, cake, cheeses, just small things, he claimed, but she knew how much time and effort they must have cost, especially since he preferred foreign brands. When he took Shagun to see a film he always bought a ticket for her as well, to assure her that she was not losing a daughter, but gaining a son. His words were backed by actions that shone in her imagination as large as he had intended.

Once the couple were engaged, Raman became even more indispensable. 'Now you have me,' he told Mrs Sabharwal, as he took care of her bills, as he dealt with recalcitrant plumbers and electricians, as he replaced her carpenter with a better one, as he helped with the wedding arrangements, talked to the caterer, talked to the pandit, beat the prices down. Everything he did was an indication of the great joys to come once he was properly part of the family.

The years of struggle and misery that had followed Mr Sabharwal's death were drawing to a close. A man was coming into the house, he would be the buffer between them and the world.

'Beta, such a good match,' the mother couldn't help repeating, 'so reliable he is, you will never have to worry about a thing. Your life will be comfortable, secure and safe.'

Shagun smiled prettily, happy to be the cause of so much solicitude. She graduated from Jesus and Mary College and put away her books with relief. She hadn't really liked studying though she had done reasonably well. She was looking forward to the freedom marriage would provide.

*

During her eleven years of marriage, many men had looked at Shagun, looked and looked, but none had ventured across the boundary line of matrimony. She had a settled air about her, weighed down as she was by her home, her son and eventually her daughter.

Later she decided she must have been unhappier than she realized. She had been brought up to marry, to be wife, mother and daughter-in-law. She had never questioned this destiny, it was the one pursued by everyone she knew.

Soon after she met Ashok Khanna she grew certain that he was trying to seduce her. It was when she told her first lie, a lie of omission concerning the cup of coffee, that she became complicit in those efforts. From then on, a curtain was drawn between her normal life and another secret one, more charged than anything she had previously known.

In the beginning it was wonderful, her sense of power experienced differently now that she was thirty-two. She was the mature one, he the child, helpless with passion.

'Why do you want me?' she asked at times, puzzled by his certainty when things were so complicated.

'Don't ask, I just do.'

'Is it that simple?'

His fingers twisted the lock of hair falling over her cheek, his arm circled her body. She felt more real to him than any woman he had known; why that was, he could not say, but she was his other half, the half he had been seeking all his adult life.

'That's what happens when you don't marry till middle age,' she teased. 'You'll get over it—just like you got over all the others.'

'Never.'

She half wished he wasn't so sure.

'What are you thinking?' he asked, trying to penetrate the gaze that went beyond him.

Of Roo.

He was jealous. He tried to participate in all her concerns, but his experience with children was negligible and he could offer little of substance.

What about Roo?

I know it's a bit early, but it will be easier for me to meet you if I admit her in playschool. There is one in our neighbourhood. It will do her good to learn some independence. Unfortunately her father is bound to object.

She had stopped using her husband's name. It seemed too intrusive.

Follow your instincts, darling, I am sure whatever you do will be right.

Umm.

*

Raman did object. His wife must be out of her mind. The child was only one and a half. He didn't think any school would take her. Also it was the middle of winter. Young children fell sick easily when exposed to groups.

Their paediatrician always said such sicknesses increased immunity, his wife pointed out. Children can't be protected like that. Besides, this wasn't a regular school but one especially designed for very young children. Just two hours a day. Playing. That is all they do.

Why couldn't she play at home?

She needed to get along with other kids. She was very clingy.

At her age surely that was to be expected? She needed her mother. Enough time for independence when she grew.

And Raman would not budge from his position.

What happened about Roo's school? asked the lover.

He is not agreeing. Fussing about winter. Colds, infections, that kind of stuff.

How old did you say she was?

One and a half. Her birthday's in June.

They fell silent. Ashok out of ignorance, Shagun because of having to remind Ashok how old her daughter was. This caused her a very brief insight—which she quickly ignored—as to what it would be like to live with a man who was not the biological father of her children.

School is not the only solution. There are others. You have to think out of the box, said Ashok finally.

*

Ever since Ashok Khanna had taken an interest in Mang-oh! Raman's performance had improved. Together they had worked out an increase of the non-CSD (carbonated soft drink) profits by at least 1 per cent.

Untapped markets had a lot of potential, said Shagun knowledgeably, when Raman told her of these projected figures.

Did she know what 1 per cent represented? he asked, surprised at her commercial turn of speech.

Whatever it represented, she was absolutely sure he could do it.

When he returned from his tours, prettiness flowed from her, generously, like a replenished mountain stream after the snow has melted in summer. And he, of course, delighted in the attempts she made to please him. It was a point of honour that she should never feel he took her for granted.

The reward for all the hard work was going to be the bonus that would make their projected England World Cup trip as special as it could possibly be. He would fly both of them business class, he would give her an unlimited shopping allowance. His absence would be compensated.

Eight couples were going to travel together, and there was much to decide: which matches to buy tickets for, which places needed to be seen, which relatives to venture towards.

The Mang-oh! ad had been dubbed into several Indian languages, and offers were coming for Shagun to act in other films.

'I have to go to Bombay,' she told Raman. 'To do a screen test for Nestlé.'

He looked at her, bright, restless and reaching beyond the home.

'I'll come with you.'

'What about the children? No, I will manage.'

When she came back, Raman asked how it had gone, but she could not answer satisfactorily. Apparently she had had to wait for a long time, she had been paired with a child she instinctively disliked, her screen test had been disappointingly short, and they had given no immediate assurances. What she really needed was a portfolio.

'What about the children?'

'What has that got to do with anything?'

Nothing, but one thing could lead to another. He didn't trust the world when it came to his wife.

'You don't wish me to have a life of my own?'

'I never interfere in anything you want to do.'

'All these years there was nothing I particularly cared for.'

'Shagu, what are you saying?'

Her face twisted, and she turned her head away. 'Oh, forget it.'

Raman did not know what to think. When things were not right between Shagun and himself it felt as though the centre of his world was hollow. Yet the demands of his work forced him to be away long hours, thinning the connection between them.

He turned to his parents.

'I'll be travelling more than usual in the next few months.'

'Hai Ram,' said his mother. 'What do they want? Your life's blood? These days you are looking so tired. If you fall sick then who will be there for you?'

Raman refused to rise to this bait, dangled over him these past twelve years, of an uncaring wife and him a self-sacrificing overworked provider.

'Ma, don't you understand? I am involved in a very important campaign.'

The mother, being the mother, persisted with unworkable solutions.

'Why don't you go for a holiday, beta? Let someone else do the work. Is there no one in that whole organization but you?'

'I am the Mang-oh! man, you know that. How can anyone else take my brief?'

The father said, 'Do not worry, beta. We will look after Shagun and the children. What are parents for, after all?'

Later, they commented on how drawn and pale their son looked. He was so reluctant to worry them, it was impossible to ever figure out what the matter was. They could only suffer anxiety as they guessed at his life.

Helping out their daughter-in-law while her husband was away was easier said than done. They did appear at her doorstep unannounced as he had suggested, but he had also suggested a warm welcome. This was not forthcoming.

'Beta, Raman said it is hard for you to manage alone,' they offered in explanation. 'In fact he was very insistent we come.'

'It was unnecessary for Raman to put you to so much trouble; I have always managed alone.'

'He even fixed this evening time. Said you would be home with the children.'

'Then he fixed it without informing me. I would have made other plans if I had known. Just now I am going out. My mother is waiting at Priya.'

'Priya? The movie hall?'

'Yes. The children are very keen to see a film.'

'Where are they?'

'With her.'

The thought of Mrs Sabharwal waiting with her grandchildren in a cinema complex, while Shagun was for some reason at home, was a strange one. Equally strange that their daughter-in-law, instead of including them in the expedition, should be ushering them politely out. They had travelled across Delhi for nothing and the car AC wasn't even working. Dispirited, they drove back.

'Imagine—he told his parents to check on me.'

'Poor bugger, he must be sensing something.'

'He likes to feel he is very sensitive.'

'And he isn't?'

'Why are you taking his side? Do you want me to stay with him?'

He tried to gather her in his arms but she pulled away and looked at him uncertainly.

'You know what I want,' he said.

'How do I know you are not lying?'

'Try me. This situation is not good for anybody.'

By now she had understood that he was a man of narrow and intense passions, one who lived, slept and ate business. For the first time in his life he claimed he had found someone to put above his work.

A bottle of Mang-oh! and thou, that were Paradise enow, he said.

What was 'enow'?

Archaic English for enough. Learnt it in school.

You were taught about Paradise enow?

Yup.

And you remember?

Everything I learnt.

She traced the silvering hair at his temples with her finger. 'And what are you learning now—here—with me? How to make a married woman love you?'

'How to get the married woman to follow her heart as quickly as possible.'

'You know that's not going to happen.'

'I know no such thing. Why is it so unthinkable?'

'I can't just leave, I can't—don't ask me—go if you like, but please don't ask me.'

'Darling, we have to talk about this.'

'Why? Why can't we just go on as we are?'

'Because I want you with me for ever, not just while I am in India.'

She cupped her hands around his face, and drew the full mouth to her own. 'You should have thought of that earlier,' she murmured.

'Yes, I should have. But who can think when you are around?'

She loved the hoarseness of his voice that came after they kissed, the closed eyes, the tense brow, the broad white hands that pressed her close.

'So? Who is asking you to think?'

'I wish it wasn't necessary, but this situation is not going to improve on its own.'

He was impatient with any problem—worrying it till a solution emerged. She knew that of him by now.

When she turned inwards where her life was waiting to be examined, she blamed Raman for her predicament, thinking of the years she had been satisfied with his lovemaking, tender, attentive, pedestrian, as so much wasted time.

Through her twenties she had presumed herself content, knowing she had much to be thankful for, healthy children, comfort, money.

Now the destroyer was in her heart, threatening what she had once held dear. All her energy was spent in keeping secrets. She had to be constantly vigilant, continuously invent excuses, convincingly justify absences from home, phone calls, even a preoccupied expression.

Ashok too was thoughtful. Many times he wished that he and her husband were not working in the same company. It was an obvious conflict of interest, and it needed to be resolved. He wanted Shagun and he wanted to clear the hell out of Delhi. Maybe relocate in Gurgaon—or go to Bombay.

He hated subterfuge of any kind, the feeling that he had something to hide made him vulnerable. His position would be hard to explain once it came out into the open, as it inevitably would.

As soon as he possessed her, this strange hiatus in his life would be over, and he would be able to focus better on his Indian mission, that is, help the company recover the millions it had invested.

VI

It was Mrs Sabharwal who first realized something was wrong. It started with Raman's departure, a usual event, but one of deep concern to the mother-in-law.

'Beta, did he go off all right?'

Shagun snorted. Here she was talking about her portfolio and all her mother could think of was whether her husband had managed to catch a plane. Which any birdbrain could do.

'Why are you always so worried about Raman? You should be the one married to him, not I.'

'Is this any way to talk about your husband?'

Such useless questions. That was the trouble with mothers. Their eyes were like those of a lynx, their gaze tried to pierce your being, their interference in your life knew no limits.

Mrs Sabharwal was thinking. Did her daughter's indifference to Raman's welfare suggest a deeper malaise? Shagun was too innocent, that was the trouble, and her husband too busy. Always travelling, leaving a young wife largely to her own devices.

Shagun raised her marvellous green eyes, eyes that established her as a rarity from the moment of her birth. 'Why can't I talk of my husband in any way I like?'

'Has anything happened? Tell me.'

'Nothing.'

'You and the children should stay with me for a few days while he is away. I hardly see you. Whenever I phone, you are out.'

The daughter looked through the window at the two feet of cemented space next to the gate of her old home. Here her mother's plants surrounded by concrete on all four sides slowly wilted and gradually died. The pots that contained these pathetic specimens were chipped. Yesterday's storm had broken some of them, exposing white, densely intersecting roots, raw against the mud.

'You know I can't just leave, Mama. There is the children's routine and the household.'

The logical thing to do would be to invite the mother to her place, but for this Mrs Sabharwal had to wait another two days, and then it was worse than not being called at all.

'Mama, please come and stay—I have to go out of town.'

'Good heavens, why?'

'You remember my friend—the one who settled down in Bareilly?'

Mrs Sabharwal remembered no such friend—but her memory was bad and she said nothing.

'Well, Mama, do you? Anyway, they have just discovered her husband has cancer—poor man, he is only in his late thirties, she called me in a total flap, they have to go right away to Bombay—and she has asked me if I can come—only till her parents manage to get there—so can you, Mama?

Just for the weekend—two nights? Not even two days? I'll be leaving tomorrow afternoon.'

There were many things Mrs Sabharwal didn't know, many, many. Why you had to go to Bombay if you had cancer, who Shagun's friends were, and whether they were married in Bareilly or not. But she could read the minutest change in her daughter's voice and now suspicion unwillingly filtered through her mind as she agreed to spend the time required with her grandchildren in their mother's absence.

Once in Shagun's house she was reassured. The children were as loving as ever, the servants gave no dubious replies to any of her oblique questions. But when Shagun returned two days later, the glow on her face, the radiance emanating from her made the mother's alarm wearily rise to do more duty.

She might as well rush in where angels fear to tread. 'Who is he?' she asked.

Shagun blushed. 'What are you talking about, Mama?'

'You weren't really in Bareilly, were you?'

'Of course I was. Phone Rita—I can give you her number—and ask her.'

'Phone a stranger to enquire about my daughter? No thank you.'

'Mama—if you don't trust me, you shouldn't have agreed to come. I am tired now—and I want to spend time with the children. I am sure they missed me more than you did.'

Quietly Mrs Sabharwal left the house. Her intuition made her wretched. She would have given anything to not know that Raman was no longer the centre of Shagun's life. For the first time in twelve years, she felt irritated with him. He must be to blame in some way, her daughter would not jeopardize her home so easily. If that was not true, her life's work had failed.

All night Mrs Sabharwal tossed and turned, desolately seeking sleep. The electricity went. The inverter came on, and with it the fan. Again and again Raman's face rose before her with all the urgency of a threatened species. Was this her fault in some way? Since her teens, Shagun had had an infinite number of unsuitable boys after her—she had needed to ensure her daughter's safety before the fruit was snatched and a tender life ruined. Raman was the antidote to every fear.

All that anxious care had apparently served no purpose. This was a worse situation to be in. Such transgressions seldom remained hidden. Some servant, some overheard phone call, some casual reported encounter. Raman might resort to violence against his wife, hard to imagine, but till yesterday it had also been hard to imagine her daughter going astray. And what about Raman's safety? Stories of lovers murdering husbands appeared regularly in the newspapers.

She got up to start reciting the Gayatri Mantra, praying for protection for her daughter and grandchildren. She prayed for Raman too as she had done all these years. How often had she told him that he was better than any son because she would never lose him to a wife. Now a wife was coming between them.

Next morning found her at her daughter's door. 'Why do you want to destroy my peace?' she demanded. 'You have to tell me who he is. What kind of person will take you away from your husband, such a good man?'

'You always take his side.'

'You never said that was a problem.'

'I was so young, what did I know?'

'You were of marriageable age, twenty-one, same as me.'

'Have you come all the way to tell me this?'

'Does he suspect? He must know—or guess—something at least.'

Shagun stared at her mother. Her face was drawn and tense, her hair dishevelled, her sari crumpled, the blouse even less matching than usual. For twelve years her mother had praised Raman for being the son she never had. Now she looked as though she had lost a child.

'If I tell you, you will get more upset,' she said, ordering the maid to make lemonade with lots of lemon and sugar the way Naani liked it, and to also bring the pista, still unlocked after last night's drinks.

No, no, let the pista be, it will be too heating in this weather.

The daughter paid no attention. Her mother loved pista, and denied herself routinely. 'If men can have pista with drinks that are already heating, you can have it with your lemonade, which is cooling.'

'Shagu, I couldn't sleep all night. What will happen to you? To the children? And Raman? His family is everything to him.'

'Mama, stop going on. It is hard enough as it is. Am I to stay married to Raman because you love him so much?'

That would not be a bad idea, thought the mother, but she said nothing. Her daughter looked perfect in her pale lavender embroidered organdie kurta with the purple salwar and chunni. Her small white feet were in delicate beaded jutti. She wore amethyst earrings, pale pink nail polish, purple glass bangles on one arm, a dainty gold watch on the other. The mother noticed a tiny diamond set in the dial. 'Did he give you that watch?' she asked.

The daughter nodded, her blush rising from neck to face as she remembered his insistence that she carry a token of their love into her house: jewellery was too conspicuous, a watch had seemed ideal.

Mrs Sabharwal renewed her attack. She promised not to blame, she would only try and understand.

Shagun wrapped her arms around her, whispered how sorry she was, really she hadn't wanted to do anything to hurt her husband, she too was afraid, but now this thing had happened, she was already more deeply in love than ever in her life, more ecstatic, more miserable. She knew what her mother felt about Raman, but she herself didn't care if she lived or died.

What choice did the mother have? She had to agree to keep silent, without having accomplished her goal of making Shagun follow the path of virtue. Now she was an accomplice to the crime. Society could point its finger at her and say, she knew and did nothing. How would it look? she blurted, and her daughter replied, 'Look to who?'

To God, how will it look to God?, but this was not a response that would influence Shagun.

Raman, for marketing reasons which Shagun found incomprehensible, had just returned from Singapore, and was anxious to distribute presents of cutlery sets, perfume and chocolate to both sets of parents. Shagun knew how transparent her mother was, and till her news had lost the capacity to shock, tried to postpone going to Alaknanda.

'So much chocolate is bad for her,' she said, looking at the small sack of Lindt Assorted.

'She loves the stuff.'

'Doesn't mean she should eat it.'

'Has something happened?'

'No.'

'Then? Why deprive Ma of a little chocolate? Besides, you wouldn't want your husband to visit his mother-in-law empty-handed.'

The visit was made, during which Shagun had to endure her mother's awkward behaviour. To have the knowledge she did and behave normally was practically impossible for Mrs Sabharwal.

'Ma, are you all right?' asked Raman, noticing the frown, sensing the worry.

'A slight headache,' she quavered.

'Maybe you should take Belladonna 200,' said Raman. Since the birth of his children he had dabbled in homeopathy.

'Thank you, beta.'

'Do you still have the bottle I gave you?'

'Yes, don't worry about me, beta.'

'It's nothing, don't fuss. You know she gets a headache sometimes,' said Shagun curtly.

'Shagu, I don't think we can call Ma's pain nothing. The headache could be an indication of some deeper malady. Homeopathy is a holistic medicine.'

'Beta, please, I am fine—just a little tired.'

Raman was forced to be content. Afterwards Shagun pointed out to her mother, who needed help in these matters, did she notice what a fusspot her husband was being? Going on about the headache, boring, predictable, she must have heard that stuff about holistic medicine a hundred thousand times.

How could Mrs Sabharwal find Raman's care boring? Comforting was how she saw it. If this was being scorned by his wife, what was left?

Her headaches increased.

VII

In April Shagun reiterated her desire to put her daughter in kindergarten. She was older now.

'Only by a few months. Why not wait till she turns two?'

Because admission started now. Because Roo needed to prepare for the entrance test for a big school. Even though Arjun was in VV, siblings did not have automatic rights.

'She is too young to start cramming for some entrance test,' said the father.

'Not cramming. Awareness. Toddler's Steps gives children awareness through play items, paints, clay, picture books. It's never too early to start.'

'All this can be done at home. Why take away her childhood?'

'Three hours a day is hardly taking away her childhood.'

'Big school starts at four-plus, she will have ample time to prepare, even if you send her after six months.'

'Then you will start talking of infections in winter.'

'I'm just saying wait till after summer. What has happened to you?'

Shagun's voice grew edgy. 'Things are more competitive now. Other parents think nothing of it, even if you can't bear to let your daughter go.'

Competition. The word that drove children from the moment they joined kindergarten till the moment they landed a job with a decent salary. No, there was no escape from competition. It had driven Raman his whole life, but for his baby he wanted something different. He tried another tack.

'Suppose she has to do su-su? Who will take her? She might feel too shy to ask.' Roohi did not always make it to the bathroom on time.

'They have ayahs just for this. Why don't you come and see?'

'No, it's all right,' said Raman slowly. What would be the use? They had not rushed like this with Arjun, but then his mother had not been so restless—maybe she needed time for herself.

So Roohi joined Toddler's Steps and cried every day for a week as her mother left her at the gate. 'She stops as soon as you leave,' the teachers assured the mother when she went to pick up her daughter. 'She is very happy here.'

Yes, thought her mother, looking at her closely, she didn't seem any the worse for the three hours away. And even Arjun had cried when he first started, though he had been older. Anyway, it was good for children to learn independence as soon as possible.

Roohi's favourite game became school-school, with dolls who were chastised vigorously for dirtying themselves, for hitting other children, for peeing in class, for ceaseless crying. See, said the mother to the father, you were wrong. Look at her friends, at her little works of art, at her eagerness to go to school like her brother.

His wife had been right after all, agreed Raman, trying to draw her closer to him, while Shagun, seeming not to notice, said that next term she would be made a monitor.

Raman smiled. He could just imagine his little Roo strutting around the classroom, handing out coloured pencils or whatever it was that two-year-old monitors did.

*

Raman returned from his Singapore trip bristling with ideas about beverage consumption. After a weekend at home, he immediately swung into action. The focus on educational institutions had been his idea, the targets and time frame had been Ashok's. 'Once this gets off,' he told Shagun, 'I can say I have done my bit for Mang-oh!. There are always other opportunities.'

'Like?'

'You have to think global, act local.'

'So you keep saying'—the irritation masked by the brightness of the smile.

He looked at her. 'It's what we are constantly told.'

'So how will you act local?'

'In all kinds of ways. So many Indian drinks can be packaged—think of kanji, think of all the different types of buttermilk, sweet, sour, fruit-flavoured, spicy. Once we have the Mang-oh! sales in place we can really diversify. In Singapore they package teas—black, green, jasmine, all doing extremely well. Coconut water too, sweetened, plain—I drank it all the time.'

It was nice, she thought drearily, that he was so enthusiastic, that he had his work and not a secret, that he could function in the world. Her life would have been different if she too had had a job. 'I am sure you will succeed. I can feel it in my bones,' she said.

Raman was glad he had his wife's support. His target was close to being met, but it required a spurt of effort over the next three months. His assistant had drawn up a list of a hundred schools that would have programmes sponsored by Mang-oh!. In return they would serve Mang-oh! in their canteens for at least a year. Local celebrities were approached for shows, and TV ads in Punjabi and Hindi were scheduled for local channels. In Ludhiana, they had their event in the sports college, with sports people talking about the energy value of Mang-oh! with its 27 per cent fruit pulp content. And so on through Chandigarh, Ambala, Jullunder, and Hoshiarpur. After Punjab they would concentrate on Haryana, next Uttar Pradesh, then Rajasthan, Gujarat, Madhya Pradesh. Within six months he expected a dramatic increase in sales.

With all this on his mind, it took him longer than it should have to find his wife changed in a way he could not explain. Roo was in school now, she was freer in the mornings. Was she enjoying herself? What did she do? he asked.

She went out with friends. Or sometimes to the gym.

Tenderly he looked at her: was she feeling all right?

Fine, fine, she was fine. Her assurances were vehement.

But what do words matter, when actions speak so loud?

Raman knew himself to be an ordinary man, ordinary-looking, ordinarily talented though hard-working. The extraordinary thing in his life was his wife, and his love for her, as strong as steel, as pliant as a spider's web. He hoped she would never find out the extent to which she could wound him.

Now he began to fear this hope was not going to be realized. Though he tried to tell himself he was mistaken, there was an opacity in her he couldn't penetrate.

It hurt him to look at her these days. The red lips, the white body, the gold glow of her cream-coloured skin, the bright brown of her thick hair, the long narrow face, the clean sharp jawline and high cheekbones, the variegated green of her eyes taunted him with their perfection, saturating him with insecurity.

His periodic returns brought him to a wife whose slightly dazzled look had nothing to do with him.

He sought reassurance in her arms, but she began to push him away, with all kinds of excuses: somebody would see, she was tired, later, later.

'I don't care. I miss my wife.'

He waited for her to say she missed him too, but the trite words died on her lips. She started talking of the children, the topic most easily at hand when so many others were taboo.

At night when he tried to pull her towards him, she again resisted. 'I am really tired.'

'We haven't done it for weeks. That's not fair, Shagu. If anyone should be tired, it's me.'

'And I have a headache.'

Could anything be lamer?

Later, how many times did he wish that suspicion had not entered him? Like poison, it seeped through his heart, paralysing him, making him see his wife through its dark and vicious colours.

He found himself phoning home at odd hours, asking the servants more questions than necessary. As he began to find out how much she vanished even after the children returned from school, he accosted her.

Where do you go?

Shopping, out with friends, going for ad interviews.

What are these interviews? Who are these friends?

Are you accusing me of something?

Should I be?

Look inside yourself and see.

What does that mean?

Oh, nothing. Forget it.

Shagu, can't one talk to you any more? What is making you behave like this?

I want something else in my life, can't you understand that? We always meet the same people, talk about the same old things over and over. It's boring.

He stared at her, uncomprehending. He worked hard to give her a good life. She had two lovely children and everything she wanted. Next summer they would be going to England for the World Cup. How many women had what she did?

As he attempted to explain his world view, Shagun rewarded him with tears and anger. Did he really think it was all about things?

Deeply resentful, he left the room. She belittled him. He would like to see how she did without *things*.

The next day in office, staring at the street scene below, looking at the taxi drivers lounging on cots next to the kiosk, distracted by his torment, wondering what was worse, touring or confined to the office, again and again pondering over what had caused the change in his wife, it occurred to him to have her followed. At least he would know what was going on in her life.

He toyed with the idea, then rejected it. Let sleeping dogs lie, once you began to suspect your wife there was no marriage left. He would try to talk to her again that evening. They both had to want a successful relationship, he was sure they both did.

That evening, after dinner, he took her hand and noticed she had on a different watch, a thin gold Cartier.

'Where did you get that?'

'Mama.'

'I have never seen her wearing it.'

'My father gave it to her long ago.'

He turned her wrist around. 'Looks new.'

'She kept it very carefully.'

'If you needed a new watch, I would have got you one, Shagu.'

'I didn't ask for this. She gave it.'

'Still, you don't have to take everything you are offered.'

'Suddenly you are very bothered about my mother's watch. What is it to you?'

'You are everything to me. And so is your mother—you know that.'

That was just the trouble with Raman—he swallowed her up, leaving no space to breathe. What normal son-in-law was so devoted to his wife's mother?

'Why do you make such an issue of everything?' She wished his voice would stop. Its cadences pursued her into a small dark place, delved into her soul, sought out her crimes in order to stand in judgement over her.

'I am surprised, that's all,' he said, holding her wrist and kissing the place where the watch sat, aware of the slight tension that made it stiff and unyielding. 'I sense some distance between us, and that makes me unhappy.'

'Distance?' she laughed as she drew her hand away. 'It is you who keep travelling. How can you talk about my distance?'

Raman subsequently spent a wakeful night telling himself how much he trusted her—he had no other option. In any other scenario lay madness and despair.

Next morning the Indica he had hired arrived at five. His wife rose with him, offering to make tea, to pack some sandwiches. As he refused everything, she looked at him anxiously; he moved to kiss her, but like last night her body sent its own message, and he silently let her go.

When he left she worried about that. She could tell her husband was beginning to suspect, but to have anything to do with him physically made her want to scream. While he was away she made a thousand resolutions: be wifelike, be good, docile, compliant, but the mere sight of him sent these decisions out the window.

To blot out such thoughts she dialled a number. It was very early, but she knew, day or night, he was always glad to hear her, no matter how sleepy, no matter how inconvenient. As far as he was concerned, her freedom was absolute.

In the meantime she had five clear days in which to indulge herself. And nights, nights that she would ask her mother to come and spend with the children. Only a few hours, she would be back early in the morning. No matter how disapproving, she knew her mother could not refuse her.

Raman returned with his own resolutions. This marriage was going to work or he would die in the attempt. He ignored the lack of interest about the meeting at the district level in Chandigarh, he ignored her absent-minded appreciation of the shawl he had bought her in Jullunder.

But what was harder for him to disregard was the rejection he faced in bed that night. You need two hands to clap, as his mother was fond of saying, two hands, and in this marriage he increasingly felt there was only one hand making its lone gestures.

Once in office he looked up the number of a private detective agency in the yellow pages. He had reached the point where not knowing was worse than any certainty.

VIII

Unaware of the trauma that her son was going through, Mrs Kaushik, on the other side of the river, was involving herself in the lives of her neighbours as usual.

Chief among them was Mrs Rajora, a librarian at the Arts Faculty of Delhi University. She lived three floors above Mrs Kaushik in Tower B-2. Mrs Rajora's working hours meant that she could not go to kitty parties, play tambola, or sing devotional songs in groups that met in the morning, all favoured activities among the society's non-professional women. The friends met instead in the evening, during walks around the building and for arti at the temple. On Wednesdays they took a rickshaw together to the market at Mandavili.

Occasionally they visited the elder Mrs Kaushik in the A-block flats, but the elder Mrs Kaushik was so absorbed by her grandchildren that she seemed to have little time for anything else.

The Rajoras had one child, a daughter, Ishita.

Ishita's early history had been marked by illness. Both parents worked and they had found it hard to manage even with this one child, dividing her care with a part-time maid and a neighbourhood woman who ran a crèche to supplement her income. Perhaps a mistake, because Ishita was diagnosed with TB when only four. A low-class disease, thought the panic-stricken mother, as in a fit of anger she fired the help—these people—you never knew with these people. They were the carriers, the ones who coughed all over your dishes while washing them, over the vegetables while cutting them, who never rested until their germs were plastered over every house they visited. It was the revenge of the downtrodden.

For nine months the child was on TB drugs. They sapped her strength, and made her vulnerable to the waves of cough, cold and fever that swept the city each year. Doctor after doctor, hakims, vaids, homeopaths, nature cure advocates, the parents went to anybody they thought might restore their daughter's health.

Eventually the caring paid off and Ishita grew stronger. Fortune further turned her face in their direction, for Shashtri College, Mr Rajora's workplace, acquired a tower in a building co-operative across the Jamuna, and teachers could pay for the yet unbuilt flats in three instalments. Collecting, borrowing from bank and family, withdrawing from their provident funds, they managed to produce the required lakhs.

When Ishita was twenty-two they moved from Panjabi Bagh, and within weeks Mrs Rajora had met Mrs Kaushik.

By this time Raman was married and a father and Mrs Rajora could spend a lot of time soothing the hurt that Raman's behaviour (that of blatantly preferring his wife to his mother) caused Mrs Kaushik, and Mrs Kaushik in her turn was careful to praise Ishita whenever she could.

The child was a beauty, she said, and so sweet-tempered, her future home would rejoice. This pleased Mrs Rajora, even though she knew that Ishita was sweet rather than pretty, and that without a dowry her qualities, both outer and inner, had to be the sole attraction.

Marriage was far from Ishita's thoughts. She knew it lay in her future but she wanted to work first. Having finished a BA, the family decided she should do a B.Ed., a degree that would always be useful. If she got a job in a government school, she would have security, a steady income, as well as the lighter hours that future matrimony demanded.

Ishita had begun to apply for teaching posts when a proposal was received. Should a good offer come, insisted her parents, you have to answer its call. Everything else can wait, not this.

The family was a traditional merchant one, just shifted to South Delhi from Morris Nagar. Their caste was the same, their horoscopes compatible. The boy was twenty-five, shy and inarticulate.

The prospective in-laws said they wanted a homely family-minded girl, dowry was not a consideration, they had enough money of their own. Suryakanta was their only son, and grandchildren were expected within a year.

Ishita was hesitant. The women of the family didn't work, daughters-in-law were obviously expected to devote themselves to home. What about her B.Ed., her desire to be independent?

A degree would always come in useful, God forbid should anything happen, persuaded her parents. For now, it was better to start on a good note. Stubbornness was not prized in daughters-in-law.

Ultimately, Ishita saw sense. Though they had yet to exchange a sentence, the boy had smiled beguilingly at her, and at twenty-three, that was her most intimate encounter with a non-relative male. They got married on an auspicious date in summer.

Both husband and wife found marriage liberating. For Suryakanta a female companion was a novel thing. For five years he had studied hard at the Delhi College of Engineering, now it was time to enjoy himself.

'SK, yaar, you have really changed after marriage,' said one of their friends as they sat in a restaurant after a film.

'Bhabhi, you should have seen him before. He was like a mouse.'

Ishita laughed. So far as mouselike qualities were concerned, she had her own share. She slid her hand in her husband's, felt the answering squeeze and thought how lucky she was. The custom of arranged marriages seemed replete with wisdom, the institution of the joint family a safeguard against any loneliness she might ever feel.

Her sisters-in-law, school-going Tarakanta, college-going Chandrakanta, were the siblings she had always longed for. She spoiled them as much as she could, helping them with their homework, participating in their shopping.

The Rajoras congratulated themselves on the successful completion of their life's duties. Ishita had jumped a notch in the world. Car, address, situation—all better. Her colour too seemed fairer, her hair shinier, her whole bearing more alive.

As the months wore on, there was no sign of a pregnancy, and Mrs Rajora became uneasy. The couple were young but it was better to prove that the machinery worked early on in the relationship. Producing grandchildren was a moral obligation.

'Beta, you are not taking anything, are you?' she asked.

Her daughter blushed. No, why?

Just like that, responded the mother.

There was little point in distressing the child, but she could no longer enjoy the sleep of one whose life's work has been accomplished. Instead she nagged her husband with her fears.

'Take her to the doctor,' he said finally, 'I cannot answer all these questions.'

'No, no, her in-laws will say we knew there was something wrong with her. I am not taking her to any doctor.'

'In that case don't fret, she is a healthy girl, she will conceive.'

But the mother could no more stop worrying than she could stop breathing. She looked up books on female reproductive health in her library but she didn't understand a word.

She buttonholed a gynaecologist neighbour near the elevator, but instead of assurance she got more reasons for alarm. Fifteen per cent of couples were infertile, though not necessarily sterile. Treatments were available, both invasive and drug-related; they worked fairly quickly if you were lucky.

These treatments, continued the anxious mother, were they expensive? Were they effective?

It all depended on the type of infertility, and the number of attempts that were made. There were many options even if the normal anatomy was lost, but she had to see the couple before she could give an opinion.

How could Mrs Rajora involve the couple when they had not sought her advice? All she was looking for was hope, and words such as 'infertility' and 'loss of normal anatomy' did not do the job. With a heavy heart she thought of the pre-marriage emphasis on the girl's homeliness, on the little Suryakantas she would bring into the world. Mrs Rajora decided her husband was right, she was getting tense for nothing. Ishita and SK were young, everything would be fine.

Ishita's father was pleased to note that his wife had stopped her incessant worrying. He did not know that Mrs Rajora's helplessness was so extreme that she had decided to follow the scriptures and live in the present. She redoubled her prayers, went to the society temple morning and evening, with offerings of sweets, coconuts and flowers.

Eighteen months into the marriage the boy's family began to make noises. 'They are beginning to ask, why haven't you conceived? SK says he doesn't want to be a father yet, but they say he doesn't know what he is talking about. They behave as though he were a child,' reported Ishita to her mother.

'What else do they say to you?'

'Isn't this enough?'

Was it her mother's imagination or had the girl lost the bloom that had been so evident a year ago?

'Are they treating you well?' she asked.

The girl's listless nod was further reason to panic.

'They say it is equally the boy's fault if there is no conception,' said the mother, swimming vigorously in waters she had hesitated to dive into earlier. 'Why are they not getting him examined?'

'He is willing, but it is probably something to do with me.'

'Nonsense. Keep faith in God. He will not let you suffer.'

'My in-laws have asked that I do this special jap 108 times a day. And fast on Tuesdays.'

'You must do whatever they tell you.'

'They want to take me to a doctor also.'

'That is not necessary.'

'I don't have a choice,' said Ishita, as she dragged herself out of the door and into her car.

Shortly after, the miracle occurred.

Such a crowd so early in the morning was odd, thought Mrs Rajora as she turned the corner of the building towards the temple.

Mrs Kaushik saw her and gestured violently.

'*He* was the first to discover it.'

'What has happened?'

'A miracle, that's what. A miracle.'

'Hai Ram. In this day and age?'

'Bhagwanji is drinking milk.'

'Are you absolutely sure?'

'See for yourself. Do you have any?'

'Only fruit and flowers.'

'That won't do. Has to be milk.'

'Should I go and get some?'

'Run, run. And get a spoon as well.'

Her husband was waiting for his tea.

'Hurry, hurry. Bhagwan is drinking milk.'

'Where?'

'Society temple. Leela said her husband was the first to discover it.'

From the corner of the balcony Mr Rajora could see people hurrying to the front of the building. At the elevator entrance their neighbour was holding a glass of milk, smiling, sharing his joy.

By the time they reached the temple, they could see that some of the society officers had organized the crowds into a queue. The building was home to a thousand people, and at least half of them were here. The small puja room was crammed. People were holding milk in all kinds of containers.

Everybody was excited. Could it be really true? Were the gods physically accepting their offerings? When Mrs Rajora's turn came she held out a trembling hand and watched as the milk slowly vanished from the spoon. People around stared. She reached out a finger and gently touched the dark stone cheek. It was dry.

'Arre, the god himself is drinking,' said the man behind her. 'Otherwise, wouldn't the whole floor be wet? So much has been offered since the morning.'

Ashamed, she pulled back her hand, allowing her husband his turn with the spoon. Then others anxious to have a go edged them away.

Once home, Mrs Rajora hurried to the phone. Ishu, come here, the gods are drinking milk, you must offer some, from your own hands. It is a miracle, beta, a miracle.

It seemed Ishita had no need to come there. The gods were drinking milk throughout Delhi. Later when they put on the TV, it was to find deities consuming milk all over India, and by the evening there were reports of similar phenomena in Britain, Canada and the USA.

Clips followed of scientists talking about capillary action, saying that the milk was just spread over the surface of the stone images, but people believed what they saw.

The next morning again Mrs Rajora hurried to the temple, but the people outside told her that the god was no longer accepting milk. 'That is how we know what happened yesterday was truly a miracle, no matter what the scientists say.'

Mrs Rajora agreed. And if the miraculous could occur all over the world, then why not in her daughter's life?

A few days later, Ishita phoned, jubilant. Her mother-in-law had taken her to the gynaecologist, who had said that not enough time had passed—they should wait another six months before going in for tests, which were neither easy nor cheap. A stress-free life was essential. Now they were being very nice to her.

Those six months were hard for Mrs Rajora. She prayed for good news, made all kinds of promises to the small goddess in her bedroom.

Five and a half months passed without any sign of a pregnancy.

'I have found the name of a fertility expert,' Ishita said to her mother. 'Will you come with me? Just to see what my options are. And keep this to yourself.'

The fertility expert was Dr Suhashini Guha, American-trained. Joginder Chhabra, the famous golfer, had gone to her, after which his wife had had twins. Quantities of money must have been spent.

Suhashini Guha listened to Ishita's story, then in a businesslike fashion drew a number of diagrams: maybe the fallopian tubes were blocked, maybe the sperm count was low as was increasingly common nowadays, maybe she had an infantile uterus, or quite simply, maybe there was nothing wrong with any of these.

Had she ever had an abortion? A miscarriage? Ever taken birth control pills? Or used internal devices? Ever experienced a major illness? Ever had TB?

Ishita said no to everything.

An HSG test was suggested, a hysterosalpingogram in which dye was injected into the uterus. This would give an accurate picture of the state of her fallopian tubes.

The doctor would do it herself, next month on the seventh day of her cycle. There would be a certain amount of discomfort involved so she would need to take painkillers, she might also experience heavy cramping for the next few hours. To prevent infection, she would be put on a course of antibiotics.

'And if all is not clear?' cried Mrs Rajora, appalled by this information.

'Then a laparoscopy will follow.'

'And then?'

'Then we will see.'

In the car the mother said slowly, 'I wonder what TB has to do with anything.'

'Why?' demanded Ishita. 'I never had it, did I?'

'Don't think so,' said Mrs Rajora cautiously.

'TB is hardly a disease that goes unnoticed.'

'Beta, as a child you were ill for a long time. But then you grew out of it.'

'Maybe I am damaged goods after all.'

'Don't be silly, and if you had TB, so what? It affects lots of people.'

'So,' said Ishita slowly, 'that's the story.'

The mother was silent.

'How am I supposed to keep this information from my in-laws? My husband? I don't keep secrets from him.' The strain of keeping her voice down so that nothing reached the driver's alert listening ears drove tears into Ishita's eyes. 'And the test? It's invasive after all.'

'Am I saying you should not tell? But let's find out first. What is the point of worrying other people for nothing?'

When his anxious wife related the details of the visit, Mr Rajora declared the doctor had to be told about Ishita's TB. Otherwise there was no point consulting an expert.

But what would this mean for their daughter? Would she be taunted, would her position become vulnerable, would there be pressure on the husband to divorce her? It needed no great experience of the world to inform them that the answer to all these questions was yes. As for Suryakanta's love, could they set store by that?

The father thought they could, the mother knew they couldn't. If the couple were living separately, perhaps, if it had been a love marriage, perhaps, if they had been married a long time, perhaps, but with the husband an only son, living at home with an infertile wife—no.

Suryakanta had been brought up to understand his role so far as the greater good of the family was concerned. Mrs

Rajora knew he would not put his own feelings in front of those considerations.

Let us see what Ishita has to say, said the father. She knows them better than we do.

'I told him about the visit to Dr Guha,' said Ishita to her mother soon afterwards.

'You foolish girl,' snapped Mrs Rajora, 'what was the need?'

'I am not like you,' snapped Ishita back. 'What kind of lies do you want me to go on living? If I can't trust my husband, it is no marriage.'

'He is still a child,' returned the mother.

'He is my best friend,' said the daughter, immune to her mother's fears. The night she had told her husband was particularly sweet. She had cried, he had held her, he had said she was the queen of his heart, he would die without her, of course he would come with her to the doctor, of course they would explore all possibilities. They were married and every problem had a solution.

Mrs Rajora was left speechless. Had Ishita no sense? Didn't she understand the family she had married into? Young love was fine in the bedroom, but outside that door its imperatives ceased.

'And what is more,' continued Ishita triumphantly, 'he is coming with me to do that test. Mummy, this is our problem, we will manage.'

The test that would reveal TB in infancy, that would result in accusations about the girl's health, about having hidden things in order to get the daughter married—that test.

A few days before the test Suryakanta suggested they tell his parents.

'Didn't you say it was our problem?' demanded his wife.

It turned out that 'our' meant the collective us of the joint family, for his parents must neither feel excluded nor ignored. Besides, how could the responsibility be his alone? He could no more think of only the two of them getting such a major test done than he could contemplate flying. And what about the side effects, the pain, the nausea, the cramping? A woman was needed in these situations.

For the first time Ishita felt annoyed with her husband. He was twenty-seven, had he never done anything without his parents' permission? Finally he agreed to say nothing for the moment, which meant that when the day of the HSG test came, the emphasis was more on the favour SK was doing her than on the trauma of the procedure.

Ishita lay down on a narrow hospital bed and stared gloomily at the glaring white lights overhead. As the dye was injected, a sudden hot feeling overtook her, followed by the most severe cramp she had ever known. Despite the air conditioning, sweat filmed her face. After a few minutes the doctor showed her the screen, and pointed out her faulty tubes, sealed irrevocably against both egg and sperm.

Helpless tears ran down Ishita's cheeks, soaking the neckline of her white gown, as the words 'severe blockage' drummed in her mind. What would happen to her now?

On the way back the husband was silent, and Ishita in her corner of the car was too depressed to say much. By the time they reached GK, hatred towards her body filled her. It had let her down in this most basic function and she had to live with the knowledge for the rest of her life.

'Papa and Mummy will know what to do,' said SK at last as the car neared home.

'You are going to tell them?'

'Of course. Don't you think that is best?'

'They will hate me.'

'Naah. They are not like that.'

She dared not contradict him. Already clouds were entering her soul, and shedding heavy drops of unworthiness, and such was the weight she couldn't even hold his hand and tell him that she loved him more than life itself. They never exchanged affection in public.

SK told his mother that evening. He was closeted in her room for a long time, leaving Ishita tense and nervous. 'Bhabhi, what's the matter with you today, why aren't you paying attention?' asked Chandrakanta, as Ishita fought to keep the sick feelings at bay. 'Do you have some good news?'

Oh, how far from the truth. At that moment Ishita thought it easier to commit suicide than to live. From the day of her wedding she had thought of this family as hers, revelling in the togetherness, sharing and companionship. Now instead of love all around her, there would be rejection.

That evening Ishita scanned her mother-in-law's face for signs of disgust as she said, 'I will come with you, beti, to this fertility expert. Men don't really understand these things.' There was no reproach in her voice, but Ishita felt it all the same. The knot in her stomach, squeezing her insides, tightened its grip.

'I want to understand exactly what is wrong, and what to do,' she went on. 'I believe there are options. But Sukku did not give me a very clear idea of what they were. But then I always say, he is just a boy, what does he know?'

On the morning of the second appointment with Suhashini Guha, Ishita discovered that SK was not coming. 'Mummy said there is no need.'

'You said we were in this together.'

'Why are you getting so emotional, yaar? My mother wants to understand the problem, and I have already been.'

Fearfully she looked at SK, who smiled back reassuringly.

In the car, her mother-in-law reached over and plucked the HSG report that was lying on her lap, and scanned the papers. Ishita waited for her to say something, but she didn't.

In the reception, when she gave her name to the nurse her voice sounded hoarse. She couldn't even pick up a magazine, for her mother-in-law's hands were empty. In the twenty minutes of waiting, Ishita got up three times to ask how long it would be.

Finally they were ushered in.

Smaller than the ants on the ground, smaller than the motes of the dust in the sunlit air, smaller than drops of dew caught between blades of grass in the morning was Ishita as she sat in the gynaecologist's office with her mother-in-law, watching as the doctor sketched out the messages concealed in her body. Here were the tubes, here the eggs, here was where conception occurred. The loss of normal anatomy meant fertilization could not take place without intervention. Fortunately, the couple had youth on their side. Often people turned to alternative methods only after years of trying, by which time age had reduced their chances.

They could first go in for IUI, intrauterine insemination, where the husband's sperm would be washed and injected into the woman's body—a simple procedure, with a minimum of discomfort. It was a comparatively cheap, less invasive alternative, and the success rate ranged from 5 to 40 per cent. It all depended on the quality.

'My boy is young and healthy, his sperm will be good,' said the mother.

If that did not work, they could go in for IVF, fertilization that took place in a culture medium outside the body, with egg and sperm extracted from respective donors. Including the cost of the embryologist, the package worked out to 60,000 rupees, with a fifty-fifty chance of success. Other clinics charged less, but had a lower success rate as well. If that didn't work, some people went in for a surrogate womb. She gestured to the pictures behind her: look at all those newborn infants conceived with our help. Here were some pamphlets on the subject.

'Beta, just wait outside for a minute,' instructed the mother-in-law finally, after she had followed everything the doctor said with the attention of a hawk, lazily circling the sky, alert to the movement of small innocent creatures scampering below.

Ishita got up. She could hear the shuffle her feet made as she left the room and despised her leaden legs. As she sat on the well-worn chairs she noticed she was trembling. She knew why she had been sent out. Her mother-in-law wanted to know all the long-term prospects, all the financial implications, before she decided to get rid of her daughter-in-law. They called it the sword of Damocles. Its tip was now grazing her hair, she wished it would fall and slice her in two without further ado. Hopefully the doctor's information would hasten the process, because she didn't think she could live in suspense for very long.

'Mummy says we must go in for the IVF,' said Suryakanta that night, after they made love—the love that was never going to lead to a pregnancy.

'She did?'

'I told you she would be supportive.'

Nobody had mentioned how painful the procedure would be, how tedious, how embarrassing. At the start of her menstrual cycle she was injected with fertility drugs to stimulate her follicles. The more follicles, the more eggs, the more chances of retrieval, the greater the chances of pregnancy.

Every two or three days she visited the doctor, with hope in her heart. Her blood had to be tested, ultrasounds taken. Are things going according to schedule? Are there enough follicles?

More injections. More hormones.

When it was time to harvest the eggs, she was given an anaesthetic. To extract them from the follicles, needles were inserted through the vagina into the ovaries. Once they were retrieved, she could go home, pumped full of antibiotics. After this the action shifted to a laboratory, where her egg united with her husband's sperm which had been collected, washed and prepared.

For six days her baby lay in the IVF lab. Days of tension, days in which in the deepest recesses of her mind she allowed the faintest of hopes to flicker. She whispered to herself, my baby. Also known as an embryo.

Back to the embryologist, back to the doctor, back to lying on her back and having a catheter inserted into her. The catheter which contained her baby. Three in fact, out of which one might develop.

Prayers, prayers, more prayers. Please stay, please grow. You are my only chance of happiness. So many people to love you, just come into the world. I beg you.

But it wouldn't. Even with more hormones it wouldn't.

Her period. Her bloody period. Each sanitary napkin soaking up thousands of rupees, hours of energy, months of expectation, now to be wrapped in old newspaper and discreetly disposed of.

Not so discreet was the reaction when it was known she had her period. No, there was nothing subdued about that.

She hated this baby, hated it. Even living for a few months was beyond it.

Ever since the fertilized egg had been implanted, Mrs Rajora had been asking every day, how do you feel, how do you feel? In her desperation Ishita had begun to feel nauseous, though she had yet to throw up—too soon, opined the mother, but God is with you, the biggest thing is not to worry, stress is very bad for pregnancy.

'Never talk to me of miracles again, Mama,' cried Ishita when she gave the news. 'This is my karma. Nothing will break it.'

'We can pay for another attempt, after all, these things are not so easy,' said the father breaking his heart over his daughter's despair.

'There is no guarantee, Papa, you know that. What is the point?'

'The point is your happiness.'

'Which is doubtful in this case. And why should you lose everything you have saved? No, if they really want to try, they should pay themselves.'

'They have paid. Now maybe it is our turn?'

'We didn't explore every option. We didn't go in for frozen embryos. That would have made it easier the second time round.'

'Why didn't you?'

Because the mother-in-law hadn't wanted to waste endless time and money trying, because the doctor might have told her that repeated attempts don't increase the chances of success, each try remains at fifty-fifty.

Had there been something wrong with SK, they would have moved heaven and earth to get a son's defect corrected. In an ideal world, the same resources would have been put at the disposal of a daughter-in-law. But this was not an ideal world.

It didn't take long for the loving atmosphere around Ishita to grow so thin that it became hard for her to breathe. Was it possible for them all to change towards her, SK, Chandrakanta and Tarakanta? Hadn't they valued her for herself?

Of course they had, replied the mother-in-law when Ishita's pent-up heart burst with wounded feelings in front of the most powerful member of the household. They were simple, warm and affectionate.

Unfortunately Ishita knew that was true.

'For us the girl's qualities were everything. You know we asked for no dowry?'

A small nod directed towards the floor.

'For us money is not as important as family. But beta, it is essential that Suryakanta have a child. As the only son, he has to make sure that the bloodline of his forefathers continues. And now'—she hesitated slightly—'I need to talk to your mother.'

Ishita sat as though a mountain of stones were pressing upon her.

'I will visit her tomorrow. I am sure something can be worked out. You are a sensible girl.'

'Yes, Mummy.'

In the night she asked Suryakanta, 'Why does Mummy want to talk to my mother?'

He merely grunted and she was too disheartened to insist on an answer, sure that it would make her even more miserable. Might as well live in the dark a bit longer. She would know soon enough.

Her mother phoned her as soon as her mother-in-law left. 'They want a divorce.'

'He also?'

'She says he also.'

'Then I should come home?'

'Don't be silly. They are not getting rid of us so easily.'

'What do you mean? Have you found a new fertility cure?'

The bravado in her daughter's voice broke the mother's heart. She tried to say a few encouraging words, which Ishita heard impatiently before putting the phone down.

Mrs Rajora wandered onto her tiny veranda. Discussion with her husband was useless: no matter how justified her anxiety, he accused her of needless worrying. It was his way of protecting himself, she thought.

Now she sat alone, staring at the many children playing in the square below, assailed by their rising voices, their excitement, their quarrels, their play.

The bell rang. She got up, half ready with her social face. She who loved company had not exchanged a word with anyone for weeks now. But neither Mrs Rajora nor the co-operative housing society was designed for solitude. It was Mrs Kaushik at the door demanding tea, determined to find out what the matter was.

All this was not to be resisted. The end result was that an appointment was made for Ishita and her mother to go and see Leela Kaushik's astrologer. 'See this jade—he got me this stone—I wear it because my mercury is too strong. Now I am not taking tension.'

'Is there something for infertility?'

'Of course. He will suggest something, he is very, very good, not at all money-minded.'

Next week Mrs Rajora dragged her daughter to the astrologer. There is a child in her hand, he said, after turning her palm over several times, scrutinizing it carefully by the light of a lamp.

'She is young and healthy,' pleaded the mother.

'She will know the joy of motherhood.'

'A son?'

'One girl.'

'Are you sure?'

'That is what the stars say. There is something I can give you that will help.'

The mother looked eager.

'A stone. She has to wear a white stone—pearl or moonstone—to counteract the influence of the moon. It has to be two carats, and get the setting such that it touches her skin. It has to be made correctly, only then will it work.'

'Please will you get it made for us?'

So, no son. Suryakanta's bloodline was not going to be passed on through her. Besides which, she would be forced to wear an ugly ring, sitting fatly on her finger.

'See, what did I tell you?' they demanded of each other as they left.

'You lose hope too easily,' continued the mother. 'I am doing special pujas to overcome your bad karma. There is a child in your future. Miracles do happen. We will get the stone, then we will see.'

'These people just tell you what you want to hear,' retorted Ishita. 'I can't go on living like this. He doesn't look at me any more.'

And what was more important, though she didn't say it, he didn't even touch her any more. In bed all she saw was his back. And last night, he moved into his parents' bedroom. She felt degraded, a non-person, certainly a non-woman. He was determined there should be nothing left between them.

She was only twenty-six. She could look for a job, but the meaning of her life came from SK. For three and a half years she had been surrounded by his shy and tender love, she had set down roots in this home, the thought of being expelled from it was heartbreaking.

Her parents encouraged her to stay. In time sex would wield its magnetic attractions. How long could SK ignore the wife who lived in the same house as him?

But staying was not easy. The mother began to call her shameless, the sisters refused to talk to her, the father and SK avoided her. She only saw her husband at the dining table—a place to which she now seldom came. Who can eat if they are treated as invisible? She stayed in her room, reading magazines, flicking through TV channels, waiting for it to be late enough so she could take a sleeping pill. And not have the fantasy that Suryakanta would creep into bed, put his arms around her and tell her that he loved her, now and for ever.

A month of this and it was clear that his love must be completely dead for him to treat her so cruelly.

She took off the stupid gigantic pearl ring her mother had got for her as she decided she need be humiliated no further.

If her parents did not want her to kill herself they would have to see reason.

The parents changed their tactics. Did the family think they could marry and divorce as they pleased? They wanted a cash settlement. With their wealth, 10 lakhs was nothing.

They can't get rid of us so easily, if you come home we can kiss goodbye to everything. What about your future?

Now besides barrenness his mother accused her of money-grabbing. Did we take a dowry, did we, did we? We were too simple for worldly types such as you.

You must have known you couldn't have a child.

You will never get a paisa from us.

How long do you think you can go on eating our salt?

There are ways to deal with shameless women like you.

In the dark watches of the night Ishita thought they were right, she was shameless. Who stayed where they were not wanted? When she looked in the mirror she saw a plain unloved face, eyes without expression, dull skin, dry lips. She had lost all the weight she had put on since her marriage, her collar bones stuck out, her breasts had shrunk. Even the beggars at the street crossings looked more lively than she. Was this the person holding out for happiness?

She appealed to the back of the man who now never spoke to her. I can't go home, I can't stay here. Just make it possible for our parents to settle, and then I shall get out of your life for ever. I will agree to divorce by mutual consent, otherwise you know how long that can take. I need to leave with dignity. For the sake of the love you once had for me.

'What about you? Asking for 10 lakhs.'

She heard the disgust in his voice, and for a moment she hated her mother who made her do this. But then in the West did they not give alimony?

'Give what you like. I don't care. But I must be able to live with some independence. You can marry again, what can I do? My life is over,' she tried to say without pathos, stating a simple fact.

The back did not respond, the shoulders drew a little inwards. But Ishita knew Suryakanta had understood her position. He still cared for her, no matter what his parents might maintain. Had they been living by themselves, how different it could have been.

Poor Ishita, still believing in love, even after circumstances had raked their steely claws across her marriage.

*

Two days later, her mother called. 'They are offering 5 lakhs. What is 5 lakhs—'

Ishita cut into this: 'Five lakhs is the price they are willing to pay. And it is me they are paying it to. If you do not want me to come home I will live as a tenant somewhere. I am leaving this house in one week. In fact,' she lied in a low controlled tone, 'there is a family close by willing to take me. I will die, or be killed if I continue to stay here, is that what you want? A corpse? You can have it today.'

Her parents were horrified. Did their daughter really think they did not want her home? They only wanted the best for her. And how could she leave without her jewellery, did she want to gift that to them?

Ishita had to speak to SK again. Her jewellery was in the family locker, and it was her mother-in-law who had the key. She trusted him to do what was right by her, and to return the pieces she had come with.

That evening SK handed her a plastic-wrapped packet. She put it in her suitcase without checking its contents. Her clothes were already packed in a steel trunk. She was sure that no one in that family would even consider as returnable all the linen, the kitchenware, the TV, the bedclothes, or the carved wooden bed that had been part of her trousseau. Well, if they wanted to send these things back, fine, if not, fine. She didn't care.

It was late at night. Hopefully there wouldn't be too many people around in Swarg Nivas to witness her ignominious homecoming. She dialled for a taxi, then called the servant to help with her baggage. He did so without meeting her gaze. No one came out to say goodbye.

In the taxi her tears fell silently and were wiped away silently. She needed to get all her crying done before she arrived.

Two and a half lakhs were to be handed to Ishita on the first signing of a mutual-consent divorce. Two and a half more would be given six months later when the final proceedings were over. The interim six months was a period meant for the reconciliation process. What process, thought Ishita drearily, what process? There never was a chance.

Six months later the divorce was through. Ishita was twenty-seven. Her mother tried to hide the conviction that her daughter's life was over. Even her father had to admit that the path ahead was obscure.

After the divorce Ishita resumed her maiden name. There are women who keep their own names once they get married, she told her parents bitterly, I should have been one of them.

Ordinarily the parents would have shuddered at the inauspiciousness of such an idea, but now everything had changed.

IX

The Lovely Detective Agency, Results Guaranteed required a minimum of one month to arrive at their conclusions. In matrimonial cases, they said delicately, they only relied on absolute proof. What constituted absolute proof? demanded Raman. He himself would be satisfied with a brief account of the subject's activities, places visited, people met, he elaborated, not quite meeting the eye of the sleazy individual who was going to shadow Shagun. Who else but voyeurs would choose such a profession?

Sleazy was firm. People met could only be documented through photos. In their experience the client's first reaction was disbelief. Confidentiality was their policy and the negatives would be handed over to Mr Kaushik. Half the fees were payable in advance. In addition they would charge photography costs as well as travel expenses.

It would only be necessary to confine activities to Delhi, said Mr Kaushik, staring at the man's fat fingers, drumming out a pattern on the glass-covered surface of his Godrej desk. With every suggestion, he felt his dignity crumbling. He hadn't realized how demeaning this detective business was.

'We need pics of the subject. Face, full-body, recent.'

It sounded so horribly intimate. He sat in shamed gloominess as he felt the sanctity of his family violated.

'More than one of us will be put on her trail. If we want twenty-four-hour surveillance, that is a must.'

'Twenty-four-hour surveillance? Is that necessary?'

'We always tell our clients the best results are got from this only, and therefore cheaper in the long run.'

'Very well.'

'So how soon can we expect the pics?'

'Soon enough, don't worry.'

Raman left the Lovely Detective Agency, even more sick at heart. He had not thought that possible, but he was learning something every day.

Family pictures were Shagun's department.

'Where do you keep our albums?' he asked that night.

'Why do you want to know?'

'I want to look at them. Do you mind?'

She stared at him. Perhaps he was going crazy. 'Why? In all these years you never asked to look at them.'

'In all these years I had no need to.'

What was this enigmatic remark supposed to mean? That she should break down over a veiled reference to the changes in their life? Well, he could take his albums and—an Ashok phrase—stuff them up his ass. She smiled absently and when he saw the look on her face that obliterated him completely, Raman was very glad he had gone to the Lovely Detective Agency.

'They are in the last shelf of the bookcase. Be sure to put them back carefully. I don't want to rearrange them all over again.'

Once upon a time he had liked the fact that she was so careful about the handsome leather albums that illustrated the family's twelve-year history. Now as he searched through the pictures of the past, he tried to look for the lies in them. Holidays, school and family events, smiles wreathed across every face, his wife the same charming creature from start to finish, unaffected, tender, posing, it seemed happily, with him and the children.

She had not even asked why he wanted the albums, how unnatural was that? His face grew stiff with suppressed pain. Quickly he slid two pictures out from beneath the protective sheet.

Before handing over these precious photographs, he would try and talk to her mother. He knew she would do anything to keep the marriage intact.

Two days later Shagun visited an ill-at-ease Mrs Sabharwal. 'What is this mysterious thing you wanted to see me about?' she asked.

'Raman phoned.'

'So?'

'He is worried about you.'

'Rubbish. He is just worried about himself.'

'Beta, give him some credit. After all these years you have suddenly turned against him. Naturally he will look for reasons.'

'Come to the point, Ma. What did he say?'

'He wanted to know if there was something troubling you. He finds you changed, less interested in the children and the household.'

'What a bastard.'

In the face of this reaction, Mrs Sabharwal did not know how to continue. She had tried to convince Raman that the only thing wrong with Shagun was that she needed a little change. She would look after the children if they went on a holiday, it was not healthy to work so hard, his life was of greater value. If he didn't want to say anything directly, she could make the suggestion to Shagun.

Her flustered insistence increased Raman's suspicions. Abruptly he terminated the call, he was sorry, he had not wanted to cause concern, and this formality from one who had been so close to her increased her grief.

'So? Is he now going to spy on me?'

'Such a thing is beyond him.'

'Then? What did he want?'

'Does he have to want something? Have you forgotten he has been phoning me for twelve years?'

'High time he stopped. Just because his own mother is so horrible, doesn't mean he can have mine.'

At this point, Mrs Sabharwal almost gave up, but thinking of the desolation in Raman's voice, she tried again. Maybe the couple should go on a holiday. He had said he was too busy, but she knew that was just his pride.

'A holiday? Are you mad? Why?'

'It will be good for you two.'

'Who is you two?'

'What kind of question is this? You and Raman—who else? I will keep the children.'

'Did Raman tell you to ask?'

'No.'

'Then?'

Her mother watched her lip curl, then burst out with, 'I think Raman suspects.'

'Nonsense, he is too stupid.'

'Don't talk like that.'

'Why not? Just because you love him doesn't mean I have to.'

'He is the father of your children.'

'So?'

'Give him some respect. Till now you never thought he was stupid.'

'Till now, till now. What did I know till now?'

'Beti, have you ever thought of the consequences of your actions? Even if you don't care for Raman, for heaven's sake preserve some appearances. You think all wives love their husbands? But they stay married. You are so idealistic, you don't think about the long term. What about society, what about your children?'

Shagun turned her head away. Against the word 'children' she had no defence. Drearily she thought yes, what about the children? She couldn't leave them, she didn't see how she could take them. Ashok had a transferable job: even if he got an extension, he would eventually go, and she, she would have to stay.

In this situation all she could do was live from day to day. She didn't want to hear her mother's worries, they echoed too precisely her own fears.

'Till now you were a happy wife and mother,' observed

Mrs Sabharwal sorrowfully. 'If there was something wrong, you never said. Now this man has come to fill your head with rubbish ideas.'

This was the trouble with her mother, thought Shagun, she just couldn't leave her past alone.

*

After the phone call to his mother-in-law Raman put the photographs of Shagun in his briefcase, only glancing at them briefly. She had been the woman who held his heart in her hand, and though he knew she did not love him with an intensity similar to his own, it hadn't seemed to matter.

No longer.

Once Raman commissioned the Lovely Detective Agency he began his certain descent into hell. How many men needed to initiate something like this? Was the problem that he had married someone too beautiful? His mother had thought so all along and now his mother-in-law's voice suggested it was just a matter of finding out the details.

For one month Raman lived in no man's land. Much of that time was spent on tour. Back home he dreaded the evidence his yearning heart obsessively sought, that his wife had changed towards him. When they were together he felt barriers he was not invited to bridge.

Shagun was largely unaware of this. Contrary to her mother's opinion, she was not determined to think ill of her husband, it was just that with her heart full of another man, the married occupant had to be accommodated on the margins.

It was her children who dragged her back to the reality of the past twelve years, standing like sentinels in the way of what her whole being craved, a life with Ashok Khanna.

She owed it to them to try and save her marriage. But the effort was too much, she couldn't make it in a sustained way. These days she appeared schizophrenic: one minute madly concerned with her children's well-being, the next abstracted, the next excessively attentive to Raman, the next absorbed in her private world.

Meanwhile Raman was doing really well at work. The Mang-oh! schemes were bearing fruit, and the fact that there was no one to share his triumph made his success hollow.

He was certain of a big bonus, but the plans mooted with so much pleasure about the World Cup had now soured. His friends were still going ahead with hotel and plane reservations, trying to figure out which combination would allow them to see India play. Shagun's silence at these sessions made him silent too. Why should he spend his hard-earned money on certain misery? He didn't want to be trapped with a wife who seemed unaware of his existence.

The days passed like this and nothing brought relief.

'Darling?'

Ashok glowed. It had taken so long for her to address him by any endearment that each of them struck him as an achievement.

'Say that word again.'

'No, listen. I think he knows.'

'He does seem rather pulled down.'

'You see.'

'But he is performing brilliantly. And working hard, doing promotional events, getting local celebs and sponsors. He has successfully created a demand for Mang-oh! in six cities, and incidentally increased the sales of water and beverages. We are now moving into permanent commitments, donating refrigerators, refurbishing school canteens, on the condition that only our products are sold. A huge bonus and a special mention await him at the end of the year.'

Shagun did wish that everything didn't have to ceaselessly revert to The Brand. Though perhaps inevitable, it wasn't *nice*. When she said this, he only laughed. Ashok didn't bother to remember all her wishes, her likes and dislikes. She was still getting used to this.

'That's wonderful—that The Brand is doing so well,' she now said dutifully.

'You don't really care, do you?'

'It's just a drink.'

'It's my life, or was until I saw you.'

'Well, I hope seeing me won't affect your career.'

'Are you sure he suspects?'

'He avoids me.'

'All the better for us. So what if you are married? You are mine. I don't want to share you with anybody.'

'No, seriously.'

'Seriously.'

She blushed, and he thought for the hundredth time that he could spend his whole life just gazing at her face.

'Besides, avoiding you must be good for him. He is becoming so innovative, it's amazing. After the target schools he moved to colleges, and then he thought of hiring students to promote Mang-oh! on campus. Saves us money and gets better results. Unlike earlier, he has all the data at his fingertips. People are beginning to notice the way he is campaigning.'

'Well, it will be for the first time. They never noticed him before.'

'I wonder why. He is solid.'

What business does he have to speak of Raman in those terms? thought the wife resentfully as she heard words her own mother had used so often. Ashok went on pensively, 'I think he needs to have someone behind him. Even if only notionally. He is a really good team player.'

'Is he glad you are there for him?' she asked with a difficulty he did not notice.

'Not sure. We worked together more in the beginning—now all we do is toss around ideas—look at targets—but he sees how best to meet them.'

'But don't you feel awkward? After all . . .'

'Once I am in office, I forget everything else.'

'So he is a cog in a wheel?'

'As am I.'

A silence fell between them as he played with her hair. He was forty-three, and found the distraction of being in love unnerving. For one thing his personal and his professional lives had become linked in a way that he found distasteful. Clear, straightforward, cutting to the chase, that was his temperament. It irked him not to have her when he wanted, not to call her openly, always thinking of what would be safe and what not.

In the beginning she had been so brave and matter-of-fact, now she was more fearful. Things never remained static; in business you were always fighting to keep your position, because if you didn't go ahead, you started to decline. And it was turning out to be true of love as well. Should he leave its management to Shagun, he was sure the whole relationship would be doomed.

'Sweetheart, the first thing we have to do towards planning our future is inform the company of our relationship.'

'What? Why?'

'We are in the same organization, your husband and I. We have to make a disclosure about anything that affects its working.'

'Don't bother. You will finish and go. I have to stay for my children. How will they like it when they grow up and realize their mother is a divorcee?'

Ashok lost his temper. 'What is there to realize? This is why I hate this fucking place. This obsession with what others think. By the time your children grow up the whole world will have changed. Certainly this benighted country. Things are moving so fast as it is. Ten years ago you couldn't get a Coke, pizza or burger here. There wasn't even colour TV, for fuck's sake. And now? Everything.'

'What has colour TV got to do with my marriage?' she asked, lip trembling. Ashok was always seeing connections where none were obvious to her.

'Traditional versus modern values, individual versus society,' he elaborated, putting a contrite arm around her. 'I just want to take you away from here. This narrow social set-up is all you know—that's why you are afraid. But it will all be fine, fine. Trust me, darling.'

'Yes,' she said slowly, 'even Princess Diana left her husband. She found happiness before she died. Who knows how long we have?'

'Are you saying we are going to die? In a car speeding to avoid Paparazzi?'

'Well—she just wanted to be happy too.'

'All right, let's look at Diana. So much of her identity was bound up with being the Princess of Wales. But she didn't care. She followed her heart. And you must follow yours. Something else will emerge if only you let it. In Diana's case she started saying she was the people's princess—you have to admire the repackaging that went into that. We only have one life to live and everybody wants to live it the best they can.'

'But then she had that terrible accident and her children were orphaned.'

He sighed and reverted to the original problem. 'This situation has to change. It would be disastrous for me if Raman did the disclosing. I would appear to be exploiting him and you. This will go down badly, the company frowns on anything that prevents employees from giving their best.'

'You should have thought of that earlier,' she said, giving him a sideways glance, over the naked back that had so attracted him when he had first seen her at the Oberoi party a year ago. The white curved expanse interrupted by the thin black band of her blouse and the sari tied low over her hips had seized him more powerfully than many women's cleavages had done over the years.

'I know it's difficult for you. But you'll see. It's better in the long run.'

'Disclosure to whom?'

'I could report to Hong Kong—or New York.'

'New York. That's far enough away.'

'I wish I could say distances make a difference, but they don't. He will get to know.'

'He can't get to know yet.'

'We can wait a few weeks.'

'A few weeks!'

She was panic-stricken. Why were things moving so fast? When she started her affair she had thought a lover would add to her experience, make up for all the things she had missed having married straight out of college. She had heard of other women who took lovers—their whole lives didn't change.

She thought of her nights with Raman. The last time she had refused his overtures, he had not repeated them. They lay together, tossing and turning, sleeping in fits and starts, staring into the darkness. In the morning often he looked haggard, while her eyes had faint purple circles under them.

A few days later, Ashok to Shagun: 'I mentioned our situation to a colleague in the US—Bill is a great friend as well.'

'Why? Why did you say anything? You promised to wait.' She clung to him, as though he could allow her to have her cake and eat it too.

He caressed her back gently, his hand lingering on the slenderness of her neck under the heaviness of her thick bright hair. If only he could take away her fear. Somehow manage it so that all the consequences were shouldered by himself.

'I only sounded him out,' and it surprised him how easily he could be patient. 'Just to get a sense of things. We have to be realistic.'

Wearily Shagun supposed he was right. Whatever way you looked at it, she would have to give up something, and suffer accordingly.

'All right.'

'It's only a matter of time before he finds out who it is. If you think he is suspicious, it is the next step.'

'He talks of you with great respect. All stuff about Mang-oh!—and the deliverables.'

'The deliverables are almost over.'

'So, who would you go to?'

'My own boss, who is head of South-East Asia—that's in Hong Kong. Or I could go to New York, that's headquarters.'

'Can they fire you?'

'Theoretically they can do anything. But they won't want to lose me. Perhaps they will suggest a transfer—but it's a joint decision. The Brand was built by consensus, by treating people well, by willing participation.'

'Well, do it quickly, whatever you have to do. My life is a nightmare. It's hard to be a wife when your heart is somewhere else. If only I were not a mother, how easy it would be. To leave him, to live with you, just be happy.'

He said nothing—only went on stroking her back, her face, her hair till she calmed down.

'So I have your permission to make a disclosure?'

She merely nodded, then got ready and went away.

The next evening Shagun looked uneasily at her husband. Though there was no change in his demeanour, her dread increased. Days went by, still nothing. Ashok tried to calm her, instant exposure didn't follow a disclosure, but he had never been married and didn't know how much a husband and wife can tell each other without a single word.

When the Lovely Detective Agency handed a manila envelope to Raman in his office he thought he was half prepared for what lay inside. Later he could admire their sagacity; without the pictures he would never have believed it.

It was infinitely worse than he expected. Out-of-focus photographs of Shagun leaving a place that had number 27 painted next to the gate. There was his wife getting into a taxi and Ashok bending over her, there were the two of them lightly kissing in an open doorway; Shagun was wearing different clothes, a different day. How had the photographer managed to take these without their knowledge? But of their authenticity he had not a doubt.

He had employed the agency so that the truth would dispel his confusion, but the information paralysed him even more. He could confront his wife, but his boss? How could he stay on in the same firm? The long hours and hard work he had poured into the company, that appreciative entity, were being rewarded with recognition, bonuses and incentives. If he left he would suffer financially, besides which it would be impossible to find an equally good job.

All these past months, working so closely with Ashok, planning the Mang-oh! campaign, being grateful to him for putting so much energy into his department, while the man was screwing his wife, and destroying his family. There must be rules against this—company rules. He would not rest till Ashok Khanna was publicly disgraced. Whom to approach most effectively, the PR regional head office, or the PR section in New York?

It only took a few minutes, though, for revenge to seem pointless. No protest, however strong, could get back the security he had lost. He remained bent over his desk simulating work, as the office slowly emptied. By ten he was the only one left. Then all pretence over, he pulled the tainted folder out from under its innocent covering papers and gave himself up to anguish. So this was what had accounted for her distance, and he had thought she wanted him to travel less.

The sound of the phone roused him. It was Shagun: 'What is the matter? Why haven't you come yet?'

What could he tell her? He loathed her voice.

'Raman?'

Still he could not reply.

'Raman? Are you there?'

He put the phone down. There was nothing to say. But he did get up. His children were at home, as well as his lying, cheating wife. He must go to them.

So he knew. The disclosures had done their job. She sat next to the dumb instrument, her hands cold, a sweaty film of fear on her upper lip. The minutes passed, and she could not move. She looked at the clock: 10.09. Her marriage was over at 10.09, May 20th, 1998. Her son was ten, her daughter less than two.

She lifted the receiver, and dialled her lover's number. 'He knows.'

'Are you sure?'

'Yes.'

'It is out in the open, good. Just get through this, darling. Or I can come and get you. It is what I always wanted.'

'No, it's all right. It won't be long now.'

Carefully she placed the receiver in its cradle. There was a little dirt around the numbers, clearly Ganga had taken advantage of her absent-mindedness to forget all she had taught her about cleaning and dusting. Absently she fiddled with the phone. Should she go to her mother's? Take the children? Right now they were sleeping, she would have to wake them up, answer their questions, endure the looks of the servants. Tomorrow. Tomorrow things would be clearer. There were other people who loved her, and if she could no longer hide, perhaps that was a good thing.

When Raman returned he wondered how he had never seen the guilt that was so evident in every gesture, every word. A lack of easiness, forced attention, periods of abstraction. Yes, that is how the faithless behaved. Now that she was in front of him, clearly apprehensive, pain entered the anger that had been so sharp in the car.

All the way home he had thought of what he was going to say, the harshness, the biting contempt. He would drag her screaming by the hair, out of the house, down the stairs. What did he care if she had no clothes, no money, if the neighbours heard? Should the children ask he would say she was dead. If only she *were* dead, how much simpler that would be.

But when he actually stepped through the front door, he could not even raise his voice. He wanted this agony to abate, and he knew of nothing that would help. He was still, his movements quiet. Dinner was eaten in silence. Finally, 'Arjun and Roohi were asking for you,' Shagun offered tentatively. 'Now that their holidays have begun they wanted to know what we're doing this summer. But you are always touring so I said no plans for the moment.'

He concentrated on the apple he was peeling. She noticed the slight trembling of his hands, the pallor on his face. 'Aren't you going to say anything?'

'What is there to say? You tell me.'

Bravely she continued, 'Is anything wrong? You seem upset.'

It was hard for him to look at her, the fear in her face was as apparent as the guilt, but to come out with an accusation was to make the nightmare still more real. But he had to, and when dinner was cleared and the servants gone, he started, praying for inspiration, for something to say that would make her see sense.

Was it true, what he had found out?

She only looked terrified.

Was there anything lacking in their home, their marriage, anything at all, that she should amuse herself—amuse herself—

His misery stopped his words and he half turned, wanting her to see and comfort, for this dreadful thing to be washed away, perhaps by both their tears.

No gesture or sound.

'You have nothing to say?'

'What do you mean?' Her face was shrivelled, he noticed the tight little fists in her lap.

'Is it not clear? Why do you insist on playing the innocent?'

'I have done nothing.'

'Nothing? Screwing around with Ashok Khanna is nothing?'

'What are you saying?'

'Fucking the boss. What did he promise you?'

'How dare you talk like that? What kind of husband are you?'

'So it's not true?'

She looked down.

'I have had you followed for one month. There are pictures to prove it—do you want to see them, or should I show them to Ashok's boss instead? Have him deported? Then what will you do, you and your precious lover? His career in the company is finished, finished. I will see to it, see to it, do you understand?'

So it wasn't the disclosure, he had had her followed. All of a sudden she hated him.

'This was what was behind all that acting in the ad films. Not your natural talent, though your talent for acting, yes, for acting, is worth an Oscar. Month after month to pretend to be my wife, and yet—all the time—all the time—Shagun, how could you? I trusted you. If there was something wrong, why didn't you tell me? I was working so hard—for whom do I work but my family?—and you—'

His tears did not allow him to say more, while her own trickled down her cheeks. She stood up. 'I have wronged you. I didn't mean to. But please don't tell the children.'

Alone in the room, he gradually grew calmer. He had cried more in this one evening than he had in his entire life, but clearly that didn't mean anything to anyone. He could hear his wife rustling about, the door of the room opening, closing, opening, closing. She was going to sleep separately, it seemed.

Wearily he got up, went to the bathroom, looked in the toilet case for the Anxit that he habitually took when he was travelling to help him sleep. Carefully he pressed two out from the strip. Hopefully this should take care of the night ahead—if not he would drink himself into oblivion.

The next day, with his world changed, Raman drove to office, determined to spread the change around. The walking pillar of effrontery known as Ashok Khanna should be made to pay for his sins.

Now the pleasure he had taken in the boss's interest in his work struck him as pathetic. Pathetic, too, all those brainstorming sessions that had helped create new initiatives. How had Ashok Khanna been able to look him in the eye? Seemed empathetic and encouraging?

Bitterness filled him. The man stupid enough to be betrayed by the two most important people at work and at home had to be mentally challenged.

He got into the elevator and pressed the button. Every day he told himself he should walk up to the fifth floor, but every day he was in too much of a hurry. Today, he had more time, but what was the use of looking after his health? If he were lucky he would die in the lift. All problems solved.

Once in office he heard that Ashok Khanna had reported sick. If there was anything urgent, he was available at home. Ashok Khanna, ever the fast mover. Had he already made a disclosure? Whatever it was, there should be no more delay in passing on his own information.

He picked up the phone to dial the Bombay office. He would talk to the head of HR there, it seemed easier than going international. He felt sick and weary, no longer able to calculate the repercussions of what had happened as he tried to summon up the energy needed to destroy his boss. It was all he could do to keep from being destroyed himself.

At that very moment Shagun was with Ashok in his house.

'You promised me it was safe.'

'Have you seen the pictures?'

No, their existence was humiliation enough.

'Then how do you know their contents? Could be you leaving the house, or you getting into a taxi, or us talking together—could be a thousand explanations for that.'

'He was sure I was having an affair. He said he had photographic proof.'

'It's not of us in the bedroom, so don't worry about that. I have questioned the servants closely. The house is clean.'

'Anyway, he knows, and I—I did not want to deny it.'

'Little point. Your life is with me, not with him.'

'I'm not ready.'

'It's a big step you are taking. Just do it, the readiness will come later.'

'So, you at least are glad.'

'You know I hated all this hole-in-corner stuff. If you have to get a divorce, fight for custody, let's start now.'

'These things are not so easy in India.'

'Is anything easy in India? That's not the point. Should we meet a lawyer? My old school friend is one of the best. Practises in the High Court. Has a home office in GK I.'

'What about the children?'

'What about them? They will be in your life, don't worry. And darling, I know where my responsibilities lie. That's a promise. We will ask Madz.'

'Is that your friend's name?'

'Madan Singh. We used to call him Mad. Maddy. Madz.'

Shagun was silent. It was lawyer time, the time of consequences, even though her relationship with her lover was hardly the most established thing in her life. She roused herself to bid farewell to her intense secret world, with its perilous edge of desire, its hours devoted to subterfuge.

*

In the next few days many equations changed.

Ashok took long leave, coming to a quick understanding with various heads of departments. He would work away from the Delhi office, and Raman was spared the embarrassment of facing him.

At work Raman could read sympathy for himself in glances, could read knowledge in the way nothing about Ashok was said in front of him. The grapevine declared he would not be returning, that he was going to travel soon, probably to New York.

Raman wished he too could take off somewhere, but how can you take off from your life? Wherever he turned, there was no escape; home, office, all imbued with a sense of failure.

The HR head in Bombay had been most sympathetic. The company would support him in every way they could. Pay for marriage counselling sessions, help him relocate, let him go on leave.

But Raman wanted more. He wanted Ashok punished. It was bad for the morale of the company if bosses could get away with stealing wives and wrecking homes.

He hoped the flaws in this assertion weren't obvious. This was a company, not a moral science school. It was up to the wife to defend her integrity. His wife, the weak chink in his armour.

At any rate he wanted a change of scene. He wanted nothing to do with Mang-oh! any more; he could not travel as much as this product demanded. He needed to stay in one place for a while, his children were going to need him.

The company was understanding. Since no one else had his expertise or experience, they couldn't relieve him of Mang-oh!, but they could increase his staff, so that the stress on him was drastically reduced. He told himself to be satisfied with these concessions.

Suffering continued unabated in the Kaushik household. Shagun tried to have little to do with Raman. The minute he came home she left. As he watched her go, he told himself he didn't care what she did or where she went. He ate with the children, then put them to bed. His wife would return in the morning to get them ready for school.

Unfairly, it was to the father that the son put his questions.

'Where is Mama?'

'Ask your mother, beta, ask why she wants to leave her home and her children.'

'She says she is going away, Papa. She was crying, Papa.'

'And did she tell you she has found another man to love, my boss in fact, and now my boss has left work? Too afraid to face the music. I could take them to court.'

Arjun began fiddling with his Game Boy, and Raman, recalling the rules of parenting, looked over his shoulder at the tiny screen and tried to engage with the little fighting figures.

If only he had not been so busy, there would have been more of a connection between him and his son, more of an established routine with his children. But even so, to be surrounded by their presence was the only source of healing he had.

Ashok to Shagun: 'Dearest, I have to go.'

'You will leave me now?'

He sighed, and moved to the practical, more and more they had to pitch their shaky tents there.

'Bill says head office is not pleased; India is an emerging market, but it is also a place where traditional values have to be respected, otherwise our image becomes tarnished. The only saving grace is that I am not a foreigner. Otherwise there would have been hell to pay.'

Shagun looked at him as he went on thinking of the company, of how he would present his case and to whom. In a few days he would depart with a head full of strategy.

'What am I supposed to do while you are away?'

'Think of me.'

'Raman wants me to think of him. He says the company has offered to pay for marriage counselling. Is this standard procedure?'

'In cases like this they want everybody to be sure they know what they are doing.'

'I see.'

'A little more patience, my love. When I come back it will be to take you with me.'

'And the children?'

'Them too.'

Their ardour grew more fervent. The need for secrecy had gone, and Shagun's bridges lay smouldering behind her. When the time came, she would go to Ashok proudly, unashamed of what she had done. She would do it all over again, even if a camera lurked in every twig of every bush outside, in every crevice of every tree in the park across the house.

Once Ashok left, Shagun spent her nights at her mother's. It was an uncomfortable arrangement, with Mrs Sabharwal looking at her beseechingly, begging her not to ruin her life.

In that context Shagun mentioned the marriage counselling, adding that Raman had a hope in hell.

In the pause that followed Mrs Sabharwal thought how wonderful it would be if in fact counselling could turn back the clock, call back yesterday, and have things as they were.

'He doesn't want to lose you. It is natural.'

'No one can make a blind man see.'

'Think of the children.'

'I am not leaving the children, just their father.'

'And you think it will be that simple?'

'People do get divorced, you know, Ma.'

'Are you mad? You want to destroy your home?'

'There is no home. What do you think this whole thing is about?'

For a moment they stared at each other across the unbridgeable chasm of passion versus safety.

'Raman will let you take the children?'

'Really, Mama,' said Shagun, 'what do you want me to do? You want me to kill myself, then you will be happy?'

'Beta, why are you talking like this? Have I said something wrong?'

'No—it is only me that is wrong. Me, my whole life, from this stupid early marriage, to—to having Roohi so late—Arjun is old enough. I can explain things to him—but Roohi? What can a two-year-old understand?'

'No one would have children, early or late, if they thought they were going to leave their husbands.'

'Well, I can't help that.'

'You know, counselling is not such a bad idea,' went on Mrs Sabharwal carefully. 'After all, it is a question of your whole future, along with that of your children.'

'No, Mama, too much has happened.'

'Beta, please, please, for my sake, do not rush into things. Raman will do anything for you and the children. Everybody makes mistakes.'

'This is not one of them.'

'It's not your life alone. Think of the children.' By now this plea was beginning to sound like a cracked record. Think of the children, the children, the children. She didn't want to think of them.

'You believe Raman is so nice? He is not. He had a detective follow me. He ordered him to take pictures. That's the kind of man he is.'

With Shagun doing what she was doing, Mrs Sabharwal could imagine Raman's trauma, saw easily the pain behind his actions. It was her daughter that was beyond comprehension, the child to whom she must remain ever faithful. Her fate was hard, and she felt sorry for herself.

'Now I hope you will drop your silly regard for him,' said the daughter.

'So what are you going to do?'

'I don't know.'

'What about Arjun and Roo?'

'I come with them. Ashok knows that.'

'He may say anything to get you, but how does he really feel about another man's children? Has he even met them?'

'No.'

'Then how can you be sure?'

'He loves me. That's how I can be so sure.'

'Think carefully, beta.'

The older generation were hopeless. Abruptly she got up and slammed the door to her childhood bedroom. Mrs Sabharwal watched sadly. Though she would do anything for her daughter, she couldn't understand how this situation had come about. And since when had she become so unhappy that she was not willing to give her marriage another chance? Raman was such a good man.

The next morning, driving back, Shagun thought it was useless presenting her mother with any problem, she was too old-fashioned, she had been the recipient of Raman's homeopathy for too long. Well, how could she blame her? A woman with her values was incapable of visualizing a companionship beyond the mundane of domestic life. That soul, that body that had flowered with Ashok could not now be asked to fold its petals and return to its budlike state.

As she approached Mor Vihar the feeling of being trapped intensified. Since Raman had put a private detective on her, all she felt for him was hatred, a hatred that became particularly concentrated during the hours spent at home.

She hadn't told her mother that she had already mentioned separation to Raman. Her choices were her own, Raman had said, his voice distant, but she was not to even think of taking the children. Equally frostily she had replied, she was only in the house because of them. He did not respond, but the next day she found he had told the servants he would deal with all the household matters himself, all the meals, the shopping, everything.

They had read each other's messages accurately.

Arjun spent as much time as he could in his friends' houses and Roohi reflected the brokenness of the family in constant loud wails which grated on all their nerves. In Shagun's absence, Raman began taking her to his bed at night, where she would settle down, snuggling into him, sucking desperately on her thumb.

X

It was shortly after this that Raman, sitting in office, began to feel ill. As he was staring dully at the next phase of the Mang-oh! initiative, still united with the product he now detested, pain shot across his chest, his face became dewy with perspiration, his head felt strange, while the Mang-oh! figures ceased to make sense along with everything else. Indigestion, it's only indigestion, he decided, the business lunch had been long, the food heavy. He slipped a large pink Digene into his mouth and waited. He had an important meeting with the district distributor at four o'clock and the Mang-oh! figures needed to cohere before then.

He got up to order tea from the pantry, when the room spun. Two chairs were overturned by his descent to the floor.

His leaden heart had attacked him.

The aftermath of the collapse found Raman in an ICU, with two stents in his chest, and the company poorer by 5 lakhs.

His parents took turns staying in the hospital, leaving no hour of the day or night unattended. The father did the night shifts, should there be an emergency it was better to have a man on hand. The mother stayed all day, to notice in those hours that things were not right in the marriage.

'What kind of wife are you?' she demanded on the morning of the fourth day, when Raman had been wheeled away for some tests.

'What do you mean?'

'Don't you care about him?'

'Has he complained?'

'He? He never says anything. Such a man you would not find in seven lifetimes.'

‘Then?’

‘You—I don’t know, you hardly seem bothered. Even nights you don’t spend here.’

‘The children are alone.’

‘This is the man who would give his life for you.’

Dispassionately Shagun watched her mother-in-law’s emotions vibrating through her set lips and large chin. The only thing in her life was her precious son, and everybody else had to be fodder for his comfort.

She found distraction in the friends who thronged around Raman’s bed with flowers, jokes, simple good cheer, no undercurrents, just concern and distress that another of their tribe had fallen prey to heart disease.

Mr Kaushik told his wife to leave Raman alone, but observing what she did, this was not in her power. His bed made him captive.

‘Beta,’ she started, ‘I named you after Ram, because I thought you would grow up with his qualities, but too much patience is not appropriate in a householder.’

Only Raman’s eyelids twitched.

Mrs Kaushik went on putting her heavy feet unerringly into the wounds in her son’s heart, her mother’s instinct showing her exactly where they were. Her son, the family breadwinner, was being denied his central place. Her advice was doled out with enough tactlessness to make it totally unacceptable.

For Shagun every day was torture. Raman exuded reproach without once looking directly at her. His illness put her in a false position, his poor weak heart and clogged arteries cried out for assurances that would mend the great jagged holes in their marriage. Could she love him because he had almost died? She compromised by offering him care with a warm but distant friendliness, conveying concern but little intimacy. This satisfied no one, and made her feel like a hypocrite.

She phoned Ashok on the cell he had given her, finding privacy in the hospital lobby, secure that no matter how long she talked, her lover was happy to pay for her calls. Through the somewhat bulky instrument the sound of his voice, the promise of his love, flowed like lifeblood into her veins. No, she was not a bad person, love cannot be forced.

Mrs Sabharwal came to visit. She sat next to Raman's bed and the tears never left her eyes.

Later she remarked to her daughter, 'beta, should anything happen to Raman it will be upon your head.'

'How guilty do you want me to feel?'

'The house rests upon us women. In your children's happiness, your husband's happiness, lies your own. Anything else is just temporary.'

If her mother could think this, then what chance did she have of appearing anything less than a monster in the eyes of the world?

It was part of the Indian disease. Ashok was always going on about stultifying tradition. The great Indian family, which rested on the sacrifices of its women.

Five days later Raman was discharged from hospital. He had taken his first walk down the length of the corridor, he had got his diet chart, he had been made aware of the lifestyle changes he would have to make, of the six-week rest period he needed at home, of the stress it was essential to avoid. His father saw to the payment of the bills, gathered the receipts chargeable to the company, collected all the necessary files plus the phone numbers of every relevant doctor.

His parents accompanied Raman home. 'I can't leave him alone with her,' said the mother, 'she might kill him. You saw how she looked—or didn't look after him in the hospital?'

Always a staunch defender of his daughter-in-law, for the first time Mr Kaushik agreed with his wife's assessment. Where was the deep devotion, the prayers and trauma that should accompany the heart attack of a spouse? For years he had attributed his wife's opinions to female pettiness and a grudge of beauty, and it hurt him now to find beauty so cold.

Their decision presented Shagun with a dilemma which had been lurking at the back of her mind ever since Raman had been in hospital. She knew her husband was waiting for some gesture that would allow him to forgive her completely. If she was serious about her commitments, now was the time, here was the place.

But can you starve the passion that leaves you trembling through the day, block off the scent of desire that rises from between your legs? You have only one life to live, only one life, Ashok said repeatedly, trying to find an argument that would dislodge her from the marital home.

It became clear to Raman that he had come back to exactly the same situation that had brought on his cardiac arrest. Although his wife now remained in the house she was adamant about staying out of the bedroom, spending the nights with her delighted daughter instead. Her father's illness had upset the child so much that she had begun to have nightmares, she explained to the bemused parents.

These lies made Raman's heart feel even heavier, but unfortunately it was now guarded by two stents, and medicines that regulated its rhythm, modified the cholesterol and thinned his blood to an unclottable consistency. His body was not going to be allowed to follow his feelings into the land of death.

In the interests of her son, Mrs Kaushik was forced to use money to establish a meaningful relationship with his servants. Clutching the 100-rupee notes she liberally bestowed in recognition of God's mercy in sparing Sahib's life, they were very willing to talk. Mrs Kaushik tearfully informed them of what the doctor had said, how bad stress was, how the next heart attack would definitely kill him, how he needed to be spared all worries.

The servants looked wise, nodded, agreed, declared that Sahib had been under a lot of strain lately.

Hint by hint, Mrs Kaushik gathered enough to put together a very gloomy picture of her son's life. It was much worse than she expected. Roohi's crying fits, Arjun's tantrums and sleepovers at friends' houses, Raman coming home late, late, late, this was the norm. Above all, the Memsahib spent every single night out. They didn't know where she went, but she and Sahib were not talking to each other. For weeks and weeks. Now Bari Memsahib, you are here, things will be all right, such was the pious wish in the mouths of the faithful retainers.

Armed with these fresh insights, the mother-in-law confronted Shagun.

'A husband's life is in the wife's hands,' she started.

As a gambit that would usher in peace and understanding, it was unfortunate. Every conventional assumption that her mother-in-law made stiffened Shagun's resolve to be her own woman. 'What do you mean?'

Mrs Kaushik's face began to twitch. 'I should not have to tell a wife what it means to look after her husband,' she said, outrage leaking into her trembling voice. 'God forbid you are ever left a widow,' but it was clear Shagun's widowhood would hurt the mother far more than the wife, and as Mrs Kaushik stared at the hard-set face, she could speak no further.

How deceptive prettiness could be. And she hadn't even managed to give her looks to Roohi, the boy had got them all. Handsome, intelligent, an achiever in school, he spent all his time sulking. Truly his mother's child.

In her frustration she turned to the children. They had to look after their father, he had no one but them, and they must be very careful not to grieve him, they didn't want their father to die, did they?

Roohi's tears, Arjun's fear, Papa is going to die, Shagun's anger, control your mother, she is frightening the children. Things became so bad that Raman had to beg his parents to go away.

Mrs Kaushik was extremely reluctant to leave her son. Death by poisoning, the wrong medicine wilfully administered, or a push over the balcony filled her troubled mind. Consultation with the servants followed. Should anything suspicious occur, they should let her know whatever the time, day or night. There would be plenty of rewards for them, they could see for themselves how liberal she was.

'Shagun may have many faults but murder is not one of them,' said Mr Kaushik as they prepared to leave. 'If Raman trusts his wife, we should respect that. And what is more, if you call her a whore, a cheat, and selfish to the core, you are going to make him feel worse.'

'Who gave him his heart attack? Answer me that.'

'I am talking about your tongue, not your emotions. But you will never learn.'

Mrs Kaushik looked upset, but valiantly sniffed to suggest that her husband did not know everything. When she talked to Raman he seemed to have put himself beyond her reach. Why was the boy so sensitive? Would he ever receive the love he deserved?

With the distracting presence of his parents removed, Raman bleakly acknowledged that the situation between his wife and himself was intolerable. What greater sign of his devotion could he give than a heart attack? There must have been a fault in him as well, that had driven her to do what she did. She was basically a good woman, he knew that, and now he tried to think of a way to draw her closer. We have to talk, he said, and commenced on his prepared speech, starting with love, moving on to the children and ending with forgiveness.

'Give me a little more time,' murmured Shagun, eyes on the floor.

As he stared at her glossy hair, the awareness of what a decent man he was flooded him, followed by self-disgust. Miserable dependent fellow, to be so enmeshed with his wife he was forced into a magnanimity she didn't even care for.

'I am approaching you with an open mind,' he said coldly, 'but if you need so much time, perhaps there is no point.'

'I only need to think,' protested the wife.

'Are you seeing him?'

'He is not here.'

Deprived of the distractions of office, with thoughts that fed compulsively on infidelity and treachery, Raman was forced to be more businesslike. Should she stay in this house, he told Shagun, it would have to be as his wife. Living like this was painful for him. He was a simple, straightforward man. If she found she had made a mistake, he was willing to overlook it. But if she refused to give up her other relationship, it was better to end the marriage.

Shagun looked inscrutable. There was a time when the words between them had flowed, now every sentence was blocked.

'Do you have nothing to say?' he asked.

'Why do you want to live with me? You will always think of what I have done, certainly your mother will bring it up for the rest of my life.'

'Leave my mother out of it, please. She is not me, neither does she live here.'

'She influences you.'

'If she really had influenced me, you would be out of the door by now.'

Shagun's face twisted. 'See. You may not say anything, but you can be sure that she will. As it is, she spent so much time worming information out of the servants. And of course she tells the children how bad I am. Why doesn't she publish it in the newspapers and have done?'

'When her son has a heart attack, naturally she is concerned. Imagine Arjun in my place.'

A silence in which both of them hoped Arjun would never be in a similar situation.

That evening Shagun walked slowly to the colony park. She needed to be away from the house, it was too full of her husband. Raman must have struggled to forgive her; how many men would have been so generous? Ashok did not have this gentle, forgiving streak, he would rather kill both her and himself before he let her go. She was a fool for preferring him, a fool. One day she would be punished.

How many times had her lover told her that women had a right to their own lives? Had the right to start again if they found they had made a mistake? But didn't leaving husbands screw up the children? she had asked. Not at all, he said, it depended on how you handled the situation.

Clearly she was not handling it well. Roohi's face had assumed a pinched look that made her big staring eyes seem glassy and unattractive. Every day she redefined the word 'clingy'. Only her mother could read her a bedtime story, only her mother could feed her, bathe her, change her, put her on the pot. When Shagun tried to reason with her, she would whimper—back to being a baby, anyone could read the signs.

Arjun swung between snuggling against his mother when they were alone to studied indifference in front of others. Once, when Raman was in hospital, she had tried talking to him about how he would feel if Papa didn't live with them, only to have him ask worriedly if Papa was going to die, so instead of preparing him she had left him more anxious.

She sat on a stone bench in the corner under a bougainvillea trellis and stared blankly about her. Walkers each brisk in their own way were going round and round the paved path, small children wobbled on their tricycles, there was a cluster around the ice-cream man, a vendor selling fruit chaat was passing out his wares in little donas with a toothpick sticking up from the sliced apples. The air was fragrant with the waxy white flowers of the champa tree. Absently she picked a fallen blossom, putting it to her nose, remembering the pleasure she used to take in its scent. Nothing. Her tangled life was taking away her sense of smell. She wondered how many more years she had to live.

She picked another flower from the grass and mangled it. If only she could wake and find herself with Ashok, why was that not possible? She could just leave with a note—people in books were always doing that. I have gone, don't bother looking for me, goodbye . . .

Marriage over, finished, done with.

Eyes closed, she slouched lower, until her head rested against the stone back of the bench. Her weary mind drifted about, trying to find a lifeline out of the morass that seemed to only get worse with every passing day.

Sometimes she believed Raman had had a heart attack just to spite her. If she should stay in the marriage it would have to be without ever sharing his bed again. The consciousness of her obligations filled her with a dreary sense of duty.

'Memsahib?'

Ganga was standing before her. Roohi had been screaming hysterically for fifteen minutes, not even Sahib could quieten her, she had better hurry back.

On the day of Ashok's arrival, Shagun left the house with an overnight case. She had to meet him one more time, she had to say goodbye in a way that wouldn't hurt him, then go to her life with Raman, that joyless, dismal, uninteresting life.

Everything was magic the moment she stepped into the airport, the intensity of the last minutes of waiting, the ecstasy of reunion. This was where she belonged, this was where she was most herself.

They spent the night in his house, and the next morning she cried as she described the horrible guilt, the children's behaviour, her mother's pressure, Raman's unspoken hopes. Everybody involved with her had suffered. She had come to say goodbye, she said, wrapping her long white arms around him, bringing his face close to hers, feeling the dampness of his breath upon her skin, breathing in his sophisticated scents.

Ashok listened carefully. Going to New York had been difficult. For the first time in his career, he had behaved in a way that required explanation. Though enough in love to pay the price, he was worried. His time in India was limited, in Delhi it was practically over.

With the international management head he had looked at his options. He could go to the Middle East—there was plenty of scope there for product development—or he could stay in India for a few more months, managing ad campaigns from Bombay.

Six months, maybe eight, but that would be it. He didn't pay attention to the stuff she was saying about going back to her husband. That was inconvenience talking, that and her children. They could no more be parted than a hand from its arm, the sea from the shore, the stars from the sky. But what he did understand was that she could not continue with this strain. It was better to make a clean break.

'I am not letting you go.'

'Don't be silly. It will be better for everyone. Even for you—see how you have to invent reasons for staying in India.'

'I mean it. You can't go home.'

'Don't be silly,' she repeated, but he heard the wistfulness.

'How am I being silly? It's never going to be easy—you might as well do it now.'

'But you are going to Bombay.'

'So? Come with me.'

'Come with you?'

'Yes, why not? Now everybody knows. In the company, in your family.'

He drew her face between his hands, looked at the perfect features, the tears that he had helped put in those eyes. He too wished for an end to complications.

She stared at him, lost in his face, so close she could smell the minty fragrance of his breath. With him everything seemed clear, the way out simple. Never to decipher the reproach in Raman's looks, to experience the guilt she knew was hers, to never have to deal with Mr and Mrs Kaushik—she would give anything for such a new beginning.

'And the children? How can I take them after his heart attack? What will he have?'

'Whether you bring them or not, you will always be their mother. Nothing can interfere with that. But from now on this is your home and I am your husband.'

He kissed her on the lips, drew her close and whispered 'little wife'. She sank down next to him; she knew she would have to pay heavily for this happiness, but at least, dear God, she would have a happiness she never had before. If she were to die tomorrow, it would be as a fulfilled woman.

XI

Mrs Sabharwal was given the task of explaining to a bewildered son-in-law that Shagun did not intend to return. She would call him later to sort things out. Raman was left with his hopelessness and two suddenly motherless children.

He was back at work and every day when he came home he had to first deal with his despair. He knew he was expecting that away from him she would realize the value of years of devotion and a home that was waiting for her. If he were in her place he would have realized these things by now.

In the beginning Raman prevaricated with the children. Their grandmother was ill, Mama has gone to look after her. Roohi accepted this, while Arjun just stared doubtfully at his father.

He distracted them with lies, then, as the days passed, brought himself to say Mama loved them, but she had left of her own accord. One day she would probably get in touch, but from now on it was just the three of them. They would have to be brave and learn to get along without her. He put his arms around his two young children and they huddled together for a long time.

Weekends brought company. There was no point in keeping his situation a secret from his friends any longer, and once they knew they arrived with sympathetic wives who came along with food and family. There was much toing and froing between parents and other relatives as well, everybody was determined that no free time should be allowed for sad and lonely thoughts. Eventually time would soothe his loss. Thank God, they said at various intervals, as Raman's fate was discussed outside his hearing, thank God she left the kids. They shuddered to think of his condition without them.

One month later the phone rang, and it was Shagun asking for a divorce by mutual consent. She also wanted some arrangement by which she could visit Arjun and Roo.

'What right did you have to do this to me?' he said, one of many prepared lines bursting forth. While the words had sounded strong during rehearsals, the moment they left his mouth, he felt like a pitiable beggar, bewildered by circumstances.

Her voice, quick and light, said how really really sorry she was.

'What about your children? Even if you don't care for me, you should be concerned about them. Suddenly no mother. Gone. Vanished.'

'Don't make this harder. I have left you the best part of the marriage. Surely my freedom is not too much to ask in exchange?'

'I will think about it.' He put the phone down, only for that word 'freedom' to hurtle around his head with all its implications, suggesting the prison their marriage must have been for her.

The digital numbers of the clock showed 11.30. He had not realized how strong his hope had been until this minute. Tomorrow he would wonder what kind of man would long for a wife who didn't care for him, but tonight in the darkness he let his grief overwhelm him and cried undisturbed, tears running off the side of his face into the pillow.

All next day her request echoed at the back of his mind. It was clear she had left the children behind so that he would recognize her generosity and be generous in return. A divorce was a precious, precious thing. If one partner didn't want it, it was practically impossible to get. People fought for years—years spent in lawyers' fees, postponed dates, lost in the agonizing slowness of the judicial system, dreams of a new life slowly wasting away in the sourness of legal reality.

Why should she be the one to escape this fate? Let her be punished, never know happiness and be miserable till she died. These thoughts caused him uneasiness. He was not used to thinking viciously about Shagun, it would take a little more practice.

That night she phoned again. 'So what is your decision?'

Once more her call took him by surprise. Clearly the breakup of a marriage operated on a different timescale for each of them. He needed to go through a period of mourning, for her it was a past that had to be forgotten.

Rage filled him.

'Well?' she asked.

'The answer is no.'

It was strange how exhilarated this word made him feel. For the first time in the whole sorry matrimonial mess he felt in control. He would not divorce her, what could she do?

She came next day and took away the children.

He was met with the worried faces of his servants, who

started justifying, excusing, explaining as soon as they saw him.

'Memsahib came—packed their suitcases—their school bags. What could we do?'

'You could have phoned me,' he snapped, not wanting to see the glee on their stupid faces. Ultimately it was not their tragedy, their interest was involved but not their feelings. Well, the help was hired, what could you expect?

'It was all so sudden. She had a taxi waiting,' said Ganga.

'I asked her to stay until Sahib came home, but Memsahib said she would get in touch with you later,' explained Ganesh.

The fight was on, and any means was fair. Ever the good woman, his wife was clearly trying to help him see things in perspective. He looked around the empty house. His parents, he would go and see his parents.

'Sahib, where are you going? The children will return, I am sure. God sees everything. He will not let you suffer.'

Should he aid Ganga's cinema-induced dialogue by informing her that he was going to throw himself in the river? He slammed the door on his way out.

'What will he do?' Ganga asked Ganesh, the house to themselves, TV and all.

'How should I know? What about dinner?'

'Better to cook—he may just have gone to the market.'

And they would have huge quantities to themselves should he decide to not eat.

Blindly Raman drove out of the colony, trying to review his options through a breaking heart. As he made his way to East Delhi the rush-hour traffic on the ITO bridge slowed him down. Inch by inch he edged around aggressive cars, darting, weaving scooters, and chugging asthmatic two-wheelers. The AC collapsed midway across; he switched it off and rolled down the windows. The hot, humid air infused with the exhaust fumes of a million vehicles made his headache worse.

As he approached Vikas Marg, the slight elevation of the bridge allowed him to see the conglomeration of cars, scooters, scooter-rickshaws, buses backed up before the traffic lights, honking, jostling, bad-tempered and trapped. Rayri wallahs and parked vehicles before shopfronts distributed commerce and misery along the road.

The light changed. He estimated at least three more cycles before he was within hailing distance of the crossing. A quarter-hour at least. His fingers travelled to the Sorbitrate in his shirt pocket. In this traffic death could reach him before an ambulance.

Again the light change and inches gained on the road. What would his parents think? The grief would be his father's, while his mother would feel vindicated.

Another light change. He turned around, at last the line was longer behind than in front.

Light change. He revved the engine, crawled through the crossing, slowly crept up the Shakarpur bridge. Finally, the traffic lights at Mother Dairy, and left onto Society Marg, skirting still more cart sellers, and finally one more left and one more right and there he was at Swarg Nivas.

The gatekeeper recognized him and let him in. It was almost seven—it had taken him an hour and twenty minutes to do a twenty-five-minute stretch. If his parents ever fell ill, he hoped it would not be in rush hour.

*

Mrs Kaushik prayed a lot these days, tottering down to the little temple near the gate, to sit in front of Lord Ram, an ideal husband like her son, who when his people insisted he take another wife in place of the banished Sita, ordered a gold statue in her image, rather than marry again. Of such integrity was her son, of such a sacrificial nature.

Her thoughts grew vague as she moved to her own sacrifices. She would give her life for her child; if only he would rely on her, he would see how some women can love.

Prayers over, she stood at the doorway gazing at the evening's brisk walkers, searching hopefully for Mrs Rajora, or even her sister-in-law, when she saw Raman drive in and park in the visitors' parking lot. He was alone, something had happened to the children, he would not be here otherwise.

'Beta,' she called as he started towards their apartment block.

He didn't hear.

'Beta.'

Deaf to his mother's voice, he kept on, his walk strangely jerky. It was the children. Forced into a slow run she caught his arm, too afraid to say anything.

He stared at her for a moment blankly and she looked back, her face pinched in terror. 'She's taken them.'

They fussed over him, listened, advised. The father took immediate charge, while the mother gave Raman hot sweet tea, along with biscuits to dip in it. 'I am going to phone Nandan,' he said. 'Right now he will be in his office in Mayur Vihar.'

'I don't want to meet Nandan,' objected Raman.

'When there is a lawyer in the family, why don't you want to meet him? You would rather go to a stranger and get God knows what advice?'

'I don't want anybody to feel sorry for me.'

'Beta, why do you keep such tension in you? His will be a professional opinion, what is the use of our suggestions? He won't tell anybody, he is a very good boy.'

'But why Nandan?' went on Raman, in a monotone, as he watched his father bending over the telephone, his neat grey hair shining with pomade.

'Han beta,' said the father, 'Raman is here. You know, the situation has suddenly worsened, and we were thinking—'

A silence as his father's thinking was interrupted. 'All right, we will be there. Thank you, beta, thank you very much.'

'What does he say?' asked Raman, already feeling a little hopeful as he saw his problems winging their way to Nandan's office in the Mayur Vihar Phase II market.

'He said he will see us at once—as family we shouldn't even have to ask. Now come.'

'I just hope he won't gossip. I don't want the whole building talking of this.'

'Why will he gossip? He hears such stories all the time. And he is like your brother—you can trust his guidance. Otherwise which lawyer cares for their clients? They are all out to make money.'

'Is Nandan good?' asked Raman on the way down. 'If I go to him I want results.'

'Arre beta, he is famous for his results. With his reputation he could move to South Delhi to a much bigger office, but he wants to stay where his parents are.'

'And you think I should have done the same thing?'

'Nobody thinks anything, all right? Go to a fancy lawyer if you feel Nandan cannot help you, but at least meet him once.'

They drove the short distance to Mayur Vihar, Phase II, Pocket I.

'Now your brother will know all the details of everything,' remarked Raman again, his unhealthy obsession with keeping things secret striking his father as a reflection of his son's extreme sensitivity.

'Beta, when you had your heart attack, they obviously figured out something was wrong.'

'You told them about my marriage?'

'Arre, when they came to visit you, they themselves asked where is Shagun? How is she coping? It was very difficult to keep silent. Especially for your mother. Your friends know, don't they?'

'That's different.'

They parked in a side lane and walked the rest of the way, stopping before a board that said 'Nandan Kishore Kaushik, LLB'. Inside, the room was divided by a small screen partition: an office, and a waiting room with chairs lined against the wall and a coffee table with magazines.

As relatives they got almost immediate access. Nandan stuck his prematurely balding dyed head out and said, to a couple waiting patiently, 'Just two minutes please, these people have an emergency.' Nobody believed him. A lawyer could never take only two minutes, their profession forbade it, and as for emergencies, nobody who did not feel their case was urgent would be found there.

In the office there was a cooler standing in the corner, water trickling down its khus-lined metal sides. Against the wall behind the desk was a ceiling-high bookcase, lined with thick red legal volumes.

'Beta, you know Raman has been going through a bad patch. We thought things would settle down, but they haven't,' began Mr Kaushik.

'Ji, Uncle,' said Nandan, fixing his mild neutral gaze on the pair.

The father looked at his son, but the son was staring at the trouser cuff of his waggling foot. He sighed and related the story.

'I care about nothing but my children,' said Raman at the end of it.

Mr Kaushik threw a significant glance at his nephew. See what kind of man he is, help him, it is your duty as a relative and a lawyer.

Nandan ignored the look. The law was a cut-and-dried business, once you got swamped in outrage, indignation, grief and anger, you were nowhere. His clients' minds had to turn to the practical, whether they were inclined or not.

'Now, what is it that you want from me?'

'I want Roohi and Arjun back.'

'We will have to file a custody case.'

'She has kidnapped them.'

'Not legally. It is true you are the natural guardian, but so is she. And normally the mother is given custody of girls till the age of eight, and boys till the age of five.'

'He is eleven.'

'I know—so you have a good chance with him. But with Roohi it is more difficult. Ninety-nine per cent of the time girls go to their mothers.'

'Even if their mother is of doubtful character?'

'That has to be proved. Of course we will say her morals are weak. You have any proof, letters for example?'

'I have pictures,' said Raman briefly.

Nandan looked approving. Mr Kaushik studied the law tomes.

'Is her face clearly visible?'

'Visible enough, and in the company of the man she is now living with.'

'We will file them in court and use them later.'

'But how long will that take? I want my children back now.'

'As soon as we file for custody we will also put in an interim application to grant us access. Then we will see.'

'So how long?'

'I have to prepare the case first. Only after that can we move an interim application.'

'Asap.'

'Asap, of course. We need as much evidence as you have, diaries, letters, witnesses, that will prove she is an unfit mother exposing the children to nefarious influences. You know, make it as strong as possible.'

On the way back Raman negotiated his car slowly through the traffic while the small figure of his father sat next to him looking worried. 'One way or another we will have to go to court,' he remarked heavily.

'I am sorry you have to be dragged through all this muck.'

'Arre beta, don't worry about me. You just don't get worked up—that'll be very bad for your health.'

'I am not getting worked up—I only want to see my children.'

'And you will see them. God will not allow a father and his children to be separated.'

Raman gave a dry, mirthless laugh. 'Leave God out of it. He doesn't seem to be on my side lately.'

This was so undeniable that the father kept quiet.

Once back in Swarg Nivas father and mother packed a few things and left with their son. On no account would they let him spend the night alone. Raman did not protest. The thought of his empty house was dreadful to him.

Over the next few days Raman visited Nandan every evening, forced to think of his life in terms of accusation and evidence as his cousin drafted his petition. The whole process was disgusting.

'Why do I have to say all this? Half of it is not even true,' he said from time to time.

'Do you want your children or not? Courts are naturally sympathetic to women when it comes to matrimonial disputes. We have to put forward as strong an argument as possible.'

It was not hard to do. Shagun had been a faithless wife. This fact was embroidered and extended to cover the whole period of their marriage.

The plaintiff's job meant he spent many days on tour, that was the time the respondent indulged in licentious activities, even in the presence of her minor children. Photographs taken by the Lovely Detective Agency were enclosed to prove just one instance.

The plaintiff's heart attack was described along with the respondent's callous behaviour. The plaintiff was a loving father, the respondent an indifferent mother, who abandoned the marital home to pursue her affairs, kidnapping the children only when a divorce was not immediately agreed to.

Even though the female minor was of tender years, living with the respondent would expose her to harmful moral influences.

The plaintiff prayed that he be granted custody of his children and in the interim be given visitation rights.

At the end of it all Raman recognized neither himself nor Shagun. His love for his wife was lost in a maze of lies that infected even him. To mourn for a woman whose life could be constructed in this way was to reveal all the hidden ugliness beneath the beautiful exterior.

'What do you do when there is no infidelity involved?' he asked Nandan curiously.

'There is always something. Otherwise why would people divorce?'

'Like what?'

'Alcohol, abuse, violence, exploitation, public humiliation—though that comes in more useful when the wife is filing for divorce. Husband having other women is not seen as so bad—in theory, yes, but not in practice.

'But then the judge will know that much is made up.'

Nandan smiled his cigarette-stained smile. 'Made up—yes, the judge often knows that. But there is some truth in everything we say. And usually in the end the correct decision is taken. You will see.'

'In my case? You keep saying they favour the woman.'

'But we have witnesses—we will call the servants, we have the pictures—they can be used to intimidate the other party. We can use your parents to testify to what a good father you are. We can even call her mother; of course she will try and protect her daughter, but she will probably break under cross-examination.'

'Leave her out.'

'Listen. This is not a party, where you are so nice and polite to each other. If she is easily scared, so much the better.'

'She is old, I don't want her upset,' said Raman, regretting the unmanly flaws in his character.

'We have to utilize everything we have.'

'Why can't we subpoena his servant, or chowkidar? How much can they lie in front of lawyers?'

Nandan sighed. Clearly Raman had taken his notions of the Indian judiciary from American films. 'Our system is different. We don't subpoena, for one thing. If we need to question them, we have to give their names on our list of witnesses. And they could very well say they never saw Shagun in their lives—won't be very good for us. Do you see?'

'Suppose I just go to their schools and take the children. What can she do?'

'She can then take them back. What's to stop her?'

'What's to stop me?'

'Nothing. You can go on doing this until a court decision. Or unless you come to an agreement.'

'An agreement is not in the picture. We have to fight.'

Initially they all wanted to fight. He had seen it happen time and again. Fight, despair, compromise. The courts defeated everybody. Cases like this could take years, but clients need to be disillusioned slowly.

'Right now we are focusing on direct and circumstantial evidence that we are confident about. We have to file this as fast as possible so you can get visitation rights. Once those are granted, nobody can stop you from seeing your children. Later on we will attach our list of witnesses and the evidence we mean to use.'

Raman leaned back in his chair. His father's instinct to go to Nandan had proved right. He saw the noose around Shagun tightening. How much could she deny?

'To what address should we send the notice?' he asked.

'To her mother's?'

'But suppose the mother says she is not living with her?'

'Then where is she living? That is even more suspect.'

Raman left Nandan more buoyant than at any time during the last ten days. Let Shagun see he too could fight back, that he was no longer Mr Nice Guy.

On his way to the car he met a vaguely familiar-looking woman.

'Hello, beta,' she said, a smile briefly smoothing her worried features.

'Hello, Auntie,' he replied, flashing his general all-purpose grin.

'Children all right? Haven't seen them here for a while.'

'Everything is all right,' said Raman and turned his back.

'That Raman Kaushik is very strange,' remarked Mrs Rajora to her husband later in the evening. 'I don't think he recognized me. Used to come so often. Then he had his heart attack.'

'Everywhere there are troubles,' said the phlegmatic husband.

Mrs Rajora only had to think of her daughter to agree. Would their duties never be over? Would Ishita never be happy?

But things were improving, Mrs Rajora decided, keeping in mind that she should be grateful to God, to look at what she had rather than what she didn't. And what she had was a daughter who was better off now than when she first returned home three years ago.

XII

In the early days Ishita had spent every moment moping. Free at last from pretending things were all right meant she was free to lie listlessly on her bed, make no effort with her appearance and focus full time on her loss.

Head buried in her pillow, she thought of the body that had known so much love, and then so much punishment. Stubbornly it had remained barren despite the money spent, the hormones, the injections, the painful procedures. She could not conceive, whereupon SK had decided he could not love her.

If only she could tear out her whole reproductive system and throw it on the road. She hated her body, hated it.

Everybody in the building must know why she had come back. Return to sender. Receipt for 5 lakhs attached.

Her parents were equally devastated. They held themselves responsible for her malfunctioning organs. They could say her childhood TB was karma, but the consolations of karma were meagre. Their daughter was still young, and the prospect of endless dreary years ahead was frightening.

The forty-five minutes on the bus to work each morning was Mrs Rajora's time for contemplation. All around her, it seemed, were broken marriages. Even Princess Diana, beautiful, privileged, adored, even she couldn't keep her husband. No matter where you lived, what your circumstances, women always suffered.

SK's parents were not willing to try everything, that had been the main problem. If a sheep could be cloned, why not use the same technology to clone their precious son? Ishu would have co-operated fully.

The bus came to its stop at Patel Chest, and Mrs Rajora got off to start her working day, rehearsing the half-truths she would tell if anybody asked about her daughter. For the first time she realized how inconsiderate social inquisitiveness could be. Thank God she was retiring soon.

It was dusk, and Mrs Rajora and Mrs Kaushik were ambling around the building. Birds wheeled in the sky, before settling down on some of the high trees that bordered the housing society. There were a few pale wisps of cloud, touched by the pink of a sun that had sunk beyond the tall apartment blocks that made up the jagged skyline of PPG. The air was cool, soon the navratras would start and the society temple would resound with prayers.

Now Mrs Kaushik was intrigued. Despite her patient wait, Mrs Rajora had not imparted any information concerning Ishita's sudden arrival three weeks ago.

Once before she had had to bang on her friend's door to get news of what was bothering her. Now she tried a less direct attack.

'How is beti Ishu?'

'Fine.'

Mrs Rajora, gentlest of creatures, made the word forbidding.

Mrs Kaushik rather unkindly persisted. 'Everything OK? I am sure that the stones the astrologer gave will work. You have to give these things time.'

Her friend changed the topic. 'How is Raman doing? Such good news about Shagun's pregnancy. Are they hoping for a girl this time?'

When it comes to their children, people love to talk and talk, as though those children were universal objects of concern. So Mrs Kaushik allowed herself to be distracted.

Mrs Rajora crept into her apartment exhausted. Usually she came back from walking rejuvenated, her interest in humanity piqued with its daily dose of gossip. Now her own daughter was the subject of such curiosity.

She must be getting morbidly sensitive. Mrs Kaushik had always shown such genuine solicitude that she should have been able to share her troubles with her. But what had happened to Ishita was so awful that it was impossible to confide even in dear friends.

Mr Rajora walked in the morning, with four or five of his acquaintances, practically racing around the building. Once done, he would have breakfast, then come down to the small administrative section near the entrance, where, as an elected office-bearer, he was kept busy with society affairs, its security, the lifts, temple matters, community events, lunches, kirtans, raffles.

Every day on his return he found his daughter still in bed. Grief was all very well, but she was carrying this to ridiculous lengths. She needed some occupation, brooding was good for no one. What was her B.Ed. for, if not to protect her against such eventualities?

'I wanted to work, you got me married,' was her sullen response.

'I am sorry, beta. At the time it seemed the right thing to do.'

Mollified by this admission of guilt which she was now in the habit of demanding, Ishita said she had every intention of looking for a job as soon as she was able.

'Nothing is going to fall in your lap,' said her father, 'you have to go out and try.'

Hopelessness filled Ishita. Her father was right, nothing was going to fall into her lap. But that meant she had to resume life from where she had left off five years ago. Although she had been reluctant to marry, her passion for her husband was such that now the acme of her desire was to be in SK's bed, his arms, his heart. Alone in the house, how many times had she picked up the phone to dial his number? Just to hear his dear voice one more time? And then put the phone down sadly—she was divorced, he didn't want her, he had made that so clear. She still had her pride. The only way to be close to him was to shut her eyes and fantasize herself back to the love they had once shared.

'Beti? It's just a few hours' work. Let's start with something small.'

'What, Papa?'

'Would you like to participate in the building drive to collect clothes and household items for the earthquake victims in the north-east? The trucks are already booked. Think of others more unfortunate.'

But no, she couldn't bear going door to door, speaking into people's inquisitive faces. She just *couldn't*.

The trouble was that people did talk, confirmed Mrs Rajora as she told her husband about Leela Kaushik's questions, again suppressing her own envy of her friend, another grandchild on the way and a son who was rising like a star in the corporate world.

Eventually, inspired by some of the women in the building, Mrs Rajora came up with suggestions about starting a home business with baked goods, or designing clothes with a tailor installed in the veranda. The world was open to an enterprising woman. All this Ishita rejected, repeating her offers of leaving if her parents found her a burden.

It was best to leave their daughter alone, concluded the parents. She took too much tension. They themselves would have to tell their acquaintances of Ishu's return; better they shoulder the questions, otherwise their fragile girl might well spend the rest of her life glued to the mattress.

When Ishita did eventually venture forth looking for a job, it turned out to be an unpleasant enterprise. Her standing was not high in the teacher pool. She had a degree but no experience. Every place she went to asked her to check later, or worse still to look in the newspapers, they would advertise should there be a vacancy. No assurances anywhere.

She tried the many schools in Central Delhi: OSC, St Columba's, Bhartiya Vidya Bhavan, Vivekananda Vidyaylaya, the Tamil School, the Kerala School, Modern School, Junior Modern School, Mater Dei Convent, the school of Sikh Martyrs.

Further and further away from Patparganj she tried, twenty, twenty-five kilometres. Nothing, nothing. Hadn't she already known that in the cards dealt out by life she would not get the winning deal?

Dusshera.

The halwais had put up tables in the quadrangle near the society office in Block A. Feeling self-conscious among such gathered acquaintances, Ishita took a tiny morsel of mutter paneer onto her tinfoil plate, along with a puri, careful to avoid eye contact with anyone.

'Beti, is that all you are going to eat?'

Mrs Hingorani. Ishita looked at the grey frizzy hair of the woman, the lined good-natured face, and wondered what she wanted. Everybody over a certain age was a cornucopia of prying questions.

'Not keeping so well, Auntie,' she mumbled. If she wished to eschew neighbourly interaction, she should have remained upstairs, but that would have meant dealing with her mother's disappointment, so here she was down among the wolves.

She started to edge away, when Auntie asked was Ishita free these days? If so, would she like to do a little voluntary work? She ran a school for slum children.

The sight of all children was detestable, but those from the slums were a different breed, not the adorable creatures that fate had robbed her of, but urchins who were visible everywhere with their running noses and sharp ways.

'Why don't you drop by tomorrow and see?' Mrs Hingorani suggested into the heavy silence.

Even for a person committed to lifelong inertia this did not seem too great a concession. She agreed to be by the gate next morning at nine.

Her parents were surprised to see Ishita get up early. 'Where are you going?'

'Out.'

'Where?'

'With Mrs Hingorani.'

'To do what?'

'Some volunteer stuff.'

'Be careful. She has a big heart, but she tries to get people to work for free.'

Ishita, further depressed, opened the door and left. Why were her parents always investing the smallest action with so much significance? It weighed her down, she with her broken wings, who longed to fly.

The rickshaw reached the main road, where the noise was deafening. Horns blared and the fumes of cars, buses and two-wheelers hung thickly over one and all, ensuring that if they spoke they coughed, if they breathed they shortened their life span.

Through the ride Ishita kept up polite conversation.

'How did you start a school, Auntie?'

It began five years ago, with a young boy playing marbles next to his father, the chowkidar who manned the gate. Why wasn't he in school? demanded Mrs Hingorani, her eyes on the child as he mapped out his future on the dusty pavement, each idle marble ensuring that he never rose from it.

He keeps running away.

Come to my house, said Mrs Hingorani to the truant. Soon he was joined by his sister, then his neighbours, then the neighbours' neighbours as word spread. They came to learn English, to see a flush toilet, to sit on the carpet, to watch TV, to swell the rooms with young impoverished lives, till there were fifty, before school, after school, running in shifts, and the apartment could take no more.

She moved to a two-room set-up in Mandavili. Mandavili, one street down, left from the lights, the poor and crowded colony teeming with domestic labourers, dhobis, sweepers, electricians, carpenters, drivers, plumbers, electricians, watchmen, rickshaw wallahs, small shopkeepers, roadside vendors of fruit and vegetables, pavement sellers of goods, all the people who provided services to the thousands of co-operative housing dwellers of PPG. The women here earned a living by cooking and cleaning, while their daughters stayed at home also cooking and minding toddler siblings.

They stopped outside a tall, narrow building before a flight of steps leading inside. Parked next to it was a van.

'Have you picked up the food?' Mrs Hingorani asked the driver.

It turned out she fed them as well. They came hungry, listless, unable to concentrate. A few questions, what had they eaten?, nothing, and she had taken to buttering a hundred slices of bread every day.

The van, donated by a bereaved father, picked up party leftovers twice a week from five-star hotels, allowing the youngsters a taste of cakes, rolls and pizza slices.

'Good morning, Auntie,' chorused rows of children all different sizes, neatly dressed, hair slick with oil, faces shining. Mrs Hingorani made sure her students didn't look the poor, underprivileged creatures they actually were. Appearances were important, a sense of worth even more so.

'Where are your shoes? Tomorrow, wear your shoes and come. What do you mean they are lost? Find them.'

'Why is your skirt torn? Tell Mummy to stitch the hem.'

'Where are your socks? You can't come to school without socks.'

'How many don't have shoes? The shoe seller is coming tomorrow. He will take your sizes.'

'Of course you can have a uniform. Come every day and you will get one.'

'Where have you been the last two months?'

'This is a toilet, this is the flush. No, you can't do anything on the floor. No, you have to use the bathroom one by one. You do your business in the pot, one at a time.'

'You have to wash your hands here, here in this basin. And put the soap back in the dish, don't throw it in the sink.'

It was a new world for Ishita, and one right at her doorstep. Mandavili was walking distance, but in social terms it lay light years away. Every day she now woke with a purpose. For of course she volunteered; face to face with eager children, so obviously in need, it only took a day to come to that decision. Here, who cared if she had a broken marriage, who cared if her tubes were fused together by a long-ago disease?

What had her mother once said when trying to rouse her from her apathy? A drop of ink gets lost in a bucket of water, and here in the bucket of Mandavili her grief receded. At first she had been afraid that these children might bring painfully to mind the one she had failed to conceive, but the social gulf was too vast for that to happen.

So it was with equanimity that she met the mothers at the PTA meetings which Mrs Hingorani organized, believing it gave them recognition and encouraged self-respect.

These women, battling a thousand needs, empty stomachs, drunken husbands, semi-literate children, with no chance of escape from their poverty, looked at the world with hopeful, though somewhat weary, eyes. If they had the wherewithal, a quiet tubectomy put an end to the baby stream—otherwise they were doomed to procreate, with little say over their bodies, their lives, or their money.

Yes, indeed, Mandavili was the sea in which Ishita's own sorrows could drown.

Confidence.

Ishita along with Mrs Hingorani marching to Parliament House to protest against the nuclear device tested in the Pokhran desert. Drawing parallels between herself and the women involved in the freedom struggle: they too had courted arrest. Contradicting her father, no, it was not necessary for India to assert herself as a world power, not when she couldn't feed her children, making the man think his daughter had grown more in the NGO than in her years of marriage.

Raising funds along with Mrs Hingorani, asking for donations, explaining their purpose. Every month 2,000 had to be found for rent, 400 for the helper, 1,000 for the food. Money for shoes, uniforms, books and copies, money for another teacher, where are the volunteers in our country? If only there were more like Ishita, mourned Mrs Hingorani.

To feel valued for the first time by the outside world.

In July she was offered a monthly salary of 2,000 by Mrs Hingorani, her usefulness recognized, her position in the school entrenched.

Perhaps it was something Ishita said, but one day Mrs Hingorani dropped in on her parents, to tell them how grateful she was to them for sparing their daughter, truly she wouldn't know what to do without her. The children too had grown so attached—she was now as popular as Helmut, the German boy who had chosen to work for them. Indeed, she laughed, the mark of their fondness was the lice that Ishita had already had to deal with twice. Helmut had shaved his head, but Ishita couldn't do that.

In a flat as small as theirs, how can the daughter get lice and the mother not know? Ishita quickly changed the topic, and Mrs Hingorani, sensitive to glacial currents, allowed herself to be directed into whichever channel she was propelled to.

As soon as the visitor went Ishita said, 'I didn't tell because I knew you would worry.'

'A mother is never free from worry. First they give you lice, next it will be pneumonia, or typhoid, or . . . or . . . drug-resistant TB.'

'I won't fall sick. Mrs Hingorani hasn't.'

'Did she get lice?'

'Yes, she did.'

Mrs Rajora looked distinctly cheerful at the thought of the spry Mrs Hingorani's short grey hair dotted with eggs, crawling with lice.

'I know you don't like me working there, you want me to be in better company, and this would only have proved you right,' said Ishita, patting the soft skin of her mother's ageing face.

'Beta, what do I matter? God will reward you, as he did Mother Teresa. So many people in her debt—such a grand funeral. You are following in her footsteps.'

Ishita giggled. 'I don't have it in me to be Mother Teresa. And I am sure lice would have attacked her if she didn't have that thing on her head.'

'How do you know all the eggs are dead?'

'I put the medicine on twice, Mummy.'

'Ishu,' said Mrs Rajora, struggling with herself. 'You keep saying you need volunteers, you never thought of asking your mother? You know next month I retire.'

The transition from university librarian to volunteer social worker was not smooth. Deep down Mrs Rajora never saw the point of it. See, they lose their shoes, see, you have to go after them to make them come—see, many mothers don't even attend meetings—see, that boy is teaching all those little children filthy language, I heard him, what is a nine-year-old doing in KG?—see, they come back from the village and you have to start from scratch—when they are older how much are they going to remember?—what is the point in teaching slum children English, or making them use computers?—they will only go back to the streets and forget everything—see, see, see . . .

A few weeks and Mrs Hingorani was forced to have a talk with Ishita. 'It's not her fault, this is the way society thinks. At least she is doing her best to help, which is more than can be said of many.'

But her best wasn't even scratching the surface, Ishita thought—and you are too nice to say so. Her heart swelled then subsided as two opposing claims pinched it in swift pincerlike movements.

That evening Ishita with her mother: 'It is attitudes like these we have to fight. You can't say it's no use, a journey to the moon starts with a single step.'

Mrs Rajora looked defeated. What had the moon got to do with anything? She was willing to teach slum children, willing to expose herself to lice, and still her daughter found fault with her, imagining she was not for social justice, which was a lie.

In the end Mrs Rajora was put in charge of the kitchen, or rather the little kerosene stove, on which they managed things like scrambled eggs with chopped onions and green chillies, or khichdi with curd from the market. Once she was in front of a fire, Mrs Rajora's instincts to feed knew no social checks.

And Ishita, seeing her mother squatting on the floor, working the single-burner stove, organizing leftovers from her own kitchen, buying biscuits and an occasional tin of powdered milk, witnessing all this, she herself jumped over the gap between them.

Every Sunday both parents sat with the papers, pencil in hand, circling the marriage advertisements where a divorcee was acceptable. This narrowed their choices, but surely somewhere there was a man suitable for a girl like Ishita Rajora. A girl with all the home-making qualities, with so much love to give.

Ishita watched their efforts from a safe emotional distance. There was no point trying for happiness, but it was important for her parents to imagine they were doing something about her future.

She was married to her work, not one suitor could give her a similar satisfaction.

XIII

When Shagun left her marriage, it became impossible for Mrs Sabharwal to hold her head high in the community. Every neighbour got to know as the news seeped through the walls of the clustered flats. Ami, who had arranged the introduction, felt personally offended. If Mrs Sabharwal didn't mind her saying so, there must be something essentially wrong with Shagun for her to leave a husband as devoted as Raman.

It's hard to know exactly what is going on between two people, replied the mother, and she began to avoid her neighbour.

Worse things happened.

A process server came.

'Shagun Kaushik?'

'What do you want?' asked Mrs Sabharwal, trying to sound aggressive.

'Court notice.'

'Why?'

'Are you Shagun Kaushik?'

'I am her mother.'

'She has to sign for this.'

'Give it to me.'

'If I give it to you, my job will go, I am a poor man.'

He could be a poor man, but every statement sounded like a threat. An emissary of the court promising to return tomorrow same time, determined to deliver disaster concealed in the envelope hanging from his limp hand.

No one in the family had ever been involved in a court case. There was something unsavoury about the whole thing, some profound incapacity to lead your life according to prescribed norms.

She had heard of cases lasting ten years, twenty years, property disputes carried on by grandchildren, custody cases only resolved by the child's reaching eighteen, divorce disputes lasting into old age. Which man would not tire of a woman—no matter how beautiful—who came burdened with legal baggage?

Besides, she could see no place for the children in the new set-up. Suppose there were problems between them and Ashok? What would happen?

Her daughter was not to be cowed into anxiety. Taking the children had been Ashok's idea, if only to bring Raman to the bargaining table. She had asked nicely for a divorce, been prepared to sacrifice, but the man refused to admit the marriage was over, slammed the phone down on her, what other choice did she have?

The mother could see no good end to any of this. 'Just tell me what I should do when the server comes tomorrow,' she said, her voice weighty with unexpressed fears.

A few hours later Shagun phoned back. 'He says we must accept it.'

'You have to come, then.'

'I will be there.'

Well, thought Mrs Sabharwal as she put down the receiver, at least she would get to see her daughter. Those days had gone, along with so much else, when they used to meet at least once a week. Now just phone conversations, hardly anything else.

When Shagun came the next day it was with Roohi. 'My darling,' cried the grandmother, rushing to her. 'I have missed you so, so much. Did you think of me, sweetheart? Did you miss your naani?'

Roohi hid behind her mother.

'Mama, please, give her time. She is still confused.'

Mrs Sabharwal thought the little girl far removed from the sweet smiling child she had known. 'How is school, beta?' she asked.

'The teachers say she has become quite withdrawn. I had to tell them what has happened at home—so they can be on their guard in case Raman tries to kidnap her.'

'What did they say to that?'

'What would they say? My situation is not so uncommon, you know.'

Mrs Sabharwal did not know but said nothing.

'Anyway, the child is happier, that is what matters.'

'Of course.'

They had lunch and waited for the server. 'I wonder what it is,' said Mrs Sabharwal, to fill the awkwardness between Shagun and herself.

'Couldn't be a plea for divorce,' said the daughter dryly. 'Must be custody.'

Mrs Sabharwal looked blank.

'Mama, I wish everybody were as sweet and simple as you. You think once the marriage is over everything naturally follows? No such luck. Divorce takes a lifetime and if you are not living together where do the children go?'

'Where?'

'Exactly. They can only be with one of us at a time. The question is who, how, where and when? All that is custody.'

This information made Mrs Sabharwal so sad she could hardly speak.

'I'll be the one to file for divorce,' continued Shagun. 'We are working it out with Madz.'

'Madz?'

'Ashok's lawyer friend.'

'What will you do if he doesn't divorce you? He may not want to.'

'Don't I know that? Punishment is what he is after.'

'Beta, he must be very upset. You know how much he loves his children.'

Shagun's face hardened and Mrs Sabharwal understood she must not say things like this.

All afternoon they waited. Shagun started fretting about Arjun coming home from school and not finding her.

'Surely he is used to that?'

'Things are different now, Mama. My children need me.'

It was around four thirty, when Shagun was coaxing Roohi to drink her evening glass of milk, that the server finally came. Shagun grabbed the sheaf of papers stamped with judicial insignia, signed, called a taxi and departed, leaving the mother to feel a little slighted, a little ignored, a little unimportant.

In the taxi Shagun flattened the thick wad with unsteady hands.

'What is that, Mama?' asked Roohi, taking her thumb out of her mouth.

'Nothing, beta, let Mama read.'

The thumb went back and Roohi returned her gaze to the city.

Petitioner—Mr Raman Kaushik, Respondent—Mrs Shagun Kaushik—flip, flip to the end, what did he want? If only, only a divorce, but no, his meanness made that impossible, ah, here it was, that for the reasons stated above, the petitioner's prayer was that the two minor children be restored to their father's custody.

Back went Shagun to the reasons mentioned above. She had guessed they would be awful, but this awful? One affair changed into licentiousness from the day they married, her own mother turned into a procuress, her uncaring nature in full display as she abandoned her children to co-habit with Ashok Khanna. Exposure to him threatened the minors' psychological well-being, she herself was an evil moral influence. The paper slid from her lap to the taxi floor.

'What is it, Mama?'

She could not answer.

The child shook her arm: 'Mama, Mama, what is it?'

'It is a little message from your father. He is trying to kill me.'

The grip on her arm tightened.

'You must never see him, or go to him, even if he calls you. He is a bad, bad man.'

Roohi looked down. The mother gazed at the bits of scalp that showed through the fine hair of her daughter's bent head. She put an arm around her, 'Never leave me, darling, never,' and the child bobbed reassuringly against her shoulder.

Arjun was in the drawing room when they came back.

'Where were you?' he demanded. 'I was waiting for you. Nobody knew where you were.' His face was tense as he fixed his mother with an accusing stare. A glass of milk was sitting on the table next to him, a thickened layer of malai crusting its surface.

'Beta, I was at Naani's house. Some work took longer than I thought.'

'Why didn't you tell me where you were going?'

'Papa is trying to kill Mama,' said Roohi.

Her brother looked at her with contempt. 'Don't talk rubbish, Roo. You don't know anything.'

'Mama said.'

She is going to die, flashed across the son's mind, while the daughter stared at her mother across the web of her spread-out fingers.

'Not really,' said Shagun hastily, 'what I meant was that he is trying to take you two away and that will kill me. Kill me.' She drew her children near and stared desolately out of the window over their heads. After a while she asked tenderly, 'I will get your milk heated, all right, beta?'

'My stomach is hurting,' said Arjun.

'Poor little babu. Would you like a banana instead?'

He shook his head. Shagun sighed. Of course it was the recent disturbances that were causing her son stress. If only Raman could see things rationally, there was no reason why they both couldn't continue as joint carers of their children.

They had been so delighted when she came to get them, throwing themselves on her with hugs and kisses. That scene had replayed itself in her heart many times, even though it had been a little spoiled by Arjun's assumption that she had come to stay. No, she had to explain, they were all leaving Papa, they would never stop loving him of course but things had changed and living together was out of the question. Some day he would understand. Now would he please be a good boy and help her pack his stuff?

'My stomach is hurting too,' said Roohi, picking up her brother's illness as fast as it takes an idea to travel from one sibling to the other.

'Copycat.'

'Beta, be nice to your sister.'

'She is so stupid.'

'Arjun! Please! You two must love each other, not fight all the time.'

She pushed them away, the reality of having to deal with thirty-two pages of lies making her suddenly impatient. Arjun stared at her. In his school bag lying on the floor next to his feet was a maths test which he had failed. His father had always sat with him during weekends, guiding him through many practice sums. 'In this subject the secret of success is practise, practise. Practice so that you will not make a mistake no matter how pressed for time in an exam or how nervous. Don't forget it's easy to fall behind, hard to make up.'

Now for the first time in his life he had done badly. Nine on 25. What would his mother say? She hadn't even remembered that tests were fixed for the first period on Wednesdays. His teacher had asked him to get the test signed. He would forge his mother's signature and hand it in tomorrow.

Next week was English, he could handle that. But the week after was science, again a subject his father had taught him. He could try asking a friend for help, but till now he was the one his friends turned to. What on earth would they think?

Shagun put away the ghastly court papers, then spent a long time on the pot, expelling the tension from her body. Once done, she stood looking at her face in the mirror. Nobody would have said she was in her early thirties, in certain lights she looked a young girl, and according to Ashok she had the body of one too.

Today, unfortunately, she would have to greet him with news of the case, another thing he would have to deal with. As though he didn't have enough on his plate already.

These days Ashok Khanna was a beleaguered man, but as he was fond of saying, he was used to fighting fire. Every morning when he opened the newspaper it was to find The Brand being accused of fresh instances of callous capitalist behaviour. An NGO had objected to the fact that it took 2.5 litres to make 1 litre of a drink of no nutritional value. On purely circumstantial evidence they were being linked to depleted groundwater resources and debt-ridden farmers.

Unfortunately nobody waited for allegations to be proved before multinational-bashing took place. The issue was serious enough for head office to extend Ashok's stay in India.

It's an ill wind that blows nobody any good.

That night as Arjun lay in bed, he could hear his mother and Ashok Uncle talking in the next room. At home comfort had flowed from the voices of his parents, here adult conversation seemed more ominous. He wanted his mother.

If he pinched Roohi she would cry and that would bring her, but he knew she didn't like being distracted by her children in the evenings.

What was his father doing now? Should he phone him? No, better not—he might remember about the Wednesday tests, and ask him questions. In his father's place there was instead this stranger hovering around Shagun. It made Arjun uncomfortable, the man's fingers running up and down her arm, his hands reaching out to pull her close, the little kisses he dropped on her forehead. She never resisted as she sometimes had with Raman.

Otherwise too his mother was different. For one, she was around much more. He liked that she was waiting to have lunch with him when he came from school, that she was so interested in everything that concerned him. To reward her the previously taciturn Arjun began to tell stories of what his friends had done, how they had competitions as to who could hit the fan with their tiffins, whose ruler could be broken by the other's ruler, who could harass the teacher the most without getting into trouble. She would laugh, ruffle his hair, tell him he had become a really naughty boy.

But when the man came home, the centre of attention shifted. Then he was treated on par with Roohi, to be fed, put to bed and otherwise ignored. Though he had only been in this house two weeks, he knew the pattern.

Sometimes the mother would say, Guess what Arjun did in school today. And the uncle would say 'What?' but his look was directed only at her, as was his smile, and soon she would forget what she had meant to tell him.

When Arjun left the room, his mother's footsteps did not follow him, as they so often had in the old house. Once as he loudly dragged his feet he heard the man say, Let him be, he is growing up, you have to give him space.

Roohi was not part of these exchanges. The maid who had appeared two days after their own arrival would be feeding her and then she would go to sleep.

A week after the notice was delivered Raman phoned his mother-in-law: 'Where are my children? I want to talk to them.'

Mrs Sabharwal could hear the anguish in his voice. She knew the pain this caused her was of interest to nobody.

'Beta, right now they are not here,' she said carefully.

'Where are they?'

'Safe and well, don't worry.'

'Make sure they talk to me tomorrow, otherwise I will file a criminal case in addition to the civil. She will be put in jail where she belongs.'

Melancholy triumph invaded the darkness in Raman's heart. He could picture the anxious Mrs Sabharwal, always so attentive to the children and himself, wondering how things had gone this wrong. Was she trying to make sense of all the lies Shagun must have fed her? She sounded scared; he was glad, now the daughter would have to deal with the consequences.

It was late but Mrs Sabharwal didn't care. She could feel her dreaded palpitations—avoid stress, her doctor had said, but how was that possible? She didn't doubt Raman's threats for a moment. In all these years, she had never known him to say something he did not mean. How separating the children from their father was going to help matters, she didn't know, but everything Shagun did now was with divorce in mind, and she herself was just beginning to appreciate that this dreaded state was in fact a sundering devoutly to be wished.

With shaking fingers she dialled her daughter's number.

'Raman phoned.'

'And?'

'He is going to put you in jail—he is very angry.'

'What did he say?'

'Tomorrow he wants to talk to the children, otherwise he will file a criminal case against you.'

'Empty threats.'

'Beta, he can hire goondas to attack both of you. He can have a private detective trail your movements, gather more damaging evidence. I keep saying, till things are settled stay with me.'

'Calm down, Mama. He is trying to frighten you—now go to sleep and don't worry. We will come tomorrow, OK?'

Did Shagun really think that anxiety, her constant companion, could be erased so easily? Was she that unacquainted with her mother's heart? Bewildered, Mrs Sabharwal remained seated by the phone, her hands helplessly in her lap. She had done her duty, relayed a message—the rest was up to other people. To calm herself she began to plan the next day's menu to include her grandchildren's favourite foods, rajma rice and fried potatoes with chaat masala. Shagun objected to anything fried but occasionally, where was the harm? Thank God she had baked a cake, in the morning she would make a cocoa-butter icing.

Eventually she closed her eyes and slept for some fitful, unrestful hours. In the morning she woke with a heavy head—another symptom of her daughter's troubled family life.

They came, withdrawn children, waifs in the marital combat zone, Arjun, face pinched, Roo pale with wisps of hair across her eyes.

'The children are looking so thin.'

'They are all right.'

Mrs Sabharwal bustled into the kitchen, lit the gas and started frying. The smell of hot oil, the sound of its bubbles, the faint sizzle of potato slices filled the flat. As they were eating the phone rang.

Arjun picked up. 'Papa?'

'Son. Are you all right?'

'Yes, Papa.'

'I miss you so. When I came home and found you not there, it was like hell. Just hell.'

'Sorry, Papa.'

'Would you like to come and stay with me? I will take a few days off. What do you say?'

'I don't want to leave Mama.'

'Am I asking you to do that? You can phone her, meet her as often as you like. I will never stop you.'

'She says I will never see her if I stay with you,' said Arjun.

'That's absolute rubbish. Does your mother think everybody is like her? Is she there?'

Arjun did not reply, and Raman tried to modify the hatred in his voice. 'Beta, if you stay with me I promise, there will be no restrictions—no pressure to do anything. We will do fun things together—like—like . . .'

He stopped. He couldn't imagine doing fun things with his children. Once upon a time they had gone on family outings, films, restaurants, friends' houses, but that had been in another era and always collectively.

His wife came on the line. 'He doesn't want to talk. You are scaring him.'

'Shagun, you know that is nonsense. Since when have my children been afraid of me? You are filling them with stories.'

'Goodbye. And incidentally please don't harass my mother. This has nothing to do with her.'

A click and silence.

This was worse than anything he could have imagined. It had been so artificial talking to Arjun like that—and Roohi—he hadn't even spoken to his daughter.

He dialled his mother-in-law's number again. Shagun picked up.

What?

Where is Roo?

A pause. Then, 'She also doesn't want to talk to you.'

Let her tell me that.

Pause, indistinct voices. Then,

She refuses to come to the phone. What can I do?

You have manipulated her. She has always, always wanted to talk to me. Even when I was in office.

Well, things have changed.

And Shagun put the phone down.

The whole charade had accomplished nothing. He could exchange words with his children, but not establish the connection he was craving. This realization drove him mad with frustration.

If only he could harm the mother without affecting the children, he would be so happy.

Telling the servants he wouldn't be in for dinner, he slowly went to his car to begin the drive across the river to his parents'. As he hurtled over the bridge, taking advantage of every gap in the traffic, his cousin at that very moment was thinking of him. The interim application had come up and the other side had been granted one month in which to file a reply. The man who had appeared was a junior of an expensive lawyer in South Delhi. Clearly the other party thought that high fees guaranteed victory.

'Calm down,' advised Nandan. 'You won't be able to fight if you get so upset.'

'She didn't even let me talk to them on the phone.'

Nandan looked sad. His younger cousin's distress brought out the pity he was usually careful not to feel. Years of litigation lay ahead and Ramu had to realize that now, otherwise the inevitable delays would destroy him. 'She is using the children to get what she wants. It's not surprising—that's what people do.'

'What does she want?'

'You mentioned a divorce,' said Nandan patiently.

'What kind of mother is she? To make the children pawns in her larger game plan—I would never do it, never.'

'There are not many like you.'

Raman felt vaguely soothed. It was true, in this dog-eat-dog world there were not many people like him.

'When will all this be heard?'

'Soon. Today they were given a month by which to file the reply for visitation rights. So at least the process has started. And judges generally keep the interests of the children in mind.'

Raman remained sunk in his own despairing thoughts. His cousin's wife was knitting some everlasting garment. He looked at her; a dab of red lipstick across her unpretentious face, her hair always in a loose plait. In the years following his own wedding, he had pitied Nandan his wife. The gods were punishing him now.

But, continued Nandan, if they were playing on his nerves the worst thing he could do was to succumb. This was essentially a waiting game. They were all behind him.

Involuntarily Raman yielded to the sympathy. When his mother suggested he stay the night, he gratefully slept next to his parents' snoring forms in the single air-conditioned room, remembering how he had studied on this bed for his

IIT entrance exams, in the belief that with good marks you could achieve anything.

*

In Madan Singh's office.

'Hey, Shakes, making up for the absence of all these years?'

'What to do, yaar? Stuck in such a situation.'

'Where's Shagun?'

'I wanted to see you without her. She gets very emotional and I need to understand exactly what our options are.'

'In matrimonial disputes the options are usually few.'

'How long will this thing take?'

'For ever.'

'Seriously?'

'Seriously. Unless you can bring the other side to the bargaining table. If they don't come, harass them until they do. Then of course there is the divorce petition.'

'Are we going in for irreconcilable differences?'

'These grounds do not exist in India.'

'How is that possible?'

'After living apart, if both parties agree, then a divorce by mutual consent can be initiated.'

'Shagun still hopes that Raman will eventually come around.'

'The fact is you have leverage as long as you have the children. But he is going to get visitation rights—six months, ten months, and after that the pressure will ease.'

'And then?'

'Then what? You live your life.'

'It's not so easy. She is petrified of being followed, that they will get evidence to link us, which will prove she is an unfit mother. I can't believe choosing another man suggests that, but she says I don't know.'

'Well, the courts take a conservative view of sexual morality.'

'It's the nineties. Don't Indians change partners? Or are we still living in Vedic times?'

'Indians do everything. But the legal position is another matter.'

'What about bribes?'

'The case has to come to that stage first. You can try and bribe the judge, you can bribe for delays—but what else? Bribes won't make the system speedy and efficient.'

'I hate this country.'

'It has its own dynamics. You just have to know how to work them.'

'That's what I do at office—all day long. Now it's particularly bad.'

'So I've heard.'

'Trust an NGO to discover that we, and we alone, are responsible for farmer suicides.'

'With what proof?'

'What proof is needed if you are a foreign company? All that is necessary is a few reports and a receptive press. Never mind farmers were committing suicide anyway. Now it's our fault because of the groundwater situation. We have to be holier than any national manufacturer.'

'Didn't you face something like this in Brussels?'

'Yes—but here the damage control works differently. You will be amazed at the number of water conservation programmes we are funding. Sponsoring environmental education in schools and colleges, cleaning up bawaris and lakes in affected districts, announcing our commitment to rainwater harvesting, sustainable development, and zero water balance in five years. Every effort is publicized—through ads in the media, TV, print, regional, national, the works. It's costing us millions of dollars.'

'Bad for you personally?'

'It'll pass. The wretched thing is that the rest of the world gets to know, and such negative publicity takes a while to subside.'

'Well, you were always up for a challenge, Shakes.'

His friend smiled, at this tacit reminder of an old school saying, challenges are what make a man.

'So,' said Ashok, 'you think we should file for divorce?'

'Absolutely. The sooner the better. We will need to work with Shagun for instances of mental cruelty, abuse, withholding financial support, in-law trouble, physical mistreatment.'

Ashok blanched, thinking how difficult it was to associate Raman with these words.

'Unless of course he comes to his senses and agrees to mutual consent. Then all this becomes irrelevant.'

'What else can we do?'

'Cause as much obstruction as possible on the minor petition.'

'For how long?'

'As long as we can. And hope they offer us a divorce as a way out of the situation.'

Shagun in Madan Singh's office. Ashok is with her, she is trying to think of instances of cruelty in her marriage, but can't come up with much.

'Why do I have to say all this? It's not true, and he can call witnesses to prove he never beat me, or denied me money, or insulted me in public.'

'Why do you want a divorce, then?'

'Because I love someone else.'

'Not a good enough reason. You have to make a case that is valid in court.'

'But I am the one that left.'

'Because of unbearable mental cruelty. I am afraid this is how divorce works.'

As strong a case was made as possible and sent to Raman Kaushik's residence.

Raman barely glanced at his wife's allegations. Though love was dead, his sense of justice found such lies intolerable. Nandan, however, maintained that the very wildness of the charges proved she was just throwing accusations in the wind, hoping one would stick. It was a weak petition, he had expected better from her lawyer, who was supposed to be quite good. It was all strategy, that Raman had to understand.

Days passed. Raman's whole soul was concentrated on August 10th when the reply to the interim application would be filed in court and the process of seeing his children would start. The night before, he phoned Nandan.

'When should we meet?'

'For what?'

'Isn't tomorrow the date for the interim application?'

'It is a mere formality. Supposing they actually file a reply—'

'Supposing? Don't they have to? Isn't that the purpose of the legal system, to make people do things they don't want to?'

'Yes, of course. However, the law likes to make allowances. And one of those allowances is time. Everybody knows this.'

'Still, I want to come.'

There was a little pause.

'Ramu—you don't know how these courts operate. The

other side will almost certainly try to delay, and you will have made a wasted trip.'

'The judge will be party to this?'

'If their excuse is good.'

'My presence might make the judge realize I am a caring father. This is not just any old case. Both my children have been kidnapped.'

'May I make a suggestion? Let me go and see where we are placed in the list. Then I will phone you just before our turn.'

'I don't want to miss it.'

'Don't worry, you won't.'

Nandan put the phone down. From the beginning he had known that to take on Raman's case would stress him out. To charge such a close relative was unthinkable, all he hoped was to avoid blame for the endless deferrals that were part of the system. It was a thousand-to-one chance that the other side would calmly hand in a reply tomorrow.

The tenth passed slowly. Mid-morning, still no phone call. By the end of the day, still nothing.

On the phone that evening: 'What happened, yaar?'

'Arre, hardly any of the applications got heard today. There was a bomb scare.'

The line was bad, Raman couldn't hear properly, what had Nandan just said?

'Bomb scare, bomb scare.'

'What does that mean?'

'Some joker makes an anonymous phone call—says there is a bomb in Tees Hazari. The whole building is vacated, while the police squad does a search.'

'Did they find it?'

'Of course not. Somebody probably wanted a postponement.'

'Tell me, does this happen often?'

'Often? Not really.'

'So, what are we going to do now?'

'Wait, of course. A date has been set next week for today's cases.'

'Well, let me know,' said Raman dully.

'Don't worry. This kind of thing happens—you can't help it, yaar. It's a matter of luck.'

'Luck. Yes. Well.'

The conversation ended. Raman remained sitting by the phone, in a well of self-pity, listening to a house empty of all family, the only human sound the murmur of servants. He had a good mind to bomb the courts himself. How was the ordinary man to get justice?

Ashok phoned Shagun with the news. Their lawyer's junior, all primed to take another date, had been spared the trouble. Then next week if the application came up for hearing, a date would be taken.

And after that another date. Only then would they file a reply. Only then.

What could the other side do? What *could* they do? Nothing.

Afterwards Shagun phoned her mother, the poor woman had been fretting since the morning—unable to grasp the way in which the courts functioned, unable to absorb the legal landscape that her daughter was continually trying to explain to her.

'Bomb scare? Did anybody get hurt?' she asked.

'It was a *scare*, nothing happened.'

'Beta, you must never go to court. These days, so much lawlessness everywhere. And the police are hopeless. Let the lawyer go—you are paying him so much.'

'*Ma*, I've told you before, he is an old school friend of Ashok's—he is not charging us a paisa.'

'Then how is he taking an interest?'

'That's the way their school works, the old-boy network is very strong. We are lucky, he is one of the best lawyers in Delhi.'

'Beta, I don't understand these things. Only be careful. Lots of terrorism everywhere.'

'Right now we just want to get as many dates as we can. Let him see how it feels. All I asked for was my freedom, willing to let him have the children, still he tried to blackmail me. Bastard.'

Mrs Sabharwal couldn't bear to participate when Shagun cursed the man she had lived with for so many years. 'Don't the children ask for him?'

'No. They realize it's either him or me, and they naturally prefer their mother to their father. How much time did he spend with them, that they should start missing him now?'

The man was working, he would come home tired, then both of you would go out, ran treacherously through Mrs Sabharwal's mind. Such thoughts belonged unequivocally to the past.

On the 17th of August Raman phoned his cousin.

'What is going to happen tomorrow?'

Nandan sighed. 'Why don't you come and see?'

'Really? I think it will make a difference. Let the judge realize she is dealing with suffering human beings.'

'Yes. Be there around eleven.'

'Even earlier if necessary?'

'Eleven is fine.'

'Bye.' The lightness in his cousin's voice made Nandan wince. He hoped against all experience that the application would be heard.

Meanwhile Raman told his secretary he had to attend to important legal work, and she should reschedule his meetings.

This was the first time Raman was actually visiting Tees Hazari. As he followed Nandan's junior into the labyrinth inside, he felt he was entering a large government hospital. The same mix of people from poor to well dressed, the same groups of huddlers, the same air of desperation, the smell of urine coming through open bathroom doors, pools around water coolers, paan-stained walls, a body or two stretched along corridors.

Finally they reached a court on the far end of the second floor. 'Wait here,' said the junior as they came to a foyer that opened onto two rooms. 'Court of the Addl District Judge' was flaked in white letters above both doors. Outside each was a board with papers stuck to it.

Raman looked around, his nerves on edge. Would Shagun be present?

There were two benches against the wall crammed with people. Lawyers with files under their arms could be seen sauntering everywhere. 'When will it be our turn? Where is Nandan?' demanded Raman.

'He's just coming.'

'Mr Nandan Kaushik said that it would be heard early.'

'It's last in the miscellaneous. Arranged datewise—our case is still new,' said the junior casually, ambling towards a clone, slapping him on the back, generating bonhomie as though he were at a party.

'Who was that?' asked Raman when he returned.

'The other side's junior.'

'You were *talking* to him?'

The man looked surprised. 'He's a friend of mine. Case won't come up for a while, he says.'

It seemed very wrong to Raman that his side's lawyers were consorting with the enemy. How would they fight, plot, plan, keep secrets, if they were friends?

'Where is Nandan?'

'He is just coming. Please you sit,' said the junior, gesturing to the courtroom.

Inside was space to breathe and think. At the end of the room sat the judge, elevated and cordoned off, surrounded by litigants, their lawyers, families and supporters.

Raman took a seat in front, glad to be one step closer to the process that would decide his fate.

'Your Honour,' said a woman dressed in a white-and-black sari, 'I must protest, this is the fifth time the respondent is trying to take a date. Please grant us some relief—my client is facing great financial distress.' Next to her was a thin woman in a salwar kameez, sindhoor in her hair, bangles on her wrist, henna on her feet, all the signs of marriage. She had two children with her. God knew how far she had come, and how many times she had waited.

The other side's lawyer asked for a postponement, and after some argument it was granted. The thin mother of two dully staggered out, while the clerk typed away.

At one the judge got up. Lunchtime. Nandan appeared.

'Come.'

'Where?'

'We can get something to eat in the canteen, but it's not very good.'

'When's the case?'

'I have sent Bhasin to find out—my junior.'

'He was talking to the other side's lawyer.'

'We have a professional relationship with everyone.'

Like whores.

Nandan was right—the food was bad. Raman could barely swallow the cold vadas, drink the too-sweet coffee. 'I thought I would see Shagun,' he probed.

'She might come.'

'But you don't think so?'

'I don't know. Depends on the advice she is getting,' said the non-committal Nandan, curved over his plate scooping the sambar into his mouth with a bent aluminium spoon. There was so much noise in the canteen that conversation was a strain.

'Is it like this all the time?'

'Yes.'

'And you come here how often?'

'Every day.'

'You think the judge will hear our case?'

'Can't say.'

'Why? Don't they care about people's time?'

He would look a big fool if there was no hearing, especially after he had taken half-day leave. The atmosphere of Tees Hazari was seeping into him, he could sense the hopelessness that hung in the air, the waiting that each aimless loiterer embodied.

Nandan patted his back soothingly and got up to pay. Lunch over, they returned to their designated courtroom to find only a few people. Judge gone for a meeting, said Bhasin as they entered. Nandan walked towards the clerk, who was brusquely greeting every fresh enquiry with the words 'next week'.

'Let's go.'

'What's happening?'

'Today's cases have been shifted to next week. That's still not too bad.'

'But didn't she know she had a meeting? Why ruin everybody's time?'

'Sometimes we do get to know when the judge is going to be busy, sometimes not—it depends,' said Nandan.

By now Raman knew better than to ask what it depended on. He felt sick to his stomach. Not only was one leave wasted, but he was no nearer seeing his children. 'Tell me honestly—how long will all this take?'

The standard reply, not long.

They must be lying like this to everyone. That was why the place was like hell, the air thick with the collective despair emanating from the multitudes outside every courtroom.

'But you must have *some* idea. Papa said you had never known failure. All your cases ended either in settlement or victory.'

'That's why I stick to Tees Hazari,' said Nandan modestly. 'Arre, everybody wants to practise in the High Court, in the Supreme Court. But then clients here suffer.'

'And having a High Court lawyer like the other side does? That impresses the judge?'

'Some judges do get impressed by a big name—but it is not worth it. Charges are too high, then instead of coming himself he sends his junior. Here everybody knows I am sincere.'

Eventually Raman managed to drag a time estimate out of his cousin. Around six months. The hearings for the main case would go on simultaneously, but the more interim applications there were, the more the main decision would be deferred, because those got heard first. If delays suited the other side, well, Nandan shrugged, sometimes people got lucky with a bribe that worked.

'But you are already bribing the recorder and the clerk.'

'That's hardly bribing. Just a little tea money to make sure the work gets done.'

Raman drove back to office furious and miserable. The minute he entered, the phone rang. His father.

'What happened, beta?'

'Nothing. Another date. Nandan took care of the recorder so at least we will get an early one.'

'How much?'

'Two hundred.'

'Hmmm. Nandan is a sincere boy. He knows.'

'The steno, the clerk, all get a fixed cut. What kind of system is this?'

'Arre, that's why you have a lawyer. Leave it to him. And don't worry.'

Everybody kept telling him not to worry. They did not apply that same brilliance to the problem of how to see his children.

XIV

It was around this time that Arjun started fussing over school. The first-term exams were scheduled for the end of August and he had never felt so unprepared. He had just scraped through in science, 10 on 25, and once again had had to forge his mother's signature.

As he handed in the signed test paper his teacher asked him to stay behind during recess.

'Is anything wrong, Arjun?' she started. 'Why have you suddenly begun doing so badly? All your junior school teachers thought very highly of you.'

Arjun remained silent while the teacher supplied her own answer. Students often found class VI difficult, the sudden increase in subjects, the leap from junior to middle school, the system of weekly tests all took getting used to, but he had to buck up. She would be very disappointed if he started slacking now.

Yes, Miss, he replied and walked slowly to the playground to join his friends, who would all want to know why he had been singled out. It had to be a reprimand of some sort.

The next morning his legs hurt so, he couldn't get up.

Shagun pleaded: he was her big boy, too big to fuss, too big to stay in bed. See, even Roo was getting ready.

Arjun stubbornly clung to his pains.

'What's the matter with you?' asked Shagun over a breakfast that took place three hours later. He detected the entreaty in her voice, which made her seem the weaker one. This both dismayed and exhilarated him.

'I'm not feeling well.'

She felt his forehead.

'No fever.'

After a pause: 'Do you miss your father?'

This question was dragged from her. Arjun was an intelligent child, their situation should have been clear by now. Ashok had offered to talk to him, but she had nervously refused, even though he had assured her that all he wanted was for Arjun to know he had a place in his life. But she hadn't considered her son ready for such information.

'Are we going back?'

'No. I can't go back.'

The boy played with his food. 'Why?'

'Don't be silly, Arjun, you know why.'

He didn't really. All his friends had their parents firmly in the background—to be lied to over minor matters like homework, to be avoided over baths, to be coaxed when something was wanted, to be obeyed when it came to tuition, to be pleased by doing well in tests. Nobody consciously thought about them. Now he was the different one.

'I don't want to go to school,' he said suddenly, the problem becoming clear.

'You have to.'

'Why do I have to? You said your feelings had changed towards Papa, well mine have changed about VV.'

'Don't be such a silly-billy.'

He said nothing, continuing to play with his scrambled eggs, now quite cold.

'Eat your food.'

'I am not hungry.'

'All your friends will get ahead of you if you start staying home for no reason. What—' She paused, the words—will your father say?—dying in her momentarily amnesiac mind. She drew close to Arjun and stroked his hair, hoping to achieve through love what reasoning could not accomplish; he must go for her sake, how was he going to be big and smart if he did not go to school?, etc., etc.

His mother was giving this too much importance. He knew he could not, not go to school, and this kind of attention made him uncomfortable.

'Can't I go some place else?'

'Do you know how difficult admissions are?'

Arjun got up, went to the drawing room and impatiently flicked the remote at the TV. Cartoons he had long outgrown appeared on the screen. Roohi must have been watching this stupid channel last night as she was being fed. Listlessly he gazed as Pingu the penguin led his snowy childhood in some frozen Arctic landscape.

The next morning again Arjun complained of pain.

A doctor's appointment was made.

'It hurts when I walk,' whined the child to Dr Jain.

'Since when?'

'A long time.'

'Did you fall? Injure yourself playing?'

Arjun shook his head. Where was the question of playing? He wanted to shun all those who had known him.

'He doesn't go out much nowadays, Doctor—the work has suddenly increased in class VI. He remains quite long with his books, my boy has become very studious.'

'Exercise is essential. If you fall sick how will that help your studies?' observed the doctor absently as she checked his injection schedule, examined his reflexes, palpitated his abdomen, took his height and weight.

'He is growing,' she remarked.

His mother nodded.

'Beta, wait outside,' continued the doctor.

Arjun limped his way to the waiting room.

'I can't find any physical symptom. Sometimes there is an emotional cause. Is anything troubling him?'

Dr Jain had known the children since their births. She was well acquainted with Raman, and Shagun now felt unequal to the task of explaining which of all the recent changes in their lives might be the one (if any) that was causing her child stress.

'You know how it is with children, Doctor. Somebody might have said something to him—he might be brooding.'

'No problem at school?'

'No.'

'At home?'

'No.'

The doctor hid her scepticism. There was something different about both Arjun and his mother, but there was only so much a medical practitioner can do.

'If he does not get better, we shall have to do a series of tests. Meanwhile put him on this course of vitamins and calcium. Make sure he drinks lots of milk, eats dahi, eggs or fish, two katoris of wholegrain dals . . .'

In these eleven years Shagun knew the list of the doctor's preferred foods by heart. She paid and left.

On their way home, Shagun asked, 'Is something bothering you, beta? The doctor thought you might be upset and that is why you have a slight discomfort in your leg. Mind and body are one, you know.'

'I hate school.'

Every time Arjun said anything about school he was exploring territory new to him. School was what drew his mother's attention. That and the pain in his leg.

Arjun couldn't imagine being allowed to malinger in his old house, whatever aches he might have had. His sense of the possibilities in his present life took on a different dimension.

When Ashok became aware of the situation he suggested stronger measures. It was unhealthy for the child to get his way in this manner.

And though Shagun was not unwilling, it proved impossible to effect. Arjun refused to get up; if she dragged him off the bed, he refused to brush his teeth, or have a bath, or put on his clothes, or eat his breakfast. Each step was a battle, only given up when it was too late to enter the school gates without a medical certificate.

These morning struggles were accompanied by tears on the part of the mother, while the daughter, looking on, cried in sympathy.

Whenever Shagun tried to reason with her son, or coax him into compliant behaviour, he would stubbornly look away. The pain this caused her filtered through to Ashok, forcing him to devote a whole evening to discussing Arjun's problems. At the end of Shagun's long narrative, he looked thoughtful and said, poor bugger.

Why?

The boy probably can't stand me—I possess the mother's love, and I am not even the father. His leg is probably paining because he wants your sole attention. I don't blame him. My leg would pain too in such circumstances.

Don't say that.

Why not? It's probably true.

The doctor asked if there were any changes in the family, and I said no. I didn't want her to think—

Ashok snorted into the dim light. Probably some tight-assed judgemental doctor. What would she know? But there was always boarding school.

Boarding school? Her son? No. Never. Boarding schools were for children whose parents did not love them.

And then Ashok really started. The child was reflecting his mother's guilt—she had to recognize that. It would probably do him good to be away. The world had no patience with these kinds of imaginary illnesses. He was basically a good kid, the right circumstances would make a man out of him. He himself had had to fight for all he got, including her. Success didn't come just like that—there was a connection between upbringing and achievement.

His own DPA years were the best of his life. He still remembered his school number 7901, marked on all his possessions.

Were he a son of his, he went on, when Shagun interrupted, everything he had said about Arjun weighing on her heart. She understood he could never feel for the boy, it was her fault for leaving the child's father, she would pay for her sins for the rest of her life.

It was their first serious fight, and they were still not talking to each other when Ashok left for Bombay next morning.

Ashok's two-day trip to Bombay produced no change in Arjun's willingness to get up. On his return, and another long talk later, Shagun approached Arjun's bed where he lay, leg hurting, staring at the wall.

'Beta, would you like to go to boarding school?'

'Why?'

'I don't think you are very happy here,' continued his mother, putting her arms around him. 'Ashok Uncle is finding out about the Dehradun Public Academy. He himself went there. It is rated one of the best schools in India. Didn't you say a classmate of yours was studying for the entrance test?'

Arjun turned his head away. She stared at his back. Ashok had said, don't push, just drop the idea in his head, this is not going to work if he doesn't want to go. And leave him alone, don't entertain him, don't mollycoddle him.

Someone else was determining, directing, deciding. It felt strange. But her own method had failed.

She got up and left the room.

Fed up with legal delays, Raman decided to meet his son at school. Driving towards Vivekananda Vidyalaya, he told himself that even a glimpse would satisfy him. His hands tight on the wheel, he thought of the many restless moments spent over Shagun during courtship and marvelled that not one of those could match his present torment.

The turn leading to VV was lined with buses, and Raman had to park on the main road. As he walked the remaining distance, he could see drivers and conductors standing around, waiting for one fifty.

The bell rang and 1,500 white and navy blue-clad children surged through the porch towards the gate. His eyes slid over every emerging boy roughly his son's height, but no Arjun, no Arjun, no Arjun. If he had known some of the boy's friends, he could have enquired about his whereabouts, but all the socializing had been through the mother, and he recognized no one.

The stream thinned, buses began to pull out, conductors banging on the sides.

So—either his son had not come or he had become a car child. How could he find out? How much did the school know about Arjun's new situation? To ask at the office might expose him as the unfortunate offspring of warring parents, and he preferred to wait a bit more before he did that.

He started the car and drove dully back to office, a heavy weight on his heart. Seeing his son was not going to be as simple as a trip to the school gates.

Once home he phoned Mrs Sabharwal. 'Why wasn't Arjun in school today?'

'He was feeling a little unwell, nothing serious. Leg is paining, also headache, body ache,' she improvised valiantly. Raman, hearing the panic in her voice, immediately decided he could no longer trust his mother-in-law. Blood was thicker than water: in any conflict she would be on her daughter's side, no matter the years of caring between them.

'I want to talk to him.'

'He will just call you back.'

'Make sure he does,' said Raman, putting the phone down on Mrs Sabharwal's gentle, unsteady notes.

He waited and waited, but his son did not phone.

The idea of going to a place where no one would know his parents had separated, where he would not have to avoid friends who had once visited him at home, where he would not have to read pity and curiosity in the glances of the people around him, that idea gradually began to seem like a good one to Arjun.

But how could he not live in Delhi? No matter how uncomfortable he was in this unfamiliar house, he was afraid of leaving his mother with that man. When they left their home Shagun had said she would explain everything, but instead of any explanation she behaved as though the shift from Raman Kaushik to Ashok Khanna was as natural as changing clothes.

From time to time she informed her son that he would understand the situation when he grew up. People often said this when they wanted to stop questions, and he did stop his questions. He had no desire to stress his mother, afraid of the few times she had seemed on the verge of tears.

For a moment he envied Roohi, whose interactions with people were so simple. All she had to do was begin to cry and her mother ran to her. 'Darling, what is the matter? Tell Mama, are you hurt?' And darling would cry ten times louder to prove that indeed she was hurt. He hated all this, including himself in this hatred. His heart felt like lead, and he wished he had never been born.

One week later his mother asked him whether he had thought further of the Dehradun Public Academy. No one would force him, but if that was not an option, he simply had to go to VV, in a wheelchair if necessary.

The boy's face remained inscrutable.

'I do not know why you are behaving so strangely,' continued the desperate mother. 'I cannot tolerate all this unhappiness. Don't you love me? Can't you see I am doing everything for your own good?' Here tears began to fall.

'I didn't say I didn't want to go,' mumbled Arjun.

That it was the right response he could see from her brightening face. 'Once you make up your mind, I don't see why you will not do well in the entrance tests—you always have been successful in exams,' she sniffed, already looking less traumatized.

His mother's pleasure extended into the days after, and Arjun wondered whether it was his grudging 'I didn't say I didn't want to go' that had made the difference in the atmosphere of the house. His leg felt better, it didn't hurt as much when he walked.

When the uncle was in Delhi, his mother and he spent a long time in the drawing room after dinner, both of them drinking. The room smelled of liquor and tobacco. His father hadn't smoked, this man did, and there was the smell of cigarettes everywhere, and his mother didn't object as she used to with guests in their old house.

His own departure began to preoccupy him, and soon not a day passed when he did not visualize a different setting for himself.

XV

By the time Ishita was thirty she had been working with Jeevan for three years with the search for a groom continuing alongside. Mrs Rajora's desperation drove her to mention her daughter's situation to practically everybody she met in the building, and fate did throw up a solitary offering, the brother of B-3/106, forty years old, an IPS officer, divorced with one issue.

Ishita rolled her eyes. 'What does he want? A housekeeper or a mother for his child?'

'Neither. He wants a companion, as does everybody. His wife has their daughter.'

'Why did he get divorced?'

'She got bored and left.'

'You believe that?'

'Arre, give him a chance. Otherwise what is going to happen to you after we die?'

'I can look after myself. You think all married women have their husbands caring for them. Look around you.'

The mother's face crumpled. 'We made one mistake, doesn't mean we have to make another.'

'Mummy, *please*. All this makes me feel terrible. You keep pinning your hopes on one meeting after another, and they are all the *same*. The *same*.'

'Beta, it is our duty to settle you. Just don't talk too much during the first meeting.'

'If the man doesn't like my daughter talking, he can go elsewhere,' put in Mr Rajora.

'Only for *now*. Later she can say all she likes—but let us first get to that stage.'

Mr Rajora thought of his first encounter with his own bride, and how he had to strain to hear the few words that had barely passed her lips. How much had India really changed, that a silent woman was still considered more desirable?

The man came. His paunch flowed gently over his belt, his round face was divided by a thick glossy moustache. His sister sat next to him looking pleased. They talked of his IPS job, of his small-town postings, of his loneliness. They talked of movies.

Had she seen *Titanic*? the man asked.

Yes, replied Ishita.

What did she think of it?

'It is a romanticized exposé of class distinctions,' she said boldly, plagiarizing Mrs Hingorani.

The man looked startled.

'We all loved it,' said Mrs Rajora hastily.

'I saw it with my sister just yesterday. Very nice hall.'

'We went to Cineplex,' explained the sister. 'No malls in Bhavnagar.'

'You will be happy in a small town, no?' asked the suitor.

Ishita's non-committal smile showed her exceptionally pretty teeth. The suitor brightened.

When the door closed the mother was triumphant. 'I am sure he liked you. Even though you gave a very strange reply to that *Titanic* question.'

'I also knew he would like Ishu,' said the father fondly. 'Arre, let her say what she likes. She is an intelligent, thinking girl, why should she not speak?'

The proposal came. They wanted early marriage, dowry was not an issue, but Ishita could only come to Delhi when her husband got leave.

'I knew sooner or later we would find a suitable man,' cried Mrs Rajora. 'Good qualifications, good salary, sister same building, simple early wedding. He doesn't want you to travel without him because his first wife had affairs—but once he knows you, that will change.'

Ishita glanced at her. It was the closest they had come to an acceptable proposal and in agreeing she would make many people happy. She shut her eyes.

'Beti, what is it?'

'Why does he want to marry me?'

'Is that a problem, silly girl?'

'It is, because I don't like him.'

Mrs Rajora was appalled: Ishu didn't know what she was talking about, feelings grew between man and wife, look at her and Papa, nobody she knew started out with love, it wasn't practical to expect it.

But Ishita did not budge.

She was very sorry for all the trouble she was causing, but she could not marry a man she didn't even find interesting. If a lonely life was the consequence, she would rather be lonely.

The sister took the rejection personally and Mrs Rajora was afraid she had made an enemy.

'Avoid looking in the building, it can lead to this kind of trouble,' said the father.

So Mrs Rajora went on circling ads, sending Ishita's bio-data and photograph, front and side, to the suitable-sounding at various PO boxes. Though there was occasional interest shown, the IPS man remained the best they had come across. If Ishita had known this would be the case, would she have behaved differently? mused the mother sadly.

She wondered where Mrs Kaushik was. Poor Leela Kaushik. Things were going badly for her, it showed there was no certainty in life. Five days and nights she had spent outside the ICU where her son was recovering from a heart attack. Since then she had taken to disappearing for the whole day to his house, she who hardly used to go.

Well, it made it easier to be her friend if she didn't have to be jealous all the time.

Meanwhile Mrs Hingorani's fertile mind was also occupied with the question of Ishita's future.

'Have you thought of studying further?' she asked. 'It will get you a job with more income, and that spells respect and independence.'

Ishita chewed her lip.

'Why don't you consider an MA in Social Work from DU, or from the Institute of Social Welfare in Bombay?'

'I'm not sure History Honours qualifies me.'

'You just need a graduate degree to sit for the entrance exam. Think about it. You are young, unencumbered, you can go anywhere, do anything. What is stopping you?'

What *was* stopping her? mused Ishita on the way home. They were many job options in the nineties, she knew that. A girl down their corridor was an air hostess, she often saw her in her smartly tied sari, with her little wheeled suitcase—going places, being adventurous.

Her parents would be delighted if she suddenly developed a burning ambition. They wouldn't even mind if she went to Bombay, unthinkable before her marriage.

Jeevan was a full-time occupation, but she and the itinerant Germans were the only young people in it. Social service in India was often a post-retirement choice.

She decided to try for the Institute of Social Welfare. What did she have to lose?

Painstakingly she filled in the admission forms, attached her recommendations, and was surprised when she qualified for the entrance test. Easily she answered the questions concerning general knowledge, confidently she wrote the essay concerning the future of social work and was not surprised when she was called for the interview.

It became a holiday with mother and father deciding to accompany Ishita to Bombay. Relatives in Bandra were dug up, train tickets bought and the planning done with a gaiety usually absent from their home.

On the day of the interview they all left early for the Institute, housed in a pillared colonial building with deep verandas near the Oval. In a room with narrow, tall windows, five people sat across from Ishita asking questions. This was the first time she had ever been interviewed, and she was so nervous her hands were sweating.

When she described her work at Jeevan, she sounded young and foolish, when she described what she would do with this degree, she sounded uninteresting. They looked at her CV, how had she been occupied between the years 1991 and 1995? Married, oh, she had been married. No longer? What would happen if she married again?

She realized the insult of that question but didn't know how to counter it.

Her rejection letter confirmed that she had been seen as a woman of no consequence. Why should they give her one precious seat if she had done nothing from 1991 to 1995 except be a wife? From the moment she had been born marriage had been the goal, and every choice reflected this.

Mrs Hingorani responded to the rejection by cursing the Institute. Fools they were not to see her potential. Ishu didn't have enough experience in presenting herself, that was the trouble.

Mrs Rajora too was disappointed. In Bombay her daughter might have met a nice boy.

'Just let her be,' repeated the father for the millionth time. 'She will find her way. Why do you keep on worrying?'

This was one of the phrases that periodically laced their marriage; necessary for Mrs Rajora to feel her efforts had registered, for Mr Rajora to feel he had done all he could to control his wife's behaviour.

A few months later Mrs Hingorani said, 'Ishu, I wonder, have you ever thought of adopting?'

A blank look.

'What is it that makes a child your own? The time, the care or the genes?'

'But people like to make sure there are no evil influences in the background, no abnormalities. And don't you bond more if you go through pregnancy . . . ?' offered Ishita in a small voice. She knew Mrs Hingorani would disapprove, but weren't these facts?

'As though you can ever be sure of these things. Look at our children, do they seem abnormal? Incapable of loving?'

Ishita thought of little Tulsi, dark, sharp-featured, thin pink lips, big alert eyes, high cheekbones, the daughter of Rajasthani migrant labourers, who followed her around, saying didi, didi, take me to your house. What would it be like to care for such a girl, watch her grow, send her to school?

It is a wonder what examples can do. This one came from a six-month-old baby girl adopted by a university couple. They were having a small ceremony, changing the infant's orphanage name to one chosen by their pandit. Come and see, Ishita, said Mrs Hingorani. Ask the mother questions.

That Sunday found the two of them driving along Ring Road. The overhead sky glared a pale translucent grey, dust hung in the air. At every traffic light, perspiration dampened their faces. Ishita knew she would look like a hag at the naming ceremony and this distressed her.

'This is a great day for them,' said Mrs Hingorani, dabbing violently at her face with her palla.

'Why so great?'

'It took them three years to get Sanjana.'

'Three years! I thought the city was crawling with unwanted children.'

'It's a crime, but that is the bureaucracy. And this is for a girl—boys are a thousand times more difficult.'

Ishita fiddled with her dupatta. 'Is it the same if you are single?'

'Almost. A bit more paperwork with the agency, but I know mothers who have done it.'

Mrs Hingorani withdrew into strategic silence. Ever the teacher, she wanted Ishita to realize the different ways in which women could fulfil their desires, while Ishita, mired in uncertainty, could not decide which suggestion to nurture in the stony ground of her life.

They arrived. Flowers were everywhere, presents heaped on a sideboard, the dining table laden with covered dishes. The centre of attention, Sanjana, was a tiny thin baby, dark-skinned with thick black hair. Her mother held her in her arms and from time to time stroked the downy cheek with a tender finger. The child's father hovered about, looking proud.

Why hadn't she and SK ever considered adoption? She had just endured whatever had been dealt to her. Young and the owner of a substandard body, she had been blinded by fear.

This woman, instead of being punished for her barrenness, was beaming with happiness. Her husband instead of looking for a new wife was content to beam with her. It wasn't fair.

Chandrakanta, Tarakanta, SK, her parents-in-law, how could she, young as she was, realize that their tenderness had strings attached? Maybe she and SK should have fought for the right to decide the major issues in their marriage, fought not towards the end when all she saw was his back—but earlier, when he still cared for her.

She would never understand love, its presence or absence altered you so fundamentally. And the loved Ishita was as far from the unloved one as the sun from the moon.

Mrs Hingorani noticed Ishita's withdrawn look.

'Have you met the mother?'

'Well, I . . . not really . . . she seems busy.'

The new mother was summoned and told to explain adoption to Ishita.

'Are you looking to adopt?' she asked.

Ishita shook her head.

'Arre, just tell her,' said Mrs Hingorani.

'Well, both of us always thought it's such an ego thing insisting on your own flesh and blood. The tyranny of biology is what's wrong with society—not only ours, but everywhere.'

Mrs Hingorani nodded.

'You mean you adopted despite being able to have a child?'

'Yup. We had to fake an infertility certificate. I suppose the idea is that if you do end up having your own child, you are incapable of caring for another.'

Both she and Mrs Hingorani looked disgusted.

That night Ishita lay awake for a long time, staring at the slivers of moonlight that sliced through the curtains. In everybody's life there had to be a focus for the love in one's heart. Without that, what was the use of living? Her involvement with street children did not extend beyond the school. She had her parents certainly, but eventually they would die.

She thought of the baby she had just seen. Her destiny had changed because an academic couple with a strong ideological position had hearts large enough to fake an infertility certificate. How would she turn out? Could Mrs Hingorani produce samples of older adoptees?

Mrs Hingorani could.

'I'm going out tomorrow,' said Ishita to her super-vigilant mother.

'Where?'

'With Auntie.'

'It's not enough you spend so much time with her during the week?'

'I asked her to arrange this visit.'

'Well, I don't mind coming.'

'It's to see a woman who has adopted a child. The girl is in high school.'

'Hai, Ram, what has got into you?'

To prevent the inevitable argument, Ishita quickly got up. Four strides took her to the front door and into the corridor, then into the rickety elevator, out the narrow entranceway, past the parked cars, past the dhobi wielding his heavy iron. They smiled at each other, united by the friendliness of long association, divided by their social class. She picked her way through his many children eating, studying, sleeping, playing among massive bundles of clothes.

Slowly she walked out of the gate towards the ice-cream wallah. 'One choc-bar,' she whispered.

Briskly he threw open the lid of his box and rummaged inside. Vapour rose from its depths and a faint cold smell. Choc-bar in hand, she sat on one of the benches in the housing society's green squares and breathed in the night jasmine. If she had had a wish in life it was to be a homemaker, with husband and children, something every girl she had ever known effortlessly possessed.

She finished eating, crumpled the wrapper and rose. It could be worse, she could have cancer, she could be fighting for her life, instead of just its meaning.

Sunday morning. Ishita and Mrs Hingorani were driving towards the proof, proof that adopted children were normal, proof that a warm heart need not also be a self-sacrificing one.

'Does the child know she is adopted?'

'Oh yes. You were chosen, Urvashi tells her, you are special.'

So much depended on how you looked at things. In her entire life Ishita had neither felt chosen nor special.

Mrs Hingorani turned the conversation to work. Their numbers meant they would simply have to find a larger place and spread their donation net wider to cover the extra rent. Her friend in Boston had suggested that Aid USA put them on their website. They were going to send some of their local representatives to inspect Jeevan; hopefully this would lead to greater funds. Meanwhile two more German kids were coming as volunteers, it was lucky that their experience here counted towards their school grades, would Ishita show them around?

Yes, of course, said Ishita, dragged from her useless thoughts.

*

The proof was completely charming. Small-built, with light brown skin, straight black hair, slightly buck teeth, a dimple, she perched possessively next to her mother, leaning against her.

The mother, typically, was boasting of her child's achievements, above all of the 92 per cent in the class X board exams. For one year the pressure was so intense, the poor girl couldn't pursue her painting, dancing or singing.

She must be very talented, said Ishita as she looked at certificates that primarily attested to maternal devotion. Perhaps love so dearly bought had to be constantly reaffirmed. Or was it her own limitations that made her think it dearly bought?

It took a few more weeks, but eventually Ishita did decide to investigate adoption. The agency she phoned gave her some starting points. First she had to register, then there would be a home visit. Her parents' support was *absolutely vital*, especially because she was a single woman. For the home study, it was important the family appear united.

Ishita informed her parents of all this over dinner. God willing, they would become grandparents.

Mrs Rajora took to her bed.

She lay awake for a long time, sighing so loudly that at last her husband relented. 'What is it?' he asked.

'Ishita,' moaned his wife. '*Adopt.* Who will marry her if she comes burdened with a child?'

'Who is marrying her now?'

'That's not the point. She is still so young, only just turned thirty. There is at least a *chance*.'

'We have been looking for three years, who have we found?'

'But there is still hope. You want that that too should go?'

'Adoption is a noble, compassionate act. More people should do it.'

'But they don't, do they? Why should only our daughter be noble? Let married couples who can't have children, let them be noble.'

'You used to say she was like Mother Teresa.'

'Mother Teresa was a *nun*. How can their personal lives be the same? Besides, she's dead now.'

'And still remembered.'

'Beti, are you very keen on this adopting business?'

'I'm not sure, Papa. It's a way of having something to live for, to plan for. Otherwise—otherwise—what is there?'

Pity coursed through the father as he was confronted with this idealistic solution. No one could ask for a better girl. But some are not destined for a normal family life—it was his tragedy that Ishita was one such.

'But are you absolutely certain? I know of no adopted child.'

'No one here. But in other places . . .'

'And you have met them?'

'With Mrs Hingorani. A very sweet girl. Just finished class X. Remember I told you I was going?'

'And meeting that child convinced you?'

'I am still not sure. But one day I will be all alone. Why should I go on waiting for some man to marry me? Can you guarantee that will happen?'

'There is time. We will find someone.'

The hollow words filled the room with their lack of conviction. Ishita merely looked at him, then went back to staring at the clothes line strung across the small veranda. Hanging there were her faded pink panties, from which just this morning she had washed the menstrual stains. Menstruating, month after month, year after year, her hopelessness somehow accentuated by the blood.

Whenever Ishita fell silent like this, her father imagined her to be brooding over her lost husband.

'Beta, you know we will help in any way. We want you to be happy,' he said somewhat hastily.

'I will be, but not in the way you think.'

'Come, come, you are still young.'

'I wish you would understand how sick I am of this whole marriage business.'

'We want the best for you.'

'That's why I agree to go on seeing these ridiculous men.'

The father had had no idea that Ishita was seeing suitors just to please them. He had always thought her disinclination was the result of bitter experience that could be overcome with the right man. But if she planned to adopt she was quite clearly shutting the door to one particular future. For the first time since her divorce he began to believe her.

He started to bargain. The year she turned thirty-one, they would both come with her to adoption agencies. He too would love a child in the house. 'But if you are going to be a single parent, you will need more money. It is a lifelong responsibility. Of course you will have the security of this house, but that is not enough.'

'I know, Papa.'

'Maybe do an MA in History—that means you can teach in the university, better salary, more free time. Later on you can do an M.Phil., to qualify for a permanent job, but meanwhile you will be earning.'

'Auntie will be happy if I better my prospects.'

'How long for this adoption process?'

'Two or three years.'

'In which time you should have your degree.'

'At least it will be nice to choose my fate instead of just waiting for some husband to appear.'

At the brightness in her face, Mr Rajora wondered whether independence could go so far in making his daughter happy.

He had a lengthy conversation with his wife. 'If this is what she wants we have to help her.'

'But what about her marriage?' wailed the mother.

Mr Rajora grabbed the bull by the horns. Their daughter was not very pretty, not fair, not rich, not fertile, not virginal.

It was possible she would never remarry. And then? Who would she have when they died?

His wife bridled. Their daughter had regular features, was slim, wheatish, not badly off, caring, it all depended on your perspective.

'You can't go on building castles in the air and expect others to do the same,' said Mr Rajora. 'Otherwise she will go ahead and do what she wants and we will be estranged. She has been a good girl, now we must be equally good parents.'

'We are good parents.'

'We have followed society's norms. Now we have to be the parents our daughter needs. A thirty-year-old divorcee.'

At these harsh words Mrs Rajora winced. 'I know people adopt—I too live in this world. In the university especially I used to hear . . .' said the mother, her voice trailing as she tried to find words to make this reality more acceptable.

XVI

Arjun lay on the back seat, his head on a small hard cushion. When he turned he could see the man's wavy grey hair, and, faintly illuminated by the dashboard lights, Shagun's hand resting on his thigh.

They had been on the road an hour before the man referred to the purpose of their trip. It would be the turning point in Arjun's life, he prophesied. He remembered his own mother's fears when it came to sending him away, but his IFS father was posted so frequently that she didn't have much choice.

It was still dark; on leaving the city the night seemed to grow thicker. Through the panes of the car some stars were visible. Arjun closed his eyes once more and felt the car's throb beneath his body. His mother's hand snaked around and rested on his arm for a moment, before finding its way back to the man's leg. The atmosphere in the car was intimate, the three of them held together by the darkness.

The man's voice started again, the sound of the engine and the wind straining through a crack in the window overlaying his words. But then his tone became more animated and he could hear talk of houses, Shivalik, Zanskar, Vindhya, Karakorum, Satpura, Pir Panjal, each divided into junior and senior sections. Lovingly he spoke of the fagging they had to do for their seniors, the rooms they had to clean, the errands they had to run, the cigarettes they were asked to smuggle in, the punishments they endured and then inflicted. Talking of school naturally led to what came afterwards, and it was clear that nothing subsequently quite matched up, not NYU, where he had gone as an undergraduate, not Harvard, where he had done an MBA. Ashok's career seemed to have been launched from DPA, his second home, gilded with the golden glaze of youth and nostalgia.

Finally it grew light. His mother felt around in her basket for his breakfast, omelette smothered in ketchup between two slices of bread. An orange followed, peeled and passed over.

When travelling with his father, they never departed so early, everything was disorganized and bad-tempered in the morning. And then in the car there was the gradual ebbing of tension, the determination to enjoy themselves, the rustle of chip packets, the smell of Bourbon chocolate biscuits, the feel of crumbs everywhere. Later there would be the tourist lodge where they would stop for the first meal of the day.

Six hours after they left Delhi they reached the cantonment area of Dehradun, and in ten minutes they were outside the school. While the man talked to the guard, Arjun stared at the gates. The letters 'Donated by the Class of 82' were carved into the metal framework on top while an island surrounded by a sea was embossed in the centre. Our emblem, said the man, an oasis in today's world, while the mother repeated the information in case her son hadn't understood.

Inside, a gravel path, red-brick buildings covered with ivy, a tree-lined lawn. As they walked down towards the administrative section small stones crunched beneath their triple steps.

A few boys strolled around dressed in grey shorts and T-shirts. Arjun looked at them curiously, his experience of school so far had been among masses of the young.

Headmaster was expecting them, said the secretary, but he had been called for an unexpected meeting. In half an hour, say? Would they like someone to show them around?

Genial laughter. No, they needed no one, and as they turned away the man addressed Arjun—come, let me show you where I spent the best years of my life.

Arjun had nothing to say to this. For him school was something to be tolerated, and he knew no one who thought differently. His mother laughed the laugh that had accompanied them since Delhi, giving her son the feeling that she would be of no use here.

They strolled through the main school block, through arched corridors, flanked by ivy-covered walls. Then down some steps onto the biggest playing field Arjun had ever seen. 'There,' said the man, pointing to some buildings on the right, 'Shivalik House, my home for six years. You will go here, sons are always allotted their fathers' houses. Next to it, Zanskar House. This is the oldest block; the school was started by the British over a hundred years ago, and it still is among the finest in India. Some families have an unbroken chain of father and son attending.'

His mother giggled again, while Arjun stood still for a moment staring around him, not knowing what to make of the word 'son'.

As they walked through the covered veranda of Shivalik House, they came to a black-and-white photo which had 'Mr J. A. Dingle' written under it. Ashok stopped before it. 'Great man. Legend in the school.'

'I hope he is lucky enough to get in,' remarked the mother anxiously. The man looked impatient, and said of course Arjun would get in, he came with his recommendation.

A few metres down the corridor was a tailor—some boys were chatting to him. Still further down a barber was cutting hair. All was tranquil. The rooms they passed had three beds each and not much else. Alternating with these were rooms with rows of desks. Sleep, study, play—it was obvious what the school was all about.

At last they arrived at a wall of pictures. On the one dated 1975, the man put his finger on a figure sitting in the middle of the front row, along with five others. 'There I am.'

'It doesn't say you were school captain. It doesn't say *anything*,' said Shagun, protective of the man's history.

'That's somewhere else.' Ashok turned to the boy. 'I was almost twelve when I came here. Your age.' He paused. 'And I left as school captain.'

Arjun had no idea of what the man was talking about. He was so old, older than his father, his youth was not even worth considering.

'Let's see your name as captain,' suggested the mother.

He led them to white-painted lists on long wooden boards: captains of Cross-Country, Diving, Swimming, Tennis, Basketball, Dramatics, Squash, Cricket, Hockey, Soccer, Athletics, Boxing, Chess, Music. And there School Captain—1975—Ashok Khanna.

Arjun gazed at the names. History is not really for the young, but at that point he felt that to have your name painted on boards was not such a bad thing, decrepit though you might be now.

He had to see more of the school when the man and his mother had their private meeting with the Principal.

'Do you like it here?' he asked the boy appointed to show him around.

'Yes,' said the boy. 'What do you play?'

'Cricket. You?'

'Cricket, swimming, chess, athletics. What house was your father in?'

'Shivalik.'

'Their cricket team is pretty good.'

'What house are you in?'

'PP. Pir Panjal.'

'Is it really so important, your house?'

'Hey, hasn't your father told you all about that? It's *everything*.'

'I was just checking, you know.'

'My younger brother is going to come here.'

'Yeah?'

'Next year.'

'I wish I had a brother.'

'Yeah?'

The two boys roamed around the grounds for another ten minutes, Arjun too shy to ask what was it really like, really?

Back to the Principal's office. 'So, young man, what did you think of the school?'

'I liked it, Sir.'

'Let's go and show you the dining hall, share a meal with the boys, all right?'

'All right, Sir.'

It was one fifteen as they headed towards the dining hall. The mother tried to hold her son's hand, but he pulled it away. Inside the noise was overpowering. They settled at a table with three empty places, a boy obligingly got up to make a fourth, even as Shagun was declaring her willingness to sit elsewhere.

The food was indifferent, dahi, dal, thick rotis, and a mixed sabzi that claimed no acquaintance with the vegetables inside it. For dessert a watery custard with slightly off fruit. Arjun barely ate. And how could he, thought Shagun, after a lifetime of specially catered meals? She looked around: her lover was attacking his plate, the boys were eating heartily, such appetites were persuasive.

Momentarily distracted from the leathery morsel in her mouth, Shagun went over the discussion they had had with the Principal. Ashok had explained the delicacies of their domestic situation, Arjun was effectively now his son, and the conflict at home was stultifying his growth. His academic achievements might have been excellent but DPA would foster his leadership potential as no other school could.

Just to hear the conviction in Ashok's voice was worth every kilometre of the journey. Arjun had managed to make Ashok interested in him, thus lightening the burdens of parenting.

These thoughts naturally led to how much she adored Ashok. All those people who had said that one man could not care for another man's children were wrong, wrong. Even though it was practically impossible for him to leave his work, here he was trying to make sure the boy received the same education he had had. She imagined the day when they would be a family unit, with the same unthinking love flowing between them as had once existed between herself, her children and a father in a far-off time, in a place she would rather not remember.

A final encounter with the Principal, who genially avowed that once the child was admitted they would make sure he followed in his father's footsteps, and with every indication of his life changing beyond recognition, Arjun slowly walked out of the school gates, leaving behind the island at the centre of the stormy seas of life.

On the way back he was silent. Mechanically he shoved the chips his mother had thoughtfully provided into his mouth. He was hungry, he had eaten little of the school food. Soon he felt thirsty, but unlike other trips the car was not stopped for him to drink. Water fell on his shirt as he tipped the bottle to his lips, but never mind, said his mother, it will soon dry.

The man drove on. He didn't think it was tactically advisable to ask the mother or son if they liked the place. They would only realize the rightness of this move later, and only then would they be grateful they had had such an opportunity.

By seven it was dark. Full of chips, a banana, an apple, two oranges, Bourbon biscuits and one Coke, Arjun did fall asleep to the murmur of voices in front. In his dreams there was a large playing field covered with stubbled yellowing grass. A pavilion at one end was filled with boys, they were all looking at him running, but he was alone. He didn't know where he had to run to, just that his life depended on winning. Everybody clapped. He looked around for his father, but he was not visible.

They reached Delhi at midnight.

The next morning over breakfast.

'Can I call Papa?'

'Why?'

'Just.'

'Is it about DPA?'

'No.'

'Then?'

'Nothing. Forget it.'

'Tell me, beta. I'm your mother.'

The boy pushed his eggs around his plate.

'I know it is not easy changing schools, but you heard what Uncle said, it is a great opportunity. Every DPA boy thinks of those years as the best ones in his life. The friendships formed there are for ever, maybe because they live together for six years. The sports too are very good. You will develop into a champion.'

'Does Papa know?'

'We will tell him once you get admission.'

'How do you know I will get admission?'

'Your uncle has good connections. Wasn't that obvious?'

'Then the exam doesn't matter?'

'It matters. But connections make everything easier.'

'When will we get to know?'

'Test—next month, interview—December, results—January, join—April.'

'Will you send Roohi to boarding school also?'

'No—I mean I haven't thought of it. She is too small. Besides, she hasn't stopped going to school. You have.'

The boy could think of nothing more to say.

In the next night's dream, the pavilion had disappeared. He was running in a mist. He thought he could see the boy who had shown him around, but when he came close he had no features. Disturbed, he woke up.

What were his options? Return to VV? He could tell his friends he had been ill—really ill—he knew they wouldn't ask questions. On the other hand not a single parent trod the DPA expanses, not a single sister or relative.

All he had to do was pass a couple of exams and that expanse was his.

That night.

'Well, how is Arjun? Where is he?'

'He says he is not feeling well.'

'Again?'

'Sometimes he gets a little moody,' said the mother apologetically. 'I don't know what it is.'

'Did he say anything about the school?'

'Not really.'

'Change can make one fearful—but he'll get over it, trust me.'

'I don't know how keen he is on going. He refuses to study for the entrance exams. I can't force him, though I tried.'

Ashok looked at her. Almost the only time she looked unhappy was when her children were being discussed.

'Didn't you say he always did well in exams?'

'Yes, but he studied for them. We were always very strict about that. Now I really don't know what's happening. I think he didn't do so well in his weekly tests this term. But why didn't he say anything? Oh, I just don't know.'

'Should I talk to him?'

'No, no, it's fine,' said Shagun in alarm.

'What's the matter, darling? If you want us to have a relationship you have to let us talk to each other. Stop trying to protect him.'

'Let him get into DPA. Let some more time pass. You yourself said too many changes.'

'Dearest, I won't do anything against your wishes. But he should make some effort—it's bad for him to think things can just fall into his lap.'

Shagun to her son:

'You have to revise the class VI syllabus. I have hired someone to help you.'

'I know it.'

'Are you being difficult on purpose? Go to school if you don't want a tutor.'

Arjun stared at her defiantly, his stubborn eleven-year-old face holding back babyish tears.

'Beta,' tried his mother again, 'I know this might be a strange situation, but we have no choice. The tutor will come three times a week from tomorrow. You will like him. He is a young man.'

Arjun immediately resolved to hate him.

The next day the tutor came.

'End October he will be tested in Maths, Hindi, English and Science,' Shagun said. 'It's for the DPA entrance exam. I am only interested in results. He has to get in.'

'Madam, I am here, no? What is your good name, beta?' asked the tutor, turning to the sullen child.

The sullen child did not reply.

'Your good name?' repeated Mr Kumar genially.

'Arjun, his name is Arjun.'

'First and foremost, he must do all assignments, all. Only then results will come. No magic. Hard work only.' His thickly accented English dismayed Shagun. Any visions of this man as a companion for her son vanished. Agencies obviously didn't supply big brothers.

*

'Your uncle will be so pleased you are studying hard,' said the mother to the son.

'Why?'

Out of the question to say that Ashok felt Arjun was indulged and badly behaved. She answered indirectly: 'You must do well, even though children of alumni are favoured with a five per cent advantage.'

'Papa is not from DPA.'

'Uncle said you were like his son. That is why they are allowing you to sit for the entrance exams. Otherwise you have to register a year in advance, some old students register the moment their sons are born.'

Arjun stared at her. He remembered the moment he and the man stood before the black-and-white picture dated 1975, remembered the touch of his hand on his shoulder and the confusion the gesture caused him.

Shagun drew her son onto her lap, saying he was getting so big and heavy—soon they would not be able to sit like this. She put Arjun's arm around her neck, and rocked him to and fro. One day she hoped he would see her love behind the move to DPA, a change that might have unsettled him enough to want contact with his father. Her grip around the boy tightened, as she thought angrily, how much time had Raman spent with him anyway that his loss should make such a big difference now? She was giving him a better role model—maybe in time he would realize that too.

XVII

Tuesday was Shagun's day at the beauty parlour; it was always deliciously empty. Arjun waited for her to leave before he carefully opened his old school diary to the front page: Numbers to be contacted in an emergency. There in his father's small handwriting was his office phone number, the house phone and the grandparents' numbers. They were as he had remembered them.

It was close to eleven when Raman's phone rang in the office. Irritated, he picked it up, and for a moment did not recognize the voice of his son.

'Papa?'

'Arjun—Arjun—Arjun.'

'Papa.'

Raman started speaking as fast as he could, these precious seconds must not be wasted.

Did Arjun know how much he missed him and his sister? He had gone to his school but had not seen him. He had phoned their naani for news, but she had told him nothing. No matter what lies he was told Arjun must never forget that for his father his children were his life. He was moving heaven and earth to get permission to see them, he had got a lawyer, his Nandan Uncle, and he was going to win visitation rights soon.

Arjun did not recognize this unfamiliar man. Never had he known Raman to have gone to his school, to sound so eager and breathless. Finally his silence penetrated the father's eloquence.

'Beta, at least tell me this, why have you stopped going to school? Is there any problem?' Tears threatened Raman's voice, and he struggled against them. He did not want to frighten his son, God only knew what he had been through.

Arjun began to wish he hadn't made this phone call.

'Beta, should I bring you home? Just tell me where to come.'

'Next month I will take the Dehradun Public Academy entrance test, Papa.'

'Why? You go to a very good school, the best in Delhi. What are they doing to you?'

Silence.

Wrong thing to say.

'Beta, is it your idea to change schools? Is something upsetting you?'

More silence proved that this too was the wrong thing to say.

'I want you to be happy, wherever you are.'

'It's all right.'

'Tell your mother, if you stay with me, you will see her every weekend. And if there is some trouble in school, I will sort it out with the teachers, but you have to let me know.'

As he was talking, the father heard a gentle click followed by the dial tone.

Had someone come into the room? The boy had sounded so distant. But he had called him, he was reaching out, Raman had to do something.

He would phone the Principal of DPA, tell them that he would file a case of wrongful confinement if they admitted his son. Schools are wary of legal tangles, they would immediately back away.

And such a school! Snobbish, isolated, obsessed with the old-boy network. He disliked the DPA alumni he knew, fucked up, assuming entitlement, aggressive when denied it, stuck in a time warp. Ashok Khanna was a good example of a basically intelligent person gone dreadfully wrong. His behaviour suggested a lack of moral training.

Dehradun Public Academy was a colonial hangover, VV an embodiment of modern cosmopolitan India. Arjun had finished the elementary Hindi immersion section only last year, and was barely into the very different experience of the English middle school. You had to go through all of Vivekananda Vidyalaya to benefit from its pan-Indian ethos.

That evening Raman reached his cousin's office in Mayur Vihar Market before Nandan. He sat in the small outside room sipping syrupy tea, waiting, waiting, more desperate than he had ever been.

But then every time he came he thought he was more desperate than he had ever been. So far his private life lurched from nightmare to nightmare.

In contrast to Nandan. Surrounded by his parents, wife and twins, the breadwinner and centre of his family, his cousin gleamed with contentment. He often said, 'I am a simple man and I want a simple life.' Any vindication he must have felt as he witnessed Raman's downfall, he was kind enough to keep to himself.

The door opened. Nandan entered, wiping his face which sweated easily. 'Bring two teas,' he told his peon as he gestured his cousin into the inner office. 'Do you want some samosas? The corner halwai is an expert.'

Samosas. He too had once been able to devote thought to teatime snacks. But now he merely shook his head as he entered the office to receive the relief of practical planning.

'We need to file another interim application.'

'On what grounds?'

'She is sending him away.'

'Where?'

'Dehradun.'

'Boarding?'

'Yes. He is already in a good school but she wants to uproot him only to make sure he will be far from me.'

'How do you know all this?'

'Arjun phoned.'

'Wonderful.'

'He didn't say much.'

'Did he say he didn't want to go?'

This gave Raman pause. How to explain to Nandan the variations of his son's breath, the quality of his silence, the visual image of a frightened eleven-year-old getting in touch with his father after many months?

'Not in so many words.'

'But still she is making an attempt to remove him from the jurisdiction of the court. We can certainly try to prevent that.'

'Also, why should he go away to boarding school? He is going to VV. People kill to get into VV.'

'The court will look at the best interests of the child. Did he say when he was going?'

'No, he didn't. He has to get admission first. Apparently the exams are in October.'

'That doesn't give us much time.'

'But if he gets in he will only go next April.'

'We will file a stay order against removal.'

'What will you say?'

'That he is being forcibly sent to boarding school.'

'He didn't actually say this in so many words. They might have brainwashed him into wanting to go.'

That was the trouble with Raman. He lacked the killer instinct. Arre, you want the child, you have to assert such things. But he sought to harass the mother without affecting the boy. Such things were rarely possible.

'The judge will probably talk to him. Find out what his wishes are.'

'Say the mother has prevented me from seeing the children for months. That she is living with her lover, and they are being exposed to evil influences.'

'We have already said all that in our main petition.'

'Say it again.'

'You have to keep in mind that in the case of marital disputes, boarding school may be considered a good option.'

'So she can do anything she wants? Deprive me of my children just like that?'

'No. But keep in mind that in boarding school you can visit him.'

Irritated, Raman brushed this palliative aside. Normally Nandan was quick to understand the nuisance value of legal procedures.

'I want her thwarted. She thinks she can make me invisible, that a father's rights can be ignored. I am going to fight her every inch of the way. You have to help.'

'What am I here for? Just be prepared for the judge to decide it is in the child's best interest to be away from disputing parties.'

'I am prepared.'

What a terrible life his cousin must be leading, thought Nandan, as he instructed his junior to draw up a standard plea for staying the boy's removal from the court's jurisdiction.

'I phoned Papa.'

'Why?'

'Just like that.'

'I told you he wants to keep us apart. He has filed a case against me. A case in court. Do you know what that means?'

'No.'

'Is this the first time you have phoned him?'

'Yes.'

She should have told Arjun not to contact his father. But she found it easier to treat her husband as unmentionable, unnameable, unseeable.

'Well, what did he say?'

'He sounded surprised.'

Of course. It must have been a shock. For a moment she put herself in his shoes, then quickly drew back to her own.

'Did you say anything about DPA? Going there?'

'No.'

'Are you sure?'

'We hardly talked.'

'Then why did you phone him?'

'Just.'

'Are you missing your father?'

No response.

Shagun looked at her son. He continued to eat, his long eyelashes spread against the pink and white of his cheek. She loved gazing at him, he was so handsome. And once he went to the Academy he would get that open confident laughing look many of the boys there had. Right now, the expression on his face was shut in, wary, guarded.

He had become paler ever since he had stopped playing games. She sighed. Arjun glanced at her; she took his hand and squeezed it.

*

Three days later the interim application notice was served at Shagun's official address.

Mrs Sabharwal looked at this fresh invitation to despair. By now she too felt that the best thing for Arjun would be to go to Dehradun. How long could such a situation last, not attending school? If his father had been around, this would not have happened. She picked up the phone.

Her daughter's silence at this news unsettled her.

'Beta?' she asked into the void.

'Still here.'

'I am saying this notice from the court has come.'

'I heard you the first time, Mama.'

'Shall I open it?'

'You won't understand the contents.'

That was true enough, but one had to say something, do something.

Shagun and Ashok in Madan Singh's home office, GK I:

'You have to understand that they will do everything to prevent the child's being removed,' pointed out Madz.

'Even if it is in the child's best interest to go to a better school?' demanded Ashok.

'We will make a case of course, but not everyone will think it is better.'

'Right now he is not going to any school,' put in Shagun.

'We will say all that, don't worry. And of course the judge will look at the child's best interest, ask him why he is not going to school, what does he want?'

'How soon before it is heard?'

'If nobody tries to delay, shouldn't take too long.'

And then visitation rights? asked Shagun. If granted, wouldn't that deprive Raman of all incentive to divorce? Why would he want her happy?

'You can't do much about visitation rights—you have to reconcile yourselves to that, the judge will grant them.'

'It's confusing for the children—first there then here then there,' reasoned Shagun, 'surely that can't be in their best interests.'

'They do link best interests with the biological parents, rightly or wrongly,' reasoned Madz in turn.

'Admissions can't wait,' said Ashok impatiently.

'The judge knows that. I have every expectation that this application will be heard quickly.'

A few days later Raman received a call from his estranged wife.

'Why have you filed this application?'

'Why have you withdrawn him from his school? A perfectly good school, where he was happy, had friends, did well.'

'He needs to start a new life.'

'That's what you think. You want to send him to a self-obsessed all-boys institution where he will be subject to the kind of bullying and fagging that will scar him for the rest of his life. You need my consent, or hasn't your lawyer told you that I am the natural guardian?'

'And hasn't your lawyer told you that custody can go to either parent?'

'And hasn't your lawyer told you that custody of a male child belongs to the father?'

'Goodbye,' said Shagun as she slammed the phone down to look at her problem and to come to one conclusion. The child had to personally reject the father, personally choose DPA, personally convince the judge.

XVIII

In October Arjun took the DPA entrance exam at Vasant Valley School, the Delhi centre. For three hours parents waited outside, chatted, drank coffee, compared schools, compared children, looked nervous. Shagun sat in a corner, her eyes fixed unmoving on a magazine. She saw her son's face in the pages, saw his eight school-going years, contented successful years, from which he was now being torn because of the complications in her life.

A little older—or a little younger—and this situation would not have arisen. Roo went wherever she was sent, while a more mature Arjun would not have developed pains no one could explain.

Her mind went unwillingly to Raman's words. Bullying and fagging. Lifelong scars. All boys. She had asked Ashok, had there been any molesting cases? Were younger boys bullied by older ones? Were teachers sufficiently vigilant? Ashok had laughed, did she want to protect Arjun from the world? Would she say he was scarred? Immediately she became defensive and the question was never answered.

Well, it was no longer in her hands. If Arjun got through, that would be a sign, if he didn't, that would be another sign, she thought, rustling more magazine pages, not really wanting to know what Fareed Zakaria had to say about the world, but opinions were useful in social conversation.

Arjun passed the written exams, and was now eligible for the interview in December, one of 200. The three of them drove to Dehradun the day before, Arjun sitting next to the man in front, preparing for possible questions in general knowledge and current events. Ashok grilled him on his reading, his interests, his strong points, his talents, sport preferences, how would he contribute to the school?, what would he do if . . . various hypothetical situations followed.

Shagun listened from the back seat, noticing how well her boy performed in these tests of Ashok's. If nothing else, DPA had brought them closer.

Next morning at school. An hour of hanging around then finally Arjun's turn. He disappeared into the Principal's office from which he would emerge fifteen minutes later, his fate decided.

Never before had he been in such a position, said Ashok, as they waited anxiously outside, but the boy would do well, he was clearly bright.

Well, smiled Shagun as she used the word for the first time in this connection, he had never been a parent before.

Arjun emerged. They pounced on him: how, what, and did you? Nothing unexpected was asked, he replied. He read out a poetry passage, did the mental maths, defined temperature without using the word temperature, answered questions about his likes and dislikes.

These fifteen minutes could be the most important in his life, said the new father expansively. Now they could only wait and see, but Arjun was not to get tense, he had a good feeling just from his conversations with the teachers.

And Shagun could kiss the ground her lover walked on, she was so grateful for everything he had done.

By end-January the phone call came: your son has been selected. Out of thousands, he had been one of the few to cross the finish line. He was such a lucky boy, wasn't he?

The intervening two months were spent in getting medical tests done, getting clothes made, sending measurements to the DPA tailor, and stitching number 2341 onto every blessed thing. Through all these preparations was the cold fear that Raman could stop Arjun's going.

A date in February had been fixed for hearing of arguments. They had a month in which to make sure that Arjun was so keen to go to DPA that he would steadfastly maintain this in the face of the most sceptical judge.

Shagun alone could not create this enthusiasm. Her son would leave all he knew, and her own heart was too wavering. Ashok knew no such uncertainty. There was now a point to sharing his memories: the boy needed to be inspired, and through him his mother. During dinner he described going to the roof of Shivalik House at night, staying there till dawn without a teacher knowing. He spoke of stealing lichis from the trees in the compound given out on hire, how they distracted the old guard, threw stones to bring down the fruit that though still unripe had all the sweetness of the forbidden. He spoke of their mid-term mountain expeditions, the most fun in the upper classes, when they arranged the trek by themselves, and knew the unfettered companionship of being alone with friends.

Once a boy wrote up the mandatory logbook—sights seen, money spent, halting points, etc.—all in twenty-four hours and then had taken the train home to Jullunder for the remaining four days! Another made up the whole log but was caught—foolishly he had described flaming rhododendrons when the season was over. PP house got many demerit points as a result.

Mother and son giggled. Arjun's after-dinner thoughts were full of what he heard—could he ever talk like this about VV? He liked it, but once he left, he left. Even his father had never shared school stories with him.

Meanwhile in a tiny part of her heart Shagun fantasized about the day when Ashok would share similar anecdotes with Roo, show a similar interest in her schooling and her future. She could see he found it difficult to relate to such a small girl. When Roo was there, Ashok at best bestowed an absent-minded caress, at worst ignored her completely.

When she tried to get him involved, he looked uncomprehending. Once he laughed and said, give me time—I'm not an instant father, you know.

But you were an instant lover.

Look who I had to love.

He reached out to touch her, and the children slipped from both their minds.

February 16th.

The day for arguments. Raman is so nervous he spends a lot of time in the bathroom. He will meet his son after months, in a court, with the devil woman by his side. Nandan had cautioned him not to expect too much—and he did not expect too much, he really didn't.

'Remember you must focus on the larger issue,' said Nandan.

'What is the larger issue? All I want is to see my children. It's seven months, do you realize, seven months?' His voice broke.

Nandan wished for the millionth time that family obligations did not extend to the legal sphere. But they did, and he carried on his shoulders the burden of Raman's anguish, along with the knowledge of a system that was not going to provide any relief soon. 'With the removal-from-jurisdiction application, the judge will most probably, 99 per cent, resolve the visitation rights as well,' he now said. 'They won't be able to delay, so good for us.'

As Raman remained unresponsive, Nandan tried to buck him up by pointing out the many silver linings in this particular cloud. No matter what the decision, he would be better off than before.

'You remember all I have told you?' Shagun asked on the way to Tees Hazari.

Arjun nodded, though in fact it was humanly impossible to retain everything she had said over the past two weeks.

Now she did a recap. He had to tell the judge he hated VV, she had a letter from school to prove that he hadn't been attending for months. His uncle Nandan, who was his father's lawyer, might try and suggest he was being kept home by force. All he had to do was tell the truth.

His father might want to speak to him, but he must only do what he felt like, OK, beta?

Above all, no information about their private life. Nothing about Uncle. Officially they stayed with Naani in Alaknanda. The court did not understand that people could change, no, they had to go on living with the same person till they died. They had the power to take away her children, put her in jail. This was a very hypocritical country—narrow-minded and censorious.

The judge would probably ask him who he wanted to live with. In this unfair system, fathers had greater rights over male children so he had to say very, very clearly he wanted to live with his mother, and even then they would *consider*, though it was so obvious that he was part of her, he looked like her, everybody said so.

She reached for his hand and held it, driving somewhat dangerously as a result, but Arjun's hand in hers was more important than safety considerations.

In the parking lot, just before they got down, she slipped a black thread with a little Om medallion around Arjun's neck and tucked it into his shirt. 'To protect you,' she murmured. He hoped whatever it was they had come for would soon be over.

Once inside the lower courts, mother and son picked their way through hawkers, lawyers and their assistants, public notary wallahs, litigants and associated family. Madan Singh's junior was waiting for them inside the main entrance.

'Is everybody here?' asked Shagun significantly. The assistant nodded. He wore grey-and-black striped pants, a black coat, and a high-collared white shirt. His glasses straddled a thick and shiny nose.

The way to the court of Additional District Judge Mathur led them across corridors, up flights of paan-stained staircases to a lobby with benches against the wall. For a nanosecond Arjun did not recognize the man standing to one side at the head of the stairs looking at him, smiling, stepping forward. His mother's grip tightened. He panicked, then his hand was jerked and he knew what to do, look down and quicken his step. Anyway he didn't really want to see his father, it unleashed more emotions than he knew what to do with.

Nandan to Raman as they waited for their turn inside the courtroom: 'Such things happen. Don't take it personally.'

'The child turns away from his own father? How else can I take it?'

'Arre, it's a matter of dispute. Relationships change when there is a dispute.'

'Even this?'

'Especially this. In a custody issue, the parent in possession usually coaches the minor, particularly if they want to prove a point.'

Raman's gaze fastened onto the back of his son sitting in the front row. Everything was manipulation and deviousness, nothing was straightforward any more. This was the corrosive game his wife had elected to play.

'It will be OK. The judge will 99 per cent grant you visitation rights. You will be able to see both your children.'

The judge was still in her chambers. If only Arjun would turn around, give a smile, a glance, some kind of acknowledgement, he would be reassured. But nothing was bestowed on this pining man.

How cruel children can be, thought Nandan. Of course he was following his mother's instructions, but he could tell Raman this till nightfall for all the difference it would make to his suffering. He looked at his watch: their time was scheduled for two thirty, it was two fifteen. The minutes dragged on. Raman was mumbling something under his breath, probably a prayer. Well, perhaps his prayers were working, the judge was in, and they were going to get a hearing.

Their name was announced. The boy was led into the judge's chamber; the mother remained in her seat, pulled out a magazine from her red purse and opened it, oblivious to all. The white hand with its shiny polished nails could be seen from the last row where her estranged husband sat, ill with anxiety.

Such calculated coldness puzzled Nandan. He could not understand the heart that could inflict this pain on a husband of twelve years. Going to court, making sure the son be kept permanently away, the son who, till Roohi came, had absorbed both of them completely and equally.

He wondered as he often did about the things husbands and wives did to each other. This case was worse because it involved his relatives.

'I hope she burns in hell,' muttered Raman uselessly.

'Whatever decision the judge takes, at least your waiting will be over,' said Nandan.

'Are you telling me I will go from the frying pan into the fire?'

'In these cases, it is often considered better to send the minor to boarding school, especially if the child is desirous. And think, he will be away from their influence, you want that, don't you?'

'Her only aim is to send him away from me.'

'You will also get visitation rights.'

Raman grunted. No matter how often he repeated the facts he still hadn't accepted his situation, thought Nandan. Only time would help.

Twenty minutes later the parents were called. The judge was sitting on one side of a low Sunmica coffee table next to Arjun. Her dyed black hair was pulled into a bun, drawing attention to her bright red mouth and large glittery earrings. She had a deliberately remote businesslike manner, and an English that was somewhat unsteady.

Each side was asked to speak.

Were the differences irreconcilable?

A few minutes were enough to show they were. She had filed for divorce, he for custody.

They were meeting to decide what to do in the child's best interest. The application filed sought to prevent removal from Delhi. Why was such removal taking place?

'Your Honour,' said Shagun, 'I have tried to send him to his school, but he keeps saying he doesn't want to go. Only then I took this step of finding out about Dehradun Public Academy.'

'Beta, what is wrong with this school?' asked Raman.

Arjun said nothing.

'Are you afraid of anything? There is nothing really to stop you from returning to your school, the best in Delhi. Your friends miss you, they keep phoning. I miss you.'

'I object, Your Honour. He is putting words in the child's mouth.'

It did not take the judge long to decide that the child should be allowed to go to boarding school, and the father should have access to his children every weekend, from

Friday six to Sunday six. Half the children's school holidays would be spent with him.

The steno recorded this, then typed it on court paper, while they waited outside for a copy. Raman knew Shagun so well, he could feel her relief even in this room of legalities. What did she care about his anguish? She would never be happy in her new relationship, never. Ashok had the reputation of being a womanizer, no charms had been strong enough to ensnare him over the last twenty years, none until he set eyes upon his wife. And then he had reached into the heart of his family and stolen its essence.

On the way home it was an exhausted Shagun who drove, almost as silent as her son. Arjun was going to DPA. That was the main thing. With one hand on the steering wheel she caressed his head. 'Beta, you are my intelligent, smart boy. You managed to convince the judge that it was best to go to boarding school. Uncle will be very proud.'

'What about Papa?'

'What about him?'

'The judge said I had to see him.'

'Well, yes.'

'So?'

'You don't want to see him?'

No answer to this one.

'It will just be for the weekends. Now that you are going to the Academy it won't even be for that long.'

Arjun still had nothing to say.

'Beta, you must answer when I am talking to you. Otherwise Mama is going to be very sad.'

'OK.'

You can take a horse to the water but you cannot make it drink, and all Shagun got was monosyllables. Though she consoled herself with how pleased Ashok would be with the news about DPA, an insidious melancholy crept in. The upset she felt about Raman's visitation rights would not be shared by him, nor the pain of her impending separation from her son.

It wasn't. You can't keep the kids away from him for ever, he said.

She felt betrayed, his rationality was too cold. And to think she had not told him about the efforts Arjun had made to contact his father, uneasily imagining such news to be detrimental to the newer relationship.

XIX

When Raman went to pick up his children that weekend it was from the grandmother's flat. This place once so welcoming was now effectively barred to him. Waiting in the parking lot he tooted, then tooted again in five seconds. There he was, on the dot, at six o'clock, Friday evening. If they didn't come out he would burn the building down with Mrs Sabharwal in it. He leaned on the horn and made enough noise to suggest a heart attack right there at the wheel.

The door opened, she came across the angan to the outer metal gate, waving goodbye. He looked away. Once he had worshipped every inch of her body, covering it with kisses night after passionate night. For a temporary infatuation, she had nullified their past, trampled on his home and set out to destroy him. There was poison in every inch of her.

He jumped out and opened his arms to the slowly approaching children. As he held them his happiness was so severe, it broke his breath into sharp quick gusts.

'My darlings, my precious ones, my babies,' he said, over and over again, stroking their hair, touching their faces. Roohi put a tentative arm across his shoulder, Arjun remained wooden.

Once in the car, Arjun taxied imaginary airplanes across the window, while Roohi clutched her new Barbie. At a stop light she shyly showed her father the doll's special attaché case. As he examined the tiny items inside his eyes grew wet, and Roohi quickly snapped the case shut.

They went to Nirula's for lunch—pizzas, burgers, Coke, ice cream, anything they wanted was theirs. 'So, my sweethearts,' started Raman, his tone hearty and bluff, 'I have been trying to get in touch with you for a long time. Did you know that?'

Silently they shook their heads. She must have warned them what to say or not to say. 'Can't you talk to me? Will your mother scold you?'

Again they shook their heads.

'Where are you living?'

'With Mama.'

'But where?'

'With Naani.'

'Why are you never there when I phone for you? I won't get angry—just tell me the truth.'

At this Roohi opened her mouth for the first time: 'Mama says we will never see her again if we talk to you.'

'What, you are not going to talk for two days?'

'Mama didn't say that—Roohi is lying.'

Roohi looked down at the Barbie in her lap, and placed a bit of pizza next to the plastic lips. Raman looked at his kids. Seven months and they seemed little strangers, his and not his.

First of all, the school issue. Though the judge had declared that Arjun's future lay in DPA, he was convinced that the child's desire could only be the result of brainwashing. And how involved was Ashok with Arjun that he would expend the time and effort required to change a school? Shagun had neither the contacts nor the resources to manage such a transfer.

'Beta, when are you leaving?'

'April.'

'Are you sure you want to go?'

The boy nodded.

'You do realize what DPA means? It's an all-boys boarding school, which makes it a completely artificial environment. If anything happens to you, you have no parents to turn to. People who go there talk very highly of it, but that is because they don't know anything else.'

'I have been there, Papa. Two times.'

'Is it true you stopped going to VV?'

The smallest nod.

'But why, beta? For eight years you were happy there, had good friends, got all-rounder prizes.'

They were beating around the bush. Raman knew why he had stopped going. With everything changed, why should school remain the same, especially for a boy as sensitive as Arjun? Helplessly he reasoned, 'beta, you know even if Papa and Mama live separately, there is no need to inflict greater changes upon your life. In school who will care about what goes on at home?'

To this lame statement there was no reply.

'Why don't you consider living with me?' he continued. 'Nobody else can take the place of your father. And I will never stop you from visiting Mama. At least give it a try, you can always go to DPA next year.'

'I have to go this year, Papa. It's the starting year.'

'Don't you have to pass the class VI exams? And how will you do that if you don't go to school?' Raman had done a little research of his own.

'I don't have to.'

'What makes you so special?'

'Nothing.'

'But you don't have to?'

'No.'

'How come?'

'Just.'

Ashok, of course. For this too he must have pulled the requisite strings. This was a school in which the old-boys network was very important. Where connections were all that mattered, and rules not as important as who you knew.

Calm down, he told his agitated heart. He is not going tomorrow. This has to be a fun weekend, they have to feel your love, realize that they can tell you anything, that their home is with you, now and always.

But it was difficult to be calm. His children appeared so different, he couldn't handle the change he saw in every gesture, the many months that he had missed out on their lives.

The children accepted his fevered attentions as their due, but they said little about the trauma the mother's kidnapping had caused. He had always assumed the trauma was mutual, indeed that was the source of much of his grief. But even as he gently probed, searching for clues, it seemed otherwise. How were they treated? Did they miss him? How was that other uncle? Fine, fine, fine to everything.

He had imagined their reunion very differently—at the very least that the joy would be shared. Absent were the tales of longing and separation, absent too the combined unburdening of hearts. There was therefore no chance for the subtext he had been set to convey, ally yourselves against the enemy, call me secretly, lie to your mother. In the face of his phlegmatic children, his own enthusiasm seemed overstated.

Raman was deeply disappointed.

*

Next day. 'Beta, look, I got you a new video game.'

'Oh, really? What?'

'*RollerCoaster Tycoon*. The man in Palika Bazaar said it was selling a lot. I even played a bit of it.'

'Why would you play a game?'

'To learn the rules, so when you came the two of us could get into it faster. We don't have much time together as it is,' said the father carefully.

'Are there fights in it?'

'Let's see.'

The computer was switched on and the little magic figures of *RCT* appeared on the screen. As Raman explained the game, the parks, the roller coasters that had to be constructed, the paths that had to be built, the kiosks, the facilities that had to be maintained, the entrance fees that had to be charged, some of the wariness left his son's face. A few hours of *RollerCoaster Tycoon* and Arjun was hooked. 'I'm sure Sumant has nothing like this.'

'Well, why don't you call him over? We can go and pick him up.'

Arjun's face darkened. 'No.'

'Why not?'

'Just.'

'You can tell me. I am your father.'

'He's from VV. I don't want to see him.'

And Raman had no choice but to focus on the corkscrew rollercoaster they were building, check the number of guests, check the park rating, and increase the cost of the tickets to hire more security men, there was so much vandalism at the moment.

Just then Roohi got up from her afternoon nap and clambered onto her father. Arjun looked at her with disgust. She was like an animal—always wanting to be petted, like the cat they once had, rubbing her back against any leg that happened to be nearby. He wanted his father to concentrate so they could plan more park attractions, but he knew Roohi would go on interrupting, demanding attention and getting it.

In a few weeks, though, he would be away from all this. And in his mind he returned to the red-brick buildings, the ivy-framed windows, the estate full of trees, the butterflies darting among the flowerbeds.

That night again he dreamt of a large playing field. This time he was running in circles, sweat dripping from his body. All around him were impenetrable hedges, and beyond those were boundary walls, high walls with iron-barred gates, guarded by men in sentry-type kiosks.

Arjun was smart enough to see that he dreamt when he was troubled by his parents, and this disturbed him. No one he knew dreamt, but then no one he knew had separated parents. His father, noting his pale morning face, asked him what the matter was, but he couldn't say. He didn't trust his father to understand anything in his new life.

Sunday evening and with a heavy heart Raman put his children in the car to take them back to their grandmother's. He had wanted to keep them but that would be contempt of court, said Nandan when he floated the idea past him, and why would he want to get into that?

So the children were loaded into the car, and the father drove them slowly, slowly towards Alaknanda. 'I imagine,' he said as they turned into GK II, 'it must be nice, living with your naani.'

'Yes,' said Arjun.

'We don't live with Naani,' said Roohi, flush with the two-day proximity with her father, and quite forgetting her mother's warnings, which she had never really understood.

'We do,' said Arjun quickly.

'We don't,' repeated Roohi.

'What day is it today?'

Roohi was silent.

'See, that's how stupid you are.'

'You stupid. We live with Mama.'

Raman could not see what was going on in the back seat, but he heard the girl cry. 'He kicked me,' she wailed.

The father had to pull over to the side of the street, and put Roohi in front with him, with the big seat belt around her. Arjun scowled in the back. Why was his sister like this? Why couldn't she remember that their mother had repeatedly warned, they were not, *not*, in any circumstances to reveal that they did not stay in Alaknanda? Maybe his sister was retarded. He had seen a retarded child living opposite his grandmother, going to the park in the evenings with his maid, trying to approach other children, who ran when they saw him coming, he was so ugly with his flat face and animal noises.

By now they were turning into the apartment gates.

'Children, next week I will come Friday six o'clock. And I love you, remember that.'

They grunted.

'It was nice at Nirula's, nice playing all those games,' went on Raman. The pleasures of the week should be bursting from their lips as soon as they saw their mother, even now standing at the gate, showing an eagerness to receive her children that she had never shown throughout their lives together. She must have been watching from inside, looking at the hands of the clock. A minute later than six, she would report his transgressions to the court.

For the next few weeks life continued its unhappy way. Raman lived for the children's visits, only to experience on Sunday night a loneliness even more intense now that they had come and gone. Thanks to medical vigilance his heart had become an organ protected against the strains of his emotional life. Such a pity, he thought, death would be preferable to this terrible agony, but wouldn't that just suit her? His parents would suffer but she would get everything she wanted with no hassle. No, he would live, he would fight.

Unfortunately the legal system didn't allow for clean conflict. He had stopped phoning Nandan obsessively before each date. Anticipation and disappointment were inevitable, he must try and distance himself from the process.

Possession was nine-tenths of the law. In the case of children it was the whole law. If only his conscience allowed him to kidnap his children, but despite repeated pleas, even begging, they never said they wanted to live with him. And because he still believed in the necessity of a mother's love, he could not insist.

Meanwhile Arjun was getting ready to depart for DPA.

'If for any reason you don't like it, or if somebody troubles you, phone me. I will come and get you. You don't have to stay in this school, you know.'

'It's all right, Papa.'

The week before he was to go he clung momentarily to his father. 'Come and see me, Papa. Parents can visit Sundays.'

At this voluntary statement of love and need, Raman grabbed his son, looked solemnly into his eyes and promised that wild horses wouldn't keep him away. If it was allowed, he would come every weekend. And he would bring him lots and lots of goodies—institutional food could get boring.

Arjun giggled. 'Mama says the food at the Academy is healthy, even if it doesn't taste very good.'

'I can drive you down. See where my son is going to study?'

'It's all right.'

Arjun's way of saying no.

XX

April 1st.

Mother and son left by the early morning Shatabdi. For the first two hours of the journey Arjun slept, his head sliding onto Shagun's arm, his mouth falling open, a bit of drool wetting her kurta sleeve. His small tender face with the downy cheek looked so vulnerable that all Raman's warnings rushed into the mother's mind, making her writhe with anxiety. Just nerves, she reassured herself, how many times had she told Arjun that she would bring him back whenever he wanted to leave?

What indeed was wrong with VV? Only that Arjun wouldn't go, and Arjun wouldn't go because she had walked out of her marriage. Because of that, he was leaving home, as determined a consequence as the turning of the wheels on the railway tracks.

She tried to replace her uneasiness with Ashok's conviction that boarding school would bring out her son's leadership qualities and connect him to an old-boys network that would support him till he died. Besides, the admission process had allowed Ashok to grow warm towards Arjun, strengthening the fragile foundation of her new family.

On the luggage rack above she could hear the locks making gentle clicking sounds against the metal rims of Arjun's suitcase. In it was contained all that the school allowed its pupils, and compared to the comforts her son was used to, it did seem pitifully little.

Dehradun, Cantonment Station, DPA.

All was friendliness, invitation and welcome. There were people at the gate to help, indicating the way to the junior houses at the end of the main road, next to the science block. On seeing other boys, Arjun relaxed slightly. He didn't mind that his mother helped him arrange his clothes and put away his stuff, other parents were doing the same. They met the housemaster and matron, were introduced to the linen-room bearers, shown the changing room and the three pegs that would be Arjun's.

Mother and son lunched in town, then hurried back for a meeting with the staff at four o'clock. The Principal started with a speech that spoke eloquently of the qualities of an Academy boy, words meant to calm the fears of parents, as well as inspire the children. Shagun could see the attention Arjun gave as he listened to the Principal recite some lines from a poem by Henry Newbolt.

This is the word that year by year,
While in her place the School is set,
Every one of her sons must hear,

And none that hears it dare forget.
This they all with a joyful mind
Bear through life like a torch in flame,
And falling fling to the host behind—
'Play up! play up! and play the game!'

Shagun was moved. Arjun would be the son of the school, just as Ashok had been, the bearer of a torch that would burn brightly all his life.

Afterwards the senior staff was introduced, tea consumed, and reassurances delivered by the junior housemaster. At seven the matron ushered the parents briskly out, no lingering farewells, no indulgence of sentimental anxieties. For a dangerous moment, Shagun wished Raman was with her. She knew she would have dealt with the parting better if both of them had been involved.

She hoped the matron would look after her son, but how would she ever know? Arjun was allowed only two five-minute phone calls a month. Write, write, she had said, and he had nodded, but what writing could one expect of a twelve-year-old?

By nine o'clock she was lying on her train berth, trying to ignore the smell of urine that seeped in from the corridor, praying for Arjun, promising God all manner of things if only her son kept well. That was all she wanted from life, that and a divorce.

Ashok would be back by the time she came home. They would have the house to themselves; she would go to pick up Roohi from her mother's next morning. As she bathed away the grime of her journey he would enter the bathroom to watch her drying herself, and then he would open the perfume bottle, take out the glass stopper and begin touching her in all the places that needed scenting.

As he touched her she would look down to check on the burgeoning swelling, slide her hands around his waist, teasing him by not immediately opening the knot that held up his pyjamas. It amused her to see how long he could stand to be teased, never more than a few minutes, while where she was concerned, he could resist gratifying her for hours, making her beg and plead till she thought she would go out of her mind with desire. Not fair, she shook her head involuntarily. This time he would be the supplicant. She could sense her power over him growing stronger, and often she waited impatiently for the moment in bed, so that her hungry heart could feed on such straightforward proof.

She felt guilty for dreaming of sex on Arjun's first night away from home. Had Raman been with her, her thoughts would have been forcefully confined to their son, he would have talked obsessively of him, would have worried so irritatingly that there would have been no rest from weary reflections, certainly no room for *amour*. That was a word Ashok had taught her, *amour*, *amore*, he said, and now she said them too.

*

April 1st evening. The children have all changed into white kurta pyjamas and at seven thirty were seated in the junior section of the dining room. The new students were asked to stand, welcome to DPA. Everybody clapped.

'Let me tell you what to expect,' started a concerned senior.

The boys looked nervous.

'You will be given punishments: you will have to wash our clothes, clean our toilets, you will have to give us your phone chits; if anybody hears you complaining, the first time you will be slapped, the second time you will be beaten with hockey sticks. For starters, every morning at five thirty, you will have to run around the field.'

Everybody cheered and laughed.

All this was to toughen their character. Day boys were woefully ignorant, they thought school was just studies, but their Academy was so much more than that. As they would see.

Titters.

When they grew up they would be grateful and thank their seniors.

'New boys, say thank you.'

'Thank you,' muttered some.

'Louder, we can't hear you.'

'Thank you,' they shouted.

And then the whole school chorused, '*April Fool!*'

The new boys grinned, they had known the seniors could not be serious, they had not been taken in, not for a minute. They were also playing along by saying thank you.

For the first time in his life Arjun was with only boys. The information they demanded of each other was cursory: where are you from, which school did you go to? All their attention was on how to manage in these unfamiliar surroundings.

That night, as Arjun lay in bed, he could hear crying from the boy on his left. The sound made him uncomfortable, thank goodness he didn't feel like that. He turned over and pulled his sheet over his head to muffle the noise.

The next day was filled with books, classes, the mysteries of the timetable and the condescension of monitors appointed to show new students around. The senior boys were enviable in their assurance. One day they too would be like them, one day.

Five days later, the mid-term break. None of the new children wanted the scheduled trip to the mountains. They had just gotten used to the many bells that guided them through the day, the early rising, the toilet queues, the quick bed-making and clothes-folding, morning milk and morning PT, just begun to figure out what was where, who was who, and what to wear when.

'Why do we have to go?'

'Why?'

'We have been to the mountains, Sir,' they chorused in collective protest, never alone, always several, as they learned the security that came from groups.

They had to go because trekking was an Academy tradition—and wait and see, they wouldn't want to come back. Their destination was Dak Pathar. Into the bus and away up the winding roads. Some boys were quietly sick out of the windows and hoped no one would notice. Four hours later they were deposited at the gates of the Garwahl Mandal Vikas Nigam guest house.

The school cooks were with them, along with sacks of provisions. One hour later, they sat on rocks, beneath the fragrant rustle of pine trees, eating off steel plates, caressed by the coolness of the sun.

Archery, a short trek, and a campfire took them to night. Arjun looked at his fellow students by the light of the flames; these would be his companions for the next six years. His home seemed achingly distant.

Faint sobs could be heard. He cast a covert glance at the housemaster, wasn't he going to do anything? But the master was strumming a guitar, he wanted to know what songs the boys knew. After 'Hotel California', 'We Shall Overcome', and old Kishore Kumar songs, the three teachers started talking. Their new school devoted itself to developing leaders and responsible citizens. Missing home was natural—it would be strange if they didn't feel strange (weak giggles). Hundreds went through initial homesickness—why, said the housemaster, he remembered a boy who threatened to kill himself if he couldn't go back. That boy went on to become his house captain, his name was up on the boards. They might not believe him but one day it would be the holidays that would seem long. As the words flowed the snivels became less audible, and maybe the housemaster was not so unobservant after all.

Each succeeding day was better than the one before. They woke by five, and by six the thirty children had begun their trek. One day it was to a dry river bed, on another to a village, a picnic spot the third, with tiffins of butter sandwiches and cutlets. Everything they did was together, and thus they formed the ties they needed to survive.

On the night before they left, the housemaster dressed up as a ghost, terrifying the boys so much that they slept two to a bed. It provided all the conversation on the return journey, who had been scared and who not, who was lying about who was scared and who not, and who had been foolish enough to believe in the existence of ghosts.

Back in Dehradun, they found the five days away had changed everything. Already each child was more of an Academy boy, with memories of home drifting beneath the impressions of school and the mid-term.

XXI

'Beta, is Arjun nicely settled? I am so worried about him all night I cannot sleep.'

It was 6.05 on Friday evening. Roohi had just departed with Raman.

Shagun looked at her mother with despair. If there was anything that allowed her to sleep, she didn't know what it was. Probably her old life with Raman, everything safe, dull and boring.

'If Raman would leave him alone, he would be settled. Imagine, he went all the way to Dehradun to see him. Naturally Arjun didn't like that.'

'Why didn't Arjun like that? He is his father.'

'Mama! Sometimes I think you deliberately misunderstand the situation. Ashok went with us to Dehradun the first time, Arjun was introduced as his son. They allowed us to register Arjun's name so late because Ashok is an old boy, and he was school captain. They put Arjun into Shivalik House because it is Ashok's old house. They even allowed Arjun to not officially pass class VI because they were so understanding about the situation at home. And then Raman comes and says I am the father. How does that look?'

It looked as bad and as messy as her daughter's life was.

'Poor boy,' she said now.

'Exactly. Poor boy.'

'Did Arjun tell you all this?'

'More or less. I had to drag it out of him when I went to meet him. Raman came, he was not prepared, someone asked who was that?, he said, my father, then they asked who was the other man with your mother last month?, not that children care, but he didn't know what to say.'

'Yes, I see.'

'I told him, write to Papa suggesting it is difficult to meet in school, you will meet him during the holidays. I told him, if I say anything, he will file an application accusing me of contempt of court. Judge Mathur said the father has to have visitation rights.'

'Did he write to his father?'

'I didn't ask. People have such ugly minds, they will all say I am trying to influence Arjun. Raman might even produce the letter in court.'

'But has Raman gone again?'

'How should I know? It is not as though we talk.'

Mrs Sabharwal was getting increasingly upset. She got up to put the food on the table, unfolding her legs from the takht, groping for her chappals.

Shagun stared at her mother's feet. The nail polish was chipping—why couldn't she be more careful? She was young enough—unlike other grandmothers she knew. In the old days, when she came to visit, she and her mother used to go to the beauty parlour in the Godavari Housing Society across the road, in what had once been a garage. Every homeowner in the complex had converted this valuable space into boutiques, tailoring establishments or offices, while their cars jostled around on the inner lanes.

'When did you last have a pedicure?'

The mother slid her feet under her sari. She knew how particular her daughter was about grooming.

'If I am not with you, you are going to neglect yourself?'

'With all this happening you want me to think of pedicures?'

'Even your hair is looking terrible. All white and patchy at the back.'

'What to do? If I go there, they will ask me about you. What can I say?'

'You lie. What business is it of Mrs Mehra's anyway? People love to pry into the lives of others, I have noticed that. My ex-in-laws were the worst. Thank goodness I will never have to see them again.'

'Don't say things like that—they are the children's grandparents. I wouldn't like it if I couldn't see my two sweet little babas.'

This brought the children back into the conversation, which put Shagun in a ferociously bad mood and forced her mother's speedy exit into the kitchen.

Next Friday, 6.05, Shagun approached her mother, a look of determined reconciliation on her face. Mrs Sabharwal had spent a wretched week, sleeping badly. How Shagun was sleeping, she could only guess. The sleek gleam on her, the roseate look, the satisfaction that seeped from every pore gave her to understand the nature of the happiness her daughter kept talking about. There were even times when she had to avert her gaze from the girl's face, what was on it was all too palpable.

'Now Mama, you know I hate quarrelling with you.'

'I know, beta, I know,' said the mother uneasily.

'Give me some tea, because I have news and I want to tell it to you nicely.'

This so alarmed Mrs Sabharwal she could barely add leaves to the pot, barely notice the chocolate pastries that Shagun now laid onto a plate, or the muduku she put into a bowl, bought for her from the stall outside Sagar in Defence Colony.

'You shouldn't buy so much for me, beti,' she said mechanically.

'Let me, Mama. Who knows what the future will bring, or for how long I can do it?'

'Are you going somewhere?'

'Ashok has finally got his posting to the US.'

'The US! What about all the cases? The children? The divorce petition?'

'He was offered this post a year ago, and instead of accepting it, he chose to spend his time in airports, travelling to all the major centres in India, and of course there was that groundwater crisis that made it worse. How can I go on allowing him to be so dislocated?' said Shagun by way of explanation.

'What do you mean?'

'He needs to accept this offer for his career.'

'Is that what he is saying?'

'Mama! Obviously not. Should he say he is leaving me and going to the US? He is too much of a man to do such a thing.'

'But beta, how can you go? But if you don't go, that also is not good. You must have thought something.' It was one of Mrs Sabharwal's fears that having chased too much love, Shagun would die alone and friendless in her old age.

The tea tray was now on the little round dining table in one corner of the living area. Shagun poured her mother's tea, pushed the chocolate pastries closer, shook some savouries onto a plate and slowly started nibbling. Her eyes fell on the worn sofas, the lamps with their permanently tilted shades, the cushions bought when she was a college student. The posters she had put up on the walls, those too were still there, and from where she sat she could see the thin film of dust on the curling bottom edges.

'What are you thinking?' asked her mother.

'Of how my life has turned out.'

There was no response the mother could trust herself with.

'You must think it's all my fault.'

'No, I don't,' said Mrs Sabharwal bravely.

Her mother was such a bad liar, thought Shagun. But once everything was settled she would find it easier to accept her broken marriage. As of now the simplest things caused her worry.

'So if Ashok goes, what about you, the children? Their schools?'

'When parents have a transferrable job, children end up in boarding school. It's not so uncommon, you know.'

'But Roo can't go to boarding school. And will the courts allow you to take her?'

'Raman will make sure I can't take her anywhere. Once he gets to know about the US posting he will promptly get a stay order. Until custody is decided I am stuck. Ashok says he is willing to stay in India as long as necessary, but I can't allow so much sacrifice, can I?'

No, agreed Mrs Sabharwal. Temporarily he might be blinded by passion, but it was wiser to plan for the moment when his vision returned.

Shagun was silent, her thoughts in Judge Mathur's chambers. Everybody said that in a custody dispute, the father was awarded the boy, but effectively she had got her son. With each visit to the Academy, Ashok and Arjun bonded. She could see things continuing this way till he finished school at eighteen. After that he would probably study abroad, especially if she was there. Even if Raman did get to see Arjun, the boy was essentially hers. Home, safe and plain.

But Roohi? Roohi was not even three. Suppose she gave her up in order to get a divorce? She could always claim her later. With visitation rights, she would be able to maintain contact, and it would be easy to get Roohi to say she wanted to stay with her mother.

On being explained Shagun's strategy, Mrs Sabharwal tried to look intelligent. It was of the utmost importance that Shagun get a divorce, but at such a high price?

'If it will work, nothing like it,' she said cautiously.

'Of course it will work, Mama,' exclaimed the daughter. 'You don't think I could give Roohi up just like that? You saw what happened with Arjun?'

'Yes, I saw. But beti, Roohi is very small.'

'And I am only going for a short time. I will come back to see her, take her there with me for a while. Raman won't insist on this jurisdiction of the court nonsense when everything has been settled and he has what he wants. If there is any other way I can get a divorce, tell me.'

There didn't seem to be.

If Raman was not agreeable, she would never get a divorce. She could go with Ashok, but without marriage the company would neither pay for her ticket (a comparatively small amount) nor for her health insurance (astronomical sums involved).

She could give power of attorney to her poor mother to represent her in court, continue to fight her cases through Madz, but what would be the good? It would take a lifetime and then some. The Indian legal system stank. Justice delayed was justice denied, a truth experienced every day by countless litigants throughout the country.

*

The estranged wife phoned. 'I want a divorce.'

Raman knew that. She had filed a petition, kidnapped the children, fabricated myriad cruelties, committed perjury, for what but the freedom to marry?

He held the phone tightly, longing to wound. 'Why ask? It's already in the court.'

'I want one now.'

'I am not going to give you a damn thing unless custody is decided and that too in my favour. If the children become too old, and the issue irrelevant, I will never free you. Never.'

'So take the children and give me a divorce.'

'What?'

'Take them.'

The voice on the other end thickened and the phone was put down. Was this another trick? He didn't trust her a millimetre, not a millimetre. He dialled Mrs Sabharwal's number: Shagun is in the bathroom—I will tell her to call you as soon as she comes out.

Ten minutes later the phone rang.

'So how was your visit to the bathroom?'

'What do you want?'

'Were you serious?'

'Yes.'

'Why should I trust you?'

'Ask my lawyer.'

Again the phone was put down. He knew she couldn't bear to talk to him, but that was all right. Superstitiously he tried not to hope, but hope came nevertheless in the thought of his children restored, in the freedom from court and the anxiety of its transactions.

Through the day the conviction of her desperation came. Obviously she wanted to marry fast. So, the rumours he had heard were true, Ashok was posted to the US. So far as visa, insurance and ticket were concerned, he knew it was easier to leave India married, but was marriage worth the price of custody? Roohi, who would have almost certainly been awarded to the mother, yes, she would be a gift indeed. Even if it meant Shagun getting what she wanted.

It was a genuine offer. The other side's lawyer contacted Nandan with a settlement so good that he could not believe his cousin's luck, nor incidentally his own. He had given him free time, free attention, free advice; everything family loyalty demanded. Moreover, Raman's misery made it easy to pity the man. Now the light at the end of the tunnel.

That evening the family gathered together in muted

triumph. Right had prevailed, the vice-ridden had given in, now to discuss the details, further strengthen their position, and to secure what was theirs.

Mrs Kaushik sat cross-legged on the sofa, raised her nose to the winds and smelt blood. Her hackles rose, her eyes gleamed and the knife she had in her heart, so far too little used, came out. 'This boy really loved her. He was a generous, good husband. We will see to it that she gets nothing. Nothing. Everything that was joint must be returned to Raman.'

'She is willing to give up all claims to his property, all maintenance for herself. All she wants is divorce by mutual consent, the custody case dropped and visitation rights. Half the holidays and weekends. Just what the father had.'

'What about jewellery? She hasn't said anything about returning that. We gave her so much when she married,' snapped Mrs Kaushik.

It would have enraged the mother beyond words to know how many more gems Raman had hung on Shagun over the years. Any occasion had warranted a trip to the jewellers. Now he didn't want to think of those times or that love. He was ashamed of his devotion to his wife, so little had it been returned. In future he would be a different person, harder, wilier, less easy to deceive.

'Eventually the jewellery will go to Roohi. Let her keep it,' he now said.

'Suppose she has another child,' demanded the vigilant mother.

'Mummy, Papa, I do not want to discuss this. All I want is to make sure she will not kidnap the children.'

'If you have custody, where is the question?'

'You never know—they have already been taken away by force once—I don't want it to happen again.'

'Yes,' said the mother excitedly. 'She may only be pretending to give the children for the sake of divorce. Once she is abroad it will be easy to just keep them. In this building alone, Mrs Sharma's daughter-in-law left her husband and quietly took a flight to her sister's in America with their baby. Mrs Sharma's son can do nothing.'

This fresh possibility generated a lot of discussion and the evening passed with many scenarios mulled over, as the family united in speculation that covered as wide a territory as possible, physical, financial and emotional.

'If she can take them out of the country, I will not agree to a divorce,' Raman eventually said. 'Even if it means I don't get Roo.'

Two days later she called. 'What are you so afraid of?'

'You.'

'How can you prevent children from meeting their mother? I did not stop them from meeting you.'

'After I won visitation rights.'

'Well, now I am offering you custody, what more do you want? That I should never see them? No judge will agree to that. And if I am abroad, I should be allowed to bring them on a visit.'

What did it matter what the court allowed or disallowed? In the end it was a question of endurance. Of who had the edge over whom.

'Raman? Are you listening? We can both benefit, is that so hard to understand?'

'When have you tried to benefit me?'

'If that is your attitude, no point talking.'

Next week Shagun's mother phoned him to say that Roohi was ill and could not see him. If he so desired, she could produce a medical certificate.

They both knew a medical certificate was not worth the paper it was on, any quack doctor would sell you one.

That he could not live without Roohi was something Raman had become conscious of only recently. He had been so used to associating his children with each other that after Arjun left for Dehradun he had found himself, to his surprise, enjoying a totally different parent–child experience. The things he did with his daughter had an added pleasure, partly because there was no attack and counter-attack from an older sibling. He hadn't realized how much of his attention had been taken up with the more complicated equations the elder brother invariably generated.

Now with Roohi he felt some of the completeness that had been so unthinkingly his for twelve years. He was in bliss when he held her on his lap while he read stories at night, lay next to her while he watched her eyes slowly close in sleep, sat by her side while she ate, stood at the corner of the neighbourhood park watching her play.

Once, twice, thrice. Over three weekends Raman was told that his daughter was sick and couldn't see him.

'What is the nature of this illness that lasts so long?' he demanded of the lying, uneasy grandmother. 'I have given her the benefit of the doubt, but one more week and I am going to file another application.'

'Beta, she is really keeping unwell. Nothing serious, though. Just cough, cold, fever, sometimes it gets OK, then again it comes. She is quite weak. The doctor says it is in the air.'

Something or the other was always in the Delhi air.

'I suppose Roohi is not going to school either,' he enquired sarcastically on the phone.

'No, beta,' said Mrs Sabharwal. 'Only one day—two days.'

Shagun was not the only one to know that Mrs Sabharwal was a terrible liar.

Eventually he gave in, as his wife must have known he would.

Take your divorce and fuck you. But the children are mine. If you dare mess with them, you see what I will do.

Nandan was very pleased at this happy outcome. You are a lucky man, he informed his cousin—I wish others could have their affairs resolved as quickly. From start to finish not even two years.

XXII

Divorce by mutual consent was initiated. The couple appeared in court, swore that it was impossible for them to live together and that they were not acting under duress. Six months later, they would reiterate the same thing, upon which divorce would be granted. Shagun was to give up all ownership of their joint assets, all claims to maintenance, the legal guardianship of the children, only demanding visitation rights in the holidays.

'I hope my generosity, my willingness to settle, gives Raman an inkling of where I am coming from,' Shagun said to her mother. 'He needs to see we have common interests, despite the fact that I have left him. Estranged partners have to keep mutually acceptable goals in mind for the sake of the children. That is the way to handle divorce. Not all this ugly fighting business.'

'Is this what Ashok thinks?'

'Ashok feels equally responsible to my kids, Mama—you

should know that by now. Look at all he did for Arjun. Obviously he wants them to be well adjusted. Our objectives are the same.'

'And Roo?'

'When the time comes he will attend to Roo. He doesn't discriminate between them.'

'I hope he continues to be so involved, beti. People change after marriage.'

'If I didn't have absolute faith in Ashok, I would not have given up everything for him. My children are his, he has said so a thousand times. You'll see.'

Mrs Sabharwal could find nothing to say to all this reasoning. Increasingly she had become the person her daughter confided in, and the ebb and flow of information about divorce, custody and Ashok was almost more than she could bear. Nothing was clear in Shagun's life, she didn't even know in which direction to turn her prayers any more.

'Ashok is already planning our holidays for when we are all together. He feels we need to bond together as a family. We will go somewhere, perhaps Bhutan, and maybe Arjun can get a few archery lessons. Ashok will no doubt arrange things down to the last detail, he is so used to multitasking, he does it even at home.'

'I'm sure he does.'

June.

It was going to be Arjun's first trip home after DPA. He had been away two months, his father thought, long enough for him to know whether he liked the school or not. And if he didn't he would record that on tape and produce it as evidence in court in order to protect him.

For now, eager to restore the sense of family his son had lost through the desertion of the mother, Raman planned a Goa holiday that included his parents. He would pick his son up from Alaknanda and after a day of preparation they would leave. Roohi's birthday would be celebrated on the beach—he bought some knick-knacks from Khan Market for a little party he planned there. It would be a surprise for her, different from anything she had ever experienced.

As the Goa Express left Nizamuddin Station Raman felt the nightmare of the past year easing with the gentle rocking of the train. This compartment contained what he loved most on earth, and as he looked at the four he thought it could have been worse. He could have lost a child, for instance, instead of a wife who, all said and done was replaceable. One arm tightened around Roohi sitting on his lap, the other stretched out to stroke Arjun's hair. The boy was looking good, clearly it had benefited him to be away from the harmful atmosphere of his mother's home. Right now he was laughing at a story his grandfather was recounting, a story of his father as a kid, one new to Raman himself.

Panjim. From the station they hired a Maruti van that would take them straight to Vagator. As they drove Arjun focused on the newness of the landscape. Initially he had resisted Goa, all he had wanted was to stay at home, eat, watch TV and sleep without a bell ringing in his ears every twenty minutes. Now he relished this first encounter with the sea.

Finally Vagator. The hotel was a long low white building, with rooms on three sides of a pool, criss-crossed by red-gravelled walkways flanked by overarching green palms. Raman had booked a villa with rooms upstairs and down, and how the children loved the novelty of the little internal staircase! The grandparents had never stayed in such luxury before, and if breakfast and dinner were not included they would probably have starved to save their son money.

Everybody was charmed by everything. Mornings and evenings were spent at the beach, playing, walking along the shore, the rolling water and crashing waves imparting joy to all. Raman wondered sadly why he had waited to lose his wife to take this kind of holiday, but there had never been any time. Now every moment with his family was precious, and he went to sleep each night thanking God for his children, and for the medical intervention that meant he was still alive to enjoy them.

The highs lasted all the way back to Delhi. Even the train being late didn't matter so much, thought Raman, when they were together. His mother told Roohi stories from the Mahabharata, and he saw that Arjun was listening too. After all, his name was from the Mahabharata: how come neither he nor Shagun had ever told their son about the Pandava Arjun? Too busy, that's why, and not enough time with grandparents.

Unfortunately Goa had also liberated the grandparents' tongues. They were mindful of their son's interests, and in that connection thought it vital to know what was going on in the boy's head. They couldn't trust Raman to give the child an adequate idea of his sufferings.

Now they seized this opportunity. What was school like?, didn't he miss his father?, his father loved him so much, kept thinking of him all the time, had been so eager about the Dehradun trip, remember, beta, when he came to see you. We all wanted to come, but your father said no, that might be too much for you, would it have been too much, beta? Do other grandparents visit?

Raman said, 'Leave him alone,' but the grandparents knew nothing of child psychology, they were willing to allow their curiosity all the room it needed to flourish.

'Does your mother write to you?'

'Yes.'

'From where?'

'Different places.'

'What does she say?'

'Nothing.'

'She must say *something*.'

'How are you? That's what she says.'

'And?'

'*Nothing*. Why don't you ask her?'

Later they told themselves that the boy had become very proud, very stand-offish.

Eventually Raman became firm enough for the questions to stop, while Arjun grew wary of his grandparents.

Back in Delhi, the boy was at his most eloquent when confronted with Roohi. 'You are so stupid, you don't understand anything' was the burden of his song.

It hurt Raman, this dismissal of the little sister. Who else did these children have but each other?

'Be nice to Roo, she could hardly wait for you to come,' he repeated to the boy's scowl and a repetition of how retarded she was. 'You have to be tolerant, she is still very young,' but the baiting continued.

Arjun had behaved so well in Goa; was it something about this house or the memory of his mother that triggered such aggression? He could think of no other explanation.

At night when Roohi was asleep, and things were peaceful, father and son watched the Cricket World Cup, the event that was to have brought Raman and Shagun closer. Now they discussed the likelihood of India's winning, went through the A and B team rankings, discussed players, their scores, their merits.

'Do you miss your mother?' Raman once asked.

'No.'

'Where is she now?'

'I don't know.'

'You don't have to tell me anything you don't want to, son—only don't say you don't know when you do.'

'She keeps travelling, Papa, how should I know where she is?' The child had begun to whine and Raman told himself never to ask about his mother again. The secret desire to be assured of her unhappiness was a sign of weakness, besides which it was really none of his business.

The only topic of conversation Arjun was enthusiastic about was school. In a mere two months he had become a proper Academy boy. Won't you like to go back to VV, beta? the father had tried asking, but the answer was such a clear no that Raman had to reconcile himself to DPA being Arjun's school.

All too soon the children's time with their father was over. Shagun phoned: please pack Roohi's things and drop the children at my mother's place.

How convenient it was to have her mother as a postbox.

Gloomily he drove them to Alaknanda. With Roohi at least things would change after the divorce, but the separation from Arjun would continue now that he was in boarding school.

'Bye, beta, write once you reach Dehradun. Remember to phone. I will come to visit you, all right? Papa loves you, beta.'

'It's all right, Papa,' said Arjun, by which mysterious statement Raman could imagine anything he chose.

*

Over the summer the nation flexes its muscles as it goes to war with Pakistan.

Everybody is glued to the TV. Patriotic feelings run high.

Kargil becomes a household word.

Collection drives for our brave soldiers take place in every colony of the city.

Companies donate, NGOs donate, schools and colleges donate, politicians and civil servants donate.

Certain very old people whisper their desire to see the country united as it was in their youth, before Independence and Partition snatched it all away.

Parks and roads are named after martyred soldiers. Five hundred and twenty-two of them have lost their lives around the mountains near Kargil in Ladakh.

Indian cricketers visit the wounded in hospitals, movie stars turn up at railway stations, singers and actors give charity shows.

In July 1999, India declares victory, the Pakistanis have been pushed back to the Line of Control.

India increases its defence spending.

Ordinary life resumes.

So far as The Brand was concerned, it was a good time to have the nation distracted. After the groundwater fiasco, it was the turn of bottled water. Some samples had been found to contain *E. coli*. More NGO reports. These reports must have been instigated by Indian manufacturers who hate our presence here, said Ashok, But for once they have picked their moment badly.

Shagun could see how much dealing with problem after problem was beginning to tire him, and how much he really wanted to leave. In that sense her divorce could not be better timed.

With Arjun back in school and Roohi with her mother Raman felt lost. It was useless confiding in his parents, they thought cursing Shagun was the way to make him feel better.

With an empty heart and an empty house, the office was the place that seemed most natural to him. Anyway, he had to compensate for his time away from The Brand.

A new regional requirement from Hong Kong demanded his full attention. He had to work out an assessment of how India was doing based on six months of figures from thirteen different Asian countries. The data he had to deal with was considerable, and he spent hours and hours in office, relishing the freedom of being so involved in fruit drink analysis that there was no room for anything else. He began to use the nearby guest house to shower, eat and sleep. What was the point in going home anyway?

By the time he left the building it was dark and the traffic noise had dulled to more bearable levels. His mind was full of numbers and the story they told. He flexed his hands as he walked and moved his shoulders. His neck felt stiff—he knew he should take more breaks from the computer, but once he started it was hard to stop. He was reminded of his time at the IIM. Days of intense work, snatches of sleep and food, and the hope that all this would lead to a gilded future. And in terms of money and prestige it had.

But he was still the home-grown produce, still Mang-oh! compared to the international bestselling drink.

A few more weeks and the second divorce petition would be signed. He would be married no longer, a phase of his life over. Soon he would have to figure out what his world looked like with Shagun inexorably out of it. Till now, absent or present, she had dominated the scene.

*

In September, a month before the final signing, Mrs Sabharwal made her daughter take her to Tirupathi. Here she offered prayers, here she paid for fifty Brahmins to be fed, here she gave a donation of a thousand rupees.

'I don't think we need worry so much, Mama,' said Shagun. 'Raman is not the type to agree to divorce one day and refuse the next.'

'He is not the Raman you knew, beti. Cold, hostile, angry—I feel he is now all these things. His mother may influence him, anything can happen.'

'Well, if he reneges on the agreement, he will never see Roohi. Or as little as I can help it. Arjun too. The boy is old enough to be asked his opinion—and in front of the judge he can say, I do not want to meet my father. What will he do?'

'I hope it doesn't come to that. He loves the children, whatever his faults as a husband.'

(That Raman Kaushik had many faults as a husband was now the party line, and Mrs Sabharwal obediently echoed it.)

Shagun stared at her mother, this woman of mean intelligence. 'Well, he's not doing me any favours by being a caring father. I am giving him an opportunity to look after them, let's see if he takes it.'

Mrs Sabharwal in turn stared at Shagun. Nothing good could come of a mother giving up her children, but to continue to live with Ashok without marriage would in the long run be even worse.

Now that the end was near, Shagun allowed herself to fantasize about being Ashok's wife. To have that happiness legitimized! She only had to look around her to see divorcing couples, fighting over money and custody, forced to spend their lives in courtrooms, till the children were grown up, the money spent, and any chance of other relationships gone. Her freedom was miraculously around the corner, seducing her with its nearness.

So far as the children were concerned, Raman was a better and more magnanimous person than she. He would not stop contact between them, if only because it would be in their best interests.

A week before the final signing Shagun hauled Roohi onto her lap. She loved her little girl so much, but her hands were tied, tied so hard she felt the knots chafing at her skin. She longed to leave this terrible city, go far, far away.

'Babu?'

The child continued to suck her thumb.

Shagun pulled at her hand. Roohi was too old to be doing this, but she had not worked at stopping her. In all the recent upheavals, let the thumb at least be constant.

'Roohi? Listen to me.'

Raman's face looked up at her.

'Beta—how would you like to spend some time with your father?'

The child looked puzzled. She did see her father. Every weekend.

Shagun rephrased the question. 'Not like now. Longer. Go to school from there.'

'Why?'

'Because Mama has to go away for a bit.'

'Why?'

'Some work.'

'I want to come.'

'Children are not allowed. Now wouldn't you like to spend more time with your father? You really like being in that house, don't you?'

'No,' said Roohi and put her thumb back in her mouth.

'Why?'

Roohi couldn't say. She looked around quickly into the small history of her life and came up with her brother. 'Bhaiyya said to look after you. I promised Bhaiyya before he left for school.'

'Bhaiyya did not know what he was talking about. He was just anxious about leaving. How can a small baby look after a big mother?'

'I want to come with you.'

'Beta, your school is here, your friends are here, your grandparents are here. And your Papa will miss you.'

By now Roohi was looking thoroughly alarmed. 'No, Mama, no.'

Impatiently Shagun gave her a little shake. 'Beta, where I am going, children are not allowed. How will I take you? The police will send you back, and it will all be your father's fault.'

At this unexpected information Roohi began to cry. Shagun instantly regretted all she had said, but Roohi could sometimes be slow to understand. 'Shush, beta, shush, Mama loves you. Don't worry—I will come back quickly quickly—make a home for my Roohibaba. Everything will be all right, I will find you a wonderful school—don't worry.'

'But I want to come with you *nooooow*.'

'Beta, you can't. Your father has made the court stop it. I will be put in jail if I take you.'

Roohi went on sobbing.

'Nothing will change. You are still my baby girl. Remember that I love you. Always, always. Now stop, stop this crying. Come, let's see what cartoons are on TV. Let me carry you, my, you are becoming such a big, heavy girl—soon Mama won't be able to lift you. Come. Come.'

Shagun carried her to the drawing room and settled down in front of the TV. She hoped that the child would be in a better mood by the time Ashok came home. Though he never complained, the sound of children's programmes gave him a headache and Shagun tried to protect him from the noise.

It was raining a few days later, an unseasonable late September rain, when Raman came to pick up Roohi from her grandmother's house. Unlike other times there was no Shagun standing theatrically at the entrance. When his daughter emerged it was with the grandmother struggling under an umbrella, clutching a suitcase, with a school bag slung from her shoulder. In the transaction involving the child, the suitcase and the school bag, no look was exchanged, not a word uttered. The door slammed, the car reversed and sped out of the central parking lot, while the grandmother stood, holding the hem of her sari up with one hand, watching her grandchild go. Once the car was out of sight she turned and walked heavily back to her apartment where her daughter was waiting.

Did he say anything? Did Roohi cry? Did she go willingly? No, no, yes.

For the rest of the day Shagun remained sunk in apathy. It would take time to get used to her new status as part-time mother. Once they were in their own apartment in New York she would regain her equilibrium. Ashok had said they would find one overlooking Central Park. Just the name was enough to distract her. The real Central Park, not the falsely named builders' creation in Gurgaon.

Yes, she couldn't wait to start her new life. They would keep house together, they would have no servants, they would do everything by themselves, just the two of them, laying the blocks of a happy, successful union.

A week later Raman and Shagun were divorced. Thirty days had to pass before either was free to marry.

Great was the relief in the Kaushik household. At last their son was out of the clutches of that woman. Raman had been generous, very generous, he had not made his wife suffer, nor had he punished her by refusing a divorce. Such men were rewarded in lifetimes to come.

As for the jewellery, Shagun herself offered it, bringing it to court in a little attaché case: 'Please keep this for Roohi.'

Clearly, thought Raman, she wanted nothing from him—nothing except her freedom. Not a shred, not a pin, not a rupee would she keep of their former life.

It would be prudent to forget her existence as quickly as possible. From now on he would devote himself to his children.

*

Thirty-one days later Shagun returned to Tees Hazari, this time to sign the marriage register. She had sacrificed so much for this love of hers, she felt like the Heer of Heer-Ranjha, the Laila of Laila-Majnu. Only their love was not doomed, it was going to flourish. Neither Ranjha nor Majnu had had the canniness and sagacity of Ashok Khanna. Everything he touched succeeded, every step he took was imbued with thought and purpose.

She felt guilty about Raman, but she had made all the amends she could. He could hold no grudge against her, nor blame her for any misfortune. She had returned the jewellery he had not asked for. She had given him the children.

It was one in the morning, foggy outside, with rain splattering against the windshield when Mrs Sabharwal accompanied her new son-in-law and daughter to the airport.

Ashok had expressed some inadvertent astonishment at

the requirement that they spend their last night in India at his mother-in-law's place. 'Please, darling,' said Shagun, 'she is very upset we are going. She really wants to come and drop us.'

'Why is she so upset? You know she is always welcome wherever we are.'

'She says she will wait and see how things go before she visits.'

'All right,' said Ashok, not quite aware of the dimensions of Mrs Sabharwal's loneliness, nor intuitive enough to suggest alternative solutions.

To herself Shagun wondered at the difference another marriage could bring. Had she been going to New York with Raman she knew he would have spent hours with her mother, convincing her to stay with them.

Now they were driving slowly, negotiating the fog that had suddenly thickened as they left the more built-up areas of the city. Ashok, sitting in front, looked impatiently at his watch. There is plenty of time, darling, murmured his wife from the back seat, her hand in her mother's.

They reached Indira Gandhi International Airport, their car inching along with others up the ramp. In front of the long entranceway they stopped abreast two other vehicles, adding to the chaos. Ashok jumped out and darted towards a free cart, the driver pulled the suitcases from the dickey, and there stood husband and wife in the line inching towards their designated door. Mrs Sabharwal was stopped at the barricade, passengers only from this point. With a last hug, a last kiss, I will phone you, Mama, take care, and Shagun disappeared inside. Mrs Sabharwal remained some few moments standing next to the guards as she watched her daughter exit in pursuit of happiness.

XXIII

'Such good news,' said Mrs Rajora, beaming with excitement from news so good that even the difficult child would rejoice.

'What is it?' asked the difficult child, sitting in the veranda looking at the strings of coloured lights that decorated the balconies of the buildings around them. Down below children were letting off firecrackers. It was Diwali and Ishita had just delivered a box of sweets to Mrs Hingorani. Now all she wanted was to be left alone, prey to an unaccountable depression.

'Raman is divorced!'

Raman?

Mrs Kaushik had revealed this when Mrs Rajora had gone to give her some Diwali dry fruit. Seeing her friend looking so sad, Mrs Rajora had scolded her for keeping secrets. Privacy and discretion were all very well, but a friend's concern also had to be given value. Why this permanently worried expression? Hadn't she herself told Leela everything about Ishita as soon as she was asked? Hadn't she?

Then Leela cried and said it was much worse than anything that had happened to beti Ishu—here there were children involved and the fear that Raman would die.

Ishita listened silently. She remembered the younger Mrs Kaushik by reputation; so fair, such unusual green eyes, so foreign-looking. But living as she did, away from Swarg Nivas, she could not be interested in her mother's gossipy nuggets. Now she was given a quick recap of those unnoticed years: Raman, so brilliant, all the Mang-oh! sales in the country due to him, marriage always considered so perfect, now look what happened.

A woman with such looks might use her face to travel

farther than the PPG-emerged Raman, thought Ishita. If she had possessed amazing beauty, she didn't think SK would have been so keen to leave her. It all boiled down to externals.

'You can share divorce stories with Auntie now,' she said.

'I never share stories about you with anyone.'

'Well, you should. What happened to me is nothing to be ashamed of.'

'People are very narrow-minded. They don't understand how misfortune can come.'

'Explain it then. Tell them I am barren.'

'I came to give you some good news, and you talk like this about yourself. It hurts me.'

'But why do you consider this good news? Do you imagine we should get married?'

'O-ho. It's just news. Can't I share it?'

'Not if you have something else in mind.'

'Why are you always so negative?'

'Because I know you always think of one thing.'

'He is known, he is a neighbour, a man from a decent family, people like us. Perhaps, sometime in the future—'

'Mummy! When has any proposal ever worked? Don't you get tired?'

Ishita got up to suffer in her bedroom. Would the search for a husband continue into the adoption process and after? Her father's attitude was infinitely preferable, whatever has to happen will happen. It led the believer to a comfortable burial behind reams of newspaper and it led to tranquillity in the house.

Mr Rajora meantime discovered his wife in the little veranda, shivering slightly in the growing chilliness of the evening. He sighed. It had to be Ishita. Nothing else could reduce his wife to this state.

'What is it?' he asked, his exasperation showing despite the festival day.

'You know what it is.'

What he had really meant was why does it have to be what it is? 'Leave her alone. She will find her own way.'

He often asked his wife to leave Ishita alone. But how could she? She was her daughter, they had to do what they could. Sometimes she suspected her husband's attitude came from a disinclination to be bothered.

Now she gave him the news that should have been so cheering, Raman Kaushik's divorce.

So this was the information that had sent Ishita flouncing into her room, while the mother sat sadly looking at the winking Diwali lights.

'Can we have a little halwa-puri now?' he asked longingly after a while. His wife hurried into the kitchen.

Twenty minutes later Ishita, chomping on her mother's crisp dal-stuffed puris, could bring herself to mumble, 'Sorry, Mummy, I shouldn't have shouted at you. I know you worry about me, but please don't.'

It was a wonder what communal eating could do.

Even if Ishita refused to take the news of Raman's divorce in the proper spirit, it continued to be a source of great consolation to Mrs Rajora. Shame and humiliation would touch the Kaushiks; the Rajoras could count on the companionship of similar miseries. Mrs Kaushik, in her turn, was relieved to find someone at her very doorstop who understood her situation. With renewed intensity they rehashed their children's histories, trying to come to terms with offspring whose lives had fallen against the grain.

'The boy is too idealistic. We said, why give a divorce?, you have not turned her away, but he didn't listen.'

'My girl was like that also. Arre, she was such a good wife, devoted, caring. For her marriage was for life. Life. But the man lost interest, and she refused to stay where she was not wanted. Are there any such nowadays?'

If there were any such, she had not had the pleasure of their acquaintance, thought Mrs Kaushik bitterly. In her son's ex-wife's case it was the opposite. More new-fashioned than the latest fashion. Changing husbands with the breeze.

'To top it all, that boy is now married with two sons, while my daughter refuses to look at a man. And what she does for those street children, bap re. Her heart is as big as the sky.'

'Has she started her studies yet?'

'Still applying,' said Mrs Rajora, suppressing all information about prospective adoption.

Mrs Kaushik looked thoughtful. She hadn't seen Ishita in a long time, why didn't Mrs Rajora bring her over? 'Maybe she can help Raman. All the time he is brooding.'

'She is too, too shy. When you are divorced, people talk.'

'These days people get divorced, what is there? Anything can happen to anyone.'

'I know, but there is no point my saying anything. She doesn't listen.'

'Tell her Auntie is calling her. This Sunday. That is when he comes with Roohi. He wants to give the child a sense of family. He has friends of course, but Roo loves Nandan's twins.'

That Sunday Mrs Rajora told her daughter of the invitation to tea. If she didn't accept, Mrs Kaushik would personally come and get her.

Ishita took exception to this. 'What? Why?'

'Auntie only said she would come out of concern. Do you hear? If you go on like this, no one will care about you. And it will be your own fault.'

Ishita had heard these dire predictions often. Her mother only wished her to marry so that she could have an old-age companion. Suppose they had dissimilar values? All the intervening years would be hell. She wished she could explain this to her mother, but here was another whose values were not the same.

'At least go and meet the boy. He is suffering. Auntie is so afraid he will die of another heart attack, then his ex-wife will get everything, children plus CEO husband—it is too, too bad. And she has sent the boy away to Dehradun, behind his back—all to spite him.'

'So you see there is nothing common between me and him,' retorted her daughter.

'Of course there isn't. But if you could just buck him up,' pleaded Mrs Rajora.

Come Sunday, Ishita lounged around provocatively messy all morning, all lunchtime, all afternoon. Evening drew nigh, and the child had still not had a bath, was she going to go to Mrs Kaushik's in her nightclothes? It was almost five o'clock and time to leave when Ishita disappeared into the bathroom to emerge ten minutes later with defiant wet hair, dressed in a plain black salwar kameez, with a red-and-black mirror-work shawl thrown over her shoulder, her only concession to make-up a little kaajal in her eyes. She looked half her age.

'Come,' said the mother, her own silk sari rustling along the corridor towards the elevator.

The daughter followed. If it was her social duty to be treated as Exhibit A she hoped the sight of her would make the Kaushik son feel better.

As they made their way to the fifth floor, Mrs Rajora was grateful for Ishita's comparatively thoughtful demeanour.

Her sterling qualities were more obvious when she was calm.

'Yes?' asked the man as he opened the door.

Oh great, thought Ishita, we are not even expected.

Mrs Kaushik bustled into view, allowing Mrs Rajora to seem less monumental. 'Come, come. Beta, you remember Ishita and Auntie?'

Mother and daughter were herded into the drawing room, where a small girl was watching TV.

'Hello, baby,' said Ishita.

'Roo, say namaste,' admonished Raman.

The girl clung to her father and looked down.

'Never mind, let it be,' said Ishita. 'Children don't really like to perform.'

Raman looked at her. 'Do you also have kids?'

'No.'

Mrs Rajora began to feel annoyed. Leela might have done a little preparatory explaining. 'She works in an NGO for slum children,' she offered.

Raman then had to ask about her NGO. It was nice to hear of people doing such good work. Yes, said Ishita, she supposed it was, but in fact she objected to such statements, not from him, but in general.

And why was that? asked Raman, looking at her with more interest.

Because people felt they had performed a social duty if they asked about NGO work, satisfied that it was taking place, but refusing to actually help in some meaningful way.

Was it troublesome, getting helpers?

If only he knew how much.

Mrs Rajora meanwhile disappeared into the kitchen to help with the tea. 'I never know what the girl will eat, she is so fussy,' Ishita could hear the grandmother complaining. 'You can see how thin she is.'

Father hauled his daughter back onto his lap, his face in miniature beneath his own. The girl did look thin, true, but not sick.

'What's her name?' she asked.

'Roohi.'

'Pretty.'

'Yes.'

Ishita sat next to the girl. To catch her attention she put the TV off. Roohi protested, 'I was watching it.'

'Do you know what this is?' asked Ishita, making her hands into a fish.

Roohi simply stared.

'She is shy,' offered the father, thus ensuring the child's non-reaction.

Ishita looked around for inspiration. She could feel Raman observing her and that made her nervous.

'You know I teach in a school for poor children? And when they come for the first time, often they don't say anything. Not for days and days. They are scared also. Do you know why?'

The child slowly shook her head.

'They come from poor homes. Never been to school. Play in the streets, beg, work in their villages. Then you know what we do?'

Big brown eyes blinked solemnly at her.

'We take them on our laps like this'—she dragged Roohi onto her lap—'and then we show them birds and fishes like this. They sometimes don't know what they are. Do you?' Again Ishita made her hands into a fish.

'A fish.'

'And this?'

'A bird.'

'And this?'

'A dog?'

'Very good. And this?'

'I don't know. What?'

'A dog about to eat you up'—Ishita snapped her fingers over Roohi's nose. Roohi giggled. 'Now I am going to draw that dog so he can eat you up better.'

'No, not eat me up.'

'OK—it will eat me up—and then, let's see, what will I do?'

'What?'

'I'll just show you.'

Raman handed her a sheet of paper and a pen from his shirt pocket. Ishita sketched a figure, dupatta flapping, lost chappal, climbing up a tree, with a dog barking beneath. Thank God she could draw—in Jeevan sometimes she thought this her most important asset.

'Should I teach you? Or do you want to show me what you can do?'

A small hand was put out. Raman stared at his daughter's inept squiggles and fresh anger towards Shagun overcame him. He was dependent on strangers for a motherly touch—that was what she had reduced them to.

Roohi sat on Ishita's lap and drank her milk to the telling of a long and complicated tale. Then Ishita took her up the elevator to show her where she lived. Half an hour later she was returned to the fifth floor with a bindi and pink clips in hair freshly plaited.

Raman got ready to leave. 'Beta, thank Auntie,' instructed the father.

'Oh don't bother, she's just a child,' said Ishita.

'She has to learn her manners. Beta, thank Auntie, otherwise Auntie will not take you to her house again.'

'Thank you,' mumbled the girl into her father's shoulder.

And half asleep, she was taken away.

'Sit, sit, have another cup of tea,' pressed Mrs Kaushik.

Over tea, gossip began. The wife, the affair, the heart attack, the lawyer cousin, the court cases, visitation rights, the divorce, custody, the Dehradun Public Academy, Roohi, Arjun. There was a lot to tell. All the early promise of happiness in the son's life, the good job, the lovely wife, the son, the daughter, all wantonly destroyed.

The person Ishita had felt most sorry for was the little girl. She could still feel the childish fingers laced through her own.

*

Next time Raman visited his mother he asked, 'Why did she divorce?'

'Arre, why do people divorce these days? Shanti—her mother—was upset for so long. Apparently they were crude business types who found someone else with more dowry. Then they divorced her just like that. Ruined her life.'

'Arranged marriage?'

'Yes.'

'Doesn't sound quite right to me.'

'Well, you never know who is lying and who is not.'

'Why didn't she have children?'

'There was some trouble,' said Mrs Kaushik cautiously. 'I sent them to my astrologer. Things happened so quickly, I don't know . . .' Her voice trailed off.

No matter what, thought Raman in a rush of emotion, at least he had his children, no one could take them away from him, they were blood of his blood, flesh of his flesh. This girl—woman—had nothing.

To this extent, Exhibit A was successful.

But he didn't actually pick up the phone and contact her. Neither on this visit nor the next, which was when his mother decided to push things a little.

'What do you think of Ishita?'

'What should I think?'

'Roohi liked her.'

'Roohi likes everybody. She is an affectionate child,' said Raman mournfully.

'I thought she was very good with her. She works with children, you know.'

'She seemed very ordinary,' said the son, 'and Mummy, you can stop thinking whatever it is you are thinking. I have just done with one marriage, don't try and push me into another. I intend to devote my life to my children.'

'Of course, beta, of course. The children are the most important thing. But it is hard to be alone. A home needs a woman.'

'This is one home that will have to do without.'

But how long can a lonely, jilted man resist a woman so totally the opposite of his wife? A woman who has entertained his child and done her hair? And fed her when she fussed, and seemed to enjoy it? A woman who has been divorced, who has known rejection, misery and unhappiness? A woman who is casually thrown across his path by mothers who are working in tandem without a word exchanged.

Raman was essentially the giving sort. He could be friends with such a woman—they could compare notes, he thought dourly, their abandonment common ground between them.

Meanwhile Mrs Rajora was busy praying to her gods. She wanted to be first in line for any match that came for Raman. But she did not want to seem too pushy either.

'A man with two children, just divorced, it is not as though he is such a big catch,' said Ishita's father. 'They should be the ones asking us.'

'On what planet are you living? What kind of catch is your daughter?' The reality of the world was that all men were catches and only some women. That made the marriageable male–female ratio fragile, and the mother of a daughter constantly watchful.

'I am not going to agree to a match in which she will not be happy. We have had enough of that.'

Mrs Rajora let him talk. It was all nonsense what he was saying. Let the match first materialize, then they could worry about the happiness.

It was just as well she had retired, she could drop in on Mrs Kaushik more often. It was time to be more social in the building, participate in kitty parties, start playing housie and teen patti, move in the same female circles as her neighbour.

After Raman's divorce Mrs Kaushik's main desire was for a simple, home-loving girl to heal the wounds in her son's life.

To make sure Ishita justified the seal of her approval, she took the precaution of volunteering a few mornings at Jeevan. Seeing a person at work can reveal much.

She found it easy to teach slum kids elementary English. All the skills required were endless repetition, patience, and good-natured shouting. In between, her eye was firmly trained on Ishita, whose own opinion of Leela Kaushik was vastly improved by this one act of social kindness.

Mrs Kaushik found her previous impression strengthened. Capable, patient, even tender with the children, reliable and deferential around Mrs Hingorani, Ishita had the attractiveness of the sincere, the casual appearance of one who looked at the world rather than expecting the world to look at her. These are good qualities in a wife. And what was good in a wife was good for the family.

An added advantage to a building girl was that family bonds did not have to transplant themselves far. She could at last admit her envy of her brother-in-law, as the possibility increased of having a daughter-in-law like Rajni.

If something good could come out of the mutual battering she and Shanti had experienced through their children, that would be the silver lining she had heard much about but had yet to see.

Mr Kaushik figured out the lay of the land.

'I don't know why you encourage her to keep coming here,' he said, 'we are hardly in a position to matchmake. Raman is an adult, he can choose his own wife.'

'Right. You want to wait until another girl puts her claws into him, another faithless whore, who will charm you along with everyone else.'

'When will you learn to stop talking?' asked Mr Kaushik angrily.

Mrs Kaushik looked weepy; she couldn't bear it when her husband was harsh with her. In disgust Mr Kaushik got up, saying he had to buy milk and vegetables. There was always something to get in times of crisis.

Since all this started nothing had been the same, thought Mrs Kaushik mournfully as she heard the front door slam. Raman, Shagun, heart attack, hospitals, children, was there never going to be any hope of a normal life for them?

Mr Kaushik moodily loaded potatoes and onions into his basket at the Mother Dairy kiosk. He added a bunch of spinach, then half a kilo of tomatoes. They were somewhat squishy, his wife would go on about that, but he loved tomato pakoras. Crisp on the outside, soft and slightly sour on the inside. Along with the green coriander chutney that was still in the fridge.

Out of the corner of his eye he saw Ishita get down from a scooter. She hauled out a plastic packet from her large cloth shoulder bag and began purposefully poking at the apples.

'Hello, beti,' he said, approaching her.

Ishita looked up, allowing Mr Kaushik to regretfully survey her features. She had a wheatish complexion, a few scattered pimples, unremarkable black hair pulled into a bun low on her neck, eyes that were large enough, height average urban Indian five feet three inches. Her strongest points were her white even teeth and unselfconscious smile.

'How are you, Uncle?' she now said.

'I am buying vegetables for pakoras,' said Mr Kaushik, showing her his basket.

'And I apples. Papa is not allowed much sugar, but he is like a child, he has to eat sweets, no matter what the doctor says. That is why I make fruit bakes with just a little honey. Something for after dinner.' She smiled indulgently.

The girl had the heart of a homemaker. It was touching how she was looking after her parents. Dimly he remembered, somewhere in all the volumes of his wife's chatter, how much trouble there had been in this girl's personal life. Well, he could no longer be judgemental about divorce.

XXIV

In December that year a cyclone hit the eastern coast of India.

The media was full of stories of starving villagers, of

flooded homes, of cholera in camps, of the irreparable damage done to the soil by sea water, of the destruction of agriculture. Charity drives were organized for clothes, medicines, money, food, anything, everything.

Ishita spoke to Raman. One truck had already gone, but people were still eager to donate. Was he one such? Did he have anything for the next truck leaving in a few days?

Did he have anything? Indeed he had. He went home, opened cupboards he had not opened for months, looked at items he would rather not have seen. With ten thousand dead, lakhs more rendered homeless, the Orissa cyclone demanded an open heart. He gave and gave and gave.

I hope you can make use of these things, he said to Ishita.

But this is really very generous, very generous indeed, said Ishita confronted with eight huge bags parked near her door. Why don't you drop them off at the collection place outside the society office?

Raman's voice dropped, melodrama crept in. I am not sure all of it is suitable.

She had to ask what did he mean?

Go through them and see for yourself.

Normally so helpful, he departed, too distraught to even bring the bags inside.

For the next hour Ishita took out random items and gazed at them nonplussed. She called her mother to help sift through the jeans, the saris, the salwar kameezes, dupattas, even the handbags that lay strewn around the Rajora living room. A faint perfume rose from them, disturbing the sorters with its intrusive intimacy.

'Hai Ram,' said Mrs Rajora, 'is the man mad? Are they going to wear high heels in the flood?'

The rhinestone-embedded gold-and-silver strappy affairs lay insolently on their sides, while they imagined a once-upon-a-time wearer.

'Either he is using us to get rid of her stuff or he imagines the villagers so desperate that even heels will help,' went on Mrs Rajora doubtfully.

'He probably wasn't thinking. It must be his way of dealing with what she left behind,' said Ishita, preoccupied with her own sense of prying into another woman's life. Why hadn't she taken her things? Had she left in such a hurry? Felt so bad she couldn't return for them? Was she now so rich she didn't need them?

'Mummy, please can you sort these? I don't want to go through them.'

And so the job passed to the mother, who separated, organized and bundled them, gave some to the collection centre, gave some to her maid, gave some to the maid's daughter, along with a small suitcase to distribute as she liked in Mandavili.

Meanwhile the woman whose belongings were being distributed among the poor of India was at that moment sitting in New York at her husband's desk. It was early morning. Central Park lay before her, she could see the bare branches of various trees swaying briskly beneath a grey sky. It looked cold out there; the little radio that kept her company informed her of the possibility of a few snow flurries. Snow! Her children would love that.

The double-glazed windows kept the faint noise of the distant traffic out, and in the silence she could hear the water sloshing around in the dishwasher, a nice homely sound. She looked around her: would her mother be happy here? Certainly for a while. She would take her to the shopping centre, to nice restaurants, introduce her to the senior club they had in the apartment building. There was so much going on, only a moron would get bored in New York.

Take herself. She had already acquired a social circle, friends of Ashok and further on friends of friends. The wives were helpful in showing her around, something Ashok clearly appreciated. He wanted no unhappiness, no loneliness, no regret. And with such a large expat community she barely missed India. Trust Ashok to give her the best of two such different worlds.

She picked up her pen and began.

Mama dearest,

Next time I am in Delhi, I am going to buy a computer and make sure you learn how to use it. Everybody here communicates with India through e-mail. Just think—we will hear from each other every day—then no worries on either side.

If you insist I will get you a hearing aid, though I think it's nonsense that you cannot hear me on the phone. It's the cost that worries you—don't deny it. STOP converting dollars into rupees. We earn in dollars now, remember?

When you visit you will realize how young you are! Here women in their sixties think they are in the prime of life. Only in India are people considered old so quickly.

I can't wait for you to come. At night from our apartment windows you can see the city lights twinkling. In the day there is the Hudson River. When I am on my own I go to the Metropolitan, do a little shopping, at home I do all the things we had servants for in India. We are very cosy here. We cook together—it relaxes Ashok, then after dinner we usually go out.

The only thing that upsets me is seeing women with small kids. When the weather is fine, they are all over Central

Park, thank God it is getting colder. If I mention the children to Ashok he starts talking of the necessity of my working. I see no connection.

Ashok has had a word with someone in the embassy, and there will be no trouble with the visas. Raman will drop the children to your place the night before. I am glad Ami's son will drive you to the airport. We will buy Ami a nice present that will convert all her criticism of me into praise. Maybe a bottle of perfume with the price sticker attached. Let the worth of no gift go unnoticed.

Thank goodness Raman was co-operative enough to let me take the children first, even though it means Roo missing school. But then he knows he has everything to gain by remaining in my good books. Ashok is right, it doesn't do any good for divorced parents to be hostile to one another. Bad for the kids.

We will both be at the airport to receive you. I have bought toys for Roo and electronic games for Arjun. It was so nice to be able to do that!

Your loving daughter,

Shagun

Three weeks into the children's departure and Raman was still angry. Shagun had asked him to change the dates, in itself not such a big deal, but every careful distant word had been uttered as though she was doing him a favour.

It will be fun for all of you to be together for New Year, so I don't mind if you send them to me earlier. Later on it gets too cold, besides, they shouldn't have to spend time being outfitted for warm clothes so close to Christmas when shopping is a nightmare.

He had never heard such flimsy excuses. Clothes! As though she couldn't buy them ahead of time! She knew their sizes. No. Shagun did not want to be encumbered by her children on Millennium Eve. Why? Because she was probably headed towards some exotic location, perhaps Bali, where the newly-wed couple would kiss in the still turquoise waters of some lagoon that lapped gently against the steps of their exclusive villa.

It was not, not his concern, he told himself. They were separate, separate, separate, he had repeated as he drove his children to Alaknanda, their warmest clothes packed in a suitcase. How had Mrs Sabharwal arranged the visas? Again not his concern. No doubt there was a DPA alumnus who knew the main guy in the USA visa section.

What about his own millennium plans? Just about everyone he knew was planning to leave the city. A guy in his office was going to New Zealand so he could greet the New Year a few hours earlier than his fellow billion Indians. Another was going to London, another was going to be cruising in Hawaii, another was going to be in New York, in Times Square, the most happening place in the world, with the most happening party of all.

Newspapers made sure that their readers knew what every celebrity in the country intended to do that night. Mauritius, Maldives, Phuket, Bangkok, Paris, yachts, islands, cruises—anywhere so long as the glamour quotient was high. Special events were being hosted at clubs and hotels, shopping places were strung with lights. Plans, plans, plans.

He shook himself. It was the solitariness of the past weeks that was making him feel so low. The only thing that would allow him to feel better was the presence of his children, and there were still some days to go before he was scheduled to pick them up from Alaknanda. Then the whole world could go to Bali, along with his ex and he wouldn't give a damn. Not a damn.

He would gather everybody who was dear to him in his house, parents, children, relatives, and surrounded by the people he loved, ring in the millennium, and hope that every succeeding year in the new century was as happy.

*

Dearest Mama,

It is the middle of the night and I cannot sleep. My heart is full—but I don't want to disturb Ashok—he has a heavy day at work tomorrow.

It is so silent. It's only been three hours since I came home, but every minute screams of loss. Tomorrow Raman will come to get the children, and then you will feel a little of my loneliness. That's not a nice thing to say, is it? Sorry. But you will see them again in the next holidays before I do. Were Raman halfway decent he would make sure their contact with you continued but he is too petty.

If Ashok knew I was sitting here like this he would be quite hurt, especially after our dinner. He took me to this fabulous restaurant—he guessed I would need cheering up. We had the tasting menu. Tiny morsels of the most exquisite French food, with ribbons of sauce all around. The whole thing took three hours! And four kinds of wine: first white, then red, then a sweet dessert wine, then a cognac. Maybe that's why I can't sleep, too much to drink.

Now that you have been here, why is it so difficult for you to imagine yourself living with me? You are not comfortable with Ashok, that's it, no? Do you want him to give you homeopathy like Raman used to—pretending to be a doctor when he was no such thing?

How were Roo and Arjun during the flight? Ashok spent his extra miles on upgrades for all of you—he is always thinking of practical ways to make me happy.

Over dinner he again said I had to work. How that will stop me from missing my children, I don't know, but I mustn't grumble. Nobody gets everything, and if I had to do it all over again, I would.

Your loving daughter,

Shagun

*

The Kaushiks were united in wanting to make sure Raman's party overflowed with warmth and togetherness. The most important thing is family, they declared, when we have each other we have everything. His parents helped him plan the menu. To ensure a festive atmosphere he strung coloured lights around the tiny veranda off the drawing room, he bought small presents for Nandan's twins and his own children. A bottle of Black Label was ordered from the bootlegger—on this night he would serve only the best.

What about Ishita? Roohi would love to see her, his parents would approve, but he was not sure how Arjun would react. He didn't want to risk any tension, though in excluding her he knew he was being unfair, but he would explain it all to her later. After all, his children had just come back from their mother in New York.

Millennium Eve. The two Mrs Kaushiks came armed with food, Arjun really likes my shammi kebabs, Roohi loves my vadas, we will fry them here, they said, while the men drank and talked politics, and the children disappeared into another room. Raman fought away wistful memories of the times when the flat was always like this, full of life and children. He reminded himself instead of what he had. Through the nightmare months of divorce and custody his family had stood by him like buffers against the winds of misfortune. Nandan particularly had never charged him a paisa, nor ever complained about the time he had taken up. What gratitude was enough for this?

They drank, they ate, the children opened their presents. Then they decided to drive down to Rajpath to look at the lights. Crowds were gathered on the India Gate lawns. The car inched towards Rashtrapati Bhavan, the glittering dome looming between the smaller clusters of office buildings on each side.

There at the Beating Retreat stood camels. When Arjun was little they had taken him to hear it. Now Raman felt hesitant reminding his son of those long-ago family outings, everything in the present was working towards obscuring that past.

Soon the 31st would be over, thank God. He couldn't bear the hype around just another day. Millenniums were man-made. Was that dying light, the suddenly darkened sky, aware that it had been 2,000 years since Christ was born? The sun, the moon, the stars, so certain of their course, emanated their steady essence without fuss or fanfare, their regularity making them significant in the lives of men.

Crowds negotiated, traffic borne and patience held on to, at last they were home. The TV was switched on—let's see what the rest of the world is doing.

Time zone by time zone they were privy to party after almost identical party around the world. Roohi had fallen asleep in the car and was now in bed. They looked at their watches and at twelve there it was, the new millennium. The roads outside erupted in yells, screams, toots, whistles. On and on, the sound of revelry.

At last, 1999 was over.

The relatives left looking tired. Now he and Arjun were the awake ones, the TV gazers.

'When are they going to show New York?' asked the boy.

'New York is ten-and-a-half hours behind us, beta. It is still daylight there. You can get up in the morning and watch. Now go to bed.'

The boy just remained, sleep in his eyes, secretiveness on his face.

'Is there something in particular you are looking for?'

No reply. Flick flick with the remote, that was all.

'As you can see, they are not focusing on individual people. Only crowds.'

Just then the camera zoomed in on one swaying woman in Cairo. Arjun looked reproachfully at his father.

'That woman is performing. In Cairo. On a stage.'

He knew his mother would be at Times Square that night, witness to the lowering of the crystal ball. Be sure to watch it, beta, I will try and stand where the cameras are, and wave to you on the eve of this new millennium, my darling boy. It will be a link between you and me. I miss you so much.

'Your mother will be in Times Square?'

Arjun nodded.

'Along with thousands of others. I doubt you will see her on TV.'

'Papa, please. I feel like watching.'

Raman got the boy's quilt and pillow and arranged them around him on the sofa, then put most of the lights off. The sounds from the TV filled the room, attracting Arjun's drowsy, staring eyes. He was going to be disappointed and there was not a thing his father could do.

In the morning he found his son sleeping on the sofa, the remote near his pillow, the TV on, images from New Year festivities still being displayed.

Ishita also spent Millennium Eve in front of the TV with her parents. She was somewhat withdrawn and her mother looked at her worriedly.

It was cold outside, but still the celebratory noises continued relentlessly. The Society had hosted a dinner, and there had been a fire. Many had stood around it, but the Kaushiks could not be seen among the people looking at the flames. Ishita searched, then despised herself for searching. She could see Mrs Hingorani, the fire flickering over the features she loved, but she didn't want to go and talk to her. At this moment her lonely heart demanded a father and a child and nobody else would do.

Mrs Kaushik had told her mother that in two weeks Arjun would be back in school. Then maybe Raman would come over with Roo, but she was not sure she wanted to see him if she was just a convenient auntie for his daughter, someone who would amuse her while they visited. If that was the case, she must watch herself, she was in danger of growing too fond of essentially borrowed goods.

It was a long and mostly silent trip to Dehradun with Arjun strapped into the front seat, looking out of the window, Raman driving the six hours with the usual heavy heart that accompanied him on this journey.

They stopped at Cheetal for lunch. Arjun banged his legs against the white plastic chair and ordered chicken tikka roll. Raman had the same.

'You will miss such food,' he remarked.

'It's all right.'

'I will come and visit you.'

Arjun didn't say anything and Raman wondered why he felt the need to say 'I will come and visit you' quite so often.

'Did you go out much with Ashok Uncle when you were in New York?'

'Some. Mostly Mama. Naani was there too.'

Mrs Sabharwal in New York? Why not? She was Shagun's mother, it was natural that she should visit her newly married daughter, natural, only natural. He should stop asking Arjun questions. There were some things it was better not to know.

'We all went to Niagara once,' continued Arjun, bits of onion falling from his mouth. 'Roohi was scared.'

'Poor thing. I imagine the water makes a lot of noise.'

'Like thunder. You haven't seen them?'

No, Raman hadn't. So Arjun must tell him about the falls. Were they as wonderful as people said?

Yes, they were.

'What else did you do? Lots of things going on in New York?'

'Yes. We went to a show.'

'Which one?'

'*The Lion King*.'

'Broadway?'

'Ya. It's walking distance from us. It was so cool.'

'Didn't Roo get tired?'

'Roo wasn't there. She was home with Mama.'

'Oh?'

'Yes—Mama says she is too young to be taken to such places. She needs her bedtime.'

'Then who did you go with?'

'Some people.' And that was all that Arjun would say.

From this Raman had to gather what he could. Although Arjun was reluctant to share his experiences, he had learned enough to depress him thoroughly.

Mama dearest!

Happy 2000! Did you get my card? And the flowers I sent? Did you eat the Christmas cake? What did you do on New Year's Eve? Go to bed as usual? Did Ami come over?

Millennium Eve was everything one could possibly possibly wish for. Sometimes I feel so happy, Mama, I wonder how I am among the lucky ones. We were in Times Square when this huge glittering ball descended. Everybody was screaming and dancing—Ashok and I danced too, he said he would never have gone to such a tamasha if it hadn't been for me. His idea of a party is getting together with some colleagues and discussing The Brand! He says I have given him a new lease of life, that now is the time for him to cash in on years of dedication to the company.

We are thinking of renting a little cottage on a lake in New England for a month in the summer when the children come next. You will love it, Mama! There is so much beauty in America.

Ashok says he will go canoeing with Arjun. I will teach Roo how to swim. High time she learned. She tends to be timid but once I introduce her to sports she will improve.

Look at me! It is only January, and I am already talking of the next visit. Ashok is a great believer in planning. Plan A, then Plan B—the back-up plan. Do you know what the back-up plan was if I did not get a divorce? Relocate in India! Imagine—when he has lived most of his life abroad! Do you think I should believe him?

Your loving daughter,

Shagun

XXV

Back from Dehradun, one of the first things Raman did was to go over to Swarg Nivas and see Ishita.

'How are you?' she started, polite and careful.

Raman could hear the hurt, justified from a certain perspective.

'I hope your new year went well?' she went on valiantly in the face of his silence.

Fine, considering the circumstances. A month ago his children had returned from their trip to their mother in America, and from then on they had been difficult to deal with. Roo tended to whine and fuss, Arjun's behaviour was unpredictable. He could not give them glamour, but he could give them stability and love, and he had spent the past month trying to do just that.

'I am sorry,' said Ishita, slightly flummoxed.

'What for? Nothing in this is your fault.'

'Yes, but you are such a good man, such a caring father that it is upsetting to see you miserable.'

Raman sighed. Such insights into his character were very welcome. Dropping Arjun to DPA always left him a residue of pain to deal with, he said.

Didn't he think that was the right place for his son?

'Oh, it might be for all I know. Ashok got him into this place, and along with other factors, I feel my son growing away from me and I don't know how to stop it, that's all.'

A weight lifted from Ishita's heart. This is what she had hoped for, that there were problems; that Raman wasn't so happy with his children that their presence obliterated her. More confidently she now said, 'I was hoping to meet Arjun.'

'I was also hoping. But things have changed. Now I feel there is a reporter lurking in my son, he sees things through his mother's eyes. He is too young to be doing this. It makes him judgemental and as a result he can seem older than he is.'

'It's hard,' observed Ishita invitingly.

'And then it is tricky between him and Roo. He understands more of what is going on, resents our divorce, takes it out on his sister, but she is just a baby.'

'Indeed, she is.'

'Yet if I scold him all the time, he will obviously mind.'

'There is that danger, yes.'

'When I am alone with him, it's fine. But when Roo is there, he just lashes out, I don't know why, though I imagine it has to do with the divorce. I can only trust it won't cause any lasting damage.'

'Um.'

'Sorry to bore you.'

He was not boring her, she was just wondering how to help. Actually, children were enormously resilient. If he could just see her slum kids, abused from morning to night, yet they had this pliancy, this optimism—they were so different from adults—it was working with them that made her want to adopt—

Oh really? She had wanted to adopt?

Yes, but hadn't done it yet. Her parents had asked her to wait a year, hoping no doubt she would get married. But now that time was almost over. She did want the experience of being a full-time mother. Take Roohi, whenever she went away she felt sad, nobody's fault of course, but she felt sad nonetheless.

Raman looked thoughtful.

And so the ball rolled between them.

It took a few more months, a few more casual meetings, and many hours of prayer on the part of their mothers, but it became as natural for Raman to meet Ishita once he was in Swarg Nivas as it was for him to meet his parents. He would dial the number of her flat on the intercom the minute he came.

Would she like to come over? He was here with Roohi.

The fact that it was always Roohi was fine with Ishita. Her pleasure in the child's company was unambiguous, while Roohi herself was forthcoming with the many things she wanted to show Auntie. Her Barbie, her books, her new hair clips, a print of her hands she had made in art class, a clay blob, which she said was a bird.

One evening found Roohi in Ishita's lap, and such was the child's insistence that she would not leave Auntie that Raman offered to take Ishita home and give her dinner if such a thing was acceptable.

'Of course it is acceptable,' said Mrs Kaushik.

'I don't know, Auntie,' said Ishita, feeling shy. 'Mummy is waiting for me.'

'Arre, Uncle will tell your mother, don't worry, beta.'

Ishita looked at Mr Kaushik, and in that timid, hesitant look the man for the first time forgot the blue-green eyes of his erstwhile daughter-in-law. 'Yes, yes, beta, I'll tell them.'

With Roohi cradled in her arms, Ishita sat in the front seat.

'Is she heavy?' enquired Raman tenderly.

'Poor thing, she can never be heavy for me. You know how much I miss her.'

'She has had so many upheavals in her life.'

'Well, at least she has learned to cope. Does she talk about her mother a lot?'

'Not really.'

'Today she drew a picture of a happy family—mother, father, brother, sister. My heart bled for her.'

'Yeah. Nice dream. It was mine as well.'

'Mine too.'

'I can see you are very fond of children.'

'Yes.'

'Your first husband did not want?'

'He did. That was the whole problem, because I couldn't have. Some childhood illness I didn't know about. They accused me of marrying under false pretences. It was horrible.'

'How long were you married?'

'Four years and a bit.'

'That's nothing.'

'True.'

'If you are married for longer, the roots are deeper, there is more violence in plucking them out.'

'I suppose. Never thought of it that way.'

'Yes. Well.'

'Listen, don't worry about Roo. She is going to be fine.'

'Nice fate. To live with whatever circumstances adults throw at her.'

'At least they all love her. That's one good thing.'

Raman sighed. What was he thinking? wondered Ishita anxiously. Was he remembering another woman who sat next to him in all her exquisiteness?

'She is very fond of you,' remarked Raman after a while, thinking he hadn't given Ishita her due.

'It's mutual,' Ishita said in the long pause that followed. By now they had turned into the side road that led to Mor Vihar. They stopped outside the house and Raman ran around to help Ishita with the still-sleeping child.

'Thank goodness I fed her, but she was very fussy with her food. I hope she is not falling sick,' said Ishita as Raman carried his daughter indoors.

'I hope not. I don't know what I'll do then.'

'Send her to me,' laughed Ishita.

Why should he be surprised at the happiness he felt at this?

*

Ishita looked around. Instead of the spectacular living arrangements she had imagined, she saw a spacious flat, neat but bland, with ordinary furniture.

Raman noticed her gaze. 'I am afraid everything is a mess. Ganga and Ganesh tend to get a little lazy when there is no supervision. When I am home I prefer to spend all my time with Roohi rather than worrying about the house.'

'Not at all. It is very nicely kept.'

'It's a company rental, not really my own.'

'Don't your parents mind your living so far?'

'In the early days I used to fall sick from staying in office late and commuting long hours. They were the ones to suggest I stay nearer work. Then after I married, well . . . it just continued . . . I don't know.'

'Umm.'

'Would you like a drink?'

'Love one.'

'Beer?'

'Vodka with lemon?'

She sensed his surprise.

'Mummy and Papa don't know I drink, they would be horrified. We used to drink sometimes when we went to friends' houses when the elders were not around.'

He gathered she was talking of her old life. Angrily he thought of that spineless husband, pressurized into divorcing a wife just because she had a womb that didn't function. He said as much.

She gave a small smile. His was not the common thinking, she assured him. Even she felt they had reason. The family wanted a child, she couldn't produce one. And they had paid for some expensive fertility treatments.

Raman fell silent. Who was he to hold the torch on someone else's behalf, when the light in his own home was so feeble?

They sipped their drinks.

'Should we order a pizza?' he asked after a while.

'Doesn't Ganesh cook for you?'

'When I tell him to. If you prefer home food, Ganesh can make an omelette. He makes very good omelettes.'

She wondered how often Ganesh's cooking skills were employed.

'Anything, I will take anything.'

But it turned out there were no eggs, so pizza was ordered instead.

'I can't think how I forgot to order eggs. He is supposed to remind me.'

'I love pizza too.'

Raman turned to her. She smiled, the ice went tinkle tinkle in her glass, giving her a feeling of daring, enhanced when he switched off the lamp next to the sofa. His arms went around her, hesitantly she opened her mouth to him. Their vodka breaths mixed, he could taste the lemony alcohol on her tongue.

The curtains were not yet drawn, the room was lit by the white neon lights of the street. Gently Raman pushed Ishita down on the sofa. Their bodies were new to each other, and he could sense her hesitation, feel the rigidity of her legs. Tentatively he explored her clothed breasts, kissed her face, whispered her name.

Half an hour later the bell rang. It was the pizza delivery boy.

The box was flung open, slices put on plates, and the hungry couple fell to. Such cosy domesticity made this a far more erotic moment for Ishita than any on the sofa.

It had never been like this with SK. Never just the two of them, because always the whole family had to be considered.

They couldn't order pizza, because the parents-in-law didn't eat it, and to leave them out was unthinkable.

The last slice finished, the last gulp of Coke consumed, the vodka returned to the drinks cabinet and back to the sofa. It was now the smell of onions and tomato spices that mingled in their mouths as they kissed. The absence of servants made them less inhibited.

Should they or shouldn't they? If they did, would it arouse commitment expectations? Raman knew the girl was traditional and he wanted to cause no unhappiness.

For Ishita, what were the implications? Perhaps he would not respect her afterwards, but equally it was time to filter such fears out of her head. Instinctively she knew he was not prepared to give much more than his body. She considered this—as dispassionately as two glasses of vodka would allow her—then turned to him, and this time she was the one who put out the light, she was the one who, a few minutes later, asked if a bed was available.

Two hours later Ishita returned home. Her mother was waiting.

'Why did you take so long? It's late.'

'So what? I am thirty-two.'

'So? That is still young.'

'Mummy, please, leave me alone.'

That night Ishita couldn't sleep. It had been five years since a man had touched her. Five years. She felt like a young girl. Her mother thought she should be careful, but for what? Had she not responded to Raman was there any guarantee that more happiness would come her way?

This had been her second man. It made her feel worldly and sophisticated. Even if the relationship were to end tonight she would still be the richer. Not to mention all the love she had received from Roohi. She thought of the little arms around her neck, her weight on her lap, the smell of her breath, the smooth pink lips glistening with a sliver of drool, the baby-white teeth. For those moments in the car she had allowed herself to feel she was the child's mother, with an intimate connection to the man sitting next to her.

Well, everybody had to have their few moments in the sun. Those had been hers. She had given herself so easily to Raman to prolong the fantasy.

Being with him was like having a taste of what every woman she was ever jealous of had. A man and a child. People to look after and care for, people who loved you in return. Among her acquaintances she was the sole childless divorcee. Even her ex-husband was now the proud father of two boys.

She decided not to tell her mother. Though she would be pleased at the romantic turn her interaction with Raman had taken, she would immediately start fretting about marriage. Her mother didn't understand courtship. Sex, romance, love had their place but only after the engagement had taken place and the wedding date fixed.

Raman too couldn't sleep. He found himself feeling protective of Ishita in a way he never had with Shagun. Even after years of marriage he had always been the supplicant, worshipping at the altar of her beauty, never ceasing to be grateful that she was his.

How many hours had he spent trying to decipher his wife's thoughts? Was she in a good mood, was she dissatisfied or happy? He had wanted to know her inside out, but she had remained an enigma. She had taken all his youth, his passion, what was there left to give another woman? Take tonight—he and Ishita had made love, whereupon he proceeded to obsess about his ex-wife.

Mrs Rajora also lay awake. She had recognized the withdrawn look on Ishita's face, a look that suggested secrets. The nature of those had to be either romantic or sexual—both transgressive for a girl in Ishita's position. If they continued to see each other, even with Roohi as ostensible chaperone, and it all came to nothing her daughter's future would be ruined along with her reputation.

In a few years Ishita's 5 lakhs would have doubled to 10. She could never think of this sum, unperturbedly increasing as the days passed, without a frisson of excitement. But 10 lakhs was nothing for a man in a multinational. Richer divorcees were prowling the field.

Her husband was no help; 'I'm not asking anybody to take my girl. If the Kaushiks are keen they can come with a proposal.'

That meant he was relying on them to fall in love.

'Always taking the easy way out,' she muttered.

'Well, you tell me, what would you like me to do?' he countered.

'I want you to be concerned about your daughter's future.'

'You have worried about her future these past five years, what good did it do?'

'I have also prayed for five years and it has made a boy like Raman see Ishita's qualities.'

Mr Rajora looked at his wife with weariness. If Ishita married, at least he would be spared the drama he was treated to so often.

Her maternal antennae up, Mrs Rajora watched her daughter, watched the colour come into her face, watched the way the beauty parlour gave her a soft perm that added body and curl to her hair, watched the new clothes and the care taken over appearance.

A mother's love will dig in the stoniest of soils. Mrs Rajora waited for Ishita to be at work before she began. She opened her cupboard, felt under the clothes, her bathroom shelf, her drawers, looking, looking for something that would give her a clue.

As she searched she wondered, where should her attention be focused? No birth control needed for her daughter, so none of that. Sexy underwear, that her daughter was too good to indulge in—presents from Raman—a possibility. Maybe some note, a letter? A diary?

No. Intimacy, imagined or otherwise, had not inspired the pen of either party.

She fumbled beneath a pile of woollens, when she touched something hard. Nestling at the very back was a big bottle of J'Adore perfume still in its white box. Christian Dior. Expensive.

Ishita could not afford to buy such things, therefore it had to be a present. A present without the ritual of showing, examining, assessing the price.

The girl appeared in the late afternoon. The mother let her have her lunch. Then she let her have her nap. Then she let her have her tea, in fact she brought it with her own faithful hands.

'I found a bottle of perfume in your cupboard. Looked costly.'

'Why were you looking in my cupboard?'

'The dhobi came. I had to put your clothes away, didn't I?'

'The perfume was in the back, under my shawls. You would not have found it unless you were looking.'

'Beta, never mind that. I only want to be sure that you are not doing anything to harm yourself. Once we were friends, since when have we become enemies?'

Ishita stirred the sugar in her tea.

'Beta, say something. I have stood by you, suffered, and you keep secrets.'

'Mummy, please. There is nothing to tell. I am not doing anything to ruin my life. I am thirty-two, Mummy, *please*.'

Mrs Rajora looked wounded, while Ishita got up to leave as she always did in these circumstances. She made her way into the little park, to sit on a cement bench.

Around her were the long dark dried leaves of the amaltas tree; another week and the branches would be completely bare. There was still a slight chill in the evening air, but Holi was around the corner, and after that the long unrelenting months of summer. She could see men and women taking their evening walk, briskly round and round the many apartment blocks of the society complex.

How she hated every narrow-minded conservative individual around her. Swarg Nivas indeed, it was just hell, full of nosy people who made it their collective business to know what she was doing every day of her life.

Easy game. Careful, careful, divorcees were easy game. That's what her parents thought—but in all these five years she had yet to come across anyone who thought she was any kind of game, easy or otherwise.

She stared at the tall buildings outlined against the never completely dark sky. She didn't like the clandestine part. It made her relationship seem insubstantial, more fraught. Yet, till Raman declared himself, what could she say to anybody? She just had to go on thinking that she had nothing to lose, that whatever romance she got was worth the risks she was taking. So far as love was concerned, she was a beggar, and beggars can't be choosers.

In what way could she make her mother understand? For her she was still a princess, albeit a somewhat tarnished one.

XXVI

The summer of 2000.

It is time for the children to visit their mother.

Ishita knows some anxiety. With Roo gone, how much will they meet? Even though they are lovers now, she doesn't want to presume.

'I will miss Roo.' She finds it easier to work through the girl.

'I won't,' he replies.

'You won't?'

'No, I need some time with you. The two of you are always clinging to each other.'

A bashful love gleams from Ishita's face.

*

A week into the children's departure and it was clear that Raman intended this to be playtime.

'Did you ever assume a position besides the missionary with your husband?' he asked.

She reddened and hung her head. He had found her wanting.

'Tell me.' He turned her face towards him. 'Why are you feeling shy?'

'Some things you don't talk about.'

'What? Where did you get that idea?'

Where? From her upbringing, of course. Everybody knew what decent girls should and shouldn't do.

It was Raman's task to remove these ideas from her head.

He gave her long lectures on pleasure, on the right to experiment with their bodies as they pleased—if there was anything she didn't like, she only had to say. And by the way, just how incompetent had her husband been? Had he ever left his mother's lap?

She blushed again and refused to answer. But though it was hard for him to get her to fantasize, or to take initiatives, she proved an adept pupil otherwise. When he hesitantly introduced her to oral sex, it was clear how willing she was to learn.

Once moved by passion, he was also moved to make a comparison between her and Shagun: 'She was an ice queen compared to you. What a fool that SK of yours was. Don't you think so? At least now?'

She nodded. Her present activities made her relationship with SK seem childlike. A child's directness, a child's lack of subtlety. How she had learned to be so uninhibited, she didn't know, but she imagined it had to do with some deeply reassuring quality in Raman; whatever she did, he would never judge her.

*

Flicking channels one night in Raman's house, they came across the Miss Everywhere beauty contest.

'Lots of Indians are winning these things,' remarked Ishita.

Raman looked at her: so?

'I wonder what it is like to be really beautiful,' she went on. 'The most beautiful in the universe.'

'It's like nothing. It's what's inside that matters.'

'That's poor consolation. You watch. This woman will go on to become a film star, and all the world will run after her. They won't think of what is inside, it's only people like me who have to think that.'

'It's a company that runs these beauty pageants, they have a profit motive. I know how commerce works—lots of hype—some substance, sure, but it's blown all out of proportion. She will have a string of affairs, essentially withhold herself, drive many men crazy, because it will be too constricting for her to be confined to one man.'

Was he talking about Miss Everywhere or the ex-wife?

'And that is why you are more attractive. You don't play games, you are what you seem, you have a heart and a soul.'

He bent to kiss her. The intensity of her response made him feel like a pasha. In the unexamined shadows of his heart, it pleased him that she was so insecure.

Ishita's lies at home grew more fluent. She was going to spend the night here, there, with this friend and that, unconvincing plans, but necessary as face-saving devices.

'I wish my mother wouldn't worry so much. It's hard for her, I know, but I am thirty-two,' said Ishita to Raman. 'She knows I am lying, but still I have to do it.'

'Does she mind a lot?' asked Raman, shifting his weight so he didn't press down on her too much.

Ishita rolled her eyes. 'If only you knew. On and on she goes—neighbours, reputation, vulnerable position. At my age why should I bother about anybody?'

Raman glanced speculatively at his lover, plain-featured like him, the same sallow complexion, but with a smile that lit her whole face. If marriages were between soulmates, this woman whose body he was even now preparing to enter for the third time was more naturally his partner.

What would his children think if they got married? Roohi loved her, that he knew, but there was Arjun to consider. He was so close to his mother, he was not going to accept a replacement easily.

'You also worry too much,' said Ishita. She drew his tongue into her mouth, and wrapped her legs around his back. Raman groaned, shut his eyes, clung to her body, raking her skin with his nails, printing trophies which she would stare at in her bathroom mirror, reliving every moment spent acquiring them.

Mrs Hingorani marked the change in her.

'Beti, you are looking happy.'

Ishita looked down and fiddled with her dupatta. Was her joy really so transparent?

A little later she did feel at liberty to treat Mrs Hingorani to a small panegyric on Raman's virtues, followed by how adorable his daughter was. Of Arjun she said nothing.

Shortly afterwards, Raman suggested they go to Tanishq to pick a ring. He reached out and held her hand. 'We both have a better chance of happiness this time round, don't you think?'

She allowed herself a small nod, yes, she did think. For months he and Roo had been firmly lodged in her heart. As she confessed this she reddened; for a woman like Ishita, saying things was tantamount to feeling them less—emotions clothed in words lost something in the transaction.

Neither mentioned the word love, but in the days that followed Ishita's sexual initiatives grew more abandoned, her passion more intense. He responded with ardour, and when they entered the shop in Connaught Place it was with an air of mutual self-satisfaction.

'A ring,' announced Raman to the salesman.

'What price range, Sir?'

At jewellery counters unfortunately love needs to be translated into rupees.

'Any price range,' said Raman grandly. Those words were more important to Ishita than the diamonds they indicated.

They settled on a mid-range one for 30,000. The diamonds were VVS1, their colour G-H, and though small, cunningly clustered in a way that made them look larger. On Ishita's hand true love sparkled.

When Raman dropped her off at a scooter stand, she went back to gazing at her ring, turning her hand, admiring its tiny glints. It was much nicer than the big ugly thing she had had the first time round, a solid lump of gold with many inferior yellow-grade diamonds plastered over it. This was delicate, refined, simple, elegant. Reluctantly she took it off in the elevator and tucked it inside her bra. It was her sweet secret.

Raman insisted upon concealment. 'I don't want her to know. Don't tell anybody.'

'But you told me she is married by now.'

'She might use it as an excuse to take Roohi.'

'How?'

'Saying stepmother and all.'

'Is that what Nandan says?'

'No.'

'Then? Besides, you have an agreement.'

'You think she is like you, but she's not. Laws are nothing to her.'

'Still, what can she do?'

'You don't know her.'

'Please, please let me tell my parents, please. It won't go further and will make them happy. They have suffered so much because of me.'

After a lot of sex he agreed reluctantly.

'I kept waiting and waiting for you last night. Where were you?' asked her mother.

They both knew where she was.

It was breakfast time.

They were sitting around the dining table squeezed against a corner of the room. As Ishita wiped her parantha against the last little bit of white butter on her plate, sucked the last little bit of mango pickle dry, she thought her news would in a small way compensate her mother for all the years of devoted care.

'Mummy?'

'Beta?'

'I have something to tell both of you.'

'Good news?'

'For once. But it is a big, big secret. He is very apprehensive of his ex-wife coming to know.'

'He has proposed?'

'Yes.'

'When? When? Oh, I knew this would happen, I knew it. You could not be so self-sacrificing for nothing, care for all those slum children for nothing.'

'Beta, congratulations.'

'Thank you, Papa.'

'He is a good man. Straight, mature, responsible.'

There were tears in Mrs Rajora's eyes. It was a miracle that her daughter had got this chance of returning to the status so rudely snatched from her.

'Does Roo know?'

'Not yet. Raman gets very tense about anything to do with the children.'

'Hai Ram, the man has a heart of a girl.'

'Mama, you don't know what all he has been through. She poisons them against him, especially Arjun. Thank God he is in boarding school.'

'So when is he going to tell the boy?'

'Probably never. Because of *her*.'

Mrs Rajora thought that the more people knew, the more secure her daughter's prospects. She didn't approve of this hole-in-corner stuff, it smacked of the insincere. Raman was divorced, even if his ex-wife were to know, what could she do? With all the haste she herself had shown, why should she care about Raman's own plans?

Ishita took to dropping in on Mrs Kaushik, who in her mind was her mother-in-law. And Mrs Kaushik welcomed her, inviting her over when it was her turn to host a kitty party, watching the ease with which she mingled with the other aunties. This was something she had never done with Shagun, there had never been an opportunity.

*

Uneasiness marred Raman's pleasure in his engagement. He would be a fool to trust to the permanence of love: it changed, that was its nature. But Ishita was a steady girl, and he made an effort to enjoy his courtship, though in a cautious, discreet way. But one area where he couldn't be cautious or discreet was in the matter of the flesh. The fact that he was an object of so much desire to Ishita, that a cross word could create sorrow, that she strove to please him, that he and his daughter were becoming the light of her life—all this made him want to respond in kind.

Slowly his flat registered the changes in his life.

'Why do you have so many pictures of her?' Ishita demanded.

'Do I?' he asked. He looked blankly at his bedside table, at the bridal Shagun, at the two of them mounted on their wedding-reception thrones.

'Not only here,' she elaborated, 'but downstairs as well. With her and the children, you two, alone, then with the parents . . .'

There was no need for her to go on. The documents of a family that had produced his children were engraved in his heart. Those pictures were his past, what good would it do to remove them? 'I keep them for the children's sake.'

'I know, darling, I know. But do you think they need to be reminded daily that their mother has deserted them?'

She could feel him shrink, but she forced herself to go on. Just like you needed to clear the ground to build a house, so in relationships too ground had to be cleared. 'Roohi was saying the other day, don't go, Auntie, stay with me. Poor thing, she must be afraid that I will also disappear. But Roohi is like my own, how can I ever leave her?'

Whenever Ishita talked of Roohi, the words fell like balm into Raman's ears. 'I hope', she continued, 'that the child will not be torn between her biological mother and me.'

'Why should she be? Children are not so complicated.'

'Oh, you don't know how their minds work. She may believe that it will be disloyal to love someone else. After all, how many mothers can a child have?'

How many?

The answer depended on Raman.

His mind went back to the moment in July when he had picked up his children from Mrs Sabharwal's. It had been wonderful to see them looking so well, and that pleasure continued till Arjun left for Dehradun.

Whether it was this departure that triggered the stress, Raman didn't know, but every night Roohi wet her bed. He would find the mattress soaked through, her legs curled up, shivering in the AC-cooled air. He bought a thick plastic sheet to place under her and started sleeping with the child.

Had she come to some harm in the US? Was she missing her mother? Bit by bit he coaxed his daughter to talk about her summer.

What was the uncle like? Was he OK?

The uncle usually drew a blank look from Roohi.

What about Mama? Did they spend a lot of time together?

She nodded. Books, they had read books, swum in the lake, stayed in a hut just like the one in Three Little Piggies.

Three Little Piggies?

Yes. Only the wolf was going to come to huff and puff and blow it all down. That was why they had to leave to catch the plane and come here, because the wolf might eat them up. But Mama was left behind.

Here Roohi started to cry.

Raman imagined the grief at this parting, the story that had been told to facilitate such a separation. Was Shagun equally distressed? He doubted it. And with what rubbish had they filled the child's head? It was not enough to demand this insane to and froing across the world with the inept Mrs Sabharwal, they also had to frighten her to bits.

Each night he held her, through each tear and whimper. As he felt the thin body tremble next to his chest he thought of how much he loved his daughter and how inadequate that love had been so far as her protection was concerned.

She had just turned four. Her mother must have celebrated her birthday in very different circumstances from his own treat last year on the beach. Both events had one parent missing and the result was a child who cried and wet her bed at night. He found himself hating Shagun for the damage done to his baby.

What had Ishita said, how many mothers can a child have? Where could a child as young as Roohi place her trust? The least he could do was to ensure that the next time around that place was solid and secure.

He started by replacing the pictures, selecting photos of the children, getting them blown up and framed. Arjun in DPA receiving a medal for athletics, Roohi on sports day. The grandparents on his side increased, the grandmother on her side removed along with the errant daughter. In a few months, new narratives were in place on the walls and tables.

*

Raman's pain was now Ishita's, his hesitations entirely understandable. She would heal him, teach him to trust. Every time they made love she felt the renewal of his commitment. He could not have enough of her, and she, she would serve him with her life.

'What have I done to deserve such devotion?' he once asked. In truth he had done nothing, he owed her devotion entirely to the fact that he was not Suryakanta.

The day did come when Raman suggested they apply for a marriage licence, and when a month was over, get married in court. He made it absolutely clear that he wanted no fuss. They would tell their parents after it was all over, everything was to be as different as possible from their first times.

To the superstitious pair, that was one indicator of the success of the present venture.

Ishita felt a bit strange, being so free from family in this important moment. Uncomfortably she wondered if her new in-laws would blame her for their exclusion.

'Don't be silly, I will tell them myself,' said Raman.

With that she had to be content.

It took two hours at Tees Hazari for them to be married.

As they walked down the corridor Raman's attention was caught by the bridal rose colour of his wife's salwar kameez and he decided on rage. These courts had been the scene of his greatest humiliation, his deepest misery, and here was Ishita dressing up in pink. Maybe women were all the same, maybe he was making a big mistake, it had been fine just him and his children. They were the most important thing in his life, not fulfilment with some woman.

Ishita was aware of his distance, and felt immediately miserable. Whatever he was thinking, it was sure to be something against her, otherwise he would have shared his feelings.

They emerged into the parking lot.

'I hope this doesn't come as a shock to the children,' said Raman.

If he was trying to wound his wife he succeeded. She didn't expect a whole lot, but some words of love just after they had signed the register would have been welcome. Was he already regretting his choice?

'Our parents will be glad,' she replied carefully.

She put a tentative hand through his arm. He pressed it. She could feel his solid warmness, knew that together they could create a happiness Raman would not be able to deny, no matter what he was feeling now. He too had been tossed on stormy marital seas, such vessels liked to rest quietly.

'Are you all right?' she asked in the car.

'I'm fine. Anxious about the children.'

Again there was nothing to say. Time would show that the step he had taken was the right one, she had to be patient.

'You can stop worrying about me now, I am married.'

Mrs Rajora was in the kitchen, tending to the chickpeas in the pressure cooker, when the daughter announced this. As her jaw dropped, the pressure cooker whistle blew. 'What?'

'Married.'

'Where? How? Why so hush-hush? Are you sure?'

Marriage. That sacred word. Back and forth it went, it could not be said enough. Finally the whole story told, the need for subterfuge explained (husband's paranoia—what could the wife do?).

They acquiesced. What could a wife do?

But here, see, here was the paper to prove it. Yes, this very morning, when they thought she was going to work, she was actually driving to court, that was the way he wanted it, she repeated again and again, the way he wanted it.

They all agreed, as they sat excitedly round cups of tea and biscuits, that the man was very sensitive, but his present marriage would help him recover his equilibrium and face the world with confidence.

Her new son-in-law had too much tension, declared Mrs Rajora. One had only to look at his health history to know this, and in that case, yes, their daughter had no option but to listen to him. He had proved his intentions honourable, so much was forgiven.

In another part of the building things were not as smooth. Such clandestine behaviour could not be regarded so indulgently, this was the son of the family, another woman was involved, ownership issues were at stake.

As he tried to pacify them, Raman marvelled at the storm created over someone they had always approved of.

Eventually the owners calmed down. Where was she?

Telling her parents.

Ha! They must have known. The parents of a girl not knowing? What world do you live in? So innocent you are.

Raman was sick of talking, explaining, justifying. He just wanted things to be normal. A simple, predictable, boring life, filled with the humdrum of the usual, this was his heart's desire.

'Call her,' demanded Mrs Kaushik. 'I must see my new daughter-in-law, even if you think there is no need.'

Ishita was summoned over the intercom, and came running over in one minute flat, bending down to touch the feet of her new in-laws the moment she entered the door.

'Beti, why did you listen to him? What is the need for all this secret-vekret?'

And for the first time Ishita said Ma. Ma, Papa, please forgive us. We cannot live without your blessings. A few more hours and both sets of parents had exhausted every reaction, blame, recrimination, wonder, congratulations, happiness.

It became time for Ishita to leave with Raman.

'Is that all?' her husband joked as he picked up the tote bag.

'I can come back for my things.'

She didn't tell him that first she needed to be in his house as a wife.

They went down in the elevator, clank clank, the two of them, standing in the slowly juddering box.

Home to Roohi.

They found Roohi in front of the TV watching cartoons, with Ganga next to her, also watching. From time to time the maid said, drink your milk, and held the glass up to the child's lips. If that milk would finish in an hour it would be a miracle.

Ishita wanted the news over and done with. She nudged Raman.

'Beta,' he started.

Roohi's gaze remained fixed on the cartoons.

'Beta, I have something important to tell you.'

'What?'

'Listen, na.'

He was so clumsy, did he have no idea of how to compel a child's attention, why didn't he put the TV off? Ishita bit her lip, don't say anything, don't say anything, let him handle it, the child needs to hear it from him, but isn't he going to send the maid away, or are they both to hear the news together?

Ads came and Roohi was momentarily diverted.

'Beta, Auntie and I got married this morning. She will now live with us. Isn't that nice?'

Roohi said nothing, while Ganga, whose understanding of English was comprehensive, kept her face carefully blank as she speculated about the changes that would come about in her own position. Raman, duty done, marched into the bedroom.

'Tell Ganesh to get me some tea,' Ishita said, to get Ganga out of the room.

She put the TV off, lifted the child onto her lap. 'Babu, beta.' She nuzzled her hair, smelling of sweat and feeling sticky. How long since it had been washed? She looked at the strands and located some crumbs. God only knew the extent of her neglect, children needed to be looked after every second of the day.

Roohi's thumb went back into her mouth. Ishita tilted her face towards her own and looked at the long eyelashes against the roundness of the childish cheek, the pink wet mouth, the slightly sallow skin. At four she was too old to be sucking her thumb. She pulled it out and held the glass next to her lips.

'Drink your milk, beta, and I will tell you a story.'

'What?'

'Start drinking first. Can't tell you a story just like that, can I?'

Roohi took a few sips then waited. 'There was once a papa who had a little girl whom he loved very, very much. That girl did not have a mother.'

'Why?'

'The mother had run away. She was never coming back.'

'Never?'

'No. Before she left she prayed to God, please send someone to look after my darling Baba. You see, in her own way this mother did love her child, but there were other people calling her and she wanted to go. And the little child was very lucky because another mother came who loved her very, very much.'

'Who?'

'Can you guess?'

'No.'

'Well, one day the child's papa, who was lonely, decided to marry this other mother. That way all three of them could live happily ever after. Now do you know who it is?'

Roohi stared at her milk. The glass was still not empty. Ishita tilted it against the girl's mouth and held it there till she swallowed the last drop. 'Good girl,' she said. Roohi probably felt some vestiges of attachment to that woman, and so could not answer the question. She vowed that one day of her own accord the child would say that she loved her and only her. That would be her greatest triumph. She stroked the grubby hands. 'Come on, darling, let's wash,' she said and led her to the bathroom.

In his room Raman cleared out one of his drawers to put away Ishita's things. He could hear his wife and daughter talking, could see the little girl's head against the woman's shoulder. Already there was a change in the atmosphere of the house, and his own mood lightened. Thank God the child had accepted the marriage, for him that was ultimately the most important thing. Now only Arjun left.

XXVII

Ishita started her life with Raman and Roohi, morphing suddenly into wife, mother and mistress of a large flat along with servants. Every dream had come true.

'What time does Roohi leave for school?' she asked Raman the first night as she nestled among sheets smelling satisfyingly of husband and sex.

'Well, I get her up at seven.'

'Then?'

'Milk, bath, breakfast, then Ganga and the driver take her to school, which starts at eight thirty.'

'You are such a caring papa,' said Ishita, caressing his chest.

'My daughter after all.'

'Our daughter now.'

He sensed the anxiety in her voice and smiled to himself, as he repeated after her, our daughter.

'Do you think I can help get her ready? Of course I don't want to startle the child . . .'

'Darling, she loves you, you know that.'

Ishita melted into him. 'You think? I wouldn't like to presume.'

'I know.'

That was his wedding gift to her.

Overnight Roohi's life changed. 'I don't want to rush anything,' Ishita repeatedly told her husband, convinced of her own sensitivity to the exigencies of treading carefully, while Raman watched bemused, as day by day a new regimen was put in place. Pottery classes once a week at the community centre, neighbours' children who started coming over to play, smarter dresses with matching accessories, clothes that matched Ishita's own outfits stitched by her Swarg Nivas tailor.

He objected to nothing because he saw the pleasure Roohi took in the attention, saw her flower under the regular routine, which was so much more carefully thought out than the structure he had provided.

That the child would be eventually graceful was ensured by dance classes at the Sri Ram Bhartiya Kala Kendra where Ishita discovered Justin McCarthy, once American, now Indian, versed in Sanskrit, Oriya, Tamil, and all the classical dance traditions of the south. Beginners were taught by his students, and parents were allowed to sit against the wall, eyes fastened on the backs of their daughters, imagining the day when they would be danseuses.

After Roohi's dance lesson was over, Ishita usually brought her to the nearby Bengali Sweet House for a dosa and ice cream. These treats were very dear to her, and she listened indulgently while the child chattered on about everything under the sun.

When she heard that Justin was in addition the foremost piano teacher in town, she rented a piano and signed up for his twice-a-week lessons, making sure the child practised every day. It gave Raman great satisfaction to hear the rudimentary tunes his daughter confidently banged out. 'Beta, play something for Papa,' Ishita would say and Roohi would run to the piano and show off.

On weekends Ishita planned family get-togethers, first checking with Raman whether it should be just themselves or all the grandparents, for now her own parents were included in that category. Raman knew his wife wanted to bind them into a cohesive unit and he did his best to fully participate in these schemes.

One Sunday at the zoo. Roohi walked between her parents holding each by the hand. All things considered, they were happy. Roohi because she was wearing new clothes, looking at animals, and the adults with her were in a good mood. Ishita because they presented a picture of a normal family to the world. She didn't think the day would ever come when she took this for granted.

Raman was the least content. He missed Arjun, he was not used to outings in which his name was never mentioned, nor his absence marked. He realized this sorrow was not fair to his present wife and he made an effort to participate as fully as possible in their enthusiasm.

Roohi jerked at his hand. Look, Papa. Before them was a large pond, overrun with flamingoes, herons, storks, ducks and swans. Ishita peered at the board, and read out the names. Flamingo, native of Africa—do you know what Africa is, darling?

Country.

No. Continent. With many countries. Say continent.

Con—con.

Ti—nent.

Ti—nent.

Raman wished his wife was not so keen on his daughter's education, but it was early days and he felt it unwise to interfere with the bonding process. Ishita drew out a plastic bag with stale roti. Here, darling, let's feed the ducks.

Roohi eagerly stretched out her hands. They leaned over the railings, and threw the roti into the water despite warnings displayed prominently everywhere. The ducks gratified them by squawking excitedly, diving after the food slowly sinking into the green opaque water.

They trudged and trudged. They passed tigers, giraffes, lions, and scores of brilliant exotic birds. Roohi started to drag her feet, October was still too early in the season for a comfortable outdoor expedition. The old fort was a big place and their energy was swallowed by heat and fatigue. Expedition over, they were going to eat at It's Greek to Me in Defence Colony Market with the grandparents.

Patiently Raman waited for the zoo to pall, for the endless succession of birds and beasts to assume the dreadful sameness it already had for him. He hid his dulled spirits, some things were not possible the second time round.

Once home he observed the glow on Ishita's face that came from a successful family outing, heard mother and daughter discussing the animals, the parrots so colourful, the lions like the ones they saw on TV, the hippo, so fat, and the black swans? Like dancers almost. The pleasures of the outing appeared retrospectively heightened as he listened to them.

*

A few days later Ishita suggested a visit to Roohi's school. 'They will want to be informed of the changes in her life.'

'In that case they will get to know a lot at once. I never told them Shagun left. People are so conservative.'

'Well, there are more families like ours than you think. Besides, they should be aware that now she has a mother who is dependable.'

'They'll really like you, Ish.'

Ishita allowed herself a small smile. Her husband's praise was very sweet to her, but she didn't let him see this, in case he thought there would be no need to compliment her further.

'I hope it is not too late to start the applications for admission into big school.'

'Really, there is no need to think of every blessed thing in her life all at once,' said Raman without thinking, amazed at how constantly the child appeared in his wife's thoughts.

Ishita looked down, but he could see from the tightening of her lips that tears were being suppressed.

'Now please, don't start crying.'

'Roo is my responsibility too, you know. I must do my best.'

'But you don't have to prove you are doing your best. Let things take their natural course. The child loves you, I love you.'

The lips softened, white teeth glinted through a small smile. 'You men are all alike. How can I just let things be? Where schools are concerned it is all law of the jungle. Don't you know that?'

He took her hand and squeezed it.

Let him say what he likes, she thought, but it had been her love for his child that had set her apart from other women. A love that, all said and done, had made him look beyond her defective fallopian tubes.

Her first marriage came to haunt her in disturbed dreams. Despite the six years that had passed, her inadequacies now appeared more vivid, her innocence more pathetic. Maybe it had something to do with being a wife again. She told herself repeatedly, wipe the past from your memory, focus on the present. You are lucky enough to have the chance of a new beginning.

Next evening, Ishita to Raman:

'The teachers were delighted to see me. Turns out they did know about the marriage breakup.'

'How come? I never told them.'

'But she did.'

'Not one to waste any time, huh?'

'Anyway, they said children are getting ready for big-school interviews, and they were wondering what was happening about our Roo.'

Raman looked down. Shagun had done all the school formalities for Arjun. He knew they were of vital importance; once the child had missed the date, admission was horrendously difficult. But with everything so uncertain he had wanted his daughter to enjoy the continued familiarity of Toddler's Steps.

Ishita stared at the guilty head. He was the girl's father, it was his duty to make sure things got done on time. What would have happened had she not arrived on the scene?

It was November. Raman was following the American elections closely. How could one of the most developed nations in the world have such a problem counting votes? He hoped Al Gore would emerge the winner, and he tried to make Ishita feel the same interest in the outcome. 'I dread what will happen to the world if George Bush becomes president. How can they take such a man seriously?'

But Ishita had issues nearer home to dread. They both concerned the children. Shagun had announced that she expected both Roohi and Arjun to be dropped at Alaknanda on January 1st. Surely Raman would not let Roohi go, she was too young to handle change. Earlier it was different, but now with two loving parents there was no need for her to be sent anywhere.

She brought this up tentatively one night. They were sitting on their first-floor balcony on cane chairs squeezed together. The street light threw its fluorescent glare on the tiny yellowing leaflets of the gulmohar in the garden below. It was the perfect tree, in winter its falling foliage let the sun through, in summer brilliant red flowers lit up the dusty bleached cityscape.

'I don't know if I have a choice,' said Raman. 'It's only for a few weeks. She has probably come to India to be with the kids.'

'What about her interviews for big school?'

'There won't be any in the holidays.'

'There might.'

'I don't think Shagun has a long visit in mind.'

'But we don't know when she will get an interview call. Then what will we say? After all my work explaining our late application—I have just married, etc., etc., marital disputes, etc. etc., child shouldn't suffer, etc. etc.'

Ever since Ishita had realized the importance of Roohi's admission she had set about it with zeal, going from school to school finding out details, making notes in her diary. Why should she work so hard if she was not to have even this basic assurance, that the child would be there for the interview?

She went on, 'Not to mention the confusion in her mind. You know they ask all kinds of questions—about Mama—Papa—school—just trying to gauge the child's awareness of the world around her. How on earth do you expect her to say anything in this situation? I know what will happen—'

So did Raman.

'She will just be silent. With thousands of children seeking admission—do you know how many applications there are for Kirloskar International?'

'Tell me.'

'Six thousand! For ninety seats! Can we afford to play with her future like this?'

'We may not have a choice.'

'Of course we have a choice. We don't have to send her.'

'Ishu, just remember, we don't have complete control over her destiny. Her mother does have visitation rights, and even if by some miracle we manage to have her not go these holidays, there will be others.'

'Let's cross those bridges when we come to them. I am worried about now.'

'I am just trying to warn you. We may not be able to control everything that happens to Roo.'

'Are you telling me not to love her?'

'Don't be silly. You are the best thing that could happen to her, we both know that.'

'Then what are you saying?'

'I don't want your heart to break like mine did.'

'It won't, don't worry.'

Raman remained silent. If hearts were in one's control . . .

'Now you tell her. Tell her—oh, tell her something. If you need a med certificate, we can do that.'

Med cert. That was what Shagun had used to wear him down when she stopped sending Roohi for the weekends. It would serve her right.

'What illness?'

'Measles? Chickenpox?'

'Isn't that a little extreme? Which doctor is going to say that?'

'Can't say the usual—diarrhoea, cough, cold, that sounds frivolous.'

They sat wondering what illness to give Roohi, but in the end decided that school admission was something that any court would understand, no need to go in for overkill with an illness. Nobody would believe it.

Issue number two.

You will meet Arjun, said Raman.

That was undeniable, but she was apprehensive. When Raman wrote letters to Arjun, she had taken to adding a few lines at the bottom, how much she was looking forward to seeing him, how much Roo talked of him, but complete silence met these offerings.

Well, now they would meet. From her side, she would do everything to make the boy feel at home.

'I hope he doesn't hate me,' she managed, 'and think I have taken his mother's place.'

'One has to understand the psychology of the boy. It is natural.'

'I understand psychology. I have also worked with disturbed children in Jeevan.'

'Things will sort themselves out. Can't put pressure—anyone will tell you it is counterproductive.'

'Children have to be guided. If we trusted alone to time, nobody would do anything about anything.'

'Put yourself in the boy's shoes, and everything will be fine. It is the first time he will be seeing another woman in his mother's place.'

'He must be used to such things. After all, he has been seeing another man in his father's place for a while now.'

Raman remained silent. In the darkness, Ishita could not see his face clearly. Afraid that she had hurt him, she drew closer and stroked his knee. His voice changed when he talked of his son's visit. A bit of a drawl, trying to sound casual. Would the son bring the mother to mind? Many had described the similarity in their appearances.

'He is adolescent, a delicate age. We have to be patient. You are so good with children, you will know how to handle him,' he now said. 'They are very close, always have been.

Though how Arjun functions with her and the stepfather is a closed book to me.'

Ishita clung to these soothing words. How can you want to have anything to do with a closed book? What is there to see in it? She herself was open. Her pages turned easily and her story was told in clear, transparent prose.

XXVIII

November 30th. The DPA buses would arrive at Nehru Stadium around two thirty.

'Would you like us to come with you to fetch him?' asked Ishita the night before.

It was obvious she wanted Arjun to feel welcome, but perhaps it would be better to go alone. It would be the first time he would be meeting Ishita, he could prepare him in the car.

He looked at his wife. Earnestness, sincerity, hope, tension, anxiety, a willingness to feel excluded, a readiness to fight for her rights, all this shone from her large intense eyes. Sometimes he thought that for her marriage was a series of tests she had to pass. Usually the times he did feel she was at ease were those in bed, when for hours nothing mattered but the pleasure they gave each other. Her ardour encouraged his own sexual passion. That gratitude gave him the patience to deal with everything else.

As he stood around the Nehru Stadium parking lot, he went over his prepared sentences, that Arjun must know he had a father who would stand by him through thick and thin, but just as his mother had married again, so had he. Now his wife was waiting eagerly to meet him. As for

Roohi, his baby sister, she was getting to be a big girl now. Ishita had been preparing her for the school entrance exams. He hoped she would get admission in VV—alma mater to both Raman and his son.

Up and down he paced the parking lot, avoiding the groups of waiting people, clearly known to each other. He himself knew no one, no one knew him.

The buses began to come. Parents crowd around each one. Hugging their sons, exclaiming over them, grabbing their bags, marching them to the car, palpably happy. Joy is where these children are.

Arjun appeared. It took time for easiness to flow between them, so it was a little awkwardly that Raman started in the car, 'beta, I wrote to you about my marriage. Auntie is very keen to love you. You will give her a chance, no? She kept sending you messages at the bottom of my letters, but you never responded.'

The boy grunted.

'She has made delicious brownies for you. I told her you don't like nuts in them.'

'Why isn't Roohi coming with me to Mama?'

'I told you, beta, she has to go to a big school next year. That is the time of entrance tests and interviews. Each school gives a different date, and it goes on till January end. Maybe you don't remember, but we had to do the same for you.'

Arjun stared sullenly out of the window. This was not the homecoming Raman had imagined. He only had four weeks with the boy. 'Anyway, this is not really your problem.'

'Mama said to make sure she comes.'

'Mama must have forgotten the problems with school admissions. You had better remind her.'

The traffic noise was loud, it seemed every driver drove with one palm pressed to the horn. Acrid city fumes swept around them. Arjun coughed.

'Not like the air in Dehradun, huh?'

'No.'

'It's the one good thing about living away from Delhi. The air you breathe is clean.'

'Yeah.'

'Are any of your new friends from Delhi? You can call them over.'

'Nah.'

By now they were reaching home. Raman thought of all the other children in all the other cars who would be tracing familiar landmarks, chattering happily to their parents about what they had done in school. Did Arjun reserve that kind of greeting for his mother? His heart felt heavy as he told his son of the films in town and the things he had planned they do together.

At the sound of the horn, Ishita looks out of the window. The chowkidar unlatches the gate, the car draws into the little driveway. The door opens and a thirteen-year-old boy gets out. Black hair falls over a white forehead. Later she will observe that the lips and cheeks are pink. The face is long and narrow, the eyes large, lashes thick. His teeth are slightly crooked.

She hurries to open the door. Roohi follows, skipping. Raman takes the boy's bag and says, 'Beta, this is Ishita Auntie.'

Ishita steps towards him, smiling, smiling. 'How was your trip?' she asks.

'Well, beta?' says the father.

'Fine,' he reluctantly replies.

'Would you like something to eat? I have kept lunch for you.'

'No thanks.'

'Eat something, you must be hungry,' added Raman.

'We ate on the way.'

'Are you sure? I thought the buses were coming straight.'

He shook his head, went to his room and shut the door.

Raman holds Ishita's hand. 'Give him time.'

'He is very handsome,' she responds carefully.

'Takes after his mother.'

'I gathered that.'

Raman looks at her. 'Are you OK?'

'Of course. Now let's hope he eats dinner. It's chicken tikka.'

'How long can he not eat? He is bound to feel hungry.'

They step on eggshells the rest of the day. Arjun eats his dinner, doing everybody a favour, but is sparing with his words.

Next day. Roohi stood next to her brother's bed, and poked him. 'Bhaiyya, get up, get up. Look what I made for you.'

A greeting card under the tutelage of the hopeful, putative mother. Welcome home, Bhaiyya. And three figures were drawn. Father, mother, sister.

The boy opened one eye and took the paper.

'Who's that?' He jabbed a finger at the female standing in the middle.

Roohi fell silent.

'Huh—who's that?'

Still she said nothing.

'Looks like Auntie,' he said.

'Yes,' she replied.

'Who?'

She giggled. 'Auntie.'

'Clever girl.'

That pleased Roohi. 'Play with me, Bhaiyya, I have got some new games.'

He opened his quilt. 'Come.'

She dived into the warmth and wriggled close to her brother. He shifted an infinitesimal bit to make room for her. They lay there, neither saying anything.

Raman could hear Ishita in the kitchen. He made his way to the children's room, and the two heads together filled him with the strong sentiments parents experience at such a sight. Hope for the future, bonding that goes beyond the father and mother, a connection that no divorce can sever. Raman went to fetch his camera, this scene needed to be recorded to buoy him in his downcast moments.

'What are you doing?' asked Ishita, coming to announce breakfast. Yesterday was bad, but she would leave no stone unturned to make today better. She had especially made puri-aloo, the boy might appreciate that after months of hostel food.

'See how sweet they look.'

'Who?'

'Arjun and Roohi. Just peep from the door—they are lying in bed together, I am going to take a picture.'

'Sounds nice,' smiled Ishita.

At that moment Arjun was murmuring to his sister, 'Do you remember Mama?'

She nodded.

'Not the auntie living with you in this house. Mama in America.'

Again she nodded.

'She loves you very much. Now don't you forget that. She is your real mother, no matter what anyone says. All right?'

Roohi lay still.

'You saw her six months ago. Remember the big lake? Remember the cabin next to it? And the canoe which you were too scared to get into? Remember?' he repeated impatiently. He must have the dumbest sister in the world.

She nodded.

Arjun drew a long breath.

Roohi got up.

'Where are you going?'

'Su-su.'

'Come back then.'

She ran out of the room as her father was coming. 'Where are you going, beta? Come, let's take a photo of you and Bhaiyya together.'

'Su-su.'

'Come back quickly.'

'Roohi!' Ishita follows her, helps her onto the pot. Roohi does not always remember to wash her hands, but this morning she concentrates on her tasks seriously. The child is adaptable, thinks the mother, she tries to please. She seems a little withdrawn, it must be the brother coming—well, they all had to get used to things, that was life.

'It must be nice, no, seeing Arjun after all this time?'

Roohi nodded. The safest thing to do in practically all circumstances was to nod.

'Is anything the matter?'

She shook her head.

'What was Arjun telling you?'

'Nothing.'

'Are you sure?'

Roohi had not yet learned to lie. Ishita wiped her hands, put the lid of the pot down, sat on it and took the child in her arms. 'I love you, my precious. You are the best thing that has happened to me. Now you will remember that, won't you?'

The head under her chin bobbed.

'Doesn't matter who was here before me. We are fated to be mother and daughter, you and I. It is our karma that joins us.'

'What's karma?'

'Destiny. Nobody can change it. Yes, another woman gave you birth, yes, you saw her in America, but now you are with me. Let people say what they like. OK, darling?'

'OK.'

'I am the person who looks after you, sees to your food, makes sure you do your homework, buys you pretty things, who will never leave you, no matter what.'

The child pushed her head further into Ishita's chest.

'Let's go and tell Arjun that, shall we? Perhaps he doesn't know there are two kinds of mothers. The ones who give birth to babies, and then forget about them, and the other ones who look after the babies for the rest of their lives.'

In the bedroom Raman was sitting on Arjun's bed, his hand on the boy's back, occasionally reaching out to stroke his hair. 'I have missed you so much, beta. You have no idea.'

The boy smiled absently.

'I keep wondering how you are. You hardly write to me, and then such short letters.'

'There is nothing much to say. Just studies and games.'

'Still I worry about you. As it is, there is hardly any contact between us.'

'I'm all right.'

Raman looked at Arjun, saw his ex-wife's face, thought of the measly four weeks he was going to have with his son before he departed and sighed. Whatever it was, he was destined to always feel pain, and an anxious tortured love that put him in hell over one or the other of his children.

What was taking Roohi so long?

The child came, Ishita stood by while Raman fussed with the camera. 'It's good the camera will put a date on the picture,' said Ishita. 'It is Arjun's first day home.'

'Yes,' beamed the father.

The photo taken, brother and sister sitting together on the bed. They are both smiling, but their bodies don't touch. The morning bed scene suggestive of love and closeness was no longer there to capture.

At the breakfast table. Raman sees how carefully Ishita piles Arjun's plate with puri, pickle and potato, how she asks him what his favourite foods are so that she can cook them, how the effort she is making is palpable to the meanest intelligence, and how Arjun's intelligence is anything but mean.

'You eat, you eat, enough feeding of us all,' he tells her.

Towards the end, when all is done, she thinks carefully before she says, 'Beta, I am like Roohi's mother. I hope to be your mother too, at least your mother in this house.'

'We can discuss all that later, Ish,' said Raman.

'Of course we can. Only I thought best to get things clear in the beginning. After all, Roohi has to live here with us—she shouldn't feel confused.'

Arjun glared at his sister, who was making potato gravy dots around her plate.

'Don't play with your food, beta,' said Ishita. Roohi paid no attention. Ordinarily Ishita would have let this go, but this moment was not ordinary. Raman was not backing her claims as he should.

'Beta,' she repeated, 'don't play with your food.'

'Let her be,' said Raman.

Ishita rose, gathered the plates that normally the maid gathered, and let her husband know through thin, tightened lips, through unnecessary clattering of spoon on china, that things were going to go badly unless he did something. He got up to follow her.

'Arjun is just a child. It's difficult for him too, you have to remember that.'

Yes, he was just a child. And her husband was just his father, unable to see that children too might have scheming minds. Her face grew tight. 'At least remember how hard I am trying to make this work. And I won't have him disturbing Roo.'

Raman clicked his tongue in exasperation. 'Don't you go behaving irrationally now. I have enough on my hands as it is.' It was the harshest thing he had ever said to her.

'I'm sorry,' she said quickly.

He put his arm around her shoulders. 'Give it time. Not even one day has passed.'

'You might have to say something to him . . . It must be hard on him to see me in his mother's place, but he has to understand this situation was not of your making. He must see we are together in this.'

'If necessary, I will. Trust me, can't you?'

A few days later Raman decided to take Arjun to Agra to see the Taj Mahal. Ishita thought it was a wonderful idea, father and son need to be alone together, she said looking at him lovingly, and he thought what a good girl Ishita was, if anything it was his fault that she was in such an impossible situation.

Raman wanted no harsh note to disturb his interaction with Arjun. He booked a package of two nights, three days in the Maurya Sheraton. He was sure the child stayed in some pretty fancy places with Shagun and Ashok. Well, he could give him fancy as well. He read up the history of

Fatehpur Sikri and the Taj to place the monuments they saw in a historical context, to fill in conversational gaps with educational fragments.

For three days father and son bonded, away from the distractions of sister-baiting and relative-hating. Arjun was now more willing to talk about the things he did at Shivalik House, the tricks they played on the teachers, the house matches, the six-or-seven-kilometre trek they had taken over Diwali weekend. Raman was careful not to ask many questions, he found that irritated his son.

Arjun clearly loved being in Agra. 'Do we have to go home?' he asked, on the evening of the third day, but yes, they had to go.

'Your sister will be very disappointed. She has been so looking forward to her elder brother's visit. When is he coming? When is he coming? A dozen times a day. And Daadi and Daada too. When is he coming? You are only with me for four weeks, after all.'

Arjun had nothing to say to any of this.

The sister and grandparents might have been clamouring for Arjun's presence, but Raman was saddened that this didn't really matter to his son. The only person he showed any preference for was himself.

Once home he insisted till Raman's hand ached that they play *RollerCoaster Tycoon* and *Age of Empires* to the exclusion of all else.

As they stared at the screen Raman used the opportunity to try and establish some mutual understanding.

'Things have changed at home, beta.'

'Do you mean your marriage, Papa?'

'Yes, and that Roohi has found a mother in her. I must ask you to respect that.'

'Mama is our mother.'

'But she left and Roo is too young to be without a mother. For better or for worse,' he went on carefully, 'she considers Ishita in that role. Ishita too dotes on her. It is best not to upset the apple cart,' he went on, laughing lightly, 'you do know what that means, don't you?'

Arjun shook his head.

'Let things be the way they are. You don't really see Roo when you are not here, but after she came from America she was very disturbed. She kept wetting her bed. And she told some strange story about three little piggies and a big bad wolf, a story that was repeated to her on the plane. For some reason this seemed to have frightened her.'

'What a baby.'

'I got quite worried. Did something bad happen there—something your mother might not be a were of?'

'Nothing. We had this game—that we were living in a house like the three little piggies—it was in a cabin by the lake, you know, Papa—anyway, she made it very difficult when Mama told her that the holiday was over. So we told her we had to go because the big bad wolf was coming to blow the place down. And cook us and eat us,' added Arjun with relish.

'She is still too young to distinguish reality from fairy tales, beta. After you left for school she really broke down.'

'It was Mama in America she didn't want to leave. You should have heard her crying and saying I want to stay, I want to stay. I didn't tell you—I knew you would be upset.'

'Beta, it is disturbing for children to be shunted around like this. You are older, you understand, but she doesn't.'

'Mama explained and explained. I was there.'

'Don't forget how young she is.'

'What'll happen to the apple cart the next time we go?'

Raman could not bring himself to answer. There was a willingness to wound in Arjun that was new to Raman. What had happened to his son? He had obviously been primed during his last trip to his mother. He looked at the face, so like Shagun's, opaque as hers had been towards the end.

For the initial meeting with the grandparents Raman arranged a family lunch at Sagar. In the restaurant there would be so much going on that any tension would be dissipated in the eating and drinking.

When they arrived they found Mr and Mrs Kaushik already waiting for them in the crowded room, seated next to the window on the second floor of this food mansion.

'Beta!' they exclaimed. 'How are you? We have missed you so much, you never wrote to us, hanh? You forgot us, did you?'

For the millionth time in his life Raman wished his parents were not so tactless. Even Ishita flinched.

'School keeps children very busy,' she said quickly.

'So busy that you forget your father, forget everybody?'

The waiter bustled up. They ordered multiple combinations of dosa, idli and vada.

Raman used the time waiting for the food to sink into depression. Gone was the sense of father and son that he had experienced in Agra, lost in transit from the two of them to the six of them.

The grandparents continued to ask Arjun questions which Raman tried to answer so that the boy's surliness was not noticeable. The food came, distractions occurred, they ate, they drank, they paid, then made their way down, pushing through people charging up the narrow staircase, and finally started on their separate ways home. Mr and Mrs Kaushik found it odd that they were not invited to spend the rest of the day with their son, but things had changed, they told themselves in the car, Raman would call them over when he thought it best. At least they got to see a lot of their granddaughter.

The tension continued during the remainder of Arjun's visit. Ishita looked as though each second was torture. She wanted Raman to understand her position, and not blame her later for anything. She was trying, if only he knew how hard. Four weeks were not much she realized, but Arjun was making trouble between Roohi and herself.

'You are imagining things.'

'No, I am not. He just stays in his room the whole time you are away, or he calls Roohi to him and shuts the door. What am I to think? And she only calls me Mama when he is not there.'

He is just a child, thought Raman, but he said nothing, merely continued going out with his son. Those were the best times when they were alone, and he tried to create these situations as much as possible. They saw a film at Priya, ate potato skins and pizza at TGIF, wandered around the shopping complex before returning home. They didn't talk much. Raman said, 'I love you, son, you are my own flesh and blood, I want you always to remember that.' Arjun said 'I know,' thus gratifying his father. Raman was not about to spoil any outing with the parental strictures that Ishita so wanted. There is a time and a place for everything.

*

For the first time Ishita began to think it had been a bad idea to give up her job with Jeevan. It meant that in times of stress there was never any relief from the torment. And wasn't it better to devote oneself to many children than to obsess about one little girl?

Yet it had seemed the obvious course. How could she allow herself to miss precious months of Roo's rearing, when so much had already gone wrong in the child's life? In both their lives?

She sighed as she returned to the papers in front of her, pushing other things out of her mind. There was plenty of time to spend on the phone, asking the mothers she knew about school interviews, because Raman was usually with his son. She tried not to look directly at him when he came back to their room, she hated his air of dreamy self-consciousness, almost as though he were in love with the boy.

Be calm, she told herself, think of your husband, think of his health.

She often thought of his health—so much easier when the man was not in front of her.

Raman, seeing her marking school prospectuses, was grateful. She is a good girl, he thought, he didn't know of anyone else who would be capable of this kind of devotion in these circumstances. She hadn't even demanded his participation, knowing how preoccupied he was.

He offered some non-Arjun thoughts. 'I keep telling you she has a very good chance in VV, my old school, you know.'

'I know. But I found out that children of alumni do not get any extra weightage. They said if they started doing that, they would never have room for anybody else.'

'We didn't have a problem with Arjun.'

'Things are tougher now.'

'When are the interviews?'

'Gandhi Smriti and Kriloskar this month, Modern and VV in early January, after that Springdales, Our Saviour Convent—'

'I don't want a convent,' said Raman.

'We may have no choice. It's the school I went to, that might increase her chances, so I thought it better to fill in the forms.'

'Are you saying no school will take her?'

'I am saying we cannot be sure of anything.' She did not look up as she said this. On her lap was a manila folder, scattered around were passport-size pictures of Roohi—he didn't even know when she had got them taken. In these few months she had already become indispensable. Because of her Roohi was happy and being looked after as children should be looked after. If there was a little trouble now, it would blow over.

'Do you need help in filling out the forms?'

'Most of it is already done. But if I do, I will ask you.' There was a slight distance in her voice.

'But do you have all her injection records and everything?'

'I got them from the paediatrician.'

'And her blood type?'

'That too.'

'Her likes and dislikes? Those too?'

She smiled. 'Those too.'

'The child couldn't be in better hands.'

'Let's hope the teachers who interview us think so too.'

He was glad it was admission time. That was enough to keep any concerned mother occupied for months. He edged closer and put his hand under her hair. He loved her neck, it reminded him of a little girl's.

She pretended not to notice.

He slid her dupatta off her shoulders and threw it on the bed. 'So stupid, hiding your breasts from your husband,' he said as his hand wandered.

'You are not the only man in the world, you know.'

'But I am the only man in this room.'

She giggled. 'So you want me to do a striptease for you?'

'Why not? It would be nice.'

'Well, I am not going to.' She pulled her dupatta towards her.

Again he tugged it away. 'Don't do a striptease, but there is no need to wear this ridiculous garment. It hardly ever does what it is supposed to do.'

He threw the dupatta across one shoulder, and mimicked a mincing girl. 'See, this is how fashionable people wear their dupattas—or like this'—wrapping it around his neck—'or like this'—some more neck-twisting.

Ishita was now openly laughing. Encouraged, Raman went on, 'And madam, if you won't do a striptease for me, I will do one for you.'

Off came the shirt, down came the trousers, and now there was just the underwear and his dick peeping through the opening. Ta-da, crooned Raman, suggestively jerking his hips in Ishita's direction.

She looked wildly at the door—it was unlocked, the overhead lights brightly lit the room. Locks in place, folder pushed hurriedly into a drawer, only the night light on, Raman slid down his underwear to display a large erection. Until she took her own clothes off, this organ was going to remain exposed.

You take them off then, she said, her face glowing, laughing at the erection that was now visible under the thin flapping material of the dupatta, tiny sequins flashing coyly as they caught the sparse reflection of the embedded light next to the bathroom door.

And there she was naked at his feet, drawing him into her mouth, caressing his thighs with her fingers, gripping him more ferociously as her excitement grew. He dragged her to the bed, where they continued indulging themselves.

In the morning Raman thought he had been unduly pessimistic. Things would work out. He had said this to himself before, but now the conviction was greater.

Ishita thought to herself, he is just a child, if he is loyal to his mother, that is quite natural. It is stupid of me to mind, I have Roohi, I should be content with that.

Just before he left, Arjun cornered his sister.

'I am going tomorrow.'

She stared blankly at him.

He sat near her and showed her something in his cupped hand. It was a small passport-size photograph of Shagun.

'Who is this?'

'Mama.'

'Don't forget her. All right?'

'All right.'

'She doesn't live here any more. She is in the States where I am going now. If you weren't so stupid you would also be coming.'

He had called her stupid so many times she was almost used to it.

Arjun felt proud that he had ended his visit on the same note with which he had started it. He had not succumbed to the enemy. He touched the photograph lying crumpled in his pocket. It was his talisman. From time to time he looked at it, knowing that the eyes that smiled from the glossy paper were always ready to smile at him in exactly the same way. In two days' time she would receive him at JFK Airport, waiting at the barricade, embracing him so tightly his breath would stop. Later on he would tell her all she wanted to know about Roohi. Then back to DPA where the home scene mattered not at all.

*

Was it wrong to feel such relief at the departure of a child? Wrong or not, Ishita hid her feelings. To reveal anything remotely truthful was to invite blame and censure.

'You must be missing Arjun,' said everybody, even her own parents. 'With two children in the house there is so much life.'

What was it about a child that you were supposed to miss no matter what he/she had done to you? Even with children there had to be some kind of reciprocal love. If things had been the least bit congenial with Arjun she would gladly have joined the general chorus of how terrible it was that brother and sister, father and son had to be separated. But his malevolent influence lingered in the things Roohi said, starting from the day of his departure.

It was Saturday. Raman was busy with extra work in office and nap time found Ishita curled around Roohi in bed. She felt an immense weariness, as though she had run a hundred-mile race every day for the past month.

Roohi stirred, Ishita pressed closer to her. The child opened her eyes, Ishita gazed at her intently. 'How's my little girl?'

'Are you sure you are my mother?'

She recognized Arjun's voice behind the sweet, sleepy bewildered tones. At that moment she could just murder him, murder him in cold blood, and not regret the years spent in prison.

'Who else?' she asked.

The girl lifted her frock to her mouth and chewed it.

'What I mean to say is that once you did have another mother but she ran away. When that happened, I married your papa. Mamas and papas live together, isn't that so?'

'Umm.'

'When your birth mother divorced your father, he chose me to look after you. That is our karma. Remember I told you?'

'What's divorce?'

'The opposite of marriage.'

'What's marriage?'

'Marriage is when two people decide to live together for ever. Should they change their minds they go to court and get their marriage cancelled. Finished. Divorced. They become strangers, sometimes they never see each other again.'

'Oh.'

'Your mother decided she loved another man. She wanted to marry him and live in America. You saw him when you were there, no?'

'Yes.'

'But she couldn't take the children with her. Children belong to their papas. So she left both of you here.'

'With you?'

'Well, in a manner of speaking. I married your papa because I love both of you—I will never, never leave you.'

Here Ishita allowed herself a sob. Roohi heard her and began to cry as well. They clung to each other for a while, before Ishita dried the child's tears. 'Come, darling, let's get your milk.'

'Mama, can I watch cartoons?'

'All right, sweetheart.'

If Roohi had only known, she could have asked for the moon and the stars, and Ishita would have tried to put them in her lap.

XIX

The first rejection came while Arjun was still with them. In mid-December they received a curt letter, telling them that their daughter would not be called for interview at the Gandhi Smriti School.

'You should have pulled some strings,' said Ishita, staring in despair at the form letter in which the box Ineligible for Interview had been ticked.

'What strings could I pull?'

'Surely there is a string you know. People on the governing body?'

'I don't.'

'Then find someone who does.'

'Ish, you are going mad. Listen to what you are saying. Approach people to approach people I don't know. As though this is going to help.'

'Something has to help. Or somebody.'

'It's not the end of the world. There are other schools. We never worried like this for Arjun.'

'Times have changed.'

'Not that much, all right?'

He looked a bit ferocious and she had to retreat.

Two weeks later massive earthquakes hit northern India. Thirty thousand died. Ishita collected bundles of old clothes and bedding from the house and drove to Swarg Nivas, to deposit them in the society office. The Brand donated money, medicines, drinking water and juices. 'It's our corporate sense of responsibility,' said Raman. 'We know how to give back.'

Ishita hoped that the good they were doing would be reflected in the ease with which Roohi would gain admission into one of the preferred schools of the city.

So far as the next interview, at Kirloskar International, was concerned, Raman did make sure they were called. A school belonging to a business conglomerate, it was easier for him to find a contact on the board.

'Sathe says he is doing this as a special favour to me.'

'Thank you, darling,' said Ishita, as she put her arms around her weary husband and kissed him.

'Hey, don't thank me. She is also my daughter, you know.'

His wife giggled at the compliment.

Since Arjun was with them, she made it a point to announce the date of the interview, information to be conveyed to the mother so that she would know Roohi was not travelling for bona fide reasons.

'There is no need to do all this,' said Raman. 'We can't really make messengers out of the children.'

'Who will tell her, then? Will she trust anything you say? At least her son she will believe.'

'My son too, Ish.'

'That's what I meant.'

Arjun departed before the Kirloskar interview, which heartened Ishita, though as the date approached, Raman had to warn her. 'They only have twenty-five seats, and they are very strict about not exceeding their limit. Not even if the prime minister asks.'

'Her chances are good. I have been preparing her.'

'Just don't get your hopes up.'

He always saw the dark side. Why shouldn't Roohi be one of twenty-five, rather than one of the many rejects?

Their slot was fixed for January 15th, 3.30 p.m.

Ishita's sanguinity knew a check. 'That's her nap time, she's never at her best in the afternoon. Maybe they are doing this only in order to disqualify her.'

'Don't be silly. How else will they fit so many in? They are interviewing two hundred children a day.'

On the appointed date they collected in the school along with many others. Along the paths bordering the auditorium were stalls with hot and cold drinks. Student volunteers took down their names, then escorted them inside, where they were solicitously seated according to their appointed times in rows. Their helpfulness filled every parent in the hall with lust. This was what they wanted for their child, this, this, this.

Every half-hour groups of ten were led by a teacher into the belly of the school.

Some social souls began talking. Where all have you applied? Where all have you heard from?

There were some who had received affirmative responses from other schools.

Then what are you doing here, ran the collective thought, spoiling our chances?

They wanted options, they felt it was their right.

Selfish, greedy parents, with their stupid precocious brats. This is the mentality that gives our country a bad name. No sense of the collective good, every man for himself.

But still all kept smiling, all kept asking, what questions were put to your child?, what answers expected?, hoping in the general accretion of information to glean a few nuggets that would help open the gates of a good school.

By the time Roohi was called, Ishita was a mass of anxiety. Her earlier confidence seemed misplaced.

'Do your best, darling,' she whispered into the child's ear. 'Good luck.'

The child barely acknowledged this as she left.

'Oh don't worry,' said Raman for the millionth time.

What was the use of going on saying don't worry? Couldn't he see the kind of children gathered here, smart, bright, confident? Not that Roohi wasn't all these things, but she was also indubitably shy.

Slowly they walked to the Nestlé kiosk. Ishita needed coffee to calm her nerves. Judging from the crowd, lots of people needed to calm their nerves and it took Raman a while to buy two cups. They sipped the hot frothy instant coffee, and while they were only halfway through they saw a teacher leading ten small children towards the auditorium, Roohi among them.

Ishita threw her coffee cup into the trash and darted towards the child.

'How was it?'

'Fine.' The child's face revealed nothing.

They smiled at her, grabbed her hands and started walking towards the car.

On their way home, Ishita asked, 'What did they ask?'

'My name.'

'And?'

'My mama's name.'

'What did you say?'

'I said Mama!'

'Then?'

'Papa's name.'

'And?'

'I said Raman.'

So. She had not taken her name. Understandably she was confused. But the teachers would never realize why.

'Beti, did they ask you any nursery rhymes?' put in Raman. He knew Ishita had focused on nursery rhymes.

'Yes.'

'Which one?'

'Any one I wanted.'

'Which was that?'

'Ring-a-ring-a-roses, Pocket full of posies . . .'

'Good girl!' exclaimed Ishita.

Thank goodness the rest of the interview had gone well, thought Raman.

'And—what else?' continued Ishita.

'They asked what "posies" was.'

'What did you say?'

'Nothing.'

*

That night Raman spent a lot of time in close proximity to his wife's anguish. 'I am sure other children do not know the meaning of what they sing.'

She sniffled.

'There is always VV.'

'That's what you think.'

There was a gloomy strain in Ishita that had burgeoned in these two months of applications and interviews. For his own sanity if nothing else, he hoped Roohi would find admission someplace.

'Should I go and talk to Mother Superior at OSC? She was very fond of me.'

'A convent is our last choice. Let's wait and see first.'

But Ishita couldn't go on trusting to Raman's optimism. Among the thousands of children lining up for admission, there were many who were going to be stuck in mediocre schools through no fault of their own. And whatever Raman's opinion of convents, he would be grateful to have her in OSC if other options failed. So unbeknownst to him she did visit her old school.

In OSC, Ishita's talents had been rewarded steadily through the years. She had been class monitor, prefect, house captain, sports captain, vice head girl. She knew Mother Superior would claim helplessness in the face of a mountain of applications, and to forestall that she related her own recent history. Deprived children at Jeevan, Raman the abandoned divorcee, Roohi the neglected child, her own love for the little girl.

When she walked out the gates it was with the feeling that Mother had been moved by her story. And in OSC at least Roohi would not be asked irrelevant questions such as the meaning of 'posies'.

*

The admission procedures in VV were spread over a weekend, from morning to night.

An intelligent school, commented Raman. They know if they want both parents present they have to do their admissions on Saturday and Sunday.

Ishita, staring at the forms they were meant to fill out, said nothing. Eight pages of questions. One would think the child was applying to do a Ph.D., or enter the secret service, the list was so exhaustive.

She looked at the other parents in the brightly coloured kindergarten room. Every low chair was filled to overflowing with a bulky parental form. From the frowns she could tell they too were finding the questions difficult. Well, it was Raman's second time round, he knew what kind of responses the school would approve of. It did say on top that the objective was to understand the child, there were no right or wrong answers. And she was born yesterday.

Raman was muttering—

Any siblings in the school?

Parents' educational history?

Jobs?

Salary?

Child's favourite food?

Favourite game?

Story?

Toy?

Bedtime?

The activities you do with your child?

What are your child's likes and dislikes?

In one sentence, how would you describe your child?

What do you think is your child's greatest weakness?

Greatest strength?

How much media entertainment do you allow your child?

Her favourite programmes?

What will you say if your child wants to buy a balloon?

An ice cream?

What will you say if your child wants a toy she has seen?

What will you tell your child when she asks you why you are smoking? (Do not say you do not smoke.)

At the smoking question Ishita rebelled. 'Surely that is the reason many people don't smoke, they don't want to set a bad example. Do they want us to lie?'

That was the trouble with Ishita. Literal-mindedness did not cut it there. She would never make it in a multinational where they were always having to project scenarios and consider possible reactions.

Form filled, the three of them were called. One teacher engaged the parents' attention, the other engaged Roohi at some distance.

Ishita saw a paper and drawing, saw a sweet being given, saw the wrapper left on the table, saw the teacher prompting, saw silence from her daughter. Saw all this through sidelong glances.

Inevitably there were questions that concerned the son whom they all remembered; he was such a promising boy. Where was he now? How was he adjusting?

Ishita could see the teacher observing her, and immediately this made her feel inadequate. Somewhat gruffly she said that the adjustment process had been successful for everybody. Arjun was happy in boarding school, he was developing in sports and academics, Roohi was happy in playschool. And as anybody could see she looked upon Ishita as her mother.

*

When the rejection letter came Raman went to meet the Principal. He was an alumnus, his son an ex-student, why had this happened, there must be a misunderstanding?

No, no misunderstanding. The child had seemed disturbed during the interview. They wanted to take her, but she hardly answered any questions. She could only recite a nursery rhyme and that was a function of memory, not comprehension.

The circumstances are special, pleaded Raman. But the school had little patience with such presumption. There was no situation in which silence could be considered favourably, nor were they in a position to allow second chances. With only room for eighty, they had to evaluate hundreds of applicants impartially. Parents have to understand.

As Raman drove home, impotent rage filled him.

Now Ishita was the one to console. Whatever happened was to the good. Even their questions showed how judgemental they were. If the worst came to the worst, she was sure OSC would be more receptive to the daughters of alumni. The old-school network was strong there.

Raman did not have the heart to argue. His alma mater was considered one of the best schools in Delhi. He hadn't found the teachers judgemental, they only wanted a fair evaluation and in Arjun's case he had approved the methods used to select the boy.

The same methods that meant Roohi was out in the cold.

Roohi did get admission in OSC. Raman and Ishita fitted the criteria the nuns were looking for. The child wrote her ABC, rattled off her nursery rhyme, recited her numbers, and drew intelligent connections between a bottle of milk and a cow, a lace and a shoe, a bird and a nest, the moon and stars, a cup and a saucer.

Her daughter would do well in this environment, of that Ishita was determined. Maybe Raman was right, they emphasized rote learning more than some of the newer schools. But students performed well in exams, and it was a competitive world out there.

In April, Roohi joined a class of fifty little girls. Every morning Ishita went to drop her, every noon to pick her up. KG children kept shorter hours than the rest of the school, and Ishita saw no reason why a five-year-old should be burdened by a bus, when they had the option of a car.

'It's a lot of time to spend on the road,' commented the father. 'I hardly get to see you in the morning.'

'I know, but what to do? From next year we will send her by bus. By then she will know other children. Right now she is still so small, poor thing.'

'Nothing poor, since she has you dancing around her finger.'

'Who could do less for her?'

From Ishita's demeanour Raman knew she expected him to say her biological mother, but the words stuck in his throat.

XXX

Arjun was by now nearing the end of class VIII, his second year at the Academy. Once a month when parents were allowed to visit, his father would drive to Dehradun. Ishita refused to accompany him, claiming that the bonding between father and son would be more effective without her. This however meant that Roohi never came, and Raman worried that circumstances would contrive to pull brother and sister so apart that as grown-ups there would be nothing to connect them. He tried to compensate by talking of Roohi to an Arjun who had very little time for girls. A sister just didn't register on his radar.

Though it was not allowed, Raman always went armed with food, biscuits, chips, chocolate, hoping that his son would get to eat at least some of it. He knew the way things worked in boarding schools, you could claim nothing for your own, unless you were at the very top of the pecking order.

For lunch they drove into town where they ate pizza or dosa. The talk involved a jargon that Raman was beginning to be familiar with. The drinking chocolate cake, the Maggi cooked in the sun, the chits he needed, the house colours, house marks, house activities, and worst of all the fagging that seemed to go on all hours of the day and night.

'Doesn't this kind of treatment bother you?' he asked. 'And that too dished out by other students?'

Arjun shrugged his shoulders. 'It's all right.'

How it was all right, Raman could not imagine. The image of a young beautiful boy—and no one looking at Arjun could deny his beauty—at the mercy of whichever sadistic senior happened to cross his path assailed Raman painfully. Having to change his clothes at the slightest excuse, running endless chores for seniors, being punished for the most minor infringements, all this was related with casual aplomb. Whenever he tried to probe, his son stayed with 'It's all right'. Maybe in the end it would be all right, but how would he ever know?

'Don't worry,' Ishita tried to reassure him when he came back from these trips. 'Hundreds of boys go to schools like this. By the end of it they seem fine.'

'How do you know what goes on in their emotional lives? Look at Ashok, wouldn't you call him damaged?'

In their house Ashok was the fucked-up one and Shagun the one who would bear the consequences.

'Still, times have changed. Schools are not what they used to be.'

Raman said no more, distrusting the calm reassurances of his wife.

Arjun's final report card came. The boy had scored in the 80s and 90s in every subject, surpassing his performance of the previous year. At least some of the fears concerning a traumatized child in a hostile environment could be laid to rest. Whatever treatment was meted out to him, it wasn't bad enough to hamper his academic achievements.

Raman stared at the card lovingly, the figures speaking to him, caressing him with their consolatory powers.

'Look, look at how well he has done,' he boasted to Ishita.

'Yes, indeed,' she exclaimed, but she didn't take the report card in her hands, gaze at each high mark, examine the teachers' comments or phone the relatives immediately. This was the time he felt the loneliness of a single parent.

Later that night he sat down at his computer and e-mailed Shagun the news. Here was the other person in the world who could equally share in this joy.

When she replied he discovered she took all the credit.

Arjun had performed as she had expected. At DPA excellence was inculcated right down the line. Children had to be taught to live in the real world, where competition was endemic to everything.

Where on earth had she got such ideas from? Not from him—must be from the man she lived with—the man with cut-throat competition bred into his blood and bones—who saw the world as a marketplace with all its wares for sale.

Ishita meanwhile was focused on Roohi's life in OSC. Convents too had changed. Roohi's class was large, it was true, but she seemed none the worse for it. School presented no terrors for her, nor were holidays a time of escape. Far from being taught to learn by rote, all she did was draw, paint, and make things out of plasticine. Letters and numbers were approached through large coloured books.

Her friends too were many. Ishita had talked to the teachers, read the list of student addresses, and made a note of the neighbouring children. She had taken Roohi to their houses, and they had come to hers. To the Justin McCarthy classes were added swimming lessons, and story-reading sessions at the children's library at the Gymkhana Club. A whole shelf in the dining room was devoted to her creations; there was even a framed collage, splashes of gory colour and awkward strokes. Raman saw no need to puff the daughter's head up so much, it was not as though she were a genius.

But could Raman see how she was growing in confidence?

Yes, Raman could.

'Now let's see how she doesn't talk in an interview. You have to understand a child's psychology.'

Roohi was a lucky little girl, said the father, to have someone who cared so much about her. He didn't recall going to such lengths for Arjun, he added carefully, aware by now that Ishita resented statements of this nature. Would a real mother, doing all she could for her child, be subject to such compliments?

Raman was analysing some spreadsheets in his office when Shagun phoned. For a moment he was startled. Did she have trouble sleeping, that she had rung at 2 a.m. American time? He tried to judge the nuances of her voice. Irritation with him as usual, but loneliness perhaps, regret and misery?

'I want to discuss Roo.'

'What about her?'

'Don't play games with me, Raman. You didn't send her last time. Now I want to be sure that you don't repeat this.'

'Don't repeat this? You think her admissions could have waited?'

'You know what I mean. I can make the arrangements, in fact I am coming there, but will you co-operate?'

'These trips are unsettling for her. You have no idea how she suffers going back and forth. Last time she had nightmares. Kept crying about a wolf. It took me weeks to settle her down.'

Silence on the other end.

'God only knows what rubbish you filled her head with. Arjun continued this game in the plane, scaring her out of her wits.'

'It was very traumatic sending her back. She wanted to stay with me.'

'This is what you have subjected our children to.'

'Don't moralize, Raman. You are so fucking righteous I can't stand it. I sent her back only because of our agreement.'

'The point is she finds this kind of dislocation extremely unsettling. She is not even five—what does she understand of anything?'

'Are you refusing to send her? I will be in Delhi, I keep telling you.'

'She is refusing to go.'

'Impossible. Put her on the phone. Let me talk to her.'

'That will be difficult.'

'Why?'

'Because I am the one who has to deal with her after you have finished your talking and your visiting.'

'It will be in everybody's best interests if we co-operate about the children,' said Shagun coldly before ending the conversation.

'Shagun phoned today.'

'What did she want?'

'Roo in the holidays. She is coming to India to make sure.'

'I'm not sending her anywhere.'

'It's part of the agreement.'

'If the agreement says push your children in the well, will you do that?'

'Explain your objections to a judge when she charges me with contempt of court, OK?'

His tone brought forth tears. 'Aren't we on the same side?'

It was his daughter and therefore, yes, they were on the same side. But this was a problem which was not going to be solved by stubbornness or weeping. He drew her close. 'I thought you would look forward to time alone with me. We will go somewhere—have a real honeymoon. Won't that be nice?' he said into her hair.

She was not to be distracted. Roohi was turning five, old enough to find this see-sawing between real and biological mothers very stressful. When she had first met the child, she had been so withdrawn, did he want that again?

'What is best for the child has already been decided, it is

not for us to reinterpret the issue,' said Raman. 'Why do you feel so threatened? Don't you see how loving she is? You think her feelings will vanish, just like that? What's your problem?'

Ishita sat silent for a moment, then said, 'Raman, haven't you heard of parents circumventing the law so far as custody is concerned? Now Shagun knows we don't send her easily. Suppose she decides to keep Roo, what will we do? We don't have the resources to fight her there. It's not as though you can retaliate through Arjun. We will simply lose her. Are you ready to take that risk?'

'Why should she keep her? She sent her back not once, but twice.'

'She is more settled; there is more scope for deceit, because she has you lulled.'

'Her husband will not want a child there all the time.'

'Are you sure?'

'How can I be sure of anything to do with them?'

This was the problem that led them, next Sunday, to Swarg Nivas, to the small room that Nandan used as a study.

'Contempt of court is a serious matter,' said Nandan.

'But what if she doesn't send the child back? What can we do?' asked Ishita.

'Then you can do nothing. But why do you think she won't?'

'In her place, I wouldn't.'

'She is not you—I keep telling you that,' said Raman impatiently.

Looking at his wife struggling against circumstances, Raman felt bad. What did she want, after all? Only to be able to love Roohi as her own. He cleared his throat: was there no way out?

Nandan thought of his twins, Abhi and Adi. How would he feel if they were removed? Even for a day?

'She is doing so well in school, settled and happy—the judge can send someone to see,' pleaded Ishita.

The men smiled indulgently. Women knew nothing.

Ishita saw the look and continued to sound naive. 'I am only talking about the welfare of the child, that's all. Such things can cause psychological damage, then the whole life is ruined. Otherwise what is it to me?'

'Bhabhi, the law doesn't work like that. Contempt is a serious thing, you can't go against the rights a judge has given. All you can do is delay. That's the best I can offer.'

'Delay the case?'

'No. Contempt cases are decided quickly. You can delay sending the child for one reason or another. Illness, camp—whatever you think will be plausible. Above all, you should not be accused of obstructing justice.'

Walking back to her parents' flat, Ishita was a little subdued.

'She runs off, abandons Roohi, and now we say, here, take. It's simply not right. And parents from abroad do kidnap their children.'

'I know.'

'Then?'

'Then what? I don't think she will, that's all.'

'She did once.'

'That was to get a divorce. And it might be worse for us in the long run if we don't send her. She is certain to fight.'

'To fight she will have to come here, no?'

'Not if she gives someone power of attorney,' said Raman tiredly. He looked at the children running about in the park although the sun was burning. Children will be children, playing at all hours, no matter what. How much does it really matter who looks after them?

Everything about the situation tore at him. It would be futile consulting anybody else, they would judge Roohi's interests according to their own loves and grievances. The child herself was too young. What did she know of mothers except that they were replaceable?

'I think my heart will break,' Ishita said as they got into the elevator. 'I can't bear this half-here-half-there. I have given her everything—not because of you, but because of her.'

'I know, dearest, I know.'

'Sometimes I think I was better off at Jeevan, caring for many children, but loving none as a parent. Now only one child—but I feel this constant tension in my head with the fear of losing her.'

She smiled at him faintly, a twisted smile. Eventually they decided that when the time came to send her, they would provide a medical certificate. The details could be figured out later.

Raman's thoughts now inconveniently wandered in a direction Ishita thought completely unnecessary. 'I wonder if Roohi might object when later on she discovers we kept her from her mother.'

'Don't you think it's our duty to keep her from being manipulated, while she is still so small? Besides, she will not object.'

'How can you be so sure?'

'How? Because she is better off with us. Besides, we are not *keeping keeping* her away for ever.'

'I have heard stories of children who go to considerable lengths to establish relations with their birth mothers when they grow up.'

'Where are these children?'

And Raman had to confess they were abroad.

'Here people are not so bothered,' replied Ishita. 'Roo will be fine, I will explain everything to her when she is older.'

Raman was left with the bleak realization that he could empathize with Shagun pining for her daughter, because he pined so much for Arjun.

Meanwhile Shagun to her mother:

Dearest Mama,

Yesterday was our fourth anniversary, imagine four years since we met at that fateful party at the Oberoi! To celebrate he took me to Veda where they have fusion Indian cuisine. He wanted to eat desi khanna, rare for him. To commemorate the country of our love.

Tomorrow we are going to the Lincoln Center, to hear some symphony, the last of the season. He has bought me a gown to wear for such occasions. He says nobody will guess I am Indian, not in a million years.

I can't wait to see you and the children. I have timed my visit to India to coincide with their holidays, so I can take them back with me. You know my initial efforts have borne fruit, and I am setting up a small import business. Once I establish my sources I will be on more secure ground.

Ashok helped me in the initial stages, mainly by getting me introductions to buyers here. He thinks I brood too much, nothing I say makes any difference.

You have a bug in your head about pilgrimages—now you want to go to Vaishnodevi! On your own! Don't you know that there can be avalanches and stampedes, and what all, what all. I will take you as soon as I can, I promise. And please don't fast for me, I am fine.

Do you ever get to see Roo? Raman must know she

misses you. Do please phone him Mama—and ask if she can come over—he can be there the whole time if he wants. He is beginning to show signs of paranoia, as though I would kidnap the children! True, one does hear of such cases, but Ashok would never allow it.

Mama, also find out if Roo is happy in school? Of all places OSC!!!!!!!!!!!! Trust Raman to send her to a convent. He is so boring and conventional. Look at Arjun's school, the best in India, then look at Roo's, a has-been convent. Honestly.

Lots of love, Shagun

PS—Don't forget to call Roo over.

Three days later.

'What's the matter?'

'I got a phone call from Mrs Sabharwal.'

'Can't they leave us alone?'

'She says she misses the children.'

'Whose fault is that?'

'She wants to see Roo. At one time we used to go over a lot. Now she sounds so sad and lonely.'

'Go, by all means. I don't know how much this will remind Roo of that woman, but yes, I suppose it will look bad if you refuse.'

The careful tones of his wife were not lost on the husband. Later, as Ishita was putting the child to sleep, Raman turned on the TV, and spent a long time staring at successive images of the world's misery. In the light of all this, he wished he could consider his own tribulations minor.

The high voice of his daughter penetrated his thoughts in the drawing room. Ever since his marriage she had been the centre around which both their lives revolved.

Clearly Ishita did not feel threatened by a visit to the grandmother, or perhaps she felt her objections would seem more reasonable if only confined to Shagun. So it was up to him.

He thought of all those times he had parked outside the Sabharwal gate in Alaknanda, waiting for his children. Not once had his ex-mother-in-law ever tried to talk to him, let alone sympathize with him. So much for the years of caring. How often had she said, you are like a son to me. Now another son had taken his place.

Thinking of all this made him far angrier with Mrs Sabharwal than he had ever been before. Even the memory of the fried potatoes and rajma chawal he had once enjoyed made him sick. There wasn't anything in court agreements about the rights of grandmothers, why then should he acknowledge them?

The next time Mrs Sabharwal phoned, Raman was distant and polite. He was sorry, but Roo refused to visit Alaknanda. Maybe the place had bad associations for her. But he thought it detrimental to the child's mental equilibrium to be exposed to the past. Cruelly he used words she would not understand, speaking in English that she was not comfortable with.

Stammering, Mrs Sabharwal got off the phone. No matter how mean it made him feel, Raman was determined to look after his own interests.

Dear Papa,

The school buses will come to Nehru Stadium on June 1st. Next day Roo and I will go to Naani's place. Mama will be waiting for us there. I won a point for my house because I did so well in my exams. Rest is fine.

Arjun

The morning of May 30th.

'I was thinking,' said Ishita.

'What?' Raman was looking moodily at his breakfast. Ishita had made him an egg-white Spanish omelette with low-fat cheese, chicken, ham and mushrooms. But she might as well not have bothered for all the appetite he was exhibiting.

'Why are you so—so unlike yourself?'

'I am fine.'

A wise wife does not push, and this one now continued as though nothing had happened. 'Anyway, I was thinking that perhaps Roo and I can spend the night with my parents?'

'Why?'

'Sweetheart, you know he is allergic to the sight of me.'

'But I think Arjun would like to see his sister. You can say what you like about two mothers, but he is her only brother.'

'Boys that age are usually impatient with little girls,' she said carefully.

'Arjun is not like other boys.'

'Well, I don't know about that. But I do know that Roo never mentions him.'

'Are you going to make sure brother and sister never meet?' he asked.

'Isn't it more sensible? If we send a medical certificate, and Arjun says Roo is perfectly fine, he saw this with his own two eyes—then we will have a contempt-of-court case on our hands.'

Raman knew this logic was unanswerable. He said nothing as he watched her pack a small bag and tell her daughter they were going to spend the day with the grandparents, wouldn't that be nice?

'Papa too?'

'No, beta, not Papa. He has some work to do.'

So she was not even going to tell her that her own brother was coming. The injustice of this smote his heart and as they put their things into the car he said, 'Bhaiyya is coming, darling.'

'Bhaiyya?'

'Yes.'

'From where?'

'School. Dehradun.'

Once one starts to tell, more things yearn to be let out of the bag in order to gambol in the wide spaces of the hitherto hidden. 'Would you like to meet him? He often asks about you.'

'Not this time,' said Ishita quickly. 'Now say bye to Papa.'

A nervous shadow crossed Roohi's small features. Ishita took her daughter's hand and they both waved to Raman as the car carefully backed out of the driveway onto the road, leaving the man standing there alone watching them disappear into the pandemonium that was Delhi traffic.

Why was it not possible to have everybody he loved under one roof? thought Raman. If he was another sort of man, perhaps he would have handled such things better.

Nehru Stadium, the Academy buses, and in the second one, Arjun.

Raman's eyes greedily drank in his son. Dehradun certainly suited him. There was a rosy glow on his face which brought great pleasure to the father's heart.

'You look good.'

'This midterm we went to Tope Sarai.'

'Midterms?'

'I *told* you about *midterms*.'

'Yes, yes, now I remember. And where is Tope Sarai?'

'In the mountains of course.'

'Did you camp there?'

'Ya. And trekking.'

Raman thought bitterly that Ashok would more readily understand every reference to DPA and its activities, even though he could never be one-millionth as interested in Arjun as he himself was. In the step-parent department, his daughter was luckier than his son.

'So tomorrow I will drop you off at your grandmother's, but today we are going to enjoy ourselves. At home I have got your favourite food made for you. Shammi kebabs and chicken curry. Later on we can order pizza. No point going out when you are with me just one day.'

At the mention of food Arjun brightened. 'That's nice, Papa.'

It only took the slightest of connecting for Raman's heart to be submerged with love. He beamed and said, 'It's a pity we have so little time now, but on your way back from your mother, we will really have fun, I promise.'

Again the boy smiled, and Raman allowed himself to think that maybe the rough patch with his son was over.

Inside the house, Arjun demanded, 'Where is Roohi?'

Oh no, no, no. 'She is not well.'

'Mama said you might say she is not well,' accused the boy in proxy rage.

'Children fall ill.'

'Where is she? In hospital?'

This was such a good suggestion that he grabbed it. 'Yes. Under observation.'

'Mama said to bring her. She *said*.'

'Well, beta, not everything is in our hands. You have done what you can. If Roohi is ill, how can you or I help that?

Don't worry. I will explain things to your mother. Tell her to phone me.'

'All right.'

By now the boy had lost interest in the matter. He chattered to Ganga and Ganesh. They made much of him. Ganga said Bhaiyya was looking healthy, growing taller too. The house was not the same without him. Ganesh asked what did he eat in school?; he always thought of Bhaiyya when he made shammi kebabs.

The day passed pleasantly enough.

At six o'clock the next evening Raman dropped Arjun at Alaknanda. Then he started on his way home. How soon before Shagun would phone?

His cell rang while he was driving. He ignored it. It rang again, then again. Rage emanated from the instrument; he switched it off. He wished he could ignore her calls forever, but bleakly realized he would have to go on dealing with his ex-wife as long as his children were young.

'Why weren't you answering?'

'I was driving.'

'Where is she?'

'Not well.'

'You told Arjun she is in hospital.'

'She is.'

'And you sitting at home?'

'I only came here because of Arjun.'

'Do you expect me to believe this?'

'It's the truth.'

'You don't know what the truth is.'

'Why talk to me then?'

'You think I want to talk to you? But we share children.'

Silence. He was sick of the whole thing. Parting from his

son had been a wrenching experience—he wanted to be alone for a few hours before Ishita and Roohi came home.

'All right. Go on, lie to me. What was wrong with her?'

'High fever. They thought she might go into convulsions. She is in the nursing home under observation.'

'Which nursing home?'

'Little Angels.'

'Who is with her?'

'That's not your concern.'

To Shagun the whole scenario screamed of duplicity. Yet Roohi had had convulsions when she was a year old. The paediatrician had said they might have to take her to the hospital, if they continued. She had sat with her the whole night, sponging her, making sure the temperature remained down. Would the new wife be careful of her in the same way? Who but a mother could do these things?

Raman sensed the slight hesitation on the other end of the line and congratulated himself for thinking on his feet. He had sounded calm and assured, did Shagun imagine she could walk all over their lives whenever she wished?

'I suppose she was also sick when you refused to send her to my mother?'

This habit of hers, of putting him in the wrong, was still functioning wonderfully.

'She didn't want to go.'

'I don't believe that. The children love their naani.'

'Love is hardly the issue here, is it, Shagun? What about betrayal?'

'Uff! Just tell me, when can you send her?'

'I don't know.'

'I have come all the way just to take her. Now this is what you do. You are a real bastard, you know that, Raman? A total fucker.' By now her voice was harsh with fury.

Her interaction with Ashok had coarsened his former wife beyond recognition. Raman put the receiver down. There was no reason why he should be subjected to insults, he was no longer married to her, besides which she was not the woman he had known.

The next day it was Mrs Sabharwal who phoned. Her voice was hesitant.

'Beta, how is Roo?'

'She is still in bed.'

'What does the doctor say?'

'Wait and watch.'

'Shagun is leaving tomorrow. It will do no good to deprive a child of her mother. After all, you do see Arjun, don't you?'

All Raman's antennae were up. Maybe Shagun was taping this conversation.

He would let them know as soon as the child was well. Right now the doctor had said travel might bring on the convulsions again, he added for the benefit of the recording device that was going to use everything he said against him.

The days passed and he heard no more. Shagun must have left, and for the time being Roohi was safe with them. As a precaution he got a medical certificate that attested to the child's high fever due to malaria. He sent a copy of this to Mrs Sabharwal's address by courier.

Two could play the same game. Shagun extended Arjun's ticket on medical grounds. He would arrive the day before his school opened to spend one night with his father.

If Raman wanted to see his son, he would have to share his daughter, hadn't he known that?

'Why on earth should the two be linked? There is no comparison. They are not the same age and have different needs,' said the wife, whose rationale for saying this was as transparent as glass.

For Ishita it was an answer to a prayer not to have the boy home. He was so completely the emissary of that woman. She refused to believe that a thirteen-year-old could behave the way he did without having been seriously primed. He probably didn't even understand the consequences of telling Roohi her real mother was somewhere else.

It was equally bad with Raman. In front of his son, the husband she loved receded into an anxious, cautious father, unable to see the woods for the tree called Arjun.

But his moping worried her, and she insisted they see Nandan the next time they went to Swarg Nivas.

'There's no point, what will he say? We can't file contempt of court, because we are also guilty of the same thing.'

Nandan confirmed Raman's suspicions: you want the son, you play fair with the daughter, then we have a leg to stand on. It's acceptable practice to delay, to prevaricate, to trouble the other side as much as you can. But you can't expect them not to do the same.

It was Sunday lunch, three generations of Kaushiks eating together, the door open between the flats, the grille that separated this two-unit section from the rest of the world securely latched. Roohi was darting around, following Aditya and Abhilasha in and out, delighting as she always did in the two mirror-image apartments. In one kitchen poories were being fried, in the other, Ishita was making rotis, the heart-attack patient had to be particular about his diet. She knew the elder women in the family approved of her care.

Her own parents were also present, her in-laws always invited them, and for this she felt a gratitude that she expressed by being all things to all relatives at all times.

XXXI

During the time Arjun was away, Raman worried incessantly about his son's return. Maybe Shagun would decide to keep the child in the US, making sure he would never see him again. At the thought of such revenge he felt faint with anticipated grief.

'Of course she will send him,' said Ishita. 'His school, studies, everything is here. Then you are always visiting him to make sure he is OK. Why would she want to disturb such a good arrangement?'

As an argument this carried no conviction, but perhaps it was not realistic to expect Ishita to regard his ex-wife as a nuanced human being.

The day before Arjun was due to arrive, Raman got a curt e-mail from Shagun giving the date and time of his flight. He would be there to receive him, he wrote back into the silent reproachful void. Well, her feelings were none of his business, he reminded himself, always reminding himself that it was none of his business. But he would see his son, nothing could take away from that joy, solitary and unshareable though it was.

The plane was landing at two in the morning. He could barely bring himself to eat that evening, his stomach was knotted, he felt sick with tension.

Ishita disappeared to put Roohi to bed, imagining a need for Raman to be alone. Somewhat forlorn, he sat in front of the TV, putting his watch on the table so he could mark the infinitesimal creeping along of minutes. He wanted a drink, but felt it inappropriate. His son should smell no alcohol on his breath when they embraced.

At the airport, how long would it take for an

unaccompanied minor to appear? To the best of his knowledge it was the first time the boy was travelling by himself.

For a moment he felt annoyed with his wife. Deliberately she had excluded herself from his worries. Her loves were around her, not hurtling home alone, through the vast unprotected skies above the earth.

Now he fooled the minutes into passing quickly by watching a rerun of *Kaun Banega Crorepati* with Amitabh Bachchan, watching the great ageing movie star with his white beard and dazzlingly shiny hair coax the audience with his charm.

From *Kaun Banega Crorepati* he flicked to a mindless film with a monster in it. A huge misshapen creature, crying for acceptance, for a wife, for the love of his creator instead of his hatred. But Frankenstein's monster was ugly. He deserved nothing, nothing.

Not like his Arjun. He saw the boy's face before his eyes, a face more beautiful than any boy should ever possess. The fair skin, the peach fuzz, the black eyebrows, the thick hair cut short so that it felt like fur. He has inherited my looks, Shagun used to say proudly. Invariably he agreed, 'The only ugly one in the family is me.' Then Roohi was born, and this particular banter had to stop.

After the thousandth glance at his watch, Raman decided to leave for the airport. He would have to wait—perhaps many hours, but he couldn't bear home any more with his fears bouncing off the walls.

Into the Esteem, driving down NH8, he put on a Pink Floyd tape, a favourite one of his son's. The sounds would tell him that he had been deeply missed, and that his homecoming started in the car.

Driving, driving, passing truck after lumbering, polluting truck, passing the small hotels, the showrooms, the dry treeless roads, the perpetual construction of flyovers on the way to Terminal 2 of the Indira Gandhi International Airport in the hot July night, listening to music he could not relate to, but which reminded him of his son and therefore he heard with ears that were not his own. Would his son have grown in the weeks away?

He parked and darted across the road, paying his 50 rupees to stand inside and watch passengers emerging. The TV screen showed that the Continental flight had not landed yet.

He sat on a sagging torn black leather seat in a row facing a screen that showed passengers descending into the immigration hall. In this way he would be able to spot Arjun once the plane arrived.

After an hour they announced the plane was going to be late. By now even the anxiety was ground out of Raman, he was just dully waiting. Waiting. Waiting.

An hour later, green lights flashed against the Continental flight number, and fifty minutes after that, a stranger walked towards him, accompanied by one of the ground staff, taller than the woman, leaner than he remembered. Two months and his son had so changed. He recognized him of course, but the face he had visualized all the way to the airport had disappeared into an older version.

Sign here, said the ground-staff woman and then she departed, leaving him with his beloved son, who greeted him with a small smile, in contrast to the greater enthusiasm of those around, the respectful feet-touching, the kisses, hugs, tears and bouquets.

'You have grown so much, beta. How did this happen?'

The boy shrugged.

Silly question. It happened because this was the age. He was his baby no longer.

As Raman reversed in the parking lot, Pink Floyd obediently welcomed Arjun.

'Why have you put that on?'

'I thought you would like it.'

'Naah. I don't listen to stuff like that any more.'

'Oh? What do you listen to then?'

'Eminem.'

'I don't know him.'

'He's really cool.'

'So, how was New York?'

'Cool.'

'You must have had a lovely time, but beta, Papa missed you. You never phoned, you never wrote, no reply to the e-mail I sent on your birthday.'

The child was silent.

'Well, now you are here, that is the important thing.'

They drove on through the night.

'Do you have any photographs?'

'Lots.'

'Maybe we can look at them together.'

'They are for Roohi.'

'Lovely. Now tell me everything you did.'

'We went to a huge place—it was as big as a stadium—where they sell games and stuff. And all kinds of equipment—really cool.'

'How nice. Did you buy anything?'

'Yeah. A GameCube.'

'Well, I hope it works here. The American system is different from ours.'

Arjun suddenly looked uninterested and simply stared ahead. Poor child, he must be so tired. These long flights were no joke.

'Soon we will be home, then you can go to sleep, beta. Hopefully you won't have bad jet lag.'

'Hoon.'

'Where's Roohi?' said Arjun as soon as they entered the house.

'She is sleeping. It's pretty late, you know.'

'Mama sent something for her.'

'That's nice.'

'She said to give it to her myself.'

'Yes, do that. But right now, do you want something to eat? I can make you a sandwich. Give you a glass of Bournvita.'

'No, I'm not hungry.'

'They feed you all the time in planes.'

While Arjun walked around the flat Raman pulled the suitcase into his bedroom. He opened it, and there on the very top was a big beautifully wrapped parcel with glitter and ribbons. On it was stuck flowered paper, which said, 'For my darling daughter Roohi, from her loving Mama.' One of the silver bows was coming off, carefully he pressed it back on.

'Where is Roohi?' repeated the brother, looking at the parcel in his father's hands.

'You will see her in the morning.'

'Mama said to give her the present myself.'

'As soon as she wakes up, you can do that. You have got all new clothes I see?'

'Yes. Mama said I had grown.'

'You have. I almost didn't recognize you at the airport.'

Arjun smiled.

'Here, here is your kurta pyjama. I hope it still fits you. I had asked Ganga to keep your clothes ready.'

The boy disappeared into the bathroom. Raman sank back on his knees. His chest felt burdened by the gladness of setting eyes on Arjun again. Just looking at his suitcase was enough to delight him.

'Will you be all right alone, beta?' he asked as the boy came back. 'I can sleep with you if you wish. Your only night home and all that.'

'Really, Papa, you think I am a baby like Roo?'

'Of course not. You are growing so fast—and going so many places. At your age I had never been anywhere.'

Arjun slept and slept, truly dead to the world. A few times his father came in and stared at him, but his gaze did not penetrate the boy's consciousness.

Twelve hours later he woke up.

'Breakfast, lunch or tea?' joked the father. 'I have made chicken curry for you.'

'Chicken curry then, Papa,' said the boy with his first broad grin. He looked younger, his dark hair tousled about his sleep-filled eyes, his Shagun face.

'Come on then. I wonder', he remarked as he spooned rice and curry onto his son's plate, 'whether New York is really as wonderful as they say. Though now you must be an old hand. Two months away is a lot, don't you think?'

'But it was so much fun. I went everywhere by myself in the subway. Mama introduced me to some boys my age—sons of friends of theirs—we hung out, took in a game or two, saw some flicks. Played pool.'

Pool? Arjun? Raman swallowed. 'Were your friends Indian?'

'Some.'

'What else?'

'We went to some shows too, but that was in the evening—with . . . you know, Mama's friends. She said she was only doing essential work from home while I was there.'

'Your mother? Working?'

'She stayed up nights doing stuff on the phone mostly—something to do with clothes.'

'Was it garment import-export? Quite a lot of that goes on between India and the US.'

'I don't know. All she said was that she loved doing what she was doing. She bought me lots of things,' he added.

'I saw that.'

Arjun went on eating.

'Papa loves you, beta.'

'Where's Roohi? I have to give her Mama's parcel.'

'You were sleeping so long she went to the market, she will be back soon. Do you want a second helping?'

Another hour and they arrived. Ishita disappeared into the kitchen, to supervise putting away the fruit she had bought, poking the mangoes to make sure none was soft, turning over each cherry to make sure none was fungus-ridden, examining the lichis chosen to make sure all were plump and red. She emerged to see Arjun handing his sister a parcel.

'Mama said to give it straight into your hands. See, see, what it says here.'

Unfortunately Roohi still could not read. The girl's eyes instinctively turned to her mother, and Ishita quickly sat next to her. 'How nice, a parcel from America, let's see what is inside it.' She took it in her lap, all the while admiring the ribbons and the paper. 'What do we have here? Oh a pair of jeans, two T-shirts, and little cartoon panties—see, Roo, how nice they are? And so much chewing gum! And this toy—let's see, how does it work?, Etch A Sketch, oh I see, look darling . . .' Etc., etc.

Raman, watching them, felt relieved. The parcel was going to be all right.

Arjun, watching, wondered if this was what his mother had in mind when she had given her son a thousand instructions—put it in her hand—be certain to tell her how much I miss her—she must come next time—tell her I had bought and kept these things for her—all for her.

By now he had forgotten half of what she had said.

Early next morning father and son set off for Dehradun. Ishita watched them go and felt free to breathe. As she turned to go back to bed, she noticed the key dangling in the drawer of Raman's bedside table. Why the key? He normally didn't lock the drawer.

She opened it and saw a pile of photographs. The ones Arjun was no doubt supposed to show Roohi, the ones he had obviously forgotten to do, perhaps left them with his father, to show them to my sister when she wakes up?

The day grew lighter, birds could be heard greeting the morning, traffic began to roar from the main roads beyond the colony. Delhi stirred into its daily routine, while Ishita feverishly shuffled through three rolls of photographs. She could feel the loathing coursing through her body, submerging her brain, narrowing her emotions to the point of that strong feeling. How could New York tolerate the presence of such a woman? How come its forces hadn't combined to kill her?

She could look at those pictures no longer. Carefully she arranged them in the same order and returned them to the drawer. Her husband was welcome to gaze at them, compare his wives, but that one had almost killed him, and this one was prepared to sacrifice everything for the well-being of her family. She turned the key and let it dangle there as Raman had done. That was Raman all over, so trusting. He might attempt to secure his things but he secured them very badly.

She vented to her mother. 'I hate him.'

'Beta, please. He is a child.'

'He is a horrible influence. Whenever he comes there is tension. Which he deliberately causes. Deliberately. I have seen him.'

'Is that what you tell Raman?'

'Do you think I am also a fool?'

'What can you do? The boy is his son, after all.'

'That's just the trouble.'

'He was here for one or two nights only.'

Ishita groaned. 'I know. And each time I think this will be a new start, but it never is. Raman only stares at the boy, for him he is an angel, we are all nothing.'

'Beti, you feel too much. What has the child done?'

'Everything, he has done everything. He goes on and on talking of his mother. His mother this and his mother that. What do you think Roohi is going to feel?'

'You are with Roohi every day, for her you are her mother, no matter what anybody says. Just be patient. How do you know she even understands what her brother talks about?'

'How much can I go on trying? I wish I were dead.'

'Hai beti, shubh shubh bolo.'

'Why? Why should I always say good things? What has it got me? I wish I were dead, so there.'

'The boy is in boarding school—think where you would be if he were home all the time.'

'Every day with him is like a year. I dread his coming.'

'Things take time. You knew this was a complicated situation before you married. There is no need to give up so easily. In your life you have faced much worse. You don't want to ruin your second chance.'

Tears came to Ishita's eyes. Why was it always like this? This time she didn't have parent-in-law issues, instead it was children-in-law. The critics, the judges, the manipulators.

That night she was especially tender with Roohi as she put her to bed. As she felt the child's face next to hers, a slight moan escaped her.

'Mama?' The small voice sounded alarmed.

'Beta.'

'Are you crying?'

'Babu—do you love me?'

The tears that the mother could not contain dropped into the little girl's heart and sent out sounds of woe.

'Do you love me?' asked Ishita again.

Roohi started to sob, clutching the older woman around the neck and rocking back and forth.

'Don't cry, beta, don't cry.'

This made Roohi cling even tighter. The child was five years old, what would she know of love? thought Ishita drearily, it was not even a fair question. Children love whoever satisfies their needs. It was that simple. It was Ishita's needs that demanded more complex inputs.

XXXII

One year passed.

In this year there were two sets of holidays.

Each time Roohi had a major illness.

Once it was measles.

Once chickenpox.

Certificates verifying the child's state of health made their way to Mrs Sabharwal's residence.

During the year Shagun's shadow hung persistently over the Kaushik household. What would her countermoves be? Contempt of court? Kidnapping? Setting Mrs Sabharwal up as a decoy, luring the innocent Roohi into her lair? How many people could Ishita warn her daughter against? Her former mother? Her former naani? Her brother (unfortunately not former)?

Day by day she enveloped Roo in a fierce and fearful love. The child was hers, if there was justice in the world she would remain hers. To this end she fasted, to this end she turned religious, to this end she surreptitiously visited astrologers and numerologists. Her fingers sprouted myriad gems glinting from thick gold settings: topaz, moonstone, ruby, amethyst. She who had objected to the pearl her mother had forced her to wear during her first marriage.

'I am told I should change the child's name,' she said to her husband. 'That will ensure she remain with us. Roohi is not auspicious.'

'Leave her name, will you? The letter R was taken from her horoscope.'

'It can be any other R. Roopali, Rupa, Rudrani, Rohini, Rehana, Rekha, Rashmi, Rasalika, Roshni . . .'

'Not one of them is as nice as Roohi. Call her what you like at home, but we cannot change her name.'

Ishita resented this disinclination to consider the child's bad stars, but she could do nothing except rename her Roopali in her mind and call her Roopi at home. Close enough to Roohi to not antagonize the father.

Isolated from Raman in these matters, Ishita went to Swarg Nivas with her troubles. A certain set for her mother—anything to do with Arjun, a certain set for her mother-in-law—anything to do with Roohi. And for Mrs Hingorani the doubts she had about herself.

'I used to be a straightforward girl, Auntie, until I married Raman. I didn't know in families everybody hears what suits them, nobody cares for the truth.'

'Perhaps there isn't one truth, Ish. We see things through the distorting mirrors of our interests. Understandable in a way.'

'But I am always suspect. Even with Raman I have to be so careful because there are always his feelings about Arjun to be considered. And to tell you the truth, Auntie, though the two children are linked in his mind, they are not in mine. That's the fundamental difference.'

'He must surely understand that.'

'He only understands what he wants to. Sometimes I think it doesn't bother him that Shagun has greater rights over Roopi than me. Though she was the one who ran off and left her. How is that fair, Auntie, how is that fair?'

'The tyranny of blood,' observed Mrs Hingorani, who applied this truth to a variety of contexts. She had long known of Ishita's devotion to Roo, and could easily imagine the child's trauma, torn between two mothers, two homes, two countries.

'And then there is all this tension of lying about Roopi's illnesses. I feel we might be punished one day by her really falling sick. It's only when I sense how much Roo needs me that I have the courage to go on. For her sake.'

Ishita was always a very intense girl, decided Mrs Hingorani. Though the child did seem to benefit from so much attention. She looked better, talked more. If anybody deserved happiness it was Ishu. And with these thoughts she accompanied Ishita downstairs to embark on her evening walk.

*

For two years, before such contact ceased, Raman saw Arjun on his visits to and from his mother. It came to a combined total of two days and four nights per annum. He prolonged the precious moments of contact by driving his son to Dehradun, taking leave from office, dispensing with the driver so there would be just the two of them during the six-hour journey.

Gone was the question of sharing any holidays. 'Mama says she is doing you a favour by allowing you to meet me at the airport and keep me the whole night,' the son informed his father. 'She doesn't get to see Roo.'

'But then how would you reach your school?'

'There is a teacher for airport duty. We spend the night in Delhi, then take the school bus the next day.'

'Isn't a father better than a teacher?'

'A mother is also better . . .' His voice trailed off; clearly this was a lesson that had been learned inadequately.

'Of course a mother has her place but she has to be around,' said Raman. 'Roo needs her routine. She doesn't keep well. Every time she has fallen sick we have sent medical certificates to your Alaknanda grandmother, who I am sure has passed them on to your mother.'

'Mama says all those certificates are fake. I told her I have never seen Roo ill.'

'How much do you see her, that you know whether she is ill or not? You are at home only one night, and that too very jet-lagged. In fact it would be nice if you paid more attention to your sister.'

'Mama says if you don't send Roohi, she will tell her lawyer to do something.'

'What?'

'Something. I have forgotten. Why don't you ask her?'

'Good idea.'

'She is very busy with her work, otherwise she would have come long ago and taken her. I said I would help her.'

'But beta, you can't just take someone. It's against the law.'

'Mama says she has rights.'

'She does, but I have custody.'

Every time his son talked of his sister in this way, Raman felt dragged into the position of respondent, making statements to the shadowy plaintiff that lurked behind Arjun's words. It made him uncomfortable, yet these were pronouncements that needed a counter-view. He was sure a similar process was not operating back in New York.

'So,' he said, determined to change the topic, 'how is your mother's import-export going?'

'Good. Some days she goes to a store. She took me there. It's really really big. Everybody knew her. They called her Shay-gun. She is a consultant now.'

'Everything in America is big. Is she a buyer by any chance?'

'I don't know.'

Raman was left with a burning curiosity that there would be no means of ever satisfying. He couldn't imagine Shagun working. Wasn't she part of all the travel Ashok did? Or maybe that wasn't as much fun as she had first thought. He hoped that was the case. Then what was she to do, this once-upon-a-time mother?

He put Shagun out of his mind and turned his attention back to his son. He had to rely on the little time he had to get an idea of Arjun's life. It was a heavy burden to place on a few hours, and the hours seldom measured up.

'So where else do you go? Last time you mentioned friends.'

'Museums.'

'You went to *museums* with your *friends*?'

'Yeah.'

'But you would never do that here.'

'It's for a school report. About Asian art. I volunteered.'

'So. You have the best of both worlds.'

Arjun looked as though this was a natural state of affairs. A smooth impermeable mantle of privilege had already begun to envelop him. Soon he would outdo his father in confidence.

'How do you feel about school now? You are bigger, things must be easier?'

'Oh, I love it, Papa. I don't even mind going back after the holidays.'

'Really?'

'Things are different now I am getting to be a senior. Even the teachers give us more respect.'

'In what way?'

'They are more like people we can relate to. That's important, you know, Papa. It's important to make people your friends. To know how to get them over to your side.'

'Yes, I am sure it is important. Do they teach you that in school?'

'Not in so many words.'

'I see. So it's just something you picked up on the way?'

'Ya.'

'What is it like with Ashok? Do you two get along?'

'Oh yes. He was head boy, you know.'

'I do know. That one achievement stands him in good stead even now, it seems.'

Arjun looked puzzled, but did not ask what he meant, and Raman did not want to tap into the resentment he still felt over his son's changing schools. He should just turn out OK. That was all he asked the powers that ruled the universe, that his innocent son not suffer for the sins of his parents.

The boy was going to be fifteen soon. He had an incipient moustache, he was taller than him, his voice was breaking, his body was more angular.

Each time he saw him Raman felt startled at the changes, the totally natural changes. And each time he worried at the rate the boy was growing, and the little time he had with him before he became a man with his character fixed.

As he struggled to reach out to his son, he felt an impenetrability that disturbed him. The earlier sullenness had gone, but slowly a stranger was taking his place.

'How was Dehradun?' asked Ishita the next evening. Always the bright cheerfulness on his return, always the husband who was tired and ill-tempered, always the fretting about the son which led to arguments about the daughter.

Dehradun was fine, he said, but for how long could they keep Roohi from Shagun?

He was careful not to say 'her mother', that phrase had caused some of their most serious fights.

'Why? Did Arjun say something?'

'He says Shagun is doing me a favour, letting me see him for the few hours I do.'

Ishita said nothing. She knew how her husband felt, but really, what could she *do*? This situation was not of her making.

'He also says she is going to see her lawyer about Roo.'

'It's just talk. If she had to file a contempt-of-court case, wouldn't she have done it by now? Not sent a message through Arjun, who doesn't even know what he is saying.'

'Maybe she was waiting. She must have accepted that some of those certificates were valid. She's not heartless, to insist her daughter travels while she is sick.'

If, said Ishita in icy tones, he still thought of Roopi as that woman's daughter, he was certainly free to send her.

Why were women so emotional? he demanded in turn. Contempt of court was a possibility they had to consider, the risk would increase the more they didn't send her—this was what they needed to discuss, not his existential freedom.

A month later when an unidentified number appeared on his mobile Raman picked it up leisurely—expecting another marketing call.

'Raman?'

'Shagun?'

'Is now a good time to talk?'

It had been a year since he had last heard her voice. Many, many times he had rehearsed speeches for just such an occasion, but at this crucial moment they abandoned him, and he responded with a concern that had lurked unacknowledged in some remote recess of his mind.

'How are you? I wondered about you when the 9/11 thing happened.'

'If we had died, you would have got to know.'

'Is it a sin to enquire after you? We still have our children in common—unless that is a link you want to deny.'

'That's just it. We don't have Roo in common. Why don't you let me see her? I have been very patient, you can't deny that.'

'I don't, but you left her when she was just a baby. You are not in her life any more.'

'And why is that? Because you don't want it. Now I am telling you that if you don't send Roohi, I am going to file a case. And you are never going to see Arjun again. *Never.* Not even that one day to and from the airport.'

'It's less than twenty-four hours. And that's the only way there is going to be any brother–sister connection.'

'You want connection, you send her here. Anyway I am

going to win my case. I am just trying to spare us both the hassles of the legal system. Think about it, will you?'

And she disconnected the phone.

Raman recounted this conversation to Ishita with reluctance. Her responses to anything to do with Shagun and Roohi were usually vehement.

Now she said, 'She is threatening you. Why hasn't she done anything till now?'

'She wanted to avoid a case. Who wouldn't?'

'It will be hard for her to fight if she is not in the country, no?'

'Not really. She can always get power of attorney.'

'Then why hasn't she?'

'I don't know. I believe she is working.'

'She? Working?'

'Whatever it is,' he said impatiently, 'I have told you the gist of the conversation. There is no use speculating about her life.'

'But you can still see him in school, no?'

'For how long? A few hours in a term. What does that mean?'

Ishita said nothing more. Her husband was not to be trusted as far as his ex-wife or son were concerned. Even a conversation about them left him irascible and touchy.

Over the next few days her sense of danger intensified. She saw a sword dangling over the family life she had created so painstakingly. That sword must be cut down, assiduously blunted, so that it never had the power to threaten.

Her husband's messy first marriage kept intruding into their present existence, and though he didn't mention it, she knew Shagun must have blackmailed him with Arjun. That was also why she could not rely on him.

Oh Mama,

Yesterday Ashok and I had a major, major fight, so major that I have not heard from him for one whole day. He is travelling, but when did that stop him? He has even phoned me from airplanes! (Costs 8 dollars a minute.)

It happened so suddenly I still cannot figure out what upset him. I just mentioned that once we are in Singapore I could devote more energy to seeing Roo. THAT'S ALL I SAID. He shouted that he was sick of my suffering, no matter how hard he tried I went on thinking of the same thing. Either I should take more concrete steps to get Roo or not miss her at all.

How unreasonable. Didn't I phone Raman, threaten him with a contempt case? Further threaten him with not seeing Arjun? Appealed to his better self? Now Ashok feels I should come up with a more effective strategy.

What strategy? I could kidnap her—I am willing to do that—once I am in Delhi it won't even be difficult. So I kidnap her, but then what? Roo is not like Arjun, she is younger, doesn't understand things, cries, whines, you have to spend a lot of time with her, be patient. Arjun on the other hand is easy to deal with, boarding school has taught him independence. He and Ashok bond whenever he is here.

Can I imagine all this happening with Roo? Not in a million years. And wouldn't that pull us apart?—I'm just a little afraid, Mama, and if this makes me a bad horrible person, then that's the way it is. But I need to feel Ashok is ready to take the responsibility of a child—I don't want to be a single parent—it won't work—not with both of us wanting different things out of our marriage.

In my heart of hearts, Mama, I want Ashok to take over. Where divorce was concerned, he was involved in each detail. Dealing with the lawyers, working out stratagems, understanding the implications of everything. It's all so complicated.

He mentioned Madz. Why couldn't I liaise with him instead of expecting him to take care of issues around the children? Didn't he have enough on his plate?

I guess I must realize that ultimately they are my children not his. That's what hurts. Arjun maybe he looks upon as his own, but he has—if I am honest—never shown much interest in Roo.

Perhaps I was foolish to believe, but he did promise to keep me happy for ever. Not that I have reproached him with anything. Our life together would not have been possible if I had regretted my past.

Still. What happened to that promise? I guess when you are in love you experience some momentary delusion, then the glow fades and things look ordinary again. Of course, I adore my life here, but sometimes I feel its foundations are fragile.

Sorry to unburden myself like this, Mama. In New York there are few people I can tell such problems to.

S

Mama! Please! I am fine!!!!

I won't tell you anything if you get so upset. Couples quarrel you know. Honestly, how on earth could you think he would leave me—just because of one fight!? In fact he is coming back today. From the airport he plans that we hire a car and go somewhere—a surprise destination. This is his way of making up.

Anyway I always go to the airport to receive him. I put on the things he likes to see me in, elegant western clothes of which I now have quite a collection. This time a white silky shirt, black pants, tan leather boots, red scarf, black coat—he says I have western style and an eastern heart.

S

*

A few weeks after the Dehradun trip, Ishita brought up the subject again. In order to protect their interests, examine their options, wouldn't it be a good idea to consult Nandan? As it was they lurched from holiday to holiday, wondering what plausible excuse to make each time. It was better to regularize the situation.

Next Sunday, the business-cum-pleasure meeting at Swarg Nivas.

Nandan said, 'She has filed nothing yet.'

'But she can, can't she?'

'Of course she can.'

'But look at how small Roo is. Besides, it wasn't possible to send her, sick, school admissions, sick again, surely when you are young childhood illnesses are believable,' said Ishita.

'We've gone through this before,' said Nandan, jiggling his pencil violently between his first two fingers, looking at Ishita. 'You have to abide by the decision of the judge, otherwise what is the point of the legal process? As for too small, if that objection was not made earlier, when she was even smaller, you cannot make it a point of consideration now. If the brother can go, why not the sister with him? And then you have custody of both children, it will look bad, very bad.'

'Custody of both children, that's all rubbish,' snorted Raman. 'Because we don't send Roohi, she doesn't let Arjun visit me. But Roohi thinks of Ishita as her mother, Ishita herself is very reluctant to have the child's heart divided, and she takes such good care of her, what am I to say? She is not your child? You have to send her away to someone she does not even remember clearly? I can't do that.'

Ishita beamed.

'It's just a visit in the holidays with her brother. The girl is with you the whole year round,' pointed out Nandan.

'Would you send your child away?' asked the emboldened wife. 'It's not just a question of holidays. It's how confused she will be, it's the distance created between Roo and me. Suppose I were to discipline her, she can always say you are not my real mother, why should I listen? When she is an adolescent she could turn completely against me.'

'At whatever cost to me, I only want their happiness,' said Raman, who had had no idea Ishita was so busy peering into the future.

That was the trouble with his cousin, thought Nandan, he kept muddying the issue with words like 'happiness', when it was rights that were in dispute. He thought for a little while, doing more violence to the pencil.

'I wouldn't ordinarily suggest this—but since she hasn't filed for contempt, let's wait. The longer she goes without doing anything, the stronger our position. I wonder why she is not being advised better.'

'Maybe because she is in the US?'

'If she wants her daughter it makes no difference where she is. She has to show she is in earnest. Otherwise her case becomes weak.'

'Can't we file contempt against her for refusing to send Arjun in the holidays? If I don't, maybe my case will also become weak.'

Don't sound so hopeful, thought Ishita. We are here for Roo, not your son. And you can stop finding reasons for your ex not strengthening her position. What is it to us?

'Arjun is—is—how old?'

'Almost fifteen.'

'In his case custody has no meaning. The boy can see you or not, as he wishes.'

XXXIII

Another year passed.

In the winter holidays Roo had typhoid. She was so sick she had to go on the drip. Copies attesting to this were signed and delivered to the grandmother's address.

In the summer holidays, still very weak from her bout of typhoid, she was advised to recuperate in the mountains. Once there her parents sent her to a ten-day camp to help build up her stamina at an even higher altitude. The camp co-ordinator gave a signed testimonial stating how much Roohi's fitness had increased. Once more photocopies were made and sent by registered post to Mrs Sabharwal.

That summer was also the first time Arjun went directly to the airport from school without the usual night with his father. Raman didn't reveal his grief to Ishita, what was the point?

She did register, though, the absence of the usual excitement that preceded Arjun's arrivals. For a while she said nothing. If he didn't want to share, she should not intrude, but his persistent air of sad abstraction broke her down.

'What's the matter? Something to do with Arjun, no?'

'He's not coming here on his way to his mother.'

'Why? You are his father.'

'You know why. No Roohi there, no Arjun here.'

Ishita silently put her arms around her husband, cradling his suddenly older-looking face against her body. 'I will do whatever you want me to,' she averred. 'Nothing is worth seeing you like this.'

But it was too late for that. No matter what happened, someone or the other would suffer. They sat like this for a while, Raman grateful that Ishita didn't make her usual suggestion of let's go and see Nandan.

Shagun phoned.

'If you'd like to meet him on the way back, let me see her.'

He said nothing.

'Raman! Are you there?'

'What on earth do you want? Just leave me alone.'

'Oh, stop being such a cry-baby. Tell me. Are you going to let me meet Roo? If not, no Arjun *ever*.'

'Why do you keep on linking the two children? The day you walked out that link was broken. And further destroyed when you sent Arjun to that school. You only care for yourself, not them.'

'Oh, stop talking nonsense, and let me see her. It's almost three years. She must have really grown.'

'She has, yes.'

'Raman, please. She is my daughter, I have rights. You can be there the whole time. What are you so afraid of?'

'She has got a settled life now, something you chose not to give her. Any meeting will only be disturbing, she never mentions you.'

'A child cannot forget her mother—Raman, what nonsense are you talking?'

'She doesn't want anything to do with you.'

'Why don't you ever let me speak to her? Are you hiding something?'

'You can't see her—why don't you understand that?'

'I will, when she tells me directly.'

'She has another mother now—one who cares for her.'

'You have turned her against me, Raman—you fucking bastard.'

'And what did you do with Arjun? I no longer have a son.'

'That was his choice. I did nothing.'

'And this is Roohi's choice—she wants to stay in the only home she has known, she wants to be with the mother who has looked after her devotedly every day for the last four years—even longer—before we were married.'

'Oh Raman, so that's why you married. I did think it was very sudden.'

'You are a fine one to talk about sudden. Everything I did was at least above board.'

The cell went dead.

The grapevine in Raman's office was activated enough for him to hear that Ashok Khanna was coming to South-East Asia as head of the region.

From Shagun's perspective it would be an ideal situation. Proximity to India meant it would be easier for her to start legal harassment. Well, time had weakened her case, she would find that out soon enough.

Idly he went on the net—to gaze at pictures the previous The Brand occupant had taken of Ashok's house in Singapore—all as far from his own little set-up as was possible. Of course Ashok was going to get the good things of life, he thought, staring at the glittering blue surface of the private swimming pool. He could just imagine them holding poolside parties on the wooden deck he could see edging the water's rim, serving drinks at the stone bar he could see tucked away under some trees to the left, cocktails in glasses that had little umbrellas sticking out of them, the cold misty alcohol smelling of lime and fruit.

So this was where Arjun was going to spend his holidays. He could imagine his tall handsome son lounging around the deck, fêted and courted by his mother, perhaps with an admiring friend in tow. Did DPA boys visit each other during vacation?

'They are going to Singapore. Head of region,' said Raman to Ishita later that evening.

'When?'

'Not sure.'

'Maybe 9/11 scared them.'

'I somehow doubt that.'

'Just our luck. They should stay in the US for ever. What is the need for them to come here?'

'Oh, God knows. He is practically CEO now.'

Her hands began to tremble. Were the little people once more going to be trampled underfoot?

'It may not be so bad,' said Raman, carrying her fingers to his lips to greet some garlic.

What did he know? It could be so bad, it had been. They were not wheeler-dealers. Her husband was such a straight man—anybody could take him for a ride—anybody.

'If that woman dares to come near my daughter, I am not responsible for the consequences.'

'What can you do? I have told you they have the law on their side, it is we who are breaking it.'

'So are you just going to wait for them to come and take her?'

Quarrels with the outside world easily turn inwards, and Raman now found he couldn't bear the high pitch in which Ishita expressed her anxiety. Abruptly he let go the haldi-stained hand.

He looked at her. She was wearing a kaftan, long, loose, unshapely, picked up from the street racks at Janpath. Her hair was unkempt, she smelt faintly of sweat and the kitchen. Don't worry, he tried to soothe, but such words were meaningless, more fragile than straws in the wind.

'I can't help it. She is everything to me—I loved her before I loved you.'

'There is no point anticipating the worst—it creates tension and upsets all of us. Think of how Roohi will feel.'

'Believe me, I think of nothing else.'

That he knew was true.

'I didn't even get ready for you,' said Ishita forlornly. 'And it's so late. I don't feel like doing anything.'

'Stop this worry,' he repeated. 'How is it going to help if you wander around like this, looking so stressed? What will Roo think?'

'What does it matter what she thinks, when I may not even have her?'

'How can you say that? At the most we are talking *visits*.'

'*Visits*. I know what visits mean. The kind of thing Arjun used to say to Roo—she's not your mother, she's not your mother. You think a twelve—thirteen—fourteen—fifteen-year-old boy can be bothered to think of all that on his own? That he would even care?'

'I don't want you to worry so much, all right? Day and night, all you do is think about this *one* thing.'

'Fine—but if she goes away, she will be poisoned by that woman. You tell me, am I wrong?'

'What can I tell you? With her present partner she has changed completely. You know I have no clue as to how her mind works.'

'Didn't she poison Arjun against me? I wanted us to have a good relationship. I knew he would not accept me as his mother. But to treat me as an enemy? If that happens with Roo I will run away and die.'

'Ishu—why are you so extreme? What'll I do if you run away and die?'

'I am just telling you what I can and cannot do. And be distant from the child who was once all my heart, that is not possible for me.'

'All or nothing?'

'Can you be a sometime parent?'

'What about her? What is she going to feel if you turn away from her?'

'What do you want from me? I am doing everything I can.'

Raman was silent, the spectre of King Solomon flitting across his mind.

'What? You are just going to sit there with your head in your hands and say nothing?'

'I have nothing to say.'

Ishita glanced at him with irritation. This whole trouble was due to his foolishness in marrying such a woman. Men were so taken in by the appearance of things, but as she laid a hand on his knee, she realized it was pointless to go on pretending to view their problem from the same perspective.

Later he thought how sick he was of children. People talked of the joys they brought; why were the sorrows so seldom mentioned, sorrows that could corrode your whole life, that far outweighed the heartache of a faithless love?

In the meantime Nandan:

'If you want to get rid of this problem, we'll have to file another case.'

'Saying what?'

'Saying it is in the best interests of the child for you to have sole custody. She cries, her health is bad, she refuses to leave her stepmother.'

'Yes, and how can we send her so far?'

'Let us not make it an issue of distance. Shagun can always say she will come here—in fact she came once to see the minor and you sent a medical certificate. The judge will probably call the child—she is, how old?'

'Seven now.'

'Too young. But still we can try. And it will take some time before the hearing. We have to prove that it is in her interests not to meet the birth mother. That is difficult, you know. But otherwise we have no case.'

'In her mind she only has one mother, and that is Ishita.'

'All the simpler then. She just has to say so. And let us hope the judge is sympathetic.'

And ruin the bloom of his daughter's innocence. Introduce her to courtrooms, biological versus actual mothers, make her renounce one in favour of another in front of a judge—why should he have to put Roohi through this?

The darkness inside Raman grew blacker. It was so palpable that it reached out and touched Nandan. He had seen parents push their children into making all kinds of statements—into saying they hated the other parent, they never wanted to see him/her again. The spirit of revenge burned bright and strong in such households. Raman's motives might be purer, his concern for wife and child deeper, but the result would be the same. His daughter would have to make such statements in court.

'We are only lucky that for whatever reason, she hasn't made a case for contempt,' went on Nandan. 'The longer she takes, the less likely it is for her to succeed. To forestall that, we are filing this petition—in response to which she can either cite contempt, which will do her no good, or prevent you from seeing Arjun. Which by now is more or less what happens anyway.'

They filed their case pleading that it would be psychologically damaging to force the minor to visit her birth mother when she had no desire to. She was happily adjusted to school, her day was full of friends, family and activities. Her stepmother and she had a loving relationship, separation would be cruel.

Ishita meanwhile organized her forces. 'Roo?' she started.

'Umm.'

Ishita stared at her daughter. Since she had married Raman, she frequently heard how alike they looked. Sometimes she could see it too. In the way the child talked, moved her hands, the expressions she used. Her looks had improved too—the little face was now open, the chatter endlessly engaging, the intelligence alert.

'Beti?'

Roohi looked up—it was not like her mother to be so tentative.

'What, Mama?'

For the first time she appreciated Raman's reluctance to swim in these murky waters. She wished she had the luxury of Raman's hesitations.

'Come here, darling.' Ishita opened her arms. Roohi crept into them. 'You are my precious, precious girl. You will never forget that, will you?'

The child's head bobbed obediently.

'I wonder, do you remember that other woman who once lived here?'

The bob was indistinguishable.

'Suppose, beta, she—or somebody—tried to come and take you away from me—'

A long pause in which the full import of this was allowed to sink into the child's mind.

'Then what would you do?'

No answer.

'You have to say—darling—you will have to say that your real parents are Mama and Papa. And if anybody asks you your mama's name, or who is your mama, you have to say . . . ?' Here she tightened her grip, to emphasize the gravity of the question. 'What will you say?'

'You.'

'Ishita. You have to take my name, and say Ishita.'

Roohi kept quiet.

'Do you want to know why I am saying all this?'

The daughter made no response, and so the mother had to tell her without encouragement. Once there was a wicked woman who was very beautiful. Despite having two wonderful children and a loving husband, she chose another man. The husband fell very, very sick. The boy was sent to boarding school. The girl, the sweetest little girl in the world, was left alone. Then Ishita came—she loved the father, she loved the little girl. Slowly the family that had been so wantonly destroyed was rebuilt.

The body beneath the chin grew rigid, but these were knives that had to be wielded.

Now the little girl was very brave. When the evil woman dragged her to court—

'What's court?'

Court was a place where a judge decided fights between people. Suppose two people are fighting over a piece of land—then they will go to court—and the judge will decide who keeps the land. When people fight over children the same thing happens. The piece of land can't speak—can't say oh I want to stay with this person who waters me, and gives me manure—but the child can speak. She can say, I want to stay with this person who feeds me, looks after me, gets my friends over, does everything a mother does for a daughter.

'I have to do my homework, Mama.'

'In a minute, darling. There is only a bit left.'

'What?'

'Only this. Do you think you can tell the judge that you don't want to see the woman who left you? You don't want anything to do with her?'

Roo nodded.

'And stay with us?'

Roo nodded again.

That night Ishita was calmer. She had taken steps to anchor what was hers. How clearly the child had understood the whole issue! Better than her father.

'Beti, what's the matter? Every time I see you, it is with a long face. Is this why you got married?'

Ishita immediately felt morally deficient. 'It's nothing, Auntie.'

'When you were here you looked much better. The children keep asking after you. Where is Didi? Where is Didi?'

'I also miss them, Auntie. They at least appreciated me.'

They had. For a few hours she had distracted them from poverty, alcoholism, illiteracy and domestic violence. Her place in their lives was there for all to see.

'You are not appreciated now?'

Ishita chose not to answer this question. Instead she told Mrs Hingorani about the case they had filed.

Now it was Mrs Hingorani's turn to look sad. Solving family problems in court was not something she approved of. Adults should behave like adults, not like the children they were fighting over. Really, why did people have babies if they were going to subject them to the messes of their own desires?

'Couldn't it be decided out of court?'

'We had no choice. She is coming here with her new husband. He is now head of region. She can kidnap the child, do anything. You have no idea of how heartless she is, how manipulative.'

'She was very pretty,' said Auntie judiciously, 'though I only saw her a few times.'

'That was just the problem. Her looks blinded everybody to her true nature.'

And then Ishita changed the subject because she didn't want Mrs Hingorani to think she was jealous of Shagun. It was only with her mother that she felt free to discuss her feelings about the ex-wife, only her mother who intuitively understood the extent of her insecurity, who would pray for her, fast for her. Subconsciously she relied on the strength of those talismans, feeling they had more or less worked so far.

The reply to their petition came. The earlier agreement was quoted. The petitioner was already in contempt for denying access to the minor. His excuses were *mala fide*. At one point he had alleged the minor was in hospital, but changed his story when the mother wanted to see her, and claimed the child was convalescing at home. Numerous other examples of malfeasance followed. In conclusion the respondent asked for custody of both children.

Nandan was right, said Raman, it was a big mistake on her part not to have filed contempt at the first cited instance. I wonder why she was so badly advised. This lawyer of theirs is just a big-name lawyer—some school connection of Ashok's, I do believe—so much for DPA. They talk as though it contained the cream of the country—when all it contains is the scum.

His wife agreed.

Every day Ishita felt she was treading on eggshells. When she looked at Roohi she saw a vulnerable creature going about her business unaware of the predator crouching in the bushes nearby. She tried to warn her against strangers, particularly a woman claiming she was her mother, whom she might even remember, but who was NOT TO BE TRUSTED. Like witches in fairy tales, she would come disguised as beautiful in order to gain the child's trust, but in reality she was out to harm her. Her intention was to capture Roo and take her far, far away.

Enough, said her husband.

'Why enough? We are not in a normal situation. She has to be able to tell the judge what is best for her. On her one answer depends our whole lives.'

'Don't exaggerate,' said Raman sharply. He hated what Ishita was doing—but exercising power over children, moulding them in order that they survive their circumstances was not something he was good at.

This was the time for tough love, said Ishita. Softness, niceness, gentleness had their place, but in other circumstances.

Raman ceased to protest. He too was afraid of his daughter being taken away, and he could trust neither himself nor the law to prevent this.

So he watched Roo's face grow tense, held her when she crept into their bed at night because of her bad dreams, silently helped change the sheets when she wet them, noticing how Ishita did her best to soothe and comfort the child. Soon the whole thing would be over, and they would be able to live a normal peaceful existence, that so many others (Nandan for example) took for granted.

His wife had a quality he knew he lacked. Maybe it was the tough love she kept talking about.

Mama dear,

We have filed for contempt of court, and demanded custody of both children. Whatever happens I can't be worse off than I am now. In the end Ashok came through and got in touch with Madz. Madz told him action should have been taken earlier, but Ashok wasted no time on that. Do your best, I have full faith in you.

I am convinced it will be resolved in my favour. Girls are always awarded to their mothers. And what can Raman do for her that I won't do better? All he could do was put her in a convent—I am still upset about that. There is a very good residential school in Singapore, called United World College, which prepares you for the International Baccalaureate. Once she graduates she can go to any university in the world. None of this struggling for admission to a third-rate Delhi college. I can just imagine my little Roo flowering as much as her brother does at DPA.

I am quite excited about our Singapore posting. For one thing you will be able to visit more often. Health insurance is also cheaper here, Mama—maybe you can be persuaded to live with me? We can give it an initial try. Singapore is only five hours from Delhi! It seems like nothing now.

If your internet connection is slow or not working CALL THE COMPUTER GUY. Don't start writing letters again I beg of you.

S

Mama—such good news—we have got a date for the court hearing. It has taken six months, but all parties are to collect in the judge's chambers on November 26th. Custody of both children will be reopened. It is in everybody's interest to decide the case quickly. The children are growing and soon it will be too late.

Both Ashok and I are coming to Delhi. We will stay in the Imperial. He is also tying this trip up with some work and as you know the company pays for some pretty fancy accommodation, so, Mama, this one time I won't be staying with you. Also Tees Hazari is closer to CP.

How is it that they feel they have the right to keep Roo from me? Me, her natural mother. Soon they will be proved wrong.

S

On the appointed afternoon Roohi and her parents drove to Tees Hazari. The idea of missing school pleased the child. She was dressed in a pink printed skirt, umbrella-cut, with a lacy pink sweater. On her feet were white closed shoes and frilled pink socks. Her hair was in two neat plaits, plastic flowers dangled at the ends of her rubber ties. A Hello Kitty tote bag was next to her, with her book and water bottle. Small gold earrings glinted in her ears. Ishita, looking at her, wondered which judge would take a child away from a mother who could produce this? Which judge on earth?

They didn't say much on the drive. Nandan's junior met them at the Tees Hazari entrance and led them up the stairs.

They emerged into the large open foyer before the courts of the Additional District Judge. Ishita's eyes quickly raked through the assemblage. She was immediately recognizable, a peacock among the hens, trying to look toned down, in an earth-coloured kameez with a black salwar and chunni, and discreet diamond jewellery. Her hair was tied back, she could see curls escaping from her ponytail. The only make-up was the touch of kaajal drawn across her lower lids, emphasizing the singularity of her green eyes.

So this was the woman Raman had loved. Poor fool, fancy putting his eggs in a basket such as this, they were bound to break. No doubt the wife would be looking at her and thinking how deplorably Raman had chosen the second time, well, she would show her.

The woman was eagerly scanning the crowd. Seeing them, she stepped forward. 'Roohi, darling,' she called.

Everybody in the foyer stared as hard as they could, some looked excited.

Ishita clutched the child's hand.

'Darling, baby.' Shagun came closer. Roohi was gazing at the woman, the woman was smiling, looking at her with all the love of three pent-up years. What an actress, thought Ishita, if you cared for your child so much you shouldn't have abandoned her. She nudged Raman. He went up to Shagun, said something, but she broke away, stepping closer.

'Darling, every time your brother came, I hoped you could come too. I came back to get you once, but they told me you were in hospital.'

This was too much. That was almost three years ago—how was the child supposed to respond? In her preparations, Ishita had sidestepped their own lies. Now she felt angry with herself, she should have anticipated this. Roohi fidgeted and fixed her glance on the dirty floor.

'I have missed you so much, my darling. I think of you every day. I have been wanting to see you for ever, but they told me you kept falling sick. Is that true?'

'Are you trying to say we are lying?'

'I am not talking to you. I am talking to my daughter.'

'Whom you deserted.'

'Raman, who is this woman?'

'Shagun, meet Ishita, my wife. She has been Roohi's devoted caretaker almost since you left.'

Devoted caretaker? Not *mother*. Had Raman lost his mind, to present her as some kind of faithful family retainer? She tugged at the child's hand: 'Let's go, beta.' Raman put his arm on hers, but she shrugged him off gently.

It was crowded and they had to push before they reached a lower floor. Once or twice she looked back, but no one was following. They would wait downstairs, said Ishita. Away from that woman who told her all kinds of lies, trying to upset her.

Roohi/Roopi said nothing.

'Soon it will all be over, I promise.'

It was getting towards four o'clock when the judge called them to her chambers.

Raman, Ishita, Shagun and Roohi slowly walked inside to sit around a low Sunmica table arranged in one corner of the large room.

'Coffee? Tea?'

They all shook their heads.

Shagun began to talk. 'The father has not allowed me to see my daughter, despite the agreement, Your Honour, for over two years. One excuse or another. One lie after another. He is guilty of contempt of court.'

'Then why have you waited so long?'

'If I had known so much time would pass, I would have filed a case sooner. But he kept sending doctors' certificates, and I always gave him the benefit of the doubt, not wanting to insist my daughter travel if unwell. I came to India to see her, but he claimed she was in hospital, a blatant lie. He even objected to the child's naani meeting her.

'The two times Roohi visited me, I sent her back faithfully. Otherwise it is so easy to kidnap, you know how many cases there are like that, Your Honour, but unlike this man, I wanted to keep to our legal agreement.

'I now want custody of both my children, particularly of my little girl, who is growing up without any maternal influence. This man is no longer trustworthy. Maybe because he has married again, and there is a stepmother in the picture. We all know what stepmothers are like.'

'Why did you give up custody of your daughter?'

'I will be honest with you, Your Honour. My marriage to this man had broken down due to irreconcilable differences, and he would only give me a divorce if I gave him custody.'

Ishita started to speak, when Raman pinched her. The judge leafed through the case files, then looked at the little girl. Three pairs of eyes stared at her.

'How old?'

'Seven and a half.' This was Ishita.

'Her birthday is the twenty-second of June,' said Shagun.

'Where is the boy now?'

'Boarding school,' said Raman.

'And he shares his holidays with both parents?'

'Yes, Your Honour,' said Shagun.

Raman glared at Shagun. 'I hardly get to see Arjun, four days in the year, that's all. And last year not even that.'

'More than I get to see Roohi,' she spat back. 'You visit him in school. You have custody.'

'The boy is how old?' interrupted the judge, frowning.

'Fifteen and a half.'

'So almost sixteen?'

'Yes, Your Honour.'

'At that age he is old enough to decide which parent he wants to stay with. No? In two or three years he will vote, after all.'

She looked at the parents in front of her expectantly and they tried to smile at this witticism.

'Your Honour, the little girl does not want to leave me,' put in Ishita hurriedly. 'How can we send her anywhere? We know there is an agreement but she falls ill, I think because of the stress of leaving the only happy home she has known. Last time she visited America she had nightmares for a month. Ever since my marriage I have put her welfare above everything. I think of her as my flesh and blood. If anybody is like a stepmother it is this lady. To be a mother you need a heart.'

'Your Honour, I object,' protested Shagun. 'They have persuaded her to turn against me.'

'You can ask the child what the situation at home is, and who she looks upon as her mother.'

Roohi shrank a little towards Ishita. Ishita put her arm around her.

The judge looked at Shagun. 'You are married?'

'Yes, Your Honour. To Ashok Khanna. He is going to be the head of The Brand in Singapore. We can give my daughter an excellent education, a really good life, the best of everything.'

'Where is your husband now?'

The moment this question was asked, the atmosphere in the judge's room altered. Imperceptible triumph, yes, where was this putative father?, imperceptible tension, who would have thought he was required?, as the air registered the changed breaths of the three litigants in the room.

'He had several meetings today, Your Honour. He is in a responsible position and many people rely on him to get things done. But he can come if necessary. He is always available if needed.'

'No, it is all right.'

The judge looked at the girl. 'Why do you not want to visit your mother?'

'Answer her, beta,' said Ishita.

But Roohi said nothing.

'You went twice? Didn't you like it?' asked the judge.

Roo shook her head.

'Your brother goes, you should also. Yes?'

Again she shook her head, as she fidgeted with her Hello Kitty bag. The judge looked speculatively at the warring parents arrayed before her.

'I would like to talk to the child alone.'

They got up to leave, Ishita with a last little pat.

The three of them sat wordlessly outside. Ishita felt Raman's heavy, solid presence as the heat from his body touched the edges of her sari and crept to her heart. Her eyes prickled. What was her little girl saying in there, what was the judge asking? Her hand crept beneath her husband's elbow.

Shagun was standing near the window, cell phone next to her ear. Ishita watched her out of the corner of her eye—she must be phoning her husband. Why hadn't the man come? Would that have strengthened their case or weakened it? Did she imagine the claims of the mother to be so strong that nothing else mattered?

It took twenty minutes for Roohi to emerge. Both women rose, but Ishita reached her first. 'You can take Roo and go,' said Raman kindly to his wife. She took the child's hand and started leading her out of the courtroom. Raman stayed behind to listen to the order, so did Shagun.

'Where's Papa?' asked Roohi as they headed towards the stairs.

'He's coming,' said Ishita. 'He has to do some paperwork.'

'Oh.'

They slowed down.

'What did the judge say, beta?'

'Who did I want to stay with?'

'And you said?'

Roohi did not say anything for a moment.

'Beta.' Ishita shook her arm, her voice quavered, her sweaty face was wrinkled with the weight of her fears. 'What did you say?'

'I said I wanted to stay with my mother. Ishita I said Ishita.'

'What did she say?'

'She asked if anybody was making me say this.'

'And?'

'I said no.'

'And?'

'She asked didn't I want to go with my brother to meet my mother?'

'What did you say?'

'I said Ishita is my mother. I want to stay with her.'

They reached the car. 'Get in, beta.'

'Aren't we waiting for Papa?'

'Yes, we are,' said Ishita, tapping out a message on her newly acquired mobile.

Fifteen minutes passed before her cell phone rang. The judge had given Roohi to them and Arjun to Shagun. If the children wanted there would be visiting but not otherwise. She was to go home, he would come in a taxi.

Maybe he was trying to work out something with the ex-wife about Arjun. She could have told him he was bound to fail, such a woman did not have it in her to be generous.

Ishita's thoughts were with her husband as they slowly negotiated the evening traffic along the stretch of Ring Road leading to South Delhi. Somewhere in the depths of the lower courts, he was mediating his past and present lives. This was something he had to do alone. Meanwhile she was carrying the most precious part of the marriage with her. She stretched out a hand and clutched her daughter's fist firmly in it.

She knew he would not realize the boy had been lost to him long ago. He would hold on to the myth that he played a part in his son's life simply because he was the father. Raman was such an idealist he couldn't see what was in front of him.

Well, she couldn't help with the boy, but she would make up to him as much as possible with the girl. Tenderly she opened the fingers of her daughter's somewhat grubby hand and kissed the palm.

The worst was over, over, thank God. Confidence flooded her. She had won this first, most difficult round. Roohi was almost eight, in ten years custody would be legally immaterial. She didn't think that woman would go on appeal, but if she did, she was armed with all the arts of delay. Another four years and she would be absolutely safe. In the meantime victory lay with the possessor.

*

ACKNOWLEDGEMENTS

For knowledge of legal intricacies:

Nidhi Dalmia — Roma Bhagat Baraya
Ameeta Rathore — Balbir Nagpal

For medical intricacies, the doctors

Malini Sikka — Sudha Marwah

For background information:

Ashish Mitter — Leena Bhavnani
Sanghamitra Bose, the founder of Sshrishti
Mala Bhagat Bali — Ira Singh
Vijay Kapur

For editorial inputs:

Ira Singh — Anuradha Marwah
Nidhi Dalmia

My writers' group, Janet Chawla, Gopika Nath, Amy Kazmin, Sujatha Mathai, Mala Bhagat Bali, Anuradha Marwah, Padmini Mongia and Charty Dugdale

Thanks to my agent,

Ayesha Karim

My editors,

Julian Loose — Chiki Sarkar

And Justin McCarthy for permission to use his name.

The lines quoted on pages 218–19 are from the poem 'Vitaï Lampada' by Sir Henry Newbolt.

A NOTE ON THE AUTHOR

Manju Kapur is the bestselling author of four novels, *Difficult Daughters* (winner of the Commonwealth Prize, Eurasia), *A Married Woman* and *Home* (shortlisted for the Hutch Crossword Prize for fiction) and *The Immigrant* (shortlisted for the DSC Prize). She lives in New Delhi.

A NOTE ON THE TYPE

Sabon is an old-style serif typeface designed by the German-born typographer and designer Jan Tschichold (1902–74). It was released jointly by the Linotype-, Monotype- and Stempel-type foundries in 1967. A unique feature of the typeface was that the roman, italic and bold weights all occupied the same width when typeset—an unusual feature, but this meant that the typeface then only required one set of copyfitting data (rather than three) when compositors had to assess the length of a text prior to actual typesetting (a common practice before computer-assisted typesetting).